Diaries
of a Lady

Diaries
of a Lady

Gillian Cox

BROWN
DOG
BOOKS

Published under licence by Brown Dog Books and
The Self-Publishing Partnership, 7 Green Park Station, Bath BA1 1JB

www.selfpublishingpartnership.co.uk

ISBN printed book: 978-1-78545-159-1
ISBN e-book: 978-1-78545-160-7

Cover design by Kevin Rylands
Internal design by Tim Jollands

Printed and bound by CPI Group (UK) Ltd, Croydon CR0 4YY

Contents

Part One

1916–1918
Memories of a War

Present day
Sara was looking through the belongings of her late grandmother at the house of her mother who had died a week earlier where she had lived with her family for some years. Sara was still in a state of great grief, as her mother had died of a massive heart attack, but was at a loss why, granted her mother had angina, but this was under reasonable control and she had kept a good diet. Sara found a large foolscap envelope which was yellowed with age, and the seal had been broken. She took it downstairs from her mother's room, not able to spend time in the room where her mother had spent her last days. She sat in the kitchen, with a mug of coffee, and took the contents out and placed them on the table. There was a large notebook which seemed to be a diary, and some envelopes wrapped in a faded red ribbon, she also found a few other envelopes, but put them to one side. Sara carefully opened the diary, which seemed to start in January 1916, which was halfway through the First World War, the Great War. What she read transfixed and shocked and puzzled her.

20th January 1916
Went to church with Father and Mother in the new motor car, it was draughty and smelly and noisy. The service was long and tedious, the sermon was hard to follow but the only part I wholly understood and said 'Amen' was for our 'boys' at the front, news was not very good, or very much. Young men from the village were away, and if not when they reached 17 or 18 years they volunteered. I

asked if I could volunteer but Father said that I was needed at home, I am 18 but I do not yet reach my majority until I am 21. It is so long to wait.

3rd February 1916

Father is letting part of our house to the military as a hospital; he said it was our patriotic duty to help the war effort. The far end of the house has been cleared, so the dining room, large lounge, and bedrooms on the first floor were set aside for wards and examination areas, and sleeping quarters for the doctors, medics and nurses. I enjoyed clearing the rooms and helping to put the beds in and making up the beds. The pictures were taken down, and dark heavy curtains hung at the windows, the servants and soldiers did that.

The downstairs wards were for the walking wounded, or had lost legs or were blinded, how awful I thought, and they were coming here those who survived the journey. We are not far from the station, which came from the seaport. I was terrified of the sights I was going to see, if I was allowed to.

10th February 1916

So much has happened in the last few weeks, I haven't been able to write. The first of the wounded soldiers arrived from Dover, to us and other large houses in Kent and Sussex to us in Three Gates in Sussex, inland but on the borders of Kent. I looked out of the upstairs window to see ambulances and bigger vehicles that stopped outside the front of the house, and fortunately we didn't have steps up to the front door. As they came out of the vehicles with nurse and orderly escorts, some of the soldiers walked with crutches, others walked with someone with them as they had eyes bandaged, and others were carried out on stretchers, some seemed to have lost arms or legs as the blankets on their stretchers did not really hide the gaps. I felt so sorry for them; as they looked so sad and listless. As I was looking a maid tapped me on the shoulder and whispered urgently, 'Please Miss Anna please come your father might see you and banish you.' She was a year younger than me, and I liked her a lot, her name is Mary Ann, almost like mine, only I am called Anna Marie and in any other circumstances we would have been friends, but our class differences made it almost impossible but we were most polite and cordial to each other. I went away quickly and smiled back at her.

17th February 1916

A week has passed, I was so unprepared for what would happen, although my sister Ellen and I were kept away from the hospital part at the front of the house and we took all our meals in another room set aside we could hear groans and even screaming from the poor injured men, and sometimes a soothing voice of a female nurse asking them to calm down. From what we were allowed to know, these were not nearly as bad as others in hospitals in Belgium or France who were so badly hurt or wounded that they could not be moved, for fear of them dying, or they died anyway. I remember praying for those who were in Belgium especially who were at the 'front' and taken back to the hospitals, those who were not killed. Oh this awful war! It began to become so real to me, as they were here in our home, to get better?

25th June 1916

Great news! As I turned 18 years old my father felt that I could do a little to help, not just making beds or rolling bandages, but I could put a calico apron on and put my hair up into a chignon and help take drinks to the soldiers and help them drink if they needed help. It was so humbling, the nurses supervised me of course, but I was so glad to help out a bit more. They seemed so grateful, I was allowed to talk to them as I helped them, especially the ones who had lost an arm, or who could not see, or see very well. I was also allowed to join with the senior orderlies and medics, and several senior nurses as well. This became much more interesting routine, and my days did not seem so long. I asked my father if I could train to be a nurse, but he said that was not an occupation for a lady. I protested that I wasn't asking to go to France, but he still refused, but he agreed that I could carry on at the house, and assist with preparations for the drinks and meals with Ellen, but she was happy to be a lady, but I felt that my life wanted more meaning than just hosting at dinner parties, and being a dutiful wife. But as a minor I had to abide with my father's wishes.

30th January 1917
We have had a new intake of injured soldiers, Americans and Canadians, as the earlier injured soldiers recovered, they went to their homes as because of their injuries they were not fit to go back to the front, so they went home as heroes. The Canadians and Americans had their own medics, although the English nurses helped with the day to day dressings but the medics and orderlies helped with their 'ablutions'. Most of the Canadian or American medics have their own 'mess' as they put it. There is one medic from Canada who seemed a bit lost, a bit like me. I just greeted him in passing. Later one of our English medics said to me during a meal as we sat together that he had been warned not to associate with us, and especially me, as I was the elder daughter of the owner of the house. I was horrified, and said that he seemed a bit ostracised by the others. The orderly said that his name was Gerard Horan and was a volunteer not a regular soldier. I thanked him and remembered what he had said.

February 18th 1917

I am beginning to enjoy my bit of helping, but wish I could do more, the nurses are so dedicated. I have also started spending a little time with the medic Gerard, and thought of having a little entertainment for the injured soldiers and asked if he had any ideas. He was quite enthusiastic and said that some of his orderlies could hold a tune and could dance. I asked if the English medics and nurses could do any turns, and they surprised me, and they had a sing song in the music room, which was big enough for about a hundred people, so I asked Father if we could hold a little show for the morale of the troops, and he agreed. It was so exciting and so Gerard and Elliott, the other medic (English) from Essex and had a wife and children at home, who said he wanted to be a doctor if he could afford it. We worked together to set up a little concert. I was so happy, and I got my sister Ellen to play the piano. From then on I was sometimes left in the company of Gerard, and he started talking about his home. As I sat at the table with him, me drinking tea and he was drinking coffee, I watched as he talked about where he lived in the country-side and his blue eyes lit up and also a faraway look came into his eyes. When he stopped to have a sip of his drink, I asked him how he could leave his country, he said that there was a war on, and although he did not want to fight, he felt he could help with injured soldiers, he looked me right in the eyes and asked me why I was so involved as I was, I told him that I was not allowed to do more, being the older daughter of the house I had a position to 'maintain'. I could not volunteer outside and I could do as there were so many men suffering and under different circumstances I would train as a nurse. He said he had similar problems at home in Canada, but as he was over 21 when he volunteered his parents couldn't stop him although he was going to medical school. He smiled and touched my hand for a moment and I hesitated before I pulled my hand away, he apologised, but I shook my head and excused myself as it was nearly time to go to bed.

March 30th 1917

From then on during the last six weeks I have been able to help a little more, with helping to feed the soldiers if they were recovering from further operations, or 'surgery' as Elliot put it, some of the poor lads had lost part or all of their arms, and were finding it hard to adjust, and the nurses and orderlies had so much to do. Their wounds do not upset me overly, I just feel so sorry for them and for their pain. Is there a nurse inside me? After finishing the clearing up, I went to my room, and shed a few tears, and Ellen came in and sat on the bed with me. She asked what was the matter, and when I told her, she was a little brusque with me, telling me that I should leave that sort thing to the nurses or the orderlies after all I was a 'lady'. I asked her if she felt there was more to life than being a 'lady' to help others, she snapped and said that was for the lower classes to do, not us. We were doing enough by giving up most of the house to be used as a hospital; she hoped the war would be over soon so that she could walk through the house and gardens without coming across wheelchairs or soldiers walking with crutches, or orderlies. I told her it was very unpatriotic and shallow of her and Father would be annoyed if he heard her. We then had the most awful argument and Mary Ann knocked on the door and came in and said very respectfully that we could be heard along the landing and our father might hear and would scold us, and send us away, Ellen said she didn't care and would ask to go to London, and I asked her not to, but she stormed out, Mary Ann went after her, and I shed a few more tears, had I lost my sister, were we so different.

April 20th 1917

Ellen was true to her word and father agreed for her to go to London to stay with Aunt Mary, and I was worried that she would take Mary Ann, but she asked for Agnes, who was a parlour maid, but she did help out sometimes as a ladies' maid, and Agnes was thrilled. Mary Ann and Agnes were cousins and quite close, and Mary Ann asked Agnes if she would write when she could. I asked Agnes to please look after my sister and she promised to be as good as a maid to Ellen as Mary Ann is to me. I loved Ellen dearly and would miss her very much but we had to go our separate ways for a while. But Ellen is only 17 years old so she would need chaperoning. Oh I agree with her one subject, I wish this awful war would end because so many young men are going and not coming back and any who do are so badly maimed.

April 15th 1917

Without Ellen's company I found that I needed another friend and Mary Ann wasn't exactly a friend as such, but I did confide in her, so in a way she is. I told her about my conversations with Gerard, and sometimes we went for a walk to the village when she had a little time off. She became serious and asked if he had tried anything else, any human contact. I said sometimes he held my hand across the table in the tea room, but moved it back when anyone walked past, and took my arm as we walked through the grove back to the house, he is a perfect gentleman, Mary Ann asked me if I knew how babies were made, and I said vaguely, but he hadn't even kissed me. 'Oh that's how it starts,' she said very seriously, and I just laughed, and she shook her head. 'Oh Miss please be careful, you are a lady and you should keep yourself pure until you marry.'

I couldn't quite understand what she meant, but said that I was only going to marry someone my father would approve of. She just said to be careful.

May 31st 1917

I have been careful when I have seen Gerard, which seems to be more often, after helping with changing the beds and also now helping to write letters for soldiers, especially for the ones who lost the use of their hands or even losing their arms, he escorted me to the post office and back as our motor car, which I came to like a little, had been taken over by officers with my father's permission. I am feeling differently about Gerard, he is more than a friend and I trust him. Last night he kissed my hand, and I felt hot and might have blushed, I pulled my hand away, and he apologised and walked away quickly. What is happening to me?

June 10th 1917

The war must end soon surely. Mama, who always deferred to Father in everything carried on as if the war wasn't happening, as she kept herself well away from everything, in the few rooms that were not being used by the army medical corps, although even if she went to the village or to the railway station one could not avoid seeing the uniforms, the army trucks and ambulances which came from the station with some regularity, and if she had had enough, she went to London to visit her sister, my aunt and Ellen, oh how I miss her, even though we used to have differences of opinions we were still sisters. The letters that Mary Ann received from Agnes, Ellen was having quite exciting times, although the officers which she met at parties, always seemed to go and others took their place, and she did not seem to be bothered. Agnes confided many things too although Agnes stayed in the house and Ellen used to go out with our cousin Melanie who seemed to have many contacts. Mama came back rejuvenated and she seemed happy to come back to our quiet village and house.

I spent time with Elliott and Gerard, who had become good friends, and they went to the public house in the village, but when Elliott had some leave he went to Essex to see his family. I was pleased that Gerard had a male friend to keep company with, but I felt a little lost, as Mary Ann had some time away too, so I managed for myself and chose my clothes and put them on myself, and I always put my stockings on and I put my hair up, and wore my older clothes as I was still helping to clean up after meals and taking crockery to the kitchen.

During this time Gerard and I spent more time together, walking in the garden and quieter areas, and I showed him the presently unused summer house. The weather in May has been very warm and the nights were light and romantic, oh where did that come from? Away from everyone we talked late, and I crept back to the house, to my room, and slept well, but in spurts. Father has been so busy and he never seems to be around.

July 31st 1917

Oh, what is happening to me, am I being wanton, a word used by one of the cooks, apparently there are some ladies in the next town who are in the hotel where some of the orderlies visit, not all single, and apparently in France, who give their bodies, I do not understand, last night just as I went into the house as I said goodnight to Gerard, he drew close to and held me by the shoulders and bent down and kissed me on the mouth, and I, I kissed him back. It was a matter of seconds, but well it felt really nice, and I didn't want him to stop, but he just turned around and walked away to his quarters and I to my room. I couldn't sleep going over what has happened during these last weeks, I think that I am caring for him more and more, am I 'falling in love' with him?

August 31st 1917
Gerard and I have been meeting in the summerhouse at least twice a week, just to be with him and sitting close to him, and he has put his arm around me and I have held his hands, which are not rough or broken like some of the men in the village, or the soldiers but clean and soft, but he does work with his hands, cleaning wounds and helping to bandage them. We talked about lots of things, the war, the wounded, his home he even showed me some pictures of his home town, which was open and he said that it was very green, with hills and mountains, very beautiful. His kisses became longer, and I did not mind. He then sat up and announced that he would soon have to go back to Belgium to the front as most of his Canadian patients would be discharged or would be, and he had orders to return. I was distraught and cried bitter tears, I was worried that I would never see him again. He said he would probably have to go at the end of September. We arranged to have a leaving party for all the orderlies and medics who had to go back to the front. I spoke to my father to see if we could host a special meal, and he said yes, not to bother him with the details, he was too busy to host it. Gosh my first party!

20th September 1917
There will be only a few days now until they go. The house seems quite quiet now as there were only about ten soldiers here now and most of them were British. Gerard and I still met when we could, and the kisses became more fervent and his hands were moving over my body, I asked him to stop, he seemed to be moving too fast, and he did and moved back a little, and made the amazing declaration,

that he loved me passionately and could not help himself, that he had not felt this way about anyone, and had not really had any experience. I told him that I felt that I loved him too, but would like to wait. He apologised and said he would try to be patient. I told him that I was saving myself for my husband; he said that he would like to be that person. I looked at him with my eyes wide. He took my hand in his and asked me to be his wife, I said, 'But when? You are going back to the front?' He then took off his signet ring from his little finger on his right hand and said that this ring was a family ring and tried to put on my ring finger, but it was a bit tight, so I put it on my chain that I wore under my dress and said that until my father gave his consent, we could not be officially engaged, but I considered myself so if he wished it. Gerard was so happy, he kissed me again, and then we went back to our rooms.

30th September 1917

The party went very well I think; most of the orderlies, doctors, nurses and medics came at intervals during the evening. I think that I drank too much wine as I seemed to get a bit sleepy. Gerard helped me to my room, but I do not remember him leaving, he helped me on to my bed, and went to the door and then came back. I am a bit muddled about what happened next, he started kissing me, and I started to undress, why did I do that? He started to undress too, and continued to kiss me, telling me how much he loved me, and would look after me, at some point I felt a sharp pain between my legs and then after a while nothing as he rolled over away from me. I fell asleep then. This morning I woke up and found I was wearing my slip but nothing else. I quickly put on my dressing gown and washed and dressed and went down for breakfast. Everyone seemed subdued as if things were going to change, coming to an end. We watched as the trucks took the soldiers away, those who could walk, and ambulances took the others who could go. Gerard came to see me in the hallway where others were and asked if I slept well after the party, after he had left me. I still had vague memories of our moments alone, but was it a dream. I muttered yes, he then pressed a piece of paper into my hand and then said firmly but quietly, 'I will come back for you, I promise, please write to me, it will be very lonely and bad out there but I must go, be brave my love.'

I screwed the paper up and put it inside my sleeve and fastened it. Elliott also came to say goodbye, I asked him to look after himself and Gerard as they had become firm friends and worked together while they were here and Elliott was promoted to sergeant and had some training to be a medic. He also gave me a piece of paper, 'If you have any problems or need to contact me, my wife will send on any letter, I have seen her and she is happy to pass on any letters to me, she is the only one besides me who knows where your affections lie.' I thanked him and wished him well and promised that I would think of them and pray for their safety.

Soon enough most of the nurses and medics and doctors left for the station back to Dover and then on to Belgium, my heart is very heavy, I have heard that the fighting is very fierce with many deaths and casualties on both sides. I went and took the pieces of paper and looked at each. Gerard was a sub lieutenant, his uniform did not give that away as it was almost nondescript, very similar to the others, as he never wore his military uniform; he wore a simple uniform when we went out for a walk or everyday wear. I hid the papers in my jewellery box under some letters.

31st October 1917
I have been unable to eat in the mornings as I cannot face the food, including the full fried breakfast at times, they are so greasy, and they make me queasy, I just put it down to something I have eaten.

I tried to hide my nausea and have been eating dry toast or put a little butter on the toast. Mary Ann has been very concerned about me, I'm not sure if I can confide in her. Also I am a bit worried that I have not had my monthly bleed since six weeks ago. Mother is not easy to talk to, she never told me much about anything personal, and she and Father do not seem to talk much to each other, she has always been more worried about how Ellen and I conduct ourselves in company, and how we dress. Ellen does with no problem but I want to do something worthwhile, like being a nurse. I am writing this in my room as I excused myself from supper as I could only manage some soup, Mother asked if I was quite well, she suggested that I visit the doctor but I said that I had an upset stomach but it would pass. What could this be? Mary Ann saw me coming out of my bathroom after I had been sick this evening, why could I not keep anything down? She followed me to my room and I let her help me undress and also to bathe my face as I had been doing this myself. She asked if she could bring me anything to eat, I said I could manage some toast and a little water so she brought me a plate of toast and a pitcher of water with a glass and I sat by the fire and managed to eat it all and drink half the water, oh God what is wrong with me.

30th November 1917

I am feeling much better now. I have been able to eat most of my meals, but avoid the fattier meats. Mary Ann is being very attentive and kind, I love her so much, she is like a sister and take away the 'class' divide and she would be my best friend, well she is in a way. My clothes seem to be a little tight and when I look in the mirror at my face it seems a little older, my green eyes do not seem to shine, I am missing the hustle of two months ago they do not seem to need any extra help as only a trickle of patients come here now. I miss Gerard of course and Elliott, they were so cheerful and Elliott was very jolly. I have written to Gerard and he sends his replies to Mary Ann's address and she brings them to me, and leaves me to read them, he talks of being busy, he cannot tell me all, but I get the impression that things are very bad, he says he misses me very much, hopes that the war will end soon. He says he brings casualties back from the front. He also sent regards from Elliott who he has been working with and is great friends with. How glad I am that they have each other to talk to.

15th December 1917

The letters have stopped coming. I have been getting a letter about every five days to six days; the last one came two weeks ago. I am going to write to Elliott's wife in Essex. I am experiencing changes in my body, my clothes are tighter again and my breasts have got bigger as they were not large but I have had to buy larger sizes in underwear and my waist has thickened, so I have stopped wearing belts. After Mary Ann had posted my letter on her afternoon off, she came in to me just before I was going to bed and brought me a hot drink with a little milk in. She sat near me as I ate the small snack before fire, she asked if she could sit a little nearer. 'Miss Anna have you not wondered why you are experiencing changes in your body in the last weeks?'

I just said that I thought that was just settling after being so busy and skipping meals and then eating normally again and the rich food that we were having, but then I stopped and thought back, the last night that the medics were there and the party, and after, Mary Ann saw my hesitation, 'Did you go to your room alone?'

I said that Gerard the Canadian medic saw me to my room, and then left I think. What she said next really shook me, 'He did not return to his bed until the early hours of the morning, I heard that

Mr Elliott asked him where he had been, and he said he had been out walking, but I am not sure I believe him.'

I was shaken to the core, 'He must have stayed with me, I thought I saw him go to the door, but he came back, and oh Mary Ann he got into bed with me!' She asked me if I remember what happened next, and I found it a bit hazy but I recounted that I remember.

She came closer and looked me in the eye, and told me what I had almost worked out for myself, 'Oh Miss Anna I did ask you to be careful, that is how babies are made, some of the girls in the village have been as foolish if I may make so bold. They have been disgraced as some of the soldiers have not come back or worse did not want to know. I will try to help you.'

I then showed her the ring that Gerard gave to me and that he promised to come back to me, and his letters said so, but I have not had one for two weeks as she was aware, so I had written to Elliott's wife to pass on to him for news. I then started to cry as I was really worried. She urged me to be strong and wait for news. I really didn't want to involve her as her job would be at risk, I asked her to be careful too, and just be neutral, so that she would not be dismissed, but she said that she was my maid and she would help me no matter what and that my secret was safe with her.

30th December 1917
Christmas came and went, Ellen is home now, and she seems happy that things are back to normal, she seems a bit quiet about my appearance, but chatters on about her time in London, where there were a few incidences of some air attacks from the Germans, but only minor, we have been very lucky. Things were very subdued, and Mother and Father seemed very distant, and not talked to us very much. Ellen did talk of one officer that she had been spending time with, who had gone to tea with our aunt. She said that he had

gone back, but was an aide to one of the generals and spent most of his time back at Headquarters in France. She has high hopes but I told her that as she is nearly 18 years old she would need permission from Father, and she said that I didn't understand, but oh yes I do.

31st December 1917
The unthinkable has happened, I received a letter in a strange hand-writing with a postmark from Belgium, I was almost afraid to open it, I was sitting in the lounge with Mother and Ellen after supper where we were drinking coffee, I did open it and it was from Elliott who addressed me Miss Anna Clarkson. It was written as follows:

> I am very sorry to advise you that the medic that you enquired about (Sub Lieutenant Gerard Horan) is registered missing in action, I was not in the same area as he was, the fighting was very fierce, and we went out to collect the wounded I got a few glancing shots go past me and my cheek was nicked. When all went quiet, he was the only medic not accounted for. I will try to find out what has happened, will check with the Canadians as he was my friend, but it may be hopeless, I am so sorry,
> Yours sincerely
> Sgt Elliott James
> British Medical Corps

The room started to swim around me and faded away to blackness. I woke up and found that I was lying in my bed with the doctor pulling the covers up. I asked what time it was, and he said it was 11.30 p.m. I must have been unconscious for about 3 hours. He said that I had had a nasty shock and then went outside to speak to my father. Mary Ann was near the fire and had been there all the time that the doctor had been there. She was told to leave by my father who did not look very sympathetic. He looked very angry.

'So you are expecting a baby and the father has probably been killed! You will stay in your room during the day and have all your meals here, if you want some fresh air you can open your windows you may use the bathroom, and walk in the grounds after dark with an escort and when the brat is born it will go to the orphanage, and I will decide what to do with you. I am very disappointed in you!'

He walked without a backward glance, I cried myself to sleep. My life is over; there is no hope for me. God Help me.

31st March 1918

New Year came and went; at least I believe so, being stuck here in my room, with my meals being brought to me. Mary Ann and Agnes bringing my meals, it has snowed and the grounds look very pretty, Ellen comes to see me sometimes, she seems sympathetic and brings me snippets of news. Her beau is still safe at the moment, but there are rumours that even he may be sent to the front. She says that everyone has been told that I have gone to London to stay with our aunt. She is giving me quick hugs, and tells me she loves me and is sorry for my plight. There is movement in my belly, which is getting larger.

31st May 1918

I feel so cooped up in this room, summer is coming and the gardens look lovely. I glanced through the bathroom windows sometimes in the morning and at sunset, before I move back to my bedroom which has become like a prison cell; don't prisoners get to walk outside? Perhaps not. I am not even allowed to walk outside now because of my size. I feel so big, and cannot walk far anyway, because my ankles are swollen a bit. I asked Mary Ann about 'giving birth', she said it comes out the same way it went, how is that. She told me about her cousin who is married to the baker. She was there with her mother last year when she had her baby boy, she did say her cousin cried a lot it is very painful, and went in to a bit of detail that I am not putting down here. I'm not sure I would like to have been a midwife, but I will not even be a nurse, Father will see to that, I am still a minor I will not be 21 until next year.

June 30th 1918
My beautiful little baby girl is here, I started to give birth late on 20th June, I have not known such pain, the doctor came and checked on me, and said everything was going well, and he would come back nearer the time Mary Ann stayed with me and Ellen spent about an hour with me, but she said she had to go, as she was not allowed to see me give birth, Mother said she was too young but she would stay in her room and think of me, she kissed my forehead, stroked my face and ran out, she does care for me. The night drew on, and the pain eased at times, Mary Ann suggested that I breathed with pains, and it seemed to help. Just before dawn when I heard the birds singing outside, the doctor came in as I felt the urge to push, Agnes and Mary Ann were with me as I gave birth, I waited and he said that it was a girl, I heard a weak cry and then after the maids started to rub her little body, (although I have heard of people smacking the infants) she wailed and I cried with relief. The doctor cut the cord, and said to the maids that they were a great help, Mary Ann said coyly that she had been with a few ladies who gave birth, and Agnes also said she had experience too.

He said that my baby was healthy, and it was a shame that I was unmarried. He seemed really sympathetic, and I thanked him for staying so long. 'It's my job Miss Clarkson, I am sorry to say that there have been quite a few births like yours but the outcome is the same, orphanage or workhouse.' He left me with the two maids who dressed my little one and put her in the cot. I also thanked them for staying with me. I looked at the baby sleeping in the cot and looked at her little face, and gently lifted the cover to look at her fingers and toes, she seemed to have my nose and eyebrows but she had long fingers which could be a surgeon's fingers and longish toes, that reminded of Gerard, and I suddenly felt a rush of love, I was not going to part from her without a fight. Then I got back into bed and fell asleep, almost happy.

15th July 1918

Father has let me come downstairs for meals now, but my baby stays upstairs in my room with one of the maids looking after her. He said he would get a wet nurse to feed her so that I would not get attached to her. I told him that it was too late, I would feed her while I can, and I would not be parted from her so he had better send me to the workhouse if he wished, he seemed taken aback and said he would still work something out. I seem to have some fire in me, being a protective mother, I have called her Ellen Mary after my dear sister, mother and dear Mary Ann, but I could not tell her.

August 30th 1918

Under normal circumstances little Ellen might have been christened but Father was adamant that this would not happen, it would depend on my new husband which he was working on. He did allow me grudgingly to register her birth at the end of July with the father's name blank.

He says that he is going find a husband for me who would take on a child that was not his, Father said not to expect any affection for Ellen, he spat her name out, and be thankful that anyone would take me on let alone her. All this for appearances, I wonder Mother cares for him at all.

One day whilst Father was out all day, Mother finally told me about her marriage to Father. It seemed that the young man she was walking with was not suitable as he was a 'humble' schoolmaster and she was discouraged from seeing him. My Father was a landowner who my grandfather knew well, and he paid court to Mother and before she knew it he proposed to her, and grandfather had given his consent so she felt her 'duty' to accept. Mother liked him but she never really loved him, and after she had done her 'duty' by having me and Ellen they seemed to live separate lives, only coming together for meals, special occasions or being a hostess. It made me feel sad, and I could understand a lot more. Was this to be my lot, do my duty be a good wife in a loveless marriage? She did say something to which shook me, 'Hold on, things might not be so bad, do something with your life, I think you wanted to be a nurse, well do it or something else, make me proud of you.' I hugged my mother and thanked her.

September 1918
Father has found me a husband, he told me, he is 35 years old, a widower who had no children and is a wealthy businessman who has a large house in Lewes. Apparently he made his fortune in metals and has three munitions factories, new money Father says, another of Father's acquaintances I suppose, he has tried to find me prospective husbands, this is the third, as each one who was invited to dinner would not accept my child, so they were dismissed as no can do. This man came to supper last week and he seemed pleasant enough and when he opened his mouth was a big put off, he had no manners, he spoke well enough, but did not seem to know how to conduct himself in company, am I being a snob? Even Mary Ann and Agnes know how to conduct themselves, the village people have good manners and are polite to each other let alone us. Is that what new money makes people arrogant and contemptuous. Father

doesn't seem to notice but Mother almost winced. He was seated opposite me and Ellen, Mother and Father sat at either end of the table and my aunt sat next to him. His name is Arthur Messen, as son of a miner from Devon who made his money from a tine mine. This Arthur is a little overweight and talks with mouth full and slurps his wine, and needs help with his cutlery which my aunt politely showed him. I have been made to put on my prettiest dress which now fits me, but the bodice had been altered to adapt to my bosom. He keeps looking at me up and down. I am uncomfortable in his gaze.

October 31st 1918
Was it only a year since they all left. Even the nurses and all the patients have gone, the house is ours again.

Apparently Mr Messen has agreed to my request of accepting child along with me, so I am to be affianced to him with a substantial sum annually from my Father as a 'dowry'. I have been worn down; I accepted a necklace from him, a pearl and diamond brooch, with a view to being engaged at the end of November and marriage just before Christmas. He looks very smug, to get a lady! But with baggage, he thinks he is doing me a favour. I am so unhappy, I seem to be doomed to a loveless marriage like my mother, oh again – God help me.

November 15th 1918
The war is finally over, on 11th November at 11 a.m. an armistice was declared, and all the soldiers are finally coming home, I have not heard any more from Elliott, the cause seems lost. My Father is planning a celebration for the end of the war and to celebrate my engagement and Ellen's engagement but she is to wait for a year. I am resigned to my fate. I have gone to London with Ellen to be

fitted for a special gown for the ball to look my best, a prize for Mr Messen. I can hardly call him Arthur, we have only met in company, is this what arranged marriages are like? Ellen is excited, but it is a little muted as she cares about me, she is marrying the man she loves, but me, last night she put a note under my door, it said, 'My dearest sister, I feel so sad for you I may be happy but you oh, how I wish your man would come back to carry you off, All my love E. Love to little E I will miss you.'

I am dreading the day when I leave this house only to become another prisoner Mr Messon looks at with half contempt and another look that I'm not sure I like, as if he is undressing me in his mind.

November 28th 1918
Only another two days and my life will be set for sadness. Father has ordered that the large lounge at the back of the house to be converted to a ballroom, with a small dais for the musicians. He seems to be revelling in the preparations; he seemed to be happy that both his daughters are to be married and to show off to the village and town what a great man he is. He has even invited the military back.

November 30th 1918
Well the day has come at last, I am dreading it, it will be the beginning of the rest of my life, I will not be able to make any decisions, he will control the money, that's how it works. The evening got off to a slow start, as Ellen and I looked over the banister rail facing the front door as the dignitaries came in, and the military, and no one familiar came in, so we finished getting ready and took a last look in the mirror at ourselves, Ellen looked lovely in her lemon chiffon gown and yellow satin shoes, with hair up she looked almost twenty years old. I wore a slightly higher necked light blue satin dress with dark blue satin shoes, and a gold bracelet from Mother, Ellen wore

a pair of gold earrings which Mother gave her. We took a last look in on Ellen who was sleeping peacefully, unaware of her not so good future, my sister planted a kiss on her fingers and on her niece's plump cheek, and thanked me for the 100th time for naming baby Ellen after her. I hugged my sister and we tiptoed out of her room, which was bare, with only a washbasin, napkins and a small drawer chest for her clothes.

We walked downstairs as elegantly as we could. Ellen's uniformed beau came forward to take her arm, but Mr Messen was across the room smoking a cigar with a glass of wine in his hands and carried on talking to his companion, a uniformed officer, he glanced at me and carried on talking. I knew my place! The music started and people started to drift towards the ballroom and started to dance. I went into the room also and sat on a chair which was among others which were placed around some tables around the wall to encircle a dance floor. Mr Messen came in and sat next to me and put a glass of wine in front of me and suggested that I drink some, after all we were going to be engaged, 'At least look as if you are enjoying yourself Anna,' he said jocularly, as if I had anything to be happy about. I did pick up the glass and was tempted to throw it over him, but kept my manners and sipped it and looked at him over the glass, he looked very smug. Another tune was started and he put his drink down and stood up and walked round to me and grabbed my hand and said, 'Dance with me Anna, after all the next time will be at our wedding.' He drew me to the middle of the room and held me a little too close, and too tight. I protested that was not how we should dance but he said that was how we danced, 'After all I am overlooking your little mistake, you should be grateful!'

I retorted, 'You are being well paid for it.' He didn't like that and shoved me around a bit roughly. Just then as we passed the open doorway I saw two familiar faces of men in uniform, and everything seemed to go into slow motion, was I dreaming? I broke away from Mr Messon and walked away from him unaware of anyone or anything else. I walked towards the two soldiers, and yes, it was Sergeant Elliott James, and Gerard, he seemed a bit tired and was walking with a stick as he had a slight limp. People were looking at me but I didn't care, Elliott did as he had promised and Gerard was back. I greeted them warmly and drew them both aside; I asked them what had happened. Elliott started by telling me that he found Gerard in a hospital near to Paris, apparently he been taken there from a German hospital, when they discharged their POWs who had been injured. Gerard took up the story, he said that he had gone too far over and was on the wrong side, he had tripped and fallen into a trench full of Germans, but as they noticed he was wearing a red cross and medical corps uniform they did not kill him, but took him to their own hospital. He had broken his ankle and grazed a knee and after a few weeks he was able to walk with a stick and with the German's fractured English and his smattering of German he was put to work helping the injured and a few POWs who had been injured. Gerard was unable to write to anyone, so was worried about me and as he could see I was with someone else, I shook my head, it was a long story and I asked Elliott and Gerard if they would come with me I had something to show them. Unaware that anyone was following us, I led them upstairs and took them to a little room next to my bedroom and opened the door to Ellen's bedroom where she was sleeping peacefully unaware of the commotion going on. Gerard followed me in as did Elliott, both went quiet, I switched the light on and Ellen stirred.

'Who is this?' Gerard asked looking at me puzzled.

'She is Ellen and she is five months old and does she not look familiar to you?' He did look at her and as she opened her eyes she looked up at him and he her.

'Five months erm, that last night before we went, we had too much wine, but I'm sorry I should have held back but I couldn't, can you forgive me?'

Just then my Father and Mr Messen walked in, asking what was going on, he said to Gerard, 'Why are you with my fiancée we are to be married next month.' I was panic stricken, what was going to happen?

Gerard stood up to his full height, which was several inches taller than Mr Messen and my Father. 'I think I have prior claim to Miss Clarkson.' I pulled out the chain with the family ring which he had given me. 'Mr Clarkson I am sorry that I did not speak to you before I went and was able to get word out. My intentions are honourable sir.' My Father was not happy and said to me, 'If you go with this young man I will cut you off without a penny, you can never come back again, you had a chance of a life of luxury as a lady and if you want to with him, make your choice.'

Gerard took my hand and said to my Father, 'If that is your attitude, I will take her off your hands as you might say, but she will be cherished and loved, and your granddaughter too. I am not without means, my father has a flourishing medical practice and I have a trust fund which I will be able to draw on in January. I am aware that she is not 21 yet, so I need your permission to marry your daughter.' My Father nodded, and Mr Messen walked out with a 'Huh'.

December 20th 1918
True to his work, Gerard and I were married in a registry office yesterday in London near my aunt's house as she had made arrangements. It was hard leaving home the next day after a virtually sleepless night. It was an emotional parting from Ellen who promised to write. I was allowed to take Mary Ann with me as a nanny and

maid, but she is more than that. I promised to look after her. My Mother gave some money in an envelope and asked to write to her, care of Agnes. We took a train to London with Elliott who acted as a witness with my aunt, who set out a meal for us. She also looked after Ellen with Mary Ann when we went to a hotel for the night. Elliott finally went home to Essex to his wife and family.

At last as husband and wife we were alone for a little while, and over supper and later we exchanged our stories, my telling him about the baby not wanting to let her go and he told me more of his time in Belgium, when he got back to the field hospital there were many casualties, and he was set to help with operations, of which many sadly were amputations, or repairs to faces and of those, returned to Paris for return to England, if they survived the first few days, as some had lost a lot of blood or were in terrible pain and there was not a lot of pain relief there. He did not have a lot of time to himself, but when he did he thought of me, and kept thinking back to the last night when we slept together, well accidentally, he wondered what he had left me to, he tried to put all his love into the letters and my letters kept him going, but I gave no clue as to what was happening to me. He was then sent to the front to go into 'no man's land' for casualties, and managed to recover six casualties with his now good friend Elliott. Unfortunately they became separated and Gerard became confused as to where he was going, there was a lot of smoke, and he could not quite see where he was going, he stumbled and fell down into a German trench, and broke his ankle and hit his head, fortunately it was a concussion but when he came to he was surrounded by German troops who were as surprised as he was, they were so young, and when they saw the red cross on his shoulders and the breast pocket of his uniform and did not shoot him straight away, with their fractured English and his smattering of

German, they made themselves understood. He was taken to their hospital, had ankle splinted, and head wound which was not serious, he lay alongside German patients, who were the less injured. After he had recovered and could walk with a stick, he helped to tend to the injured soldiers, not unlike ours, and he felt sorry for them as they were only conscripts. He did his best, sadly knowing that if they went back to the front that they might likely to be killed.

He was not allowed to write to anyone but he clung to the hope that I would wait for him, and when he was finally sent to Paris as a POW with other soldiers at the end of the war he was reunited with Elliott and Elliott told him of the letter he had sent to me. Gerard was heartbroken, but Elliott said that he would take him back and hope that I had been true to him. So when he went to the house he saw me dancing with another, he felt crestfallen, but when I turned and walked towards him, he had hope. I told him what had happened to me and the hope that I kept and once the baby was born I refused to let her go, and made conditions. We had talked far into the night and it was the small hours when we went to bed, and at last as husband and wife. There was nothing clandestine or blurred by our coming together this time, and it was an act of love.

December 31st 1918
We have obtained a passport for me, and for Mary Ann who wanted to go with us, and tickets for passage to Canada, to go to his home town to start a new life.

As the ship sailed away from the docks, I looked at the fading coastline, I felt a sadness, a little fearful as I had only been to London in my life, we were going to Canada to his homeland.

The diary ended here.

Sara was frustrated the diary or journal had taken her through the second half of the first war, of the romance and trials of Anna Mary; she wanted to know more. She had sat at the table for three hours, and it was getting dark. She put all the papers in a drawer in the kitchen and locked it, she carried on to make the supper for her husband and daughter Emily, and son Jeremy, both in their twenties and working hard, one was a nurse and the other a midwife (son a nurse and daughter a midwife.)

Part Two

1919–1936

Between the Wars

Present day

Sara was not able to look at the package in the kitchen drawer for a few weeks, she had been busy working at the local school as a supply teacher which she enjoyed, she had been offered a permanent post, of five hours a day five days a week and she had talked to her husband and children who thought that this was a good idea, and she was good with the age group that she taught, 8 to 11 years and she had a good knowledge of the subjects and how to teach them. It was the summer holidays and she had accepted the position, and was looking forward to starting in September. Sara had a free morning and again sat down with a coffee and opened the second envelope, the one with the letters in. They were wrapped in a faded red ribbon. She looked at the envelopes which were postmarked Ontario, Canada, the address on the back was from a large town.

The first letter was in the same handwriting as before, and was addressed to Miss Ellen Clarkson in Hampstead. The first letter was dated 15th March 1919.

Dearest Ellen,

Well we have arrived! The sea crossing was quite unpleasant at times, being winter, and I have never travelled for so long and so far on water before, remember the river trips we went on as children, no comparison! Mary Ann has been such a help, I hope that Agnes has been so to you. I am so glad that you could continue to have her with you. Your little niece Ellen is well. Gerard is well enough, his limp is improving, he still needs a stick, I hope that he can get help with it, as when the sea was a bit choppy at times he struggled to move around. After a few weeks at sea I seemed to get quite queasy and put it down to the choppy sea, but it continued after we arrived in Canada, and Gerard laughed, when I told him, I am expecting again! He is very happy, I'm not sure, considering how I felt last time, but there is no need to keep silent this time. We landed in Hudson Bay a lesson in itself. The journey to his home town continued by train, this took two days as we had to take another train inland. The scenery is breathtaking. I have put a few postcards in also. Maybe one day you could come and visit us, if you have six months to spare! We seemed to be on the train a long time travelling through many towns, and empty spaces but with as I said before, are many beautiful scenes and spaces. Gerard has been giving me, us, a Geography and culture lesson as we go. So much to find out about this wonderful country. Mary Ann is enjoying the journey also; she is embracing this new life as am I. There are so many horses, as the motor car has not become a reliable transport yet, and they are able to get to many places where there are not many proper roads as such. It is very cold also at this time of year as we are closer to the Arctic Circle, nearer or as near as Scotland. Remember the Geography lessons that we had, of faraway places, the Americas and Canada, we are living it and seeing it. I suppose this will be a one way correspondence for a while but I will give you our new address when we arrive. We passed through Ontario, and near Quebec, Gerard says that they have a language of their own being settlers from France, but not quite the French we learned!

We finally arrived in Montreal, which is not far from the United States border. Gerard's parents live a few miles out of the city, in what you might call a suburb, but they have a large house, near a town, and yes, there are a lot more cars here, and big trucks but they have a stable with horses, as your niece will learn to ride as we did when we were younger. Gerard did telegraph ahead to say that we were coming, but he didn't exactly get a hero's welcome, as Gerard said that he had volunteered, and he left under a bit of a cloud as his father wanted him to complete his medical studies. Gerard was welcomed by his mother, who was worried about his welfare as he only wrote sporadically, and it seems he must have written to me more. Now I know why he went to the post office, I thought he had a sweetheart here but it was to his mother, who is a beautiful gracious well born also, but has adapted well, she came from New Brunswick and, as I was, a lady without a profession as such but trained as a nurse and met Gerard's father, Gerard senior, was kind but brusque. Gerard [my Gerard] is their only son, and he was happy to go into his father's profession. After a few weeks, apparently, Gerard junior will continue his studies and be attached to the main hospital, so I may not see him very much, but I will support him to his graduation.

Shortly after we arrived at the house in Moose Falls (there are some moose in the hills, and there is a lovely big waterfall about five miles away) we went into the house being a large imposing building, with a large entrance door to the house with a large staircase to the left cross with banisters. The upstairs rooms were all bedrooms, with two en-suite bathrooms and another bathroom further down. For the guest rooms. I have just about got around knowing where everything is, as I have been looking after our rooms and them tidy and clean, I wanted to help as I am aware they have a cook and housekeeper and a maid, and have got used to looking after myself.

It was Gerard's birthday 18th March and they had a party for him (he is 26 now) and invited friends and neighbours to meet and welcome us to Canada. Mary Ann has expressed a wish to train as a nurse, and I think this is a great idea as she had some experience with me, when I gave birth, and she also helped the nurses when they needed an extra person. She has had a good education, but unfortunately left school at 14 when her time came and she came to us. I told her that if she needs any help at all, I would gladly help her with her further studies, and Mrs Horan said she had some biology books that she would be happy to lend her. I know dear Ellen that you might not approve, as we are quite different, you may be happy to be a lady and have class distinction but we may not be in a frontier town, but I was never happy just being a lady, I wanted to do something useful, and whilst I am being a mother to a baby of nine months, and in waiting for another, I think that I would like to be a teacher. Oh, and despite having people to do the cooking and cleaning, Mrs Horan senior also does some baking of her own, and she is teaching me! Please don't be angry with me Dearest Ellen. I hope that your new life with your new husband, as you will marry in June, will be as happy and exciting as mine. (Cheque enclosed for your wedding present.)

Much love, Anna Mary, Ellen, Gerard.

The next letter was dated 30th June 1919.

Dearest Ellen,

Thank you for your short letter, I received it two days ago, sea mail is so slow. Thank you also for the photographs of your wedding, you looked so solemn, are you not happy? Ah maybe it is not the thing to smile, these photographs are very abrupt, and one still has to stay still for so long, even now. I hope that you will be happy in your new home, is Agnes still with you? I hope that she may come with you, it will be a help to have someone familiar when you start afresh in a new life. Gerard works long hours, and when he is not at the hospital he is studying and he looks tired at times, but he still finds time to be with little Ellen, as they get to know each other, we sometimes go out for walks and take Ellen in her baby carriage which Mrs Horan senior gave us, apparently it was Gerard's when he was a baby, she had someone in town clean and paint it and put some bedding in, she also took us into town to buy some wool and material for baby clothes, as the clothing that we brought from London is getting a bit tight for her, she is growing so fast. We also had our photographs taken all of us, and me with Ellen as she would not sit still, see how she has grown! Mrs Horan is so kind, as when we were having lunch one day, I told her how Gerard and I met, and what transpired, she is such a lovely person, I have become very fond of her. Mary Ann continues to do well, she has passed her initial exams, and oh dear, she is getting an accent, as so will I, as I seem pick up words that people understand better. I am also getting bigger as this baby seems to be bigger than Ellen. I have also been to the hospital for a check on my progress, both Mary Ann and Mrs Horan senior suggested both being nurses and both having delivered quite a few babies. What a change around. The hospital is five miles away just outside Montreal, and is very big. They have to pay for treatment and stay in hospital as we do, but there are less well off people who cannot afford the charges, so once a week Mr Horan senior goes to visit them in the small villages and remote settlements. He goes on horseback with a mule to carry any extra equipment; Gerard has been going with him too, so the horses that they keep in the stables are not just for pleasure, but for work. They are beautiful, there are stallions, one is black with white spots around his eyes, and one is a chestnut. The mares are both white one has a brown splash on her forehead; the other is smaller and is pure white. They keep the stallions and mares apart for obvious reason, but they are loved and well looked after and the mules are also groomed and valued and when he is not working is free to run around the corral and field at the back and stays in the stable in the winter and at night. How Gerard could leave all this I do not know, but I'm glad he did for my own reasons.

There is only worry though, whilst we were back in England, Gerard had a nightmare, and woke up in a sweat, he tried to tell me that it was just a bad dream, but he has had these dreams at least once a week now, when he is tired or has been working on the surgical side of the hospital, and I have become concerned. As you know, I am not the subservient type of wife, so I asked him if we could go for a walk just the two of us, and took a picnic. I just said that it might be the last time that we could spend time together as he had big examinations coming up, and I will be giving birth early September. So we packed a hamper, left Ellen with Mrs Horan, as Mary Ann has started her formal training as a student nurse at the hospital and bless her, she works long hours, and she spends her spare time studying. He is a little worried that she is not looking after me or the little one, but I am happy looking after myself and Ellen, and Mrs Horan is enjoying being a grandmother who looks after her grandchild. Ellen is starting to talk, and her first word was Da then Dada, her next word was Mama, then Hiya, Ganda and Gamma, she will get her 'R's eventually but her 'Ganda' and 'Gamma' are thrilled to be called so. Anyway to get back to the picnic, Gerard harnessed the two stallions to a wagon and took us out to the falls, and placed the wagon in the shade, but unharnessed the horses so that they could graze and go down to the lakeside to drink but did not let them stray too far, so we sat near the tree on a blanket and set out our picnic. It was idyllic, I asked him if he came here when he was younger, he said yes, he loved it, and he even saw a moose or two walking up in the hills. As we were eating I asked him about his experiences at the front, but he was a bit reluctant to talk. I then mentioned that when I was at home, I sometimes heard the injured soldiers cry out in their sleep at night, and the nurses calmed them down or the doctors gave them an injection, as I sometimes crept down and hid in the shadows and saw more than I should have done. He looked at me a bit oddly, and asked why, I said that I had heard him cry out about once a week and asked if there was something that had happened that he couldn't tell me. I thought for a moment that he was angry, but he drank some water, took a deep breath and told me of the noise of the guns, and of the soldiers who were not physically injured, who could not sleep or could not be hospitalised, did have a problem but the doctors did not seem aware of it, or did not recognise it. Gerard had a small experience of it, he said what gave him the nightmares was the not being able to help their minds as well as their bodies, these men went home mentally scarred, those who did not ran away and went AWOL (absent without official leave) and were shot for cowardice. He was in tears as he was talking, maybe it was because of my condition, but I was in tears also, and for a time I just went over to him and held him, resting his head on my shoulder, as the shadows lengthened he dried his tears and mine, kissed me, and I said matter of factly; 'What are you going to do about it then.'

He laughed and said, 'Ever the practical one, where do you get it from?'

We cleared up the meal etc. hitched the horses to the wagon and went back to the house. I felt strangely lighted of heart and Gerard was smiling. Please keep some of this to yourself, dear Ellen.

Much love,

Anna, Gerard, Ellen.

Mary Ann wishes to be remembered too and sends her love to Agnes. She is writing to her father.

DIARIES OF A LADY

24th September 1919

Dearest Ellen,

Thank you for your letter, you do not say much, I trust that all is well with you. You say Mother is spending more time with our aunt, and less with our father, I should write to her in London as you suggest. Have you started a family yet? If that is not too probing. Things are going quite well with us at the moment. I am very occupied with Ellen, and oh yes, you have a nephew! It was quite traumatic, two weeks ago I had bad twinges, I thought that it was a bit early, as the baby was not due for at least two weeks or so the doctor suggested, but no, after about half a day, I had what they called contractions, still very painful, I do wish there was some way to make that process manageable. However Mary Ann was with me, and I stayed at home for a while, but Mr Horan suggested, nay insisted that I go to the hospital, albeit at bit bumpy, going in the carriage, and I was there within ten minutes, but I also noticed that the horses were breathing heavily but none the worse, and I know you would say piffle about the horses, but they are so good, anyhow, just as well I did go, as the baby was the wrong way around feet first, and could not be turned, and they suggested using some implements called forceps. Euggh! When I saw the instruments. They did give me an injection to ease the pain, they said! After another two hours, I was 'ready' as they and I was feeling sleepy but still aware, Mary Ann explained to me later what they did, I will not go into details, I am sure you would faint! Sufficient to say the child was delivered, and I lost some blood, I am recovering well. The child is a boy! He is bigger than Ellen was, and seems little the worse for his entry into the world! Thank God. As I named Ellen, Gerard had the choice to name our son. He is to be called Gerard Philip Horan III. He is a sweet baby, with his father's nose and a shock of dark hair, but with fingers like mine, so maybe he will not be a surgeon like his father is training to be. I am quite well now also, and seem to have recovered from the 'labour'. Gerard is happy to have a son, but I think little Ellen has his heart, Gerard III is my little man, but our Ellen is still very part of my heart, she could not be otherwise, as I fought so hard to keep her. I am so happy, but I know that they will be a handful, two children under two years old. I just wondered, are you thinking of starting a family? You tell me so little in your letters, are things all right with you? Perhaps you could tell if Mother is well. Mary Ann has written to her parents to tell them all the news and we get some back. There are so many miles between us, and the mail takes so long, but I am a little homesick, but I do love this place.

Much Love, Anna Mary.

Present day
The letters stopped and Sara was a little puzzled, so she put them back and wrapped them in the red ribbon and back into the big envelope with the journal of the early years. Sara opened the second envelope and noticed that had been read already. There was another large notebook like the first one, and another smaller envelope which seemed to have something flat and hard inside. She left it to one side and opened the notebook eagerly, hoping to find more about Anna Mary and her family in Canada and Mary Ann. She was not disappointed. The next date which carried on her story started two months later.

30th November 1919
I am a little lost and sad that I received no more letters. I waited and waited and waited to no avail. Mary Ann was still getting letters relatively regularly from her parents and she shared with me her news, of the village and snippets from the house, my old home, but

I do not miss it, but I miss the people from the village. This is my home now, with my darling Gerard, who spends as much time with me and our little ones, and his parents are very kind and seem to have adopted me too. I even call them Mother and Father H. I have grown to love them, I miss Mama more than a little, I wonder if news got back to her. Gerard is working hard to complete his studies to qualify as a doctor, not just a GP but to do surgery and he has been studying also about a mental condition called 'shell shock' after his own experiences.

Sadly though earlier in the month 11th November Gerard and other members of the military marched past a new memorial to those who have died during the last war (at least 10 young died from the town) and wore their old uniforms. We stood quietly for two minutes in silence to remember all the young men who died.

But also he asked if I would marry him again, I asked if the first marriage was legal, and he laughed, he said that we could renew our vows in church and have a proper ceremony and a party afterwards with everyone, also to have our children christened which I thought would be wonderful. The preparations were exciting and again Mary Ann was my maid of honour, and my in laws arranged for a reception or party, and invited their friends and new friends. Dear Mary Ann, she is more of a friend than a servant, come to think of it, she isn't a servant any more, she an independent woman who is training to be a nurse and especially a midwife, and she lives with us, and eats with us, and helps to look after the children, and she is their godmother. The service was lovely, Mr Horan gave me away and I had a lovely dress. Gerard's face was a picture, he seemed so happy and so handsome in his grey suit, having packed his uniform away, but he says the military have put him on the reserve list. The wedding was everything I could have hoped for and tradition for a semi rural town as this is. Gerard also did something special for Little Ellen, as she was born whilst he was away at the front and his name is not on her birth certificate, apparently it cannot be re-registered with his name on, so he did the next best thing he 'adopted' her legally so that she has the same name as us, and the wording was as this, 'As the father was not present at the birth of the said child Ellen Mary Clarkson, and the registration there of, he hereby acknowledges being father of the said child and by doing so he adopts her into his family and she will be known as Ellen Mary Horan thereafter.'

When we went back to the house with all our guests and family in the decorated carriages and carts, Gerard showed to me the document, 'It's the next best thing Darling,' he said, 'Keep this safe with her birth certificate, so that she will understand when she is older will have the same rights as our son, and it's the least I could do, as you kept her safe and with you despite the odds.' I shed a few tears. Ellen who was sitting in the carriage with us called over, 'No cry Mama.'

I then burst into tears afresh; this was the first sentence she had said. Gerard who was holding little Gerard III, 'Mama just happy, you clever girl, you are talking,' and she laughed. Mary Ann who was in the carriage with us smiled and hugged Ellen, and hid her face in the little girl's hair for a moment, as she shed a tear too, as Gerard had read the wording out loud.

When we arrived at the house Mary Ann got out first and helped to get Ellen out, and took Jarred from Gerard's arms, and he got out, and then he helped me out. We all walked up to the house, and everyone else were waiting for us and there was a photographer with his large camera on a stand, so we all stood together and froze our smiles, and it was rather cold being almost the end of November, and then everyone went inside including the horses to the stables. I asked for this to happen quickly, as they had been standing outside and blowing hot breath. Gerard laughed! 'They are working horses and they are getting their winter coats, we are in a colder part of the world, and get snow for a good six weeks if not more!'

I looked him in the eye and replied that may be, but it didn't hurt to let them be looked after well, so that they will work better. We were not overheard, and I thought that this was just as well because as in England, women tended to defer to their husbands. He whispered to me, 'Is this our first spat?' and smiled at me with a twinkle in his eye. I shook my head, and giggled.

We went into the house and saw the guests waiting for us and they clapped as we came in, before we went into the dining room for the meal. Mr Horan made sure everyone had a glass of champagne, and Mary stood by the 'best man' a tall handsome young man with dark straight hair, clean shaven just like Gerard's with a blue cravat but seemed a little uncomfortable and pulled a bit at his neck as if to loosen it. Gerard smiled when I whispered, 'Who is that man Mary is standing with?'

'Oh that is Harry Manton, a young intern, same year to me and my best friend, she is on the same ward as he is and they seem to get on well.'

Then Mr Horan raised his hand and asked for silence. 'Ladies and gentlemen, friends and family, I am very happy to welcome you to our home, and to this very special celebration, as you know our son Gerard returned from the war serving overseas as a non-combatant medic, against my wishes I may add,' a little murmur of small laughs from the guests, 'but thank God he returned relatively in one piece. He did not come alone, he brought this young lady who befriended him at her home (pointing to me and I lowered my head for a moment) and made him feel welcome. I need not go into details, but she remained constant to him and when he returned he took her away on a long journey to his homeland, and she has been a brave lady to leave everything. She has brought us our granddaughter and then a grandson and made this home ring with the sound of children's voices, even if they do wake us up in the early hours!' They laughed at that, and I also. 'Young lady, Anna Mary you have settled in so well as has your friend Mary Ann.' He indicated with his hand to dear Mary Ann. 'We, my wife and I have so much to be thankful and happy for. Finally I wish you to raise your glasses to the renewed Mr and Mrs Gerard Horan junior, Gerard and Anna Mary.'

They raised their glasses and repeated our names and drank and, and then burst into gentle clapping, after putting their glasses down. My eyes filled again, it was so gracious of him to say such nice things about me. Gerard (mine) handed me a handkerchief and I dabbed my eyes, Mr Horan came over to us and planted a kiss on my cheek and patted his son on the shoulder, I told him that he was too kind to say such things about me, that my tears were of joy and the occasion was just wonderful. He smiled down at me although he was slightly shorter than Gerard, he was a good five inches taller than me, 'No more than you deserved my dear, after all, if it wasn't for you and your friendship and love, he might not have come back at all, that was an awful thing, so many young men not coming back, let's hope there will never be another one. And I believe that you left under a cloud, with your father only too happy to let you go?'

I replied quietly as people started to go into the dining room, 'I was a disappointment to him, as he didn't want me to get involved with the hospital side, but that was what I wanted to do, not be the lady of the manor like my mother.'

'Well all I can say is God moves in mysterious ways.' He replied, 'Wait here for a moment you two, and once everyone is in their place, you will be announced.'

I looked at Gerard as his father took his wife's arm and she looked lovely in dark blue, and he smiled down at me. 'I know that you do not like grand occasions any more, but this is what you deserve, for being my wonderful brave girl, so take a deep breath and enjoy it my darling.'

We went to the opened double doors of the beautifully decorated dining room, and the 'butler' for the day announced us as, 'Mr and Mrs Gerard Horan,' and we walked the length of the room past the long tables of guests who I think were about 100 in number, I cannot be sure it was too quick, everyone stood up and applauded as we took our seats at the head of the table next to Mr and Mrs Horan senior and at the side stood the best man and dear Mary Ann, who seemed very happy. As we sat down I asked Mary Ann, 'Where are the little ones?' she smiled and said 'Ellen was falling asleep and Jarred is asleep, so they were taken up to their room.'

I smiled my thanks and listened as the minister stood up to say grace, it was a short but sweet one, and we enjoyed our lovely three course meal of French onion soup, with fresh bread rolls, then roast beef with Yorkshire pudding, and potatoes and carrots, broccoli cauliflower and Brussels sprouts. (I asked about the Yorkshire pudding and veg, and they said Mary Ann had helped with the menu and showed cook how to make Yorkshire pudding) it was perfect and reminded me of home. I am a basic cook, so I think I had better get some help to do more. The desserts were a choice of lemon cheesecake, chocolate gateau with cream and fruit salad with cream, and cheese and biscuits and coffee and more champagne 'till my head almost whirled but I wanted to remember each moment. The best man stood up and made a speech, and he said some witty things about Gerard, it appeared that they went to school together and had same interests in medicine, and went to medical college together, but Harry is a year younger, so was a year behind Gerard, and by the time he wanted to enlist the war was over, but he always read the news from the front in the newspapers, which they wrote. He was grateful to find out more from Gerard when he got home, and finished with thanking Gerard for asking him to be his man, and then raised his glass and asked for a toast to the happy couple (us). Everyone stood and toasted us. Later, we sat for a while whilst coffee was being served before we were encouraged to go and cut the wedding cake, which was two tiers round and with white and silver icing with two figures on top representing the bride and groom. The cake was quite large, and there was a sword on the table, I looked quizzically at Gerard, He said, 'It belonged to my grandfather who was a seafaring man, he became a captain and got the sword as a present from the crew as he was firm but kind.'

I smiled and with his hand over mine, cut the cake with a piece of history. Everyone clapped and the cake was taken away to be cut up for the guests. Gerard and I walked around meeting the guests and being introduced to others I had not met before. Mary Ann seemed happy to sit at the table and chat with Harry, they seemed very comfortable and at ease with each other, I was so happy that she had settled down so well, and was almost reaching the end of her training as a nurse and apparently was doing very well. She was a bit apologetic at times that she was not helping me, but I had reassured her that she was doing something so worthwhile and I was happy being a wife and mother, for her to see this as a progression, and that she was helping at times, with the children and she does love them so, I almost told her how I felt about her, more as a friend and an equal, but because of our upbringing, remained silent, but things are changing. Gerard noticed my silence and took me to one side and asked what was wrong, 'Nothing really, I was just thinking of Mary Ann, she still feels that she is my maid, but she has moved on more and doing a wonderful thing. I cannot tell her how I feel; she is a good friend and more...'

'More like a sister?' he asked, and my eyes opened wide, 'Well yes I seem to have a better rapport with her than Ellen, although Ellen and I had the same education and training in manners and deportment, I went through the motions, but I didn't always get it right. So shortly after my 15th birthday, Mary Ann came to the house, I thought that she would be a kitchen maid, but was so glad that she would be my maid, to learn to be a ladies' maid, and for her to teach me how to be a lady, I think that she did a good job, but I was a bit rebellious at times, but she always kept reminding me of my place, and although she had other jobs to do in the house, she was always there for me. Ellen had her own maid also, Agnes who is Mary Ann's cousin, who seemed more to know her place as Ellen was able to act and be more of a lady than I could ever be. But I am so glad that we came and Mary Ann can do more than just be my maid, but if you do not mind I want to be more than a wife and mother, I am fulfilled at the moment, but I have always felt I could do more than just being a lady.'

Phew! I stopped talking out of breath, Gerard just smiled, 'All in good time Anna, after all that's why I fell in love with you apart from your beauty, you have an enquiring mind. We have two little ones, look after them, but if you wish, in your spare time especially while I am working, read, gain knowledge, teach the children and if you would like, go to the local school and help them there. I don't want you to be just a hostess and mother, learn from my mother, she is so gifted and is ready to encourage you just as she did and does to Mary Ann.'

People were looking at as, as were deep in conversation, as the noise and chatter subsided apparently we were expected to start the first dance. I could dance a few dances, but I was concerned that Gerard did still have a slight limp, but he said, 'A simple waltz will be fine, my ankle is much better.'

So that's what we did, and he surprised me at times, as although he danced with small but sweeping movements, he would twirl me around, and after a few twirls around the floor, the others joined us. Shortly after we stopped dancing and other dances continued, we heard a little wail, and I knew what that meant, my little boy was hungry, so I excused myself and went to the nursery, where the 'nanny' was holding up the little fellow gently and said, 'Sorry Mrs Anna I thought he would sleep a little longer.' I shook my head, and smiled and as Gerard followed me in, he suggested that she get something to eat and drink and to come back in an hour. Little Ellen looked up from her cot and said 'Gerry hungry mummy.'

Gerard picked her up and chatted to her as I went to the adjoining room which was our bedroom, and I sat on a little sofa, and gave the baby my breast, and he suckled hungrily. It was just as well I asked for buttons down the front of my lovely cream gown, so that I could open it with no problem. After drinking his fill, I put him on my shoulder taking care to place a towel there, as my little boy was greedy and sometimes drank a little too much and lost about a quarter of what he had drunk. I was a bit worried that he might ruin my lovely wedding dress, but he did not, and as I rubbed his little back I heard a big burp, and he seemed fine. After a while he fell asleep, and I rearranged my clothing, and took him back to their nursery, and laid him down in his cradle. I noticed that little Ellen was getting sleepy too, cuddled up in her father's arms. She too had been given a drink, and I noticed her feeder cup on the table next to where they were sitting. He gently placed Ellen back into her cot, and she turned to her side and settled and he gently ruffled her hair and covered her with a blanket. He walked over to me and took me in his arms and whispered in my left ear, 'Have I thanked you for keeping Ellen safe and for my beautiful son?' I murmured, 'Several times I'm sure,' before he closed my mouth with a kiss.

There was a knock at the door, and as we separated but emerging through the door, were Mary Ann and Harry Manton who looked slightly less coy than he might have looked, Harry stepped forward and holding Mary Ann's hand said, 'We thought we would take over minding our godchildren until their nanny comes back, so that you can go back to your guests,' Mary Ann looked very happy and gave a shy smile.

'What's going on between you two?' Gerard asked with a smile. Mary Ann looked down and Harry replied, 'Well if you must know I have just asked Mary Ann to be my wife, and she has accepted me, on condition that we wait until we have both finished our training and qualified, and she also wants to wait for a family, so you are the first to know.'

Gerard laughed and shook Harry by the hand, and I was so happy that I hugged Mary Ann who was a little overwhelmed, but I said, 'No class now, we are almost equals, forget the past, you are a free woman to plan your own future.' She relaxed and hugged me back. So Gerard and I walked downstairs hand in hand and went back to the party, apparently our absence had been noticed, we had been gone for nearly an hour. Gerard explained that the baby needed feeding and he woke up his sister so they both needed attention. Comments were bantered about my having to manage when Gerard is at work and it was women's work, but I just smiled, and catching the eye of my mother-in law who smiled also. She has been so supportive to both of us, and I was aware that she is very active in the community from church socials and helping people passing through the town who need a little boost while they found work with the logging camps or until they found somewhere to live. She was very respected in the community. The evening went by quite quickly and people started to take their leave so we stood by the door as they went out into the chilly night, some walked home and some had their carts brought around from the stables where their horses were sheltered. We thanked everyone for their company and gifts. Mary

Ann came downstairs with Harry as the nanny had returned to the nursery until we went to bed. We said our goodnights to his parents, who became as much my parents; I had come to love them as such, having grown up without the warmth and care as Gerard had. I did not blame my mother as she was just as much unloved as I felt. We went through the nursery and checked on the little ones and relieved the nanny, and went to our room which had a warm fireplace as it had become really chilly. I looked through the window and could see white on the stable roof which was not frost and saw flakes of snow in the glow as there was no moon that night. I exclaimed at the sight, and Gerard laughed and said, 'Well it does snow here, as we are not far from the Arctic Circle, Alaska is on the edge and we get a lot of snow and we know how to deal with it, there may be a foot of snow at least by the morning!' My eyes opened wide with a little fear, I said that where I lived we had about six inches of snow at best and we shovelled it away and it was very slippery. He came over to me and put his arms about me, 'Come to bed my love and tomorrow and for the rest of the winter we will show you how we deal with snow!'

He gently took me to the bed and helped me to undress and then we both fell into bed and fell asleep in each other's arms.

30th December 1919
The snow got worse and thicker and the whole countryside was covered in a white blanket, and the hills looked different. Gerard was right about dealing with the snow, they were out the next morning shovelling, and hitched the horses up to a special plough which they seemed to pull effortlessly, all six of them in twos in turn, as two more had been purchased from the stables as a they had been left there by prospectors who did not return and they might have been set loose to fend for themselves and Gerard Senior felt that he

needed to intervene, as he had a sense of feeling for all animals and felt that they should be protected and looked after as progress was coming to all of Canada, motor cars were becoming more in evidence. Mr Horan was a relatively wealthy man, and he did not show it by being affluent, but helped people and animals, and looked after their welfare. He worked long hours at the hospital, and visited people who were cut off to make sure they were keeping well and had enough to eat.

Although it was bitterly cold we wrapped up warm and ventured out on to the now cleared paths and roads, on foot as the horses were being used. It was a bit too cold to take the children out so the nanny looked after them. Mother Horan and I went to the shops to look for decorations and presents for Christmas, and we were greeted by the shopkeepers and residents alike. I seem to have lost my English accent a bit and spoke with a way that would be understood, and felt accepted. We went into the post office to look for some Christmas cards when I was called over by the postmaster who said I had some mail, I was surprised and a little excited, and thanked him as I was handed a package and a medium letter postmarked from Sussex. The date on them was three months old; he explained that the train had finally been able to get through the snowdrifts with a special plough on the front. As we had finished our shopping, we made our way back home, by which time it was about 3.30 p.m. in the afternoon, as was explained to me being near the arctic circle daylight was shorter. As we got through the door I heard a familiar wail, and I excused myself, left my packages on the hall table and ran upstairs with Mother Horan's little laugh following me as I knew my baby boy was hungry, and as I took my coat off and went towards the nanny who was trying to pacify a now reed faced baby. I took him from her arms, and smiled my thanks as I went to our bedroom and sat by the fire and undid my jacket and opened my blouse and camisole so that he could feed. He stopped crying almost immediately, and he looked so peaceful as he suckled away. I looked down at my growing baby, and stroked his downy head of brown hair, and wondered what he would look like as he grew. I mused for a moment and wondered what was in the package, and the letter, but it would keep. I enjoyed my moments with my babies, as Ellen was only a year and half old, and I spent as much time as I could with both of them. As Jarred finished his feed and started to doze off, I put him to my left shoulder and rubbed his back, and he burped a few times and then fell asleep, I did not even see him open his eyes.

I changed him at times during the night as I had become a light sleeper and he was waking every four hours so I used to wake up at about four o'clock in the morning, he did not seem to wake up at midnight since the end of November and if I was sleepy, Gerard would bring him to me, and gently wake me up, so I could feed the baby. More often than not Gerard would fall asleep, but he worked such long hours I felt guilty if he needed to wake me up.

I took the baby back the nursery and gave him to the nanny, who put him back into his cot. Ellen was sitting on the floor by the fire (which had a fire guard) and she was playing with her blocks and her dolls, of which she had about five at the last count. I sat down with Ellen whilst I took off my boots, and put them to one side as I chatted with Ellen. I did remember to tell the nanny, whose name was Riella, that the baby had not brought all his wind up, as we conferred with the welfare of both children, and I trusted her completely, as she was the daughter of one of Mother Horan's friends, and had wanted to be a nurse, but preferred to work with children and was hoping to open a children's nursery, and needed experience with children. She was a modest young woman, 20 years old, slim, dark haired and dark skinned, and had some American Indian in her ancestry, she was as tall as me, which was 5'6" and she loved the children and they looked on her as another auntie. Mary Ann seemed to get on with her too and when she first came to us when Jarred was born, Mary Ann told her about Ellen as she had been with her from the start. After spending a little while with Ellen there was a knock at the door, and Mother Horan came in, and asked if I would like some tea and sandwiches, I said Yes, and she said that she would have it brought up to the nursery so that we could all be together. Riella asked if we required her to stay, and I said if she wanted to stay and have her tea with us or whether she would like to take a break for a while and have a meal elsewhere and she said if it was OK she would eat and then go to the town to do some shopping, looking at both us, I had no problem and Mother Horan nodded, so she left the room, I got up quickly and called after, 'Riella? Please be careful, it is getting dark, and it is slippery outside.'

She smiled, 'I know Mrs Horan, I'm used to it, but I will not be late, thank you.' She smiled and went to her room and then went out.

I went back to the nursery to find that tea had been set out on the table and Mother Horan was helping Ellen into her special chair at the table and was putting a little muslin bib around her neck. Ellen seemed excited that she was having tea with us. Her little feeder cup was filled with warm milk and she was given some soft biscuits on the tray of her chair. Ellen had got most of her baby teeth and she started to chew on her biscuits, and then put the feeder cup to her mouth, she dribbled a little, but we praised her for being independent, her golden hair had grown quite long, I had drawn it back gently with two little combs, specially made for children. Mother Horan and I had our tea and of scones with butter and jam and small sandwiches, and chatted about our plans for Christmas. I did mention that I would like to find out more about Canadian history and to do something to help in the community as I was not allowed to when I was growing up, and when they turned the house into a hospital, I wanted to train as a nurse but my father would not let me, it was not a thing for a lady to do, although I know that other young 'ladies' did train to be nurses at the front. Mother Horan said that being a mother was a job in itself, but she understood, coming from a similar background but she had to look after her son, but also found time to get involved in community outreach once Gerard went to school and she was his first teacher. 'If you need any help or reference books, just ask me, our house library is small but Gerard senior has collected many books, just help yourself, and if you need any more I'll take you to the library in the town.' She would take me to museums when the weather got better, the snows thawed about the end of February. My eyes opened wide, and she laughed.

We chatted for about an hour, and the tea got cold, so she went downstairs and asked for some more. By this time Ellen was falling asleep, so I lifted her from the chair, and took her to the bathroom, and washed her face and hands, undressed her and put on her nightgown. She sat a bit limply on the chair in the bathroom, and just as Mother Horan returned, changed her nappy and put the soiled one in a bucket to soak and almost carried her back to the nursery, Ellen was more awake now and wriggled to be let down, and started to climb into her cot. I helped her a little, and she managed to get in. Ellen then settled down and went to sleep. So I covered her with her blankets and went back to the table and we finished our tea.

It was quite late when Riella arrived back, as the clocks struck the half hour after five o'clock. I looked around as she walked through the door of the nursery, she apologised for her lateness, but apparently there was another arrival of mail from the train and she was called into the post office as there was a letter from England for Mary Ann and he knew Riella worked here, she handed the letter to me and I promised to give Mary Ann the letter when she got home, knowing that she would get back the next day as she often stayed at the hospital after a late shift. I was puzzled after looking at the postmark that her letter was postmarked from Sussex also, what did this mean, why had we both got letters? And from Sussex?

I put the letter in her room which was at the back of the house which was neat and tidy, and had a few pictures of her mother, and father and of Agnes, her cousin. I felt as I was intruding so came out after putting the letter on her pillow where I knew she would find it when she returned home, for this is her home. I went back to the nursery, just as Mother Horan was supervising the clearing of tea things and Riella was sitting by the fire and reading a book, and I asked her to call me when Jarred woke up so that I could feed him. It had been suggested that I let Jarred have a bottle instead with cow's milk but I said I would rather feed him as I had Ellen, and whilst I still had milk to give him, I would feed him myself, despite any inconvenience to myself, after all other women fed their babies except I know that my mother did not feed for very long as convention decreed that she had to leave me to a nurse to feed me. I was not like my mother, I had fought to keep my daughter and I stood up to feeding my son. Mother Horan understood and supported me. Mother Horan and I went downstairs and I picked up my package and letter, and joined her in the drawing room and asked if she minded my opening my mail she said she would not mind, but didn't I want to read it alone, but I said, 'I'm a bit afraid of what is in there, I would be grateful if you would stay.' So she sat down next to me on the sofa next to the roaring fire after turning up the lamp as it was quite dark, so that I could see the writing, first on the package which I opened, which had been postmarked from

a central London post office, several envelopes fell out, which had
been opened, they had my handwriting on and were addressed to
my sister Ellen, I picked them up, and put them in order of date and
looked at Mother Horan, she took them from me and found a piece
of ribbon a red ribbon and tied them together, she came back to me,
and my hands were shaking, I looked at her in alarm, she sat down
with me again, and pointed to a piece of paper which fell out with
the envelopes, it was from Elliott, I explained to Mother Horan that
he was the man who 'rescued' Gerard from France, and brought him
to my home. The letter was dated 30th September 1919.

Dear Mrs Anna Horan,
Forgive me for writing to you I was asked by your mother to
return these to you, your sister has moved out of the house she
and her husband have separated, your mother said that she
would write to you.
 Best Regards to you both, if you wish to write to me, please
feel free, I would just like to let you know that I have been
accepted to medical school, I am going to be a doctor.
 Best Regards Elliott.

I did not realise that I was reading aloud, my eyes were filling up
with tears and I could not see properly, Mother Horan gave me her
handkerchief as I rubbed my eyes, and then I dabbed at the tears
with the handkerchief. 'Please could you read the other letter I do
not think I can see properly at the moment.'
 Mother took the letter which was written in a careful beautiful script which I had never seen before. 'It is from a Mrs Eleonor
Clarkson from Three Gates in Sussex,' she said.
 'That is my mother, she has never written to me before,' I said
with a quivering voice. She read on:

'My dearest Anna Mary, forgive me for writing, I know that you have made a new life in Canada, but I wanted to tell you myself, not from a third party, so Elliott gave me your address. I assume that you have received your letters to Ellen. Unlike you she did not have a happy marriage; he apparently was only interested in her money. I'm aware from my sister that after their marriage they were seen out on social occasions but she seemed to put on a front, but not very happy. Apparently Agnes was still living with her, as well a cook and a valet. When she got your letters, she would tell my sister, and she sounded less than happy, for unfortunately she was not blessed with children as you have been. She felt obliged to write to you but could not bring herself to tell you that she was not happy. Then six months after they were married, Agnes was found to be pregnant, so she left, and although the valet was under suspicion, his attentions were elsewhere. It would seem that her husband was carrying on with Agnes, and apparently whilst Ellen was out and instead of sleeping with her he pretended to come in late and instead went to Agnes. He was quite brazen about it accusing Ellen of being shallow and not really supporting him, he seems to have some mental problems arising from the war. He packed his bags and took as much money as he could, but she told my sister, and I told your father who stopped her allowance. Of course Agnes went with him and there is a divorce going through. Poor Ellen she is staying with my sister, and they have closed the house and moved the furniture. I am so sorry to tell you, but you may understand now why when she stopped writing. By the time you get this it may well be Christmas, I wish you well my darling; please pass my wishes to your family, and Mary Ann and your lucky lovely husband. Your poor father is not very happy. All my love God Bless you. Your loving Mother.'

Then the tears came, big heaving sobs, I had thought that Ellen had a charmed life yet what I thought was a happy romance and marriage would appear to be a sham, what she must have suffered. I thought I had a hard time, but poor Ellen, all I could see was her face and I suddenly felt a feeling of loss, I blurted out, 'I do miss my mother so much, she had a difficult time, but I know she loved me, loves me.'

Mother Horan put her arms around me and stroked my head until I cried all my tears out.

'Why don't you go up and have a sleep until Gerard gets home, after all, he and his father are doctors, well my husband is. If you wake up before they get home Riella will be there, and she does care, she loves the little ones and she respects you.'

I thanked her and she walked with me to our bedroom, through the main door so that I did not disturb the children. I slowly undressed and put on my nightgown after hanging up my clothes and putting others in the drawer, I unpinned my hair. I didn't go to bed, but put a wrap around my shoulders and sat by the fire, and looked at the flames, and as they flickered thought back over the year. I had been blessed. I had a lot to be thankful for. Although Gerard was spending a lot of time at the hospital, and when at home he spent time in the study writing up his notes, but he had time for me and our children. Getting the letters back and a letter from my mother reminded me just what I had left behind. I was so lucky that I had brought Mary Ann with me, and I was so happy that she was doing so well, and that she had found a good man to marry who loved her.

My heart was so full, so sad, I found myself praying for my sister, my mother and for those I left behind and thankful for being with a loving family where there was no falseness, but genuine good people who worked hard. I must have dozed off because I did not hear the door open, Gerard was by my side and gently rubbed my shoulder, 'Mother said you had some letters and a nasty shock, she said you had gone to bed, but I find you here, oh, she gave me these,' He had the envelope and mother's letter in his hand, and the returned letters, I told him about the news, and seemed quite able talk without crying. I told him how she had been so kind and supportive. He looked at me carefully, 'Are you sure you are okay, it must have been really awful to hear such a thing would you like something to help you sleep? Father could give you a sleeping draught.'

I shook my head, and got up and looked at the mirror in the bathroom, my eyes were puffy, my hair was a loose mess, so I washed my face, and drew my hair back after brushing it, and pinned it back. Gerard had followed me in, he brushed his hair, and washed his face, he looked so tired, I said to him, 'Just being with you will be fine, I am glad your mother stayed with me when I opened the letters.' He kissed me and I hugged him back. We shall we eat up here, I'm not feeling very sociable at the moment, so much to do before my final exam.'

I nodded, if it was no trouble, so he went downstairs and came back with a tray and the maid brought in another. After we had eaten, by the glowing fire, and Gerard went to the study afterwards to do some revision, and I had fed little Jarred, and helped settle Ellen to sleep, I sat and thought what I could do next, and also wondered what Mary Ann's letter was about. Gerard came up to bed at about 10.30 and after some intimate moments, we fell asleep in each other's arms, for me a dreamless sleep.

Mary Ann returned the next day at about 9 a.m. and we were downstairs having breakfast, she put her head around the door and I went to greet her, and after closing the door behind me, I told her that she had a letter which I placed in her room, and said I had something to tell her later if she had time. She thanked me and went to her room. Mary Ann was changing; she had become more assured and almost stopped calling me Mrs Anna. After about ten minutes she came downstairs a bit faster than she had gone up, and she still had the letter in her hands. I went to her, 'What is wrong Mary Ann?' I asked as I gently led her to the breakfast room but she stopped, 'I cannot go in, I am so ashamed.' I turned her gently to face me, 'What is in the letter?' I asked.

'It's about Agnes and your sister and oh...' She broke off as tears filled her eyes. I gently took her to another small room away from the bigger room, which was not used very much, and had two chairs and a table, I sat her down, asked her to wait, and went quickly to the breakfast/dining room and got a tray and cups and saucers and Gerard picked up on what I was doing and brought a coffee pot milk and sugar, and some toast, plates and butter. We went to the other room where Mary Ann was sitting forlorn and she had her head bowed as we came in. Gerard put the tray down and excused himself, saying he had to study. I started to pour out coffee and Mary Ann started to get up to help, I motioned her to sit down, 'Let me serve you for once, dear Mary Ann,' I said and passed the cup of coffee to her and offered something to eat. After drinking her coffee and having a bite of toast, she managed to compose herself, and the words tumbled out, 'The letter was from my mother she wrote about how Agnes had carried on with your sister's husband and is expecting his baby, your poor sister!'

I put my hand over hers, and then held it, 'Dear Mary Ann, I had a letter too, from my mother, and she returned my letters to Ellen. I now understand why her letters were short, as she didn't have much to say or could not tell me what was going on, it's nobody's fault, sometimes people do not always get what they hope for out of marriage. Please do not think that will happen to you. You are a schoolmaster's daughter and your mother was a nurse. There is no reason to think that you are not a lady, and you are achieving so much.'

Mary Ann looked at me with eyes that seemed brighter. 'But you and Ellen are so different, I had such trouble trying to teach you to be a lady, but now, you are doing more, you are helping.'

We both cheered up, but I told her that I had done my share of crying, and suddenly felt so far away from my old home. I said that I wanted to write to my mother, and she said it would be all right if I sent my letters to her home and her mother would see that my mother would receive it. I told Mary Ann that if she needed anyone to confide in, I said I was so grateful to her for coming with me, and being like a... and I just about got the word 'sister' out and I saw her as a sister. 'No more Mrs Anna, we are equals. Please, please call me Anna and Gerard, not Mr Gerard after all, you are our children's godmother and they love you' (as I do I thought).

Well after we got on very well, Christmas came and went, and on Christmas Day when Harry joined us with his parents, he and Mary Ann became officially engaged, and she asked me if I would be her matron of honour, and Harry asked Gerard to be his best man. We were so happy for them. Mother and Father Horan said that Mary Ann could get married from the house, and she shyly asked if Father Horan would give her away in place of her father, he said that he would be happy to, if her father gave consent as she was still a minor not reaching 21 years of age until May 1920. She said she would write to her father, but she had already told him about Harry, and he had already said that should wait. Father Horan said that he would write to her father asking permission to give her away in his place, Mary Ann was very happy and we all toasted their engagement and to their future.

1920

Another decade, so much had happened in the last four years. I have changed so much, and so has Mary Ann, she is so assured, and although polite, she calls me Anna now. We managed to get out in January, as the snow did not thaw and it was so cold. Everything still on as usual, the men went to the hospital, and at this trekked up to the logging camps on horseback with the mules. I did worry about them as they always stayed away overnight and there was no way of contacting them. But they came back with news and good reports, and we made sure that the horses and mules were brushed and hooves cleaned which I had learned to do at home in England, when my father was away, before he sold them to the army. I made sure they were warm and well fed and watered, in fact when I could, I went out to the stables to groom the horses and fed them. I built up a rapport with all the horses and mules. Gerard was a little taken aback, but I explained that I could still be a lady as well as seeing to the horses, and he laughed and hugged me. The children flourished and grew, Ellen has been walking well, she almost runs, and needs more things to interest her, so I have started to help her with her letters and words, by showing her pictures of objects and words, simple letters. Jarred is nearly six months old, and is drinking from a feeder cup, and Ellen has progressed from a feeder cup to a cup. I was a little worried about Jarred for a little while before the end of the year as he was crying during the night and did not feed well, and I asked Gerard and his father who came with us to see the child doctor who checked him over, and kept him in hospital overnight, and Gerard and I both stayed, but it turned out to be very bad wind in his tummy, and he was given a simple natural medicine which calmed the wind and he passed very smelly stools and then seemed better. I was advised to give him a dose of this medicine if it happened again, which I did but after about four weeks he seemed to get over it. The doctor asked me some questions about his feeding, and I said that he took his feed very quickly, but didn't always bring up his wind; I never had this problem with Ellen. The doctor said maybe as a boy he was greedy and I agreed, but Jarred seemed to get better with his feeding. As Jarred got bigger, I noticed that one arm seemed slightly stiffer than the other one. I remembered when he was born and the horrific time of his birth and as he was sitting up and he put his right arm to support himself but his left arm seemed a little stiff. I talked to Mother Horan and she insisted that I talked to Father Horan and Gerard about it, she said that nurse in her felt I should, and not to worry myself but share the concern. I was also worried about Gerard's limp from his war injury was still there, although he tried to hide it, it caused him discomfort, and I shared that with her. She was also worried and had spoken to him about it but he just brushed it away. I said I would talk to him about it too, but he was so involved with final exams. So we had to be patient, but I was getting really worried, because as he suggested, I had begun reading lots of books, including Canadian history, the history of the town, and geography, and I also read the medical books, especially biology, as this had not been deemed the right subject for me to be learning, only grammar, language, maths and religion, but I found it easier to find out about Christianity at Sunday School, which I was allowed to attend and where I met Mary Ann for the first time.

Whilst I was reading the biology book I looked at joints and connectors, and the growth of babies and children and found it very interesting, but I did not just jump to conclusions, oh how I wished I had been to train as a nurse or an orderly; at least. I was sitting in the library between meals for the children, it was late February and the afternoons were getting a little lighter, Gerard came in a little earlier than usual and he seemed quite excited, and for a moment he did not notice what I was doing. 'I've done it Anna Honey, I've finished my exams, and they think I have done well. I should be an M.D. in a few weeks, and then we can go away. What are you looking at?'

I told him about my studies and about the biology books. I told him about my concerns about Jarred, and his arm, and how it didn't seem to work as well as the other, and was it because of the forceps delivery?

'Well they did suggest a caesarean section, cutting you open and delivering the baby that way, but that would have taken you longer to recover and it is not a routine surgery, the wound might have taken a while to heal, so I agreed to the forceps.' I mentioned about Kaiser Wilhelm's birth by forceps, and he sat down with me and said, 'Yes, I've read up on that, the medical reports stated that they broke the infant's arm, and did not set it properly, and causing it to grow slightly stunted and poor Empress Victoria did not bond with him, a feeling of shame that she caused the injury, but it was the doctors who did it. Now you bonded with our son, he responds to you, and I know you notice the changes in his development, which is good and I am glad, if it bothers you that much, we will take him to see the paediatrician at the hospital. I am not an expert as such, but they will check to see how bad it might be, and what they can do about it.'

I held his hand and thanked him. 'There is something else, I have been noticing your limp is still there, and you do not complain, but I can see that when you are tired you flinch. Can you go to a doctor to see if anything can be done? I know that I am a mere woman and should not question your decision but…'

He laughed and hugged me and said, 'It never stopped you before. Who has been telling you to keep your place? That is what I love about you, you speak your mind. Okay, I have been having problems, but I keep the ankle strapped up. I have asked what could be done, but I've been busy getting qualified, that I didn't notice, I think there might be something that could be done, but I may have to have my ankle in plaster for six weeks, how can I get a job or earn a living for us then?' I told him that if he was so good, they would wait for him, as I know that doctors and surgeons do a lot of standing.

So in March we took Jarred to the hospital in Montreal and the specialist who checked Jarred out, and x-rayed his arm (this was new) and Jarred cried a bit, but was otherwise very good, but I cuddled him and told him he was a good boy, the specialist asked us to call back the next day for the results. Gerard then went to see an orthopaedic specialist. I stayed outside with Jarred, who was sleepy by this time and fell asleep in the perambulator and tucked him up and he slept for a while. I looked at the old magazines and found them quite interesting as the articles told me a lot about the fashions, the adverts and stories. I made a note of the magazine and thought that I might get it when we got back home. Gerard seemed to be in the consulting room for quite a time when the door opened and he came out. He shook hands with the specialist and he nodded towards me, and said, 'When I get the results of the x-rays, I'll tell you what we might be able to do.'

Gerard said that we might have to stay for a few days so he had already left the address of the hotel that he had booked into, and they would telephone. This was a new thing, which I had heard of but this was not something that my father would have installed. I asked how we would let his parents know, and he said he would telephone the post office in Moose Falls and leave a message, and a telephone number of the hotel. We then walked back to the hotel and I looked at the shops on the way. They were quite interesting on a par with London, when I visited my aunt a few times. I stopped a few times to look at their wares. Gerard asked if I wanted anything but I said no, 'You must think me quite provincial, I have only been to cities a few times. The village was my place to shop if I was allowed to. The town in Moose Falls was great to shop.' He laughed and then as we had reached the hotel helped me lift the perambulator up the steps and went to the reception to get our room keys and to ask to use the telephone, and he called Moose Falls. I could hear him speak up; just as well the room was empty. After he had made the call, he asked them to put any calls to him into our room. We went up in the elevator and went to the first floor to our hotel room, and he opened the door and I pushed the perambulator in. Jarred was stirring and woke up. I picked him up, and found that he was wet so I took him to the bathroom, and changed his nappy laying him on the sink side which was quite wide. I found a white bucket which was kindly left for us, along which a child's cot. I filled the bucket with water and put some soap powder in. Jarred seemed quite happy, so I took him into our room and put him in the cot, where he sat up, so I gave him some toys to play with. The hotel was going to send up our meals as we had a baby, and we thought it better as there were no other people with children staying. They also put a small electric heating ring and a saucepan as a special concession so that we could heat up some milk and little jars of food that we had prepared and brought with us. I asked Gerard if he had any special connections, but he said that was a hotel recommended by the local hospital. I heated up his milk and put it in a feeder cup, which he drank well, holding the cup. I had tried him with a baby's bottle, but he pushed it away, happy to move on to the cup. He was also putting on weight and had started on solid food since January, taking small bowlfuls of mashed carrots, potatoes and a small portion of gravy. I warmed up the small jar of food prepared by the cook, who was quite excited that he was starting on solid food. I sat him on my lap, and put a small apron on him, and a towel over myself, and I fed him with a small spoon, with Gerard watching and encouraging his son. Jarred sometimes grasped my hand with the spoon and pushed it into his mouth and ate well. He seemed a little more forward than Ellen, although I noticed that he watched her feed herself, and guessed that he copied her and Ellen needed a little more encouragement. I had a little pang, we had to leave her behind with the nanny and Mother Horan, and Mary Ann who promised to spend time with her, but I missed her, and it was the first time that I had left her when she was old enough to notice. Suddenly there was a loud ring and I jumped, it was the telephone, Gerard picked it up and answered, it was his father, Gerard told him what had happened at the hospital and that we might have to stay another day before going home. He nodded and said yes, 'There is someone who wants to talk to you,' he put the telephone down for a moment, and I went over to the instrument, I looked at it and Gerard came over and helped me to use the speaking and hearing piece the right way around, I said in a quivery, 'Hello?' and I heard a little voice saying, 'Mama is that you?' it was my Ellen, I was nearly in tears when I replied, 'Yes Ellen it is me, are you all right darling?'

The little breath voice came back, 'Yes, me okay, when you come back? Is baby Gerry okay, miss you, love you Mama, love Dada.' The voice changed and Father Horan said, 'She just wanted to talk to you, she misses you. Hope everything goes well dear.' I swallowed hard and, 'It is a first for both of us, it is the first time I have used a telephone. Tell her she is a clever girl, I send my love to all.'

I handed the telephone back to Gerard who said his goodbye and placed it back where it rested. He put his arm around me, I said she sent her love to him too, and said it was the first time we had left her so far away.

'We should have some kind of a diagnosis for both of us by tomorrow, then we can pay for the consultation and hotel and go home.' That bothered me, as the fact that we came to the city and a big hospital was going to be costly. I went to my bag, and took my purse out. I had changed the money that my mother gave into dollars and had brought it with me. I said, 'I have about 100 dollars left if that helps. I feel so bad, you have taken so much on already, I feel guilty.'

He closed my hand over the notes and said, 'Put your money away, it is fine, everything has been taken care of if you want to spend some money, get some souvenirs for Mary Ann and Ellen.' I lowered my head, 'I know that you came away with no settlement or allowance, and Mother was kind enough to give me £500 and I tried to hold on to most of it.'

He held my hand, 'Now get this straight, I didn't come back for you or marry you for what money I could get for you. That's no basis for a marriage. As you have found out. I married you for the right reasons. We may not be old money or landed gentry but we are comfortable, and my parents love you and Mary Ann.'

I looked up suddenly and realised something, 'But you told my father you had a trust fund, and were very wealthy!' He laughed, 'Well would your father have let me marry you if I didn't. I had my severance pay, and some savings, but the signet ring is an old family crest handed to me from my father.'

I laughed, and shook my head and looked at the smaller ring set with stones that resembled his signet ring that you gave on our church wedding day, 'No I guess not, you are a wag, but I am so happy that you did, because I hate to think of the life that Ellen would have had if you had not come back.'

Jarred had gone to sleep, it was early, so we went to bed for time, and made love. When we woke up it was quite dark, and I put the lamp on and looked at the time, it was six thirty. I suggested that we dressed and looked at what food was on the menu. I put my clothes on and went to the bathroom and tidied my hair up, and looked at myself in the mirror, I was 21 and I seemed to have looked more mature than the naïve teenage lady of two years ago. I saw no lines, and my hair needed trimming. I put my hair up into a chignon, and went back to the room, Gerard was ordering our food, and he pointed to the dishes, and I nodded, coffee he asked, I nodded, wine, I nodded and motioned a small bottle, and he said thanks and put the telephone back onto its rest. Jarred was still asleep. We sat there for about half an hour, when Gerard also went to the bathroom to tidy himself up, and brush his hair. He came back just as there was a knock at the door. I hastily pulled the cover up on the bed, as a maid with a male servant brought in a trolley with covered dishes and dinner and dessert plates, they laid the table at the window and put the covered dishes on the table, the young man uncorked the small bottle of wine, and Gerard thanked them, gave them both a small tip and they left. It was quite a nice experience, and even better than the one in London. I enjoyed the meal which was on a par with what we had on special occasions, I did say, 'This is very pleasant, and I enjoy the experience but I'd rather be at home in Moose Falls.' He smiled and was glad that I was happy, but I just wanted to go back home.

The night passed without much interruption, as Jarred had a drink at 10 p.m. and he slept through until 6 a.m. The next morning I got up gave him another drink, bathed him in the large sink as he fitted into it, and then as he sat in his cot, Gerard got up, washed and dressed, and I got bathed and dressed and came just in time for breakfast to be served in our room again. Our appointment at the hospital was not until late morning for Jarred, and early afternoon for Gerard. We went for a walk through the city, I looked at the shops and went into a toy store and bought a little doll for Ellen and a teddy for Jarred, but had them wrapped. We looked at the clothing stores and I bought some gloves for Mary Ann, Mother Horan and Gerard helped me to choose a warm scarf for his father. I bought a picture for Riella, and some postcards for my mother. We went to the hospital and waited outside the paediatric specialist and after a short wait in the quiet waiting as we had checked in at the reception, a nurse came out to call us in. We took Jarred in his perambulator, and I went to take him out as he was sleeping. The specialist, who was of a medium height with thin rimmed spectacles, motioned for us to sit down. He looked at his notes and the x-rays and looked up at us. 'He is very lucky with obstetrician, and help, I have seen and heard of much worse birth injuries, including Kaiser Wilhelm's. This a minor injury and he will only be slightly unable to do some things he seems to have a good grip, and he may not be a weight lifter but the difference as he grows older will be minor. I see no point in setting his arm and putting it in plaster or such like, but I will write to your doctor at home to have him checked annually to see if it gets worse, but I think you were lucky. It will depend which hand he uses to write with. Now go home, enjoy your children and let them find their way in the world. Thank you for coming to see me. I am glad that I can say that he has a good chance of thriving well, and you can be commended for making this consultation.'

He shook Gerard's hand, and took both of my hands and shook them, and touched little Jarred on the cheek, but he still carried on sleeping. I was very happy, but was still a little nervous about Gerard's own results. We went to another part of the hospital to the orthopaedic specialist and registered with the reception there. We sat in the waiting area which was empty, and we only had to wait about 10 minutes before we were called by a nurse and I offered to wait with Jarred but was told to go in as well with him. Gerard sat down and I was offered a chair slightly apart from the desk. The specialist was thinner than the child specialist, younger only a few years older than Gerard, and nodded to me, called me Mrs Horan and sat down, my eyes wandered a little around the room, their plaques of qualifications, from M.D. to surgery, to orthopaedics which quoted a hospital in New York. He started to speak, and had a different accent, not Canadian, 'Thank you both for coming, I guess you wanted to know your results Gerry, well I'm sorry to have to tell you there is nothing I can do, the bone is fixed, it would have needed resetting almost within three weeks and I see that they strapped your ankle but made you walk on it almost straight away as if it were a sprain. The only good news I can give you is that it has not affected the blood supply to your foot but you should know that being a medic and practically an M.D.'

Gerard nodded, 'Yes I know but you are the expert on joints and I wanted a second opinion of course, I thought it might be a hopeless cause, if you cannot help then that's it.'

The specialist smiled, 'Well not completely, but surgically not at present, I do not want to put you through a procedure that would take time and maybe make it worse. You can do exercises and strap the ankle, and adapt your practice, know when to rest your leg, at least you still have your foot, many young men lost theirs and legs too.'

'I know Charles, thank you for your time and advice.' They both smiled, but I looked at both of them with a puzzled look on my face. The specialist smiled and said, 'Is there a problem Mrs Horan?' I said to the specialist, 'You are speaking to my husband as if you know him, and he you. Is there a connection?'

The both laughed and Gerard said, 'Well Charles was a surgeon in the hospital in Belgium and we saw a lot of activity in the hospital, and when I went back we met up again, I learned a lot, and when I resolved to continue my studies and qualify.'

I smiled and Charles said partly to Gerard and then to me, 'Is this the young lady you told me about? He couldn't stop talking about you, how kind you had been, how you fell in love and the reason he wanted to go back. I take it this is your son,' looking at Jarred who had woken up, and was moving his arms. 'Yes this is Gerard Horan

III, we also have a little girl, not too much detail, but she will be two this year, I have a picture of her,' Gerard replied taking a picture of Ellen, and handing it to Charles. 'Very sweet and pretty, she looks like you Gerry, but this little chap, well, I'd say he looks a lot like his Mom.' We all laughed and I said, 'Thank you it's my fault, I was worried about Gerard's limp so I suggested he get checked over.'

'How very caring of your wife, but she doesn't come across as a bossy lady, are you a budding suffragette?' he said to both of us.

I spoke up a little indignantly, 'I am not bossy nor am I a suffragette, whatever that might be, I am concerned and show that, and I just want to be useful not just sitting around to be waited on, is that a crime? If so I am guilty as charged,' I could hear my English accent coming out, and looked away.

The specialist gave a little cough, and I could see he was trying to stifle a laugh, 'I am sorry, I seemed to have touched a nerve, forgive me, you are a special lady, not afraid to speak up for what you believe in or care about, Gerry is a lucky man please go on doing what you are doing and encourage your husband and family.' He replied with a twinkle in his eye, and I laughed. This tall slim man with slightly greying hair, with the funny accent, later clarified as a Bostonian accent, was the inspiration that made Gerard come back to finish his studies, he said to Gerard as we made to leave, 'Gerry, let me know about your studies of post traumatic stress, I also look forward to reading about it in the medical journal.'

Gerard nodded, 'Thanks will do, and carry on with your studies on joint repair, we have to offer an alternative.'

They shook hands, and he patted Jarred on the hand gently, and Jarred grabbed his finger with his 'bad' arm and he said, 'No problem there, he has a good grip,' and bent down and gently took his finger away, but kissed the little hand, 'Keep in touch Gerry,' he said as we walked out.

Whilst we were walking back to the hotel, Gerard said, 'You sure impressed him, you're no shrinking violet, and your English accent came out!' I took his arm away from the perambulator for a moment, 'I'm sorry I spoke out of turn again, Mary Ann would be shocked. I forget I'm supposed to be a lady, but I'm not like Ellen, I want to get involved, I think I should take some more lessons from your mother on being a hostess and housekeeper.'

Gerard smiled, 'I know you have a lot to learn, but you are a good hands on mother, and I believe that you are learning to cook, but please do not change, that is what I love about you, getting involved, back in Sussex you were so helpful, despite what your father might have thought, after all, we might have lost Ellen if you hadn't fought for her.'

I agreed and he suggested that we stop somewhere to eat, and I realised that we hadn't eaten since breakfast but wondered where we could take Jarred. He found a little café in a side street which was quiet and seemed to be homely, and the proprietor was happy to warm up Jarred's milk, and he offered to make up a small bowl of mashed vegetables. The man appeared to be European, and the name above the door said 'Marinelli', and Gerard said that he was Italian, and would I like to try some Italian food, and I nodded, intrigued to try some different dishes. I was pleasantly surprised when a pasta dish was served; it had a creamy sauce with ham pieces. In between feeding Jarred and myself, and listening to Gerard talking to the proprietor in English and Italian, I was aware of some words, he told Gerard that he had emigrated to the United States of America, but as there were many Italian restaurants there, he came across the border and ended up in Montreal and people came to his café out of curiosity and they came back, and word of mouth meant that they came back, apparently we had come late for the lunch rush. I noticed that he had a meat counter under glass, and a cabinet with tubs of what might have been ice cream, but in many colours that I had never seen before. I went up to the cabinet and the proprietor went over and explained what they were and said it was a speciality of many flavoured ice creams, and asked if I would like to try some, and I asked for a green coloured ice, and a pink coloured ice, so he put two scoops into a glass dish with a little flat biscuit and I went back to the table and tasted it, Gerard smiled and tried a blue coloured ice cream and a pink coloured ice cream, we enjoyed the tastes, and finished our coffee, and Gerard paid the proprietor and before we left he picked a little packet of soft sweets for us to give to Ellen, 'Very soft and chewy, not choke little one' he said, and we thanked him. As we went back to the main street, and I saw a ladies' hairdresser, and said I'd like to get my hair trimmed, Gerard looked a little worried, 'You are not going to have a 'bob' like in the window? Mother will faint if she saw you.'

I laughed and said, 'No no I'm not ready for that, my hair has got rather long and I just want a few inches off, I haven't had a trim since I left England and my hair is almost down to my waist and it is hard to manage. So we went in and whilst Gerard looked sheepishly at a magazine, and looked after Jarred, I waited my turn to have my hair cut. When it was my turn I let my hair down and it was down to my waist. The stylist asked how much I wished to have cut off, and showed me some pictures of young ladies with very short hair, but I said, 'No thank you, just cut it to just past my shoulders so that I can still pin it up, thank you.'

Gerard looked up and then covered his eyes as she made the first cut to the hair at the side of my face, and I braced myself as the scissors cut through, she did just as I asked and as about 12 inches came away as she cut around, my head felt a lit lighter. She tidied my hair up and asked if I would like my hair down or styled up. I asked her to style it up and would try to copy it. She asked if I would like some hair ornaments and I asked what they had to offer, and she showed me a tray of pretty combs and I chose about six and asked for some new hairpins. When she had finished, I was happy with the result, and Gerard looked relieved. They put the hair together and put it in a bag, and I asked why, and was told that it was good strong hair and could be turned into a wit after it was washed, they offered to pay me for it but I said not, so they did not charge me for the hair accessories, but just the cut, so after paying for my haircut, I bought some pretty little slides for Ellen whose hair was getting long enough to pin back.

We then went back to the hotel and Gerard went to the reception and gave notice to check out the next morning, and asked for them to arrange rail tickets to go back to Moose Falls. We went to our room and started to pack our bags to go home. Jarred was still sleeping so I put him into the cot for a while and helped to pack. I did say that I wanted to get back to Moose Falls as I missed everyone especially Ellen, who was a bit tearful before we left. Gerard said that we were going to catch the first train in the morning at 10.00 a.m. and would reach Moose Falls at 5.30 barring holdups. We had our meal and then slept in that room for the last time. We all had breakfast and we went to the reception and Gerard paid the bill. I carried what I could, but Gerard came out with our two bags which looked heavy, I was concerned as the station was at least 10 minutes walk away. I knew that Gerard could walk that far without being loaded up, and when I raised the subject, he said he wasn't an invalid, and I reminded him that we didn't walk from the station, so why should we walk back. Gerard gave a wry smile, and went back into the hotel and came back two minutes later, and said that a 'taxi cab' would collect us shortly. Shortly was ten minutes later, it was a motor car, a big square black vehicle which had a small sort of box in the front, where the driver sat, and next to him was an open space covered by the front, where he put our bags and we got into the back of the car, with the perambulator, with the baby in my arms. It did not take long to get to the station, and were not late, Gerard paid the cab driver who helped to carry the bags, and lift out the perambulator. Jarred was wide awake and was looking over my shoulder and to the side. We went to the station building and Gerard checked the time of the train. I put Jarred into his perambulator, and he settled down and pushed him and carried one of the bags, to the platform, and stood by a seat. In the distance I could hear a whistle and then a whoop and I could see a pall of smoke in the distance, which got closer and closer, until the noisy engine rolled into the station, with the loud squeal as the brakes were being put on. Unfortunately Jarred was startled and screamed and started to cry, I picked him up and soothed him, as tears rolled down his cheeks, I showed him the big beast of an engine as it slid to a stop, his eyes were wide, and he seemed dwarfed, as all of us were. Then the engine let out a loud hiss, and steam rose up from the funnel, wondering what would happen next, he said, 'Choo, choo, woo woo, shshsh!' and smiled and laughed. Relieved, I told him that we were going home on that thing!'

A man on the station platform called out, 'Montreal Central,' called about ten stations and 'Moose Falls, all aboard.' So we went up the steps and the guard put the perambulator in the guard's van, and carried our bags to the carriage, and sat down facing the engine, with Jarred on the other side and Gerard on the other side and Gerard held him to the window after putting our bags on the shelf. The guard blew a whistle and there was another whoop from the engine and we moved slowly off, and got a bit faster, and we settled down for the long journey, but not as long as the one that took us from Hudson Bay. The journey was uneventful stopping six times to let people get off or get on, and the towns were well spread out. We went to the dining car and had something to eat and drink, and fed Jarred. He slept for most of the way, and he did drink but did not eat much, but Gerard said not to worry, he was tired and his routine had been disrupted, so we should see how he gets on when we get home. I was so grateful to be married to a medical man. The journey seemed so long, and we both dozed off for a while, until the conductor walked through the carriage and was shouting, 'Moose Falls next stop, ten minutes to Moose Falls.'

We started and woke up, and stretched out our arms, Gerard got our bags down, and I gently woke up Jarred and picked him up and put him up to the window to look out 'Look baby, home, Moose Falls.' He looked at us and then looked out of the window and said, 'Moo fulls moofulls home.'

Gerard said with a laugh, 'Close enough son.'

The train again slowed down with a screech of brakes, and came to a stop. We went to the back of the carriage and went back down the steps and our bags were put on the platform, Gerard retrieved the perambulator and I put our parcels in it, the perambulator near Jarred. We gave up our tickets, and walked out, it was just getting dusk, outside the station we saw a carriage and I recognised the horses, they were ours, standing by the carriage was Mary Ann and Father Horan, and with Mary Ann was Ellen, my little girl. She ran towards us, and went to me first, 'Mommy you back, baby OK? Miss you mommy.' I gathered her up in my arms and hugged her tight and kissed her little cheek. Father Horan came up and he hugged me too before he shook hands with Gerard and said 'Hello,' to Jarred. He took our bags and put them into the carriage. I said hello to Mary Ann, and held her arm for a moment and thanked her for bringing Ellen to meet us. I then went to the horses who were waiting patiently to be driven back. I stroked their muzzles and told them I had missed them too, and they huffed at me in greeting. We then got into the carriage with Ellen sitting on my lap, and Jarred on Mary Ann's lap and Gerard sat next to his father in the front and gave the horses direction to go back to the house. He was talking to his father as the horses took us home. Mary Ann and I chatted too on the way back, I asked how everyone was, and she said everyone was fine, we were missed, and they were glad to have the telephone call, that Ellen kept saying 'Talked to Mommy through the bone thing.' I laughed and said that it was the first time that I had used the instrument as well. I asked how Mother Horan was, and she said that she was fine. I then asked after Riella, and Mary Ann said that she had gone to spend time with her mother who was taken ill. So Mary Ann had taken a few days off to help look after Ellen. I expressed sorrow, and then said that Mary Ann was there, as I had missed her and it would be good to spend some time with her.

We arrived back at the house and Father Horan and Gerard put the carriage and horses away and Mary Ann and I took the children into the house with the packages. Waiting at the door was Mother Horan who looked very pleased to see us and took Jarred from my arms, and hugged him, and then put her arm out and I hugged her too. I said that Mary Ann had told me about Riella and she said that Riella had a message the day before and had asked to go to look after her mother who had been taken ill, and Mary Ann offered to look after Ellen until we got back. We all went to the dining room where the table had been laid, and Ellen said, 'Eat here Mommy, all of us?'

I looked at Mother Horan who nodded. So we all sat around the table and Ellen sat on her father's knee and Jarred sat on Mary Ann informally for once, with cold food and rolls, tea and coffee, and the children were helped to eat and drink but Jarred didn't seem to want to eat after he tasted his food, Gerard said again that it might be his routine, but I thought back for a moment, and remembered when we went to the Italian café and he ate some vegetables there and that the owner put a little sauce on the soft vegetables, and he tasted and ate it all. 'He has not had a stomach upset or cried; do you think that the food might be a bit bland? Perhaps if he had a little gravy or some tomato sauce?'

The men hummed and hawed, but Mary Ann spoke up and said, 'If I may, some babies as they get older start to like different flavours, depending on their race, and the culture, they weaken the sauces, but they start to get the proteins.' She bowed her head, as if she had spoken out of turn, but Mother Horan said, 'I have heard that, and have read it in your medical journals, Gerard, as a former nurse I would say you have a good idea Mary Ann, you are a budding paediatrician not just midwife, let us try it, I'll get cook to make up a sauce.'

I smiled at Mary Ann and Mother Horan as she left the room, we told the baby that she had gone to make his food taste better, and he said, 'Magic Soose.'

My Gerard said, 'He's starting to talk Dad, I guess we'll have to keep on talking to both of them, because I know that's how they learn language.'

Soon Mother Horan returned with a small tray with two small jugs on, she put it on the table, 'One has beef gravy and one has tomato sauce with a little herb in it she said,' she poured some brown sauce on half his food and some red sauce on the other side. The room went quiet as Mary Ann offered Jarred a spoonful of food with brown sauce on, and he looked at her, the spoon and opened his mouth and tasted it, he swallowed and then she offered him a spoonful with red sauce and he looked at the spoon, opened his mouth tasted it and swallowed. He put his hand out and Mary Ann gave him some more and he grabbed the spoon, and put it in his mouth, and he ate all of his food, surprisingly he put the hand of the arm that didn't work so well. Ellen watched as well and said, 'Magic sauce daddy me have some too please.' We laughed and Mother

Horan took the tray and put it down by Gerard Jnr. Who put both sauces on her plate, she tried the tomato sauce but spat it out with a 'Yeauggh.' And then tried the brown sauce and she liked it, and finished her food.

'Well they seem to have different tastes, I guess it's what they get used to' said Gerard senior. We laughed and then Ellen slipped off her father's lap, and said, 'Bed now, me sleepy, night Dada, Gampa, Nana Mommy take me up.' She then walked and put her arms up to her grandparents for a kiss, which they did, hugging Mary Ann who carried Jarred upstairs and Gerard carried Ellen upstairs to their room, he then put her down and said he would be back later, he patted Mary Ann on the shoulder and kissed me on the cheek, 'Better tell Mom and Dad about our visit, perhaps you would like to tell Mary Ann' and he left, closing the door quietly behind him. As we got the children ready for bed, Jarred was already asleep and Ellen was drowsy, so I got her undressed, put her on her bed and covered her up.

We then sat down at the table and I told Mary Ann about our visit to the hospital and Jarred's diagnosis and that no operation would help. 'They talked about physiotherapy and have strapping inside Gerard's boot,' I said and Mary Ann explained about how physiotherapy worked. She then changed the subject and said, 'I have heard from my father, who sent his best wishes to you, and gave me his permission to marry and sent some money towards buying a dress. My mother hoped that I was working hard, she seems to have lost interest in me.' Mary Ann looked unhappy.

'Why so sad Mary Ann?'

'She spoke so quietly,' I miss my father a lot but my mother was only interested in the money that I earned, and that I didn't disgrace myself and lose my position. She gave up her position as a nurse.'

I moved towards her, 'Oh Mary Ann as if you would. I was the one who did that, and you stood by me, I will stand by you, what are friends for? Are you not looking forward to getting married? I am, we will help make your wedding a wonderful experience.'

Just then Mother Horan walked in after knocking on the door, she noticed that I was sitting close to Mary Ann and just smiled. Mary Ann looked up and sat up straight. Mother Horan said, 'I just came up to say goodnight, to the little ones. Why so sad Mary Ann? Are you not soon to be married?' Mary Ann nodded, 'Yes I have permission from my father, but I have no one to give me away, would Mr Horan give me away?' Mother Horan said, 'Why don't you ask him? I cannot speak for him but I don't think he would refuse.'

Mary Ann looked at me and said, 'Ellen should be nearly two then, could she be my flower girl, as you will be supporting me, and perhaps she could carry the rings?' I smiled, and could not hide my happiness, 'Of course we could coach her walking, and she would love to carry your rings.' I could not contain my joy and hugged her tight, and whispered but not too quietly, 'I love you so much, we all do, we just want you to be happy.' Mary Ann hugged me back and muttered, 'I love you too, so much.' Mother smiled and put her hands on both our shoulders and she just smiled.

'Well that is sorted, let us go down and I will send Helen my housekeeper in to keep an eye on the little ones, she loves them too. She left the room and we smiled at each other, 'You are my best friend and I could not love you more if you were my own sister' I said and Anna replied, 'You are the next best thing to a sister for me too,' she turned her head to one side as if she was looking at me for the first time since we arrived back, 'Anna', she said without hesitation this time, 'Have you had your hair cut?'

I looked a bit taken aback, suddenly remembering, 'Ye-es I did but not too short, they offered to buy the cuttings, but I didn't want any money so they gave me some hair combs and ornaments.' I unpinned my hair and let it down, it reached just past my shoulders, Mary Ann walked around me and said, 'Yes you look lovely you could even wear it loose.'

I suddenly remembered that I had brought some gifts back and looked in a mirror at my hair and brushed it away from my face and put some combs in just to keep it tidy. There was another knock on the door and Helen came in 'You need someone to watch the little ones, take as long as you wish I have brought a book to look at and some menus to look at.' We thanked her and she waved us off. Helen was such a kind lady and I felt that she could help me later on.

We joined the others who were now in the lounge drinking coffee. I had picked up the bag with the present in, and handed them out. Gerard came up to me and whispered, 'You've let your hair down.'

'Mary Ann noticed that I had my hair cut and I didn't have time to put it back up.' Mother Horan noticed also, 'I see you have had your hair cut. Were you not tempted to have a bob like other young ladies in the magazines?'

I replied, 'Oh no! That would have been too drastic, and it is not my style, my hair had just grown too long,' and they all laughed.

I handed out the gifts except for the children, resolving to give them to them in the morning. I said I hoped that Riella's problem would be soon resolved soon, as taking time to visit a sick relative was not as a good time as going home for a visit, and Mother Horan said that Riella would let us know, I said that it was not out of self-ishness I really liked Riella, and only hoped that the problem was not serious. They all nodded but nothing more was said.

Mary Ann then said, 'I have had a letter from my father who gives me permission to marry before I am 21 which will be in June, I wondered Mr Horan, would you give me away as Gerard is going to be Harry's best man?'

Father Horan stood up and walked over to Mary Ann and held her by the shoulders, 'I would be honoured to my dear, and I will talk to the Pastor, and if you would kindly lend me the letter with your father's permission, I will arrange for the banns to be read, assuming that you want to get married in church?'

Mary Ann's face lit up with relief, 'Oh yes please, if it is no trouble. I will tell Harry, because he will want to make arrangements, and a guest list, and oh, what about a reception and dresses, I have some money but?' she went quiet again. I stood up and walked over to Mary Ann, and sat down next to her, 'I think you may have forgotten, when you got engaged at Christmas last year, we said that you could get married from here, after you asked me to be your matron of honour, and Harry asked Gerard to be his best man. Please don't worry about some arrangements, just tell us what you like and we will set things as you ask, you are virtually family and family helps at times like these. Please I want to help, consider it a wedding present.'

Mary Ann again looked relieved, as furrows creased her lovely brow, 'Oh yes I remember now, I'm sorry I have been so busy with my qualifying exams once I pass them I can go on the wards with less supervision. I have been taken by surprise by my father's quick reply, it is okay I will talk to Harry and see what date he would like too, and thank you, thank you so much I am overwhelmed by your kindness.'

'You know there is something to be said for having a telephone instrument in the house, then we could talk to Harry,' said Father Horan. Mother Horan did not appear to agree; she almost snapped back, 'What! And having it ring all hours of the day and night, calling you out to an emergency! How do you know if Harry's parents have a telephone thing anyway?' He smiled back at his wife and said with a little laugh, 'It was just a thought Marie Claire.' She smiled and we all laughed, I had never heard him call her by name, before, he always called her 'Honey' or 'Sweetheart'.

Shortly after we all went to bed. We relieved Helen and I thanked her, and checked Ellen and Jarred, who were fast asleep. I suddenly felt very tired and when I went to our room where Gerard was getting undressed. After a little chat we fell asleep in each other's arms.

June 1920

Several months have passed and Gerard passed his final exams and Mary Ann finished her first exams to be a nurse, I was so thrilled. The children have grown and thrived, and my initial worries about Jarred seemed to fade as his 'bad' arm got stronger, and he seemed to have no problems using it and seemed to compensate, Ellen is also growing up fast her talking gets better as everyone talks to her, spent time with her and I helped her to recognise objects, people and names, and when we went out for walks, to know the words for sights. She also went to the stables with me on days when the weather was bad, to hold the brushes when I groomed the horses, she got to know their names, and she adored them all, and the mules. When the weather was good, when spring and summer came along they were let into the paddock. She was running by now, being nearly two years old. I had to keep an eye on her to make sure she didn't trip outside and even inside. Riella came back after being away for a month, and said her mother was much better, and she had noticed the changes in the children whilst she was away. Mother Horan had got busy preparing for Mary Ann and Harry's wedding and got Harry's mother involved. As promised we all listened to the couple's wishes and organised a modest celebration, and a few family members and friends from Harry's side of the family and some of Mary Ann's nursing friends, and us. The number totalled about twenty, so although the table in the dining room would take twenty people it seemed friendly to have a buffet with people sitting at tables around the room. We had the graduation ceremony for Gerard and Harry and Mary Ann to look forward to first. Riella looked after Jarred and Mother and Father Horan and I took Ellen to the great hall at the hospital, and we used the carriage, pulled by our best horses specially groomed and with plaited manes and tails for the occasion. Fortunately the ceremony was in the morning and it wasn't too hot, but sunny, the month being April. The journey was about five miles, and they didn't have to go too fast. Father Horan sat at the front with the driver and Mother Horan and I sat inside the carriage with Ellen, who was dressed in a new dress and coat and shoes, with her hair nicely groomed with the little combs that I got in Montreal. She was beginning to look like a tiny female version of her father, and had my eyes, but with his mouth, chin and honey brown hair which was getting thicker and after a little trim was down to her chin. Ellen's eyes were bright and she was very excited to go to the hospital for a special occasion to see her daddy being made a doctor, and her 'auntie' Mary Ann and 'uncle' Harry having their diplomas too. I had tried to explain to her that after Mary Ann and Harry had got married they would go and live in a place of their own; they would not live in our house. She did not quite understand, and asked why. I tried to explain that is what married people would do normally so that they could be on their own. She was a bit puzzled only being nearly two years old, as Gerard and I lived with 'Gamma' and 'Gampa', but I told her that when she was a baby she was born in another house and then her daddy brought us all here to Canada. I was going to have to explain to her when she was older, and show her on a map or atlas or even a globe where she was born, that she was born in England and Jarred was born in Canada. The journey took about half an hour, and we were driven into the grounds of the hospital where we got out of the carriage and the driver went around to the rear of the hospital where the horses could rest. Father Horan escorted us to the entrance, and I carried Ellen up the steps and set her down as she wriggled and said, 'I walk Mummy, not a baby!' but she held my hand as we walked through the corridor to the main hall, where there was a buzz of conversation. We entered the hall which seemed to hold about two hundred people. We had seats towards the front about six rows back from the stage. The front row was empty, where there were about twenty seats on either side of the aisle, I asked Father Horan how many doctors were getting their M.D.s and how many nurses were graduating, he wasn't sure, but he thought about twenty of each, but as the ceremony was about to start, we would soon find out. Mother Horan who was sitting between us was quite happy and she looked lovely in her black suit, slightly longer than the norm but with a small black and white hat, on the top of her chignon which was just starting to go grey, and she had a few lines and they were only laughter lines.

After about ten minutes a line of nurses walked in, wearing white, with no caps, I counted twenty. They sat down to the left of the hall, I noticed Mary Ann in the middle of the row before she sat down. Then shortly after the men walked in but oh yes! There were two women among them, I remember thinking that they might have had to work harder in a man's world, and I was secretly proud to see them, but wondered what I could do or would do when the time came.

Several senior people came into the room and walked up the steps to the stage and sat behind a rectangular table which had several scrolls and nursing caps also. There was a senior nurse who introduced herself as Sister Tutor, she explained about the different courses that the nurses had undertaken, and would take specialist courses after their graduation in general nursing and that standards had been very high. She then called the names of the nursing students, and then announced the specialist courses they would go on to train. When she got to Mary Ann, she called her by name, and as Mary Ann went up to receive her scroll and her cap, and mentioned that Mary Ann had come from England and had progressed well in her first year. There were other comments and encouragements for all the nurses. But I was just so happy and thrilled for Mary Ann and her achievement, and I felt very emotional. Then a senior doctor stood up, wearing a gown like a mayor might wear (from my memory) and a funny hat with a flat square on the top with a tassel. He also said that the standards were very high, and that the assembled graduates could now call themselves M.D.s, and would also be continuing with their studies to specialise, and would be an asset to any general practice. He called out each one by name, and as they walked up the steps to the platform, made a little comment to the assembly on their merits. He said that Harry was going into general surgery, and with a view to eventually orthopaedic surgery. When Gerard was called, he said that Gerard had come back from his war service to continue his studies, and had settled in well, to carry on the line of Horan M.D.s. He said that one of Gerard's projects would be research into the effects of trauma after conflict or injuries, also going to general surgery. There was a little murmur near us about the war to end all wars and so on, and then he went on to the next M.D., after Gerard went back down the steps. Ellen was falling asleep as all the talking was a bit beyond her, but she had been alert when Mary Ann and Gerard received their diplomas, but she then lost interest. After all the diplomas had been given and the tutors gave their closing speeches everyone clapped and Ellen woke up with a start, and looked a little wide eyed but I told her what was going on, she clapped her hands too, and said, 'We see Daddy and Mary Ann and Harry now? And then go home?' I nodded. We made our way out slowly because of the crowded room and made our way to another room with my carrying Ellen so that she did not get crushed as there were a lot of people milling around. Mother Horan and I stayed close together, but Father Horan went on ahead to meet the three members of our family who were waiting for us in the hallway, along with other new nurses and doctors. When Ellen saw the three, she wriggled from my arms and wouldn't stay with me, she almost ran to them, and my heart was pounding as the room was getting crowded, and she was no more than two feet six inches tall, she cried, 'Daddy, Daddy,' Gerard saw her and started walking towards her. Fortunately she was safe, as people heard and saw her and moved out of the way, she seemed to be the only child under ten years old there, and the adults moved out of the way and she ran straight into his arms, as he scooped her up, there was a little murmur of laughter but it was a generous laugh. As Mother Horan and I joined them there were hugs all round from the women and the men shook hands and warmly congratulated each other. For the moment it was a time of release and we went home as all the graduates had a few weeks off before their starting to work on the wards in the hospital, or elsewhere, as this hospital was actually a renowned teaching hospital. We all got into the carriage and Gerard sat up with the driver to go back, I didn't mind as perhaps we could go away for a little while with the children on our own. The journey took a little longer, the horses going at a reasonable pace, they started a little when an occasional motor car went by, but Gerard calmed them, and this only happened once or twice as mostly there were horse drawn carriages. How I still hated the noisy somewhat smoky vehicles.

When we arrived home, we went into the house where Harry's parents had already arrived in their own buggy, which carried two people, so both carriages were taken around to the back where the stables were, and their horse was unhitched, like ours to have some time to relax like us.

There was a cold buffet with cold meats, pies, fresh sliced crusty bread with butter and on another table desserts, including cherry pie, fruit flans, and a trifle with sponges and fruit in with a custard topping and whipped cream decorated with strawberries which we got from a store in the town (which was imported) apparently they were out of season. This dessert was virtually prepared by me with cook Helen supervising, and Ellen helped to decorate it. I had long wanted to become more 'domesticated' and whilst I spent time in the kitchen, watching Helen cook and listening to her commentary, this was the first time I was allowed to prepare and make something. I was a little envious of Mary Ann who had spent time in her mother's kitchen, because she had to, but this had been a good apprenticeship, as she had been able to make a meal for herself when she had stayed over at the hospital and slept in the nursing home.

There was a buzz of conversation during the lunch hour as people ate and drank. Ellen sat with Mary Ann, Mother Horan and I, and she had her own plate for some grown up food. Gerard was busy talking to his father, Harry and Harry's father and mother. Soon after she had a little of the trifle, Ellen seemed to get a little sleepy, so Mary Ann and I took our leave and took Ellen upstairs to her room for a sleep. We saw Riella sitting with Jarred in a corner and she was helping him with his lunch, or rather he was grabbing the spoon and putting the food in his mouth, he seemed to be progressing well, and his lesser able arm did not seem to upset his movements. As we walked in with Ellen who was by now being carried by me and Mary Ann, Jarred saw me and put his arms out and said 'May Ann, May Ann,' as that was the nearest he could make of her name, Mary Ann walked over to him, kissed his downy head, and said that she was going to get changed into day clothes, as she had been in whites for virtually six months, and she wanted to wear ordinary clothes for a little while until she started back on the wards. As she left the room Riella asked me if the presentations went well, I said, 'Yes it was very good, the tutors said a little about each person receiving their scrolls, they said what each nurse or doctor would be going on to. Mary Ann is going into midwifery, Harry is going on to do medicine and research into antibiotics, and blood group research, and illnesses of the blood. When he got to Gerard he went on about following his father into the 'family business' and surgery but when he mentioned the after effects of war and stress related mental affects we heard murmurs of 'war to end all wars' and people just didn't seem to understand I am aware of the after effects, I remember the moans and cries of the injured soldiers and they weren't actually in pain.' She nodded, and patted my arm. I wondered if Riella had any relations who had been involved, but didn't dare to ask, and as for Gerard, that was between him and me, and if he had confided in anyone else. After about ten minutes Mary Ann knocked on the door and came in wearing a pretty spring outfit, with a calf length skirt in grey, and a blouse with pretty lemon flowers on. We went back down leaving the children with Riella, and promised to send up a tray from the buffet lunch.

When we returned they were drinking coffee, Gerard came over to me, and Mary Ann went over to Harry and his parents, who made complementary remarks on her outfit. I felt a pang I was going to lose her soon, well in a way as she was going to get married in a few weeks, and she would be going to live with Harry, possibly with his parents, and she would not be sleeping under the same roof with me, but I knew that I had to let her go, as in the beginning, shortly after she had arrived, she had started to begin her own career and path in life, and I knew deep down that this was right, and that Gerard and I would be leading our own lives, also knowing that he had to do what was right for him, and that times together were, are precious.

I must have gone quiet for a moment as Gerard said, 'Penny for your thoughts?' and I smiled; how did he get that phrase? 'Just thinking how things are going to change, you have your career, Mary Ann and Harry are getting on with theirs, where do I fit in, what can I do?' He smiled and put his arm around my waist for a moment and said, 'After the wedding we will go away for a while just the four of us, and then you can think about what you feel you can do' he said.

Just then Father Horan left the room for a moment, and returned with three packages, and Harry's father took a small package from his inside pocket. Father Horan went to Gerard, Harry and Mary Ann and gave them a package wrapped in brown paper. Gerard and Harry opened theirs, which contained a stethoscope each, Mary Ann's was flatter, and contained a book on midwifery, I remembered that I had a gift too in my handbag which I hadn't a chance to give her, it was a little bulky a short trumpet shape, which when she opened it was a trumpet shaped item which midwives used to listen to heartbeats of unborn babies in their pregnant mothers' bumps. They were all quite happy. Harry's father called Mary Ann over and Harry, and gave Harry the small package, which when Harry opened it, contained a longish key, which would fit a barrel lock, and a smaller Yale key. It also had a label on it which had an address on it, Harry's father explained that it was for an apartment near the hospital which had a kitchen living room, bathroom and bedroom, for which they had paid six month's rent, to help them out until they were able to pay their own rent. The apartment was within walking distance to the hospital, but close enough for us to visit them, and they us. Mary Ann was nearly in tears, Harry looked very happy and I nearly cried too, and went over to hug Mary Ann and Harry. I really liked Harry's parents, they were sort of middle class like Gerard's parents but Mr Manton worked in the bank as a deputy manager.

Soon it was time for them to go, and Harry took his leave of Mary Ann, and us, he went to get his horse saddled up, which was stabled at the house, and as he lived a bit nearer to the hospital, did always use her, but she has a home either in his home stable or ours. We waved the three of them off.

The wedding was a sweet and happy affair, with Mary Ann wearing ivory as she did not want to wear white, as her nurses' uniform was white. She had a little veil reaching just past her shoulders, and her hair was swept up with a little coronet of flowers. Her dress was simple but stylish as her skirt was floor length, slightly flared but hung loose. Her bodice had elbow length sleeves which were gathered and the bodice had gently un-pleated folds and a belt which was dove grey, which matched her little heeled shoes.

Ellen was dressed in a little white full skirted dress with a dove grey sash, and a little flattish hat also in dove grey which was held on her head with lilac ribbons attached to the hat. She had white slippers and carried a little basket with flowers in. As 'matron of honour' I had a lovely lilac dress, similar but plainer than Mary Ann's dress, and with a dove grey belt, and grey slippers. Mother Horan kept with the theme of dove grey, and she had a lovely lilac hat on with a broad brim, and wore grey gloves. Father Horan and Gerard and I noticed that they wore morning suits in grey, with waistcoats and lilac cravats. Gerard took and his mother went early with Jarred to meet the others at the church, which left Mary Ann, Father Horan, Ellen and I to leave later. Five minutes before we were due to leave, I suddenly remembered an old custom, and I repeated it out loud, 'Something old, something new, something borrowed, something blue. Have you got all those?'

Mary Ann reeled off, 'Something new my dress, something borrowed your gloves, something blue, er yes, something old no.'

I suddenly thought of something and left them for a moment, picked up my long skirt and almost ran upstairs, I came back down with something grasped in my hand, which held a pearl bracelet, which had a little clasp. 'My mother wore this on her wedding day, this is the only thing which she gave, she wore it on her wedding, oh and this string of pearls which my aunt gave, it was my grandmother's,' I had managed to bring both down without her seeing.

Mary Ann was taken aback, 'Oh no I couldn't.'

'Yes you can, this is your something old, take it with my love, my mother would have wanted you to wear them' I replied, as I fastened the necklace around her neck and the bracelet on her wrist. Mary Ann looked a bit bewildered, and a bit scared, I guessed that she might be nervous, and was glad she asked me to go with her to the church. The door opened again as the carriage with two of our horses was ready to take the four of us to church. The carriage was an open one and had flowers arranged at the back, sides and front of the carriage. Mary Ann and I were given a small bouquet of flowers each, hers the larger one. I lifted Ellen into the carriage as the steps were a little too high for her, but once in she managed to clamber on to a seat. I waited to help Mary Ann into the carriage, and held her flowers, then I got in and sat next to Ellen, and Father Horan got in and as tradition decreed he sat next to MaryAnn. The groom closed the door of the carriage and then got next to the driver and we set off, at a moderate trot.

Mary Ann was worried about the time, and Father Horan and I both gave a little laugh, 'You are meant to be a little, so as not to appear too eager to marry your groom' Father Horan said with a smile, and I nodded, and Mary Ann relaxed a little.

Ellen, who had watched and listened, said, 'Who is marrying Mama, you?' I smiled at her and said, Mary Ann is getting married, she is wearing the bride's white dress and veil.' She then said, 'Who is she marrying Mama?' I replied, 'Mary Ann is marrying Harry, Daddy's friend, you remember when we had a party last week and his mother and father came.' She smiled, 'Yes me remember him, he nice, I like him, and the mummy and daddy were nice to me, when Mary Ann took me to tea with them when you away with baby Jerry, she showed me her garden.'

I looked at Mary Ann, 'Oh sorry, I forgot to tell you, with everything that went on, Ellen seemed a little lost, so I took her out is that all right?' she said with a frown.

I smiled, 'Thank you, I was a little worried about Ellen, and I missed her, so that was a nice outing for you Ellen?' Mary Ann relaxed, and smiled and then Ellen said as she looked around, 'We here, Mary Ann getting married' and we all laughed.

We all got out of the carriage; I got out first, then Ellen, then Father Horan, and finally Mary Ann, helped by us both. We walked up to the church, and up the steps and I checked that Mary was ready, adjusted her veil, but before putting it over her face, kissed her quickly on the cheek and whispered, 'Be happy my dear Mary Ann, love you so much,' then stepped back, lowered the veil, and she smiled and as tradition was in this country, Ellen and I walked down the aisle first, and I saw that Mary Ann coyly took Father Horan's extended arm as he led her down the aisle. Ellen was very good and held my hand and walked slowly down the aisle to 'Here comes the Bride'. We reached the front and Ellen and I went to the left and Mary Ann and Father Horan went forward to meet Harry, and Gerard walked forward also.

The pastor went through the preliminaries, and it was time for Mary Ann and Harry to say their vows, so I went forward to take her bouquet so that she would have both her hands free. When the moment came, Father Horan duly gave her hand away, saying 'My wife and I do, on behalf of her parents.'

I was feeling very emotional, and looked over and Gerard caught my eye line and smiled, then looked back. They duly made their vows, and also said some special words of their own. I was standing near Mother Horan and could feel tears pricking my eyelids and overflowing, blessed Mother Horan touched my elbow and handed me one of her handkerchiefs which I whispered my thanks and dabbed my eyes. They exchanged plain gold rings, just like Gerard's and mine, and were pronounced man and wife and exchanged a quick kiss, after Harry had lifted her veil. They went away to sign the register, and Gerard and I went as witnesses, with Ellen coming too as she did not want to leave me. She watched as the process took place, and asked to see the book, so Gerard lifted her up to look. We then went out to the church again, and Mary Ann and Harry walked back down the aisle first as man and wife, to the strain of the 'Hornpipe' which seemed much better. We all filed out and waited on the steps as photographs were taken, and then Harry and Mary Ann went in the carriage which we came in and we followed in the carriage with Mother and Father Horan, Harry's mother and father in one carriage, and Gerard, Ellen, Jarred and I went in another carriage back to the house.

Jarred had been half asleep during the service, but he woke up once we were in the carriage which Gerard sat in front to drive. We managed to use all six of our horses, and they performed very well.

When we got back to the house the guests were waiting for us, including the parents of the groom and his family, Mr and Mrs Manton and his aunt and uncle. We stood outside as again, photographs were being taken of the bride and groom, and then Gerard, Ellen and I were called over as best man and matron of honour and flower girl. Ellen ran over to Mary Ann and held her hand and Mary Ann sweetly and gently moved Ellen in front of her and I went to her side, and we held each of Ellen's hands and Gerard went to Harry's side as we posed with frozen smiles for the ten seconds for the photograph. Then we moved away and Father and Mother Horan stood by the couple. Finally there was a group photograph by which time the carriages had been taken around to the stables. We all went into the house where there were hired waiters and waitresses holding trays with glasses of champagne to offer to the guests. Whilst people were circulating I excused myself and took Jarred up to the nursery and Riella went up with me, and I laid him in his cot. I told Riella that I would send up a tray of food for her and would get someone to relieve her later, and she smiled and thanked me, but I said, 'Thank you.'

I returned to the reception area just as people were going into the dining room, and Gerard had waited for me with Ellen, and kissed me on the cheek, and said, 'I didn't get a chance to tell you that you look wonderful, and Mary Ann looked beautiful. Ellen did a great job, she has been so good. We need to take our places at the top table.' So we walked with Ellen to join the others at the top table which consisted of the bride and groom, of course, Harry's parents on his side, and Gerard and I and Father and Mother Horan on the other, with Father Horan sitting next to Mary Ann. Ellen sat on her own chair which we helped her on and it was boosted by a pillow so she could see everyone. After the pastor said grace, everyone went to the buffet to eat, but were served with food and drinks.

We all chatted during the meal and it seemed very light hearted and convivial. When everyone had eaten their fill and were seated in their chairs at the tables around the room, everyone was given a glass of champagne, well except for Ellen. Gerard stood up and tapped a glass for a request for everyone to be quiet, and he started his speech as the best man, he talked about his times with Harry, and how they were best friends from school, and then at medical school finally he raised his glass to the 'Bride and Groom,' and we all toasted them. Then it was Harry's turn, and he talked about how he got to meet Mary Ann at the house, and later on the wards, he thanked Gerard for his return of the favour as best man and thanked me for bringing Mary Ann in the first place, I caught her eye and we shared a smile. Finally he thanked Ellen and I for attending Mary Ann and Mother and Father Horan for being the hosts for the wedding and he also thanked his parents for their support, and for their first home. Finally he asked everyone to raise their glasses to the Matron of Honour and flower girl, I told Ellen that was us, and she clapped her hands. The band had arrived and the food table was moved and put back to make space for dancing, waiting for Mary Ann and Harry to do the first dance and then others followed. Ellen was helped from her chair and she then went to Mary Ann as she and Harry went to sit down, Ellen said, 'Where you go now Aunty Mary, Unca Harry? You leave this house now.'

Harry smiled and as he sat down he took her onto his lap and Mary Ann held her hand, as she leaned into Harry, Mary Ann said gently, 'Yes I will leave to go and live with Harry now we are married, but I/we will come to visit, and you can visit us. We both love you, and nothing will change, but you will still have Mama and Daddy and your grandparents, and you will see us. We have a little present for you for being such a good flower girl' and Harry took a little package out if his pocket and opened it for her, inside was a little rigid silver bracelet with her name on and the date of the wedding and Mary Ann and Harry inside as she showed me later. He slid it on her outstretched hand, and she looked at it, smiled and hugged them both, and gave them each a little kiss. Ellen said thank you without being prompted, and then slid off Harry's knee, and came over to me and said, 'Mama sleepy, go to bed now.' And I got up with her and walked to the door after excusing ourselves, Mary Ann joined us, and said, 'Can I say good night to the little ones? Is that all right Harry?' as Harry joined her, he said, 'All right dearest, but don't be long, it is our party' he said with a smile.

So we went up with Mary Ann to the nursery where Riella was sitting at a table with a tray of food and a soft drink, she went to get up, but she had seen Mary Ann and Mary Ann explained that she wanted to say goodnight and Riella nodded. Riella said that Jarred had woken up once she changed his diaper and he went back to sleep. I thanked her and Riella excused herself for ten minutes, Mary Ann had taken her veil off earlier, and she put on an apron and helped Ellen get ready for bed. Mary Ann hugged her and kissed her goodnight, and leaned over and kissed Jarred's downy head and pulled his blanket up a little, 'I'm going to miss then, I've seen them from their births, oh this is a new step, how did you do it Anna?' Mary Ann was getting a little teary, and I replied with a little tremor, 'Well I had a good man who loved, and my best friend next to you, and my in laws are so kind, I'm sure you will be all right.'

Just then there was a knock at the door and Riella had returned, and she had a package in her hand and she gave it to Mary Ann, 'Just a little gift Mary Ann, to your new life.' Mary Ann was very touched, and gave Riella a little hug. Riella then went on into the nursery and we returned downstairs. We didn't realise or notice how long we had been but Gerard and Harry were waiting for us. Gerard said, 'We are waiting for the wedding cake to be cut,' with a smile and Mary Ann joined Harry and they walked hand in hand to the table where the cake was. It was a simple two tier circular cake with a little set of icing flowers on the top. Gerard and I followed with my hand in his. We stood slightly back so that everyone could see Mary Ann and Harry cut the cake, and then everyone clapped. The cake was then taken away to be cut into slices. The room was buzzing as Harry and Mary Ann went around to greet their guests, Father and Mother Horan were chatting to Harry's parents, Gerard and I sat down near them and I felt my eyes filling up again with tears, and I turned my face towards him, and covered my eyes, Gerard saw my tears and gave me a handkerchief from an inner pocket, 'What's wrong my love,' he whispered, and I whispered back, 'It's the end of an era, I will not see Mary Ann so much, she's been living with us for nearly two years and with me for most of my life, it's just a bit hard to let go, but I will.'

Harry and Mary Ann finally came over to us. It was early evening and the marriage had taken place at 1 p.m. Harry said, 'We will be going soon, we just wanted to thank you for being there for us and all your help.' Mary Ann looked a little teary too as she clung to Harry. Gerard noticed too, 'We have a present for you also, they are in the stables, we found two horses for sale in the livery they are young and needed a good home, you can leave them here to be stabled when you are not using them and we will look after them, a good excuse to visit us I guess.' Their eyes lit up, and I said with an almost quivery voice, 'We also got you some linen.'

Mary Ann hugged us both and Harry shook hands with Gerard, and gave me a little hug, which I reciprocated and I whispered, 'Take care of her.' He nodded and said, 'For both of us thanks for the horses and the linen, it does not need much excuse to visit because we will want to see our favourite godchildren.'

They left the room and went upstairs to her room and returned about half an hour later in ordinary clothes and Mary Ann still had her bouquet. Everyone went to the door to see them off. There was a carriage with their two horses which would take them to the station and then come back. We told Mary Ann and Harry and they went to see the horses and stroked their muzzles before getting into the carriage to leave. Gerard got up to the front to drive, and held his hand out for me to get up to the front of the carriage also, I managed with the little indignity of lifting my skirt a little higher and stepped up to the seat. Everyone waved to them and shouted; 'Good bye good luck' and Gerard tapped the reins and said, 'Gee up' and we set off, the horses walked very well. The journey to the station did not take long and we heard the whistle of a train in the distance. We stopped just outside the station, and Gerard got down and went round to help me down, and then opened the carriage door to let Harry and Mary Ann out. The men took their bags and Mary Ann and I followed arm in arm behind them. We didn't say anything just looked ahead, and we both knew that this was an end to one life, and the beginning of another. We finally arrived to the platform and the train was arriving, 'Have a lovely time wherever you are going. We'll see you in a week or two, dear Mary Ann dear Harry.' Mary Ann and I hugged each other and I planted a kiss on her cheek and she kissed mine. Gerard helped Harry with the bags, shook hands with Harry, Mary Ann gave Gerard a little hug, and Harry gave me a little hug, and he said quietly, 'Thanks for bringing Mary Ann here, I will look after her.'

They both got on to the train, walked through to their carriage and we waved to each other until the train pulled away. Gerard and I walked back to the carriage and I climbed up front with Gerard again, and we drove back to the house, and to the stable, and we unhitched the horses together and I took the traces off and led them to their stalls and took their halters off, and they turned around whinnied, and I stroked their muzzles and made sure they had something to eat. Of course all the horses looked at me and I greeted them all, including the mules, oh I loved them all!

We went back to the house and joined the others, and smiled and chatted with everyone. Gradually people started to take their leave, thanking both sets of parents, I know that I loved them all, especially Mother and Father Horan, and Mary Ann wasn't just grateful, she felt and was a member of the family. After everyone had gone home, including Harry's parents who were called Mabel and Stanley, who thanked us for taking care of them, and thanked me, yes me, for bringing Mary Ann to Canada, I just said that I couldn't think of doing otherwise because she had been there for me, when Ellen was born, and it would be a good opportunity for her to do something more important than being a lady's maid. I was very happy for her. After saying 'Keep in touch,' they went. I offered to help clear away, but Mother Horan said not to worry, the hired help would take of that, so we went to the library and had coffee and mints and talked about the events of the day. The comments that they gave back to us was that Mary Ann looked sweet, beautiful and her attendants looked after Mary Ann very well. Gerard was given praise also, for looking after Harry, keeping him composed until Mary Ann arrived. Gerard said that when the music for the arrival of the bride started, Harry glanced back quickly, and when he saw Mary Ann walk up the aisle on the arm of Father Horan, his shoulders shook a little and Gerard put his hand on Harry's shoulder to reassure him, but Harry had just said, 'She looks wonderful, I'm so happy,' and the ceremony continued.

Gerard said to me, 'He really, really loves her, no doubt about that.' I looked at Gerard, and Mother and Father Horan, and said, 'I know I believe you Harry is a nice kind man.'

We all went to bed then, after exchanging goodnights and I kissed Mother and Father Horan, Gerard kissed his mother goodnight and hugged his father. Later, as we lay in bed together, just before we were settling down to sleep, Gerard said, 'How would you like to go away for a while?' I sat up and wide eyed said, 'Where? I don't like the big city, too noisy.' He laughed and said, 'How about a log cabin two miles away in the forest, there is running water, well a freshwater stream, we could take two horses, a cart, and bedding and food and some wood, and the children they might like to have a little time in the wild.' I smiled and said, 'That would be lovely and I think if there was a log fire and an oven, maybe I could bake bread and a stew or something, I've become a lot more domesticated since I came here, when I'm allowed to, oh yes please darling.' He laughed and kissed and as we fell asleep in each other's arms, I was thinking of the tranquillity of the forest.

We had a lovely week away only a few miles into the forest with one excited little girl and a baby not so little, looking at everything, and two of our lovely horses who pulled the cart steadily making it seem easy. The cabin was an old one, clean but a little dusty, so we found brooms, and I found sacking from the cart and covered my clothes whilst I swept through the cabin, Gerard unhitched the horses and took them over the shelter and took off traces and bridles, found the water and left them to walk free in the small fenced off corral outside the shelter. Whilst the children sat in the cart watching their father, the water was brought from a stream which ran outside the back of the cabin. After cleaning the cabin, and making up the beds, one double for us and a single cot bed which hopefully the children would sleep together. Then we brought the children in, Ellen was lifted out of the dart and ran into the cabin, and I carried Jarred, but once in the cabin he wriggled down and crawled, pulled himself up, and then said, 'Up Mama,' so I put him on the bed, and Ellen joined him and they sat together watching us bring in the food, bags of clothes holdall and a metal canister which he said had milk in, for the children. There was a little wood stove which had two sort of hot plates, one to heat up water for coffee, and another for cooking. When I checked the box of food, there were cakes, oats, coffee, tea, two loaves of bread, butter jam, separately, sausages, bacon, eggs, lard, biscuits and fruit. I was astounded, and said so. All he could say was, 'Can you cook?' I gave a look to him, and said, 'Yes, I had lessons with Helen!' and he laughed teasing. I smiled and was not able to stifle a giggle, 'Where do we put these things, especially the dairy stuff?'

Gerard opened the cupboards and after I had washed them out and the sink and scrubbed the table with a brush that was in the box also with a bar of soap, and we put the dry food in the cupboards and he also brought in a metal box from the cart and showed me the slap of ice that was in the bottom, and I put the perishables in there, putting the metal plate in between the fresh and the raw food. I went out to get some water from the stream making sure it was clear, and carried in the bucket and put it in a clean metal jug and put some into the kettle, and Gerard lit a fire in the stove and I put the kettle over the hob on one side. The children watched with interest, until Jarred lay down and fell asleep. Gerard finally sat down and pulled his boots off, and I found his shoes, which he put on. 'Where did you learn to do cleaning, not here, Mother wouldn't let you?'

I smiled and said 'Well, my father wouldn't either, but he wasn't there all the time, so I got involved with the setting up of the beds and wards at Three Gates with Mary Ann and the orderlies. I was more involved than Father knew. This was a lovely challenge, but my cooking? Helen taught me, who do you think made the trifle at Christmas? Me!'

Gerard laughed and came over to me and held me in his arms and kissed, 'My own little wifey, domesticated but still a lady!' and he kissed me and I kissed him back.

'Mama, smoke!' Ellen said and pointed to the stove to see the kettle boiling, but no smoke, 'No Ellen, steam' I said, and she said, 'Steam, water hot?' and she smiled, we praised her, and I went to find a coffee pot to make coffee, and there were also metal mugs, plates, cutlery and bowls in the box, everything that we might need. I was not really aware of what time it was, but I felt hungry, so I guessed it might be late morning, I asked Gerard if he was hungry, and if he had any idea what time it was, and he said, 'Country time, we get up with the sun and go to bed at sundown.'

I asked what would we do in the dark mornings, knowing that we had a wind up alarm clock at home, and he laughed and pulled out his pocket watch and opened it and, 'Well it is 11.45 in the morning, so we could have lunch, something light, bread and cheese or something with coffee and something for the children.'

I laughed and said, 'Yes sir, right away sir!' and Gerard laughed too. Jarred woke up and started to wail, so I picked him up to see if he was wet, but he wasn't and I asked him if he was hungry, and he opened his mouth, and Ellen said, 'Jarry hungry, me too Mama, that his cry' and I thanked her, as I did know his cries as he was just making words apart from Mama, Dada, Gamma, Gampa, and Merry Ann, and Len, his attempt at his sister's name. I cut up some slices of bread, put pieces of cheese, cut some slices of ham and took the butter out of the cold box, Gerard and I had coffee, and I made some hot chocolate with some of the milk in a pan, there was also a malt drink which they would have at night, we sat around the table, with Jarred on my knee, Ellen on a chair, which she knelt on and ate her pieces of bread and butter and cheese with some pieces of cake. Jarred had his bread and small pieces of cheese soaked in some warm milk, I just hoped that it would last. It was a lovely simple meal with all four of us. After the children had their fill, and Ellen got down from the table and Jarred was falling asleep, so I tucked him up on his end of the bed, Ellen said, 'Wee wee mama,' and I looked at Gerard, and he smiled and showed where Ellen could go, it was a little hut outside with a covered bucket with a wooden board with a hole in it, Ellen went with me and I helped her sit on the 'privy' and held her so she wouldn't fall in. I helped her down and she pulled up her knickers and she scurried back into the cabin. I found a bucket and filled it from the stream and poured it onto the bucket, and I found a bottle in the box with cleaning cloths which said 'liquid carbolic'. I vaguely remember the orderlies scrubbing floors and surfaces with carbolic soap, so after checking with Gerard about the safety of using it, and he thought for a moment and said if it was diluted it should be OK I told him that I had already put a bucket of water in there, so he went outside with the bottle and came back with the bottle and told me that he had put a bit more water in and put a small amount of the bottle in, and praised me for considering it, and consulting him, and I thanked him for being so helpful to me as I was learning all the time. I prepared some meat and vegetable for a stew for later and put it in water on the stove with some herbs and a little lard, and let it simmer. I was enjoying myself doing food preparation and clearing away the lunch plates and used some hot water and some cold water in the metal bowl that I found under the sink, after giving it a good swill out with hot water and oh yes, there was a pipe out of the sink into a large bucket outside which was thrown onto an almost overgrown vegetable patch that I noticed outside and as I was using bicarbonate of soda to do the washing up it seemed all right. I wondered where the cleaning regime that I was using came from, and I remembered that I had read a good housekeeping book that I found in the library, and it was very instructional and I went to the kitchen some mornings and afternoons before, during and after food preparation, cooking and washing up. I sometimes sneaked in there with some trays for tea or coffee and took them to the scullery and if no one was there I would wash them up quickly, running out if I heard anyone coming into the kitchen, and then asked if I could have something later. Mary Ann would have been a little shocked, but hey ho, but I can act like a lady, but was not afraid to get my hands wet, or dirty or a little roughened, as I washed my hands and put some hand cream on. Gerard asked if I had brought any with me, but I said I had forgotten, but had remembered soap, and towels, and the children's powders and creams. Gerard laughed and said, 'You are an enigma, my love, but that is why I fell in love with you, don't ever change!'

I bowed my head, a little overcome with his praise, and after I had washed up the lunch things and left them to dry, I sat down on a chair at the table, and watched as Ellen explored the cabin, it seemed to be a large open plan sort of room, with one large bed in the back corner and a smaller single bed opposite on the front wall, with a table in the centre of the cabin with four wooden chairs with backs and a window over to the side where there was a sink, a board on either side. Some cupboards either side of the window which I had not cleaned out but did, with some carbolic soap, and after the cleaning was able to put the plates, mugs and cutlery away and the dry foods and ground coffee and tea away. Gerard just watched me as I was making this cabin a little home if only for a little while.

'Are you going to stop cleaning for a moment it's a lovely day out there.' I stopped and said, 'I just want to be tidy, this is going to be our home for a little while, well if the children want to, we could explore.' Ellen was anxious to explore outside, so I suggested if Gerard would take her out for a walk, unless he wanted to watch the stew cooking and not let it burn, and he chose the first choice, and Ellen ran over to her father, who stood up and took her hand, he smiled to me as they went out and said, 'Let's find some flowers and get some water Ellen,' and she nodded, and said, 'Bye Mama,' and they were gone. I looked around the cabin and felt so happy. We were away from everyone, and were almost self-sufficient, Jarred slept on peacefully for a while, his little face looked so angelic. I stirred the stew from time to time, and looked out of the window, the horses were standing quietly in the corral, occasionally whinnying, chewing some of the straw and walking around a little. It seemed a bit quiet, I looked outside the door and saw Gerard and Ellen near the stream and she was dabbing her fingers in the water, Gerard was crouching down beside her, holding her hand, so protectively. They then went behind the cabin and I lost sight of them. I felt a little uncertain thinking possibly on my own, with a baby, and I did not know the area. After about half an hour which seemed longer, they both walked in with a bunch of flowers, and some herbs, and dirty hands and fingers. 'What have you been doing?' I asked, trying to keep the panic out of my voice so as not to upset Ellen.

'We've been around the back of the cabin, over the stream and found some wild flowers, and Ellen wanted to do some digging from the old vegetable patch, but they've all died,' he came over to me as I looked a little worried and said quietly, 'Were you worried? I know you couldn't see us, we were quite safe, and besides the horses would give an alarm if strangers came. I promise you I will not go anywhere far without you all, we, Dad and I use this cabin as a half way place from the logging camp, and I will show you where we go. We'll take the horses. I'm sorry my love, I should have said we wouldn't go far.'

I hugged him and then encouraged Ellen to wash her hands at the sink, standing on a chair. I then thought about washing the children and told Gerard, and he opened a door, which I thought was the back door, but was a little room, with another bed, and oh yes, it had windows and an old fashioned hip bath. I laughed and said we could wash the children there. After Ellen had washed her hands, and face and dried herself, she got down from the chair, and I washed the herbs that she brought and asked Gerard if he felt that they were alright to put in the stew which was bubbling away on the hob over the stove, he sniffed it, and tasted it, 'Well, A, the stew is fine by itself, and B, this is sage and I think we could use it with bird not beef. Another thing for you to learn is which herbs are which, and when to use them.' He smiled, but I was a little upset. 'Well it just so happens that your mother gave me a book on herbs, and fungus, and I brought it with me, so I will explore the herb garden and compare.'

Gerard picked up on my tone, and came over to me, and hugged me and whispered, 'No criticism of your cooking honey, it must be difficult to change from being a lady of leisure to being a housewife, and I know you want to despite Mary Ann's training,' and he kissed my hair, and I remembered that we were not alone and laughed out loud.

Ellen was watching us, and said, 'Mama and Dada fight?' and we laughed and reassured her. The meal later, as the sun was still high, was served, with Jarred's food finely cut and mashed up, Ellen's food was cut small as well, but she could chew. I fed Jarred and Ellen sat next to her father and ate her meal. I had some spicy sauce to put in Jarred's meal as he seemed to have acquired the taste with his main meals, just a tiny spoonful, but he ate all his dish full. After the plates were cleared away and washed up, and covered the pot, we sat outside on the steps, and watched the sun go down. The horses seemed quite contented in each other's company and we went over to check on them with the children. After settling the horses down for the night, and getting the children undressed, and giving them a drink they went to bed, head to toe, and made sure they were safe from falling out. Gerard and I sat down with a glass of wine, and as the shadows fell, we got into bed as well. Before we went to sleep, Gerard told me that this was luxury compared to accommodation at the front during the war, even if they were in huts and not in the trenches, the constant thud of shells and gunfire was awful.

The next few days were wonderful, true to his word Gerard took us up to the logging camp, a few miles away, about an hour's ride on the horses and the hills were not steep, we had a child in front of us, and the horses trotted briskly or walked when it was bumpy, and we walked at times so the horses could keep their footing, a little foolish

I know but I loved those horses, as did Gerard, so we treated them well. We returned to the cabin late afternoon after spending time watching the loggers do their felling of trees and trimming them. We had a meal and then went back. We also went to Moose Falls further down taking care to keep the children from falling or jumping into the water and the horses went to the edge to have a drink. The week came to an end only too soon and we repacked the cart, left the cabin tidy and hitched the horses to the cart and made our way back to the town and home to the house. When we got back we had a great welcome from Mother and Father Horan, Riella, who had been on holiday and Helen the cook/housekeeper. After unloading the cart, unhitching the horses, and taking them to the stables, giving them a good brush down and settling them into their stalls, greeting the other horses, we all went indoors. I was feeling a bit unkempt and in need of a wash, as I had just had a bit of a strip wash though the children had a bath or a good wash every day, so I excused myself and went up to the nursery with the children, who were happy to see Riella, and Ellen told her in her own way about our time away, and Jarred who was ten months old just smiled and laughed as I carried him upstairs. Riella asked if I had managed at night on my own and I laughed, 'I wasn't on my own, Gerard was helping, he and Ellen went for a walk and were gone for what seemed ages, and Jarred was asleep, and it was so quiet, I got a bit worried, but oh yes it was a great experience, I felt a little like the settler wives when their men went hunting, but that was the only thing he didn't do.'

She asked if I would go again, and I said I would but not sure about in the winter. As Riella was helping the children unpack, I ran a bath and put some fresh clothes out, it was nice to be home, but I had quite enjoyed fending for myself, cooking and cleaning, it just proved I could, but also meant I was different, as my sister

Ellen would roll her eyes at the thought of cleaning or washing up or seeing to the children. We were so different, but I still missed her, and loved her.

After a nice cleansing bath and hair wash, I got dressed in fresh clothes, Gerard came in and he said he was going to have a bath and a shave, he wouldn't be long, but asked me to wait until he had done as he had something to show me. As I brushed my hair after drying it, and pinned it up, away from my face, I unpacked the two bags, putting dirty clothes in a basket, one for me and one for Gerard, and put the clean ones on the bed for him, and put mine away. Gerard always put his clothes away and I mine, as I respected his way of where he put things away. He came into our room with a towel around his waist, and drying his hair. He saw the neat pile of his clean clothes, socks and things, and I said, 'I left them for you to put away as you know where you want them.' He nodded and said, 'Thank you for respecting my privacy, such as it is.' I smiled, 'You're welcome, there are some things that I do not want you seeing, so no problem.'

After Gerard had dried himself, and dressed he said, 'Thanks for waiting, there's something I want to show you downstairs, Father has been busy while we were away.' I was intrigued, and we went back downstairs, and he took me by the hand to the side of the hallway, there on the table was a telephone, very similar to the one in the hotel room, I was very surprised, as I did not notice any wire overhead, Gerard took me outside and high up on the left of the building, there was indeed a telephone cable thing going into the house. 'Mother isn't too pleased, she's worried we will get calls during day and night, but there's only about twenty in the whole town including the post office and the hospital and the railway station; we haven't been connected yet or have a number, but I'm told it will be Moose Falls 21. Father thinks the exchange will connect us up tomorrow, I believe that Harry's parents have one, and they were going to have one in Harry and Mary Ann's apartment, so she could telephone you and you her.'

'If she is not working,' I said, looking as the two piece instrument which had a long bone shaped piece resting on a round base which had a pronged rest and a curly cable coming out of one end of the lifting piece. I lifted it up, but it was silent. Gerard laughed, 'I'll show you how to use it after we are connected.'

I smiled, and then we went to the library where Mother and Father Horan were waiting for us with a table laid with sandwiches, scones and cakes. We were gestured to sit down near the table as Mother Horan poured tea into cups, and passed them around on saucers, a maid passed tea plates out and we placed our drinks on a nearby table, as we accepted sandwiches, small talk ensued, until the scones were passed around and cake. The conversation was quite enjoyable, as Mother and Father Horan told us what had happened whilst we were away, and they gave us a postcard from Mary Ann and Harry, from Niagara Falls, to all of us, saying that they were having a lovely time, missed us a bit. And we laughed at that. They said that they would be back in a few days, and sent their love to all, especially the beloved children.

July 1920

Mary Ann and Harry returned from their honeymoon and went to their apartment near the hospital. Apparently they had a telephone installed where they lived too as Gerard had told me, and after a few days we were all connected through a local 'exchange' which when we tapped a lever, would connect us to a household or the post office or to the hospital. I expressed a hope to one day telephone England to the village that we left in Sussex, but was quite content to telephone Mary Ann sometimes. We met occasionally on a Sunday after church, if either she or Harry or Gerard were not working and we went out for a picnic on our horses, and took the children along sometimes, and went to the falls. Mary Ann and Harry seemed very happy and content, and enjoyed the company of the children and us. I noticed a slight difference in her attitude towards me; she seemed a little shy at times, being a newlywed. I wonder if it was like that for her when Gerard and I got married. Whilst the men went for a walk with the children, I had a chance to talk to Mary Ann, I asked if everything was all right with her, and if she wanted to confide or ask for help, to just ask, after all, she was there for me when I needed a friend. She looked at me sideways, and said it was nothing, but as we sat down, she sat close to me, and I could see her tearing up, I put my arm around her, 'What is wrong dear Mary Ann, are you happy, is Harry still the man for you?'

She gave a water smile, 'Oh yes, he is a wonderful man, and so patient, he agreed that we would not start a family straight away, but well, we did you know, and it was OK but he uses something, and well, it's not very comfortable.' She pulled out a kerchief and dabbed her eyes. I hugged her, and said, 'Oh dear, Mary Ann, you are trying not to have a baby, and I don't seem to be able to have another baby. If it would help, I would be happy to look after any child that you might have, after all, you helped look after mine. Talk it over with Harry, it's a decision that you both need to make, and you will be able to carry on being a midwife, looking after other mothers to be. Whatever you decide, I will support you.' She smiled and dried her eyes.

Shortly after our men came back with the children who were quite excited and Ellen ran to us, with Jarred walking behind as fast as he could, his walking was very good, I was getting a bit worried when he started to run. Ellen was getting tall, and very pretty, and her speech was getting better, and she knew lots of words and was making sentences. She ran towards and said, 'Mama we see a big brown animal not a horse, a a Dada what is...?' Gerard laughed and said, 'A moose Ellen, it was a moose.' She looked at Gerard and me and said, 'A moose, what that?' I explained to her that the creature was wild, and lived near here and promised to show her pictures and tell her about them when we got home. I was so pleased with her and Jarred called out, 'Moose, moose, moose Mama!'

Somehow I felt a bit like a teacher, and I felt the beginnings of being useful. Harry and Mary Ann walked back together, his arm around her, and he was talking quietly. The children sat on a mule as we walked back slowly together. After supper, Harry and Mary said goodnight to the children, and to us, and Mother and Father Horan. It was still quite light as they walked back to the town, and to their apartment. I loved this time of year, with the light evenings. We went out to check the horses who were out in the paddock with the mules, happily roaming around; they had a water trough which we checked to make sure they had enough, and enough food, and shelter. They came over to the fence when we called, all eight of the horses and the two mules came over to us and we greeted them in turn, and gave them a titbit, usually an apple which they took very gently. Gerard and I then went for a little walk around the gardens before going in, and then joined Mother and Father Horan for a late night drink before going up to bed and relieved Riella, who went to bed. We checked on the children who were sleeping peacefully, Jarred in his cot lay on his back with his arms thrown out sideways, with a peaceful smile on his little face, covered to his chest, and his little fists closed. Ellen on her bed lay on her side with her honey coloured hair loose and tumbled on her pillow, with her hands over her cover. They looked so peaceful, and I was so thankful that we had two healthy beautiful children, but I just wondered why I had not become pregnant again. As we got ready for bed and into bed, Gerard told me that he and Harry had been talking and asked if Mary Ann had been talking about anything in particular, and I muttered, 'Just ladies' talk, er I'm not sure I should tell you, it's kind of private.'

He looked across at me as I was in bed and sat on the edge of the bed, and he said, 'We promised no secrets, is it so private you cannot tell me?' I looked away, afraid to betray a confidence especially about Mary Ann. I took a deep breath, 'Why do you ask Gerard?'

He moved across and into bed, still looking at me, and he said very low, 'Something is not right between Harry and Mary Ann, Harry is besotted with her, but says she is not happy with something between them, he is a really great guy, been like a brother to me, since we were at school together, and I know things are not right and its hurting him, he would do anything for her even…'

I almost guessed what he was trying say, and I started to cry, 'Oh Gerard she confided in me, rather than Harry, they need to talk, she said he is respecting her wish not to start a family, but the method is uncomfortable, and she is afraid to tell him. I am happy for them and hearing what you said makes me feel very warm towards Harry. Oh Gerard I did say if she wanted to start a family I would help her with the baby so she could carry on working as a midwife, did I do wrong?'

He laughed and hugged me and kissed me, 'Oh no you two look after each other, I will have a word with Harry just as you did to Mary Ann, they need to talk to each other, that is all, and then wait and see, they are our friends, but we don't interfere, just be there when they need us, just like family.' I agreed, and we fell asleep in each other's arms.

September 1920
We said no more about the conversations, and at the end of July Harry and Mary Ann took a week off and took their horses and a

few provisions and went up to the log cabin where Gerard and I went with the children. I can only guess how they got on; I hoped that Harry would show her around the countryside too.

I could only pray that they would be all right. The children were growing fast, Ellen was very inquisitive, and I tried to answer her questions, and show her pictures, and took her out on trips into the town, and sometimes we went a bit further out into the country to part of Moose Falls, on one of the horses, it was getting easier for me to ride, and Ellen loved holding the horses mane, and she used to coo to the horse whose ears pricked up, when we got to a place where we could go on foot a little way, I used to tether the horse where it could graze, and have a drink. We wandered a little way from the horse, but not too far. These trips were fun for both of us, as I was able to show Ellen the flora and fauna around thee, and Ellen nearly shouted out loud, but I asked her to be quiet, to shush, which she did, and then – oh joy we saw a moose, we saw another bigger one, which might have been a mate, we were both transfixed, until the horse lifted its head and sniffed, and whinnied and the sound travelled across the water, and the moose went away quietly, just as they had appeared. Lesson over we went back to the horse, and I put Ellen on the horse, and I walked the horse to the town. Ellen said to the horse, 'Naughty horse, made mooses run away.' I laughed and the horse whinnied again.

We arrived back at the house, and I put the horse back in the paddock after removing the saddle. Ellen and I went in the back door as usual, past the kitchen and into the hallway, Ellen and I were just going upstairs to change, when Mother Horan called to us from the dining room, 'Hey you two come and see who have come to visit.'

Ellen ran into the dining room, and I followed Mother Horan, 'But I'm not exactly dressed for receiving visitors,' looking down at the trousers I was wearing and riding boots, and my hair was just drawn back into a rough chignon. Mother Horan laughed 'I don't think they will worry about that.'

Before I could get through the door, Ellen was already there and she whooped, 'Mama, Mama, Aundy Mary Ann, and Unca Harry!' (only she said Maryam) and as I went through, Ellen had been lifted up by Harry and Mary Ann had Jarred on her lap, but she stood up too. Mary Ann let Jarred down, and he came over to me and he put up his arms to be lifted up, Mary Ann went over to Harry and hugged Ellen too, and I looked at both of them, as I went to greet them, and just before we hugged, I noticed a glow from Mary Ann's face, and a relaxed look on Harry's face. I did not need to ask anything, but just said, 'Did you have a good time? I found it lovely and peaceful at the cabin.'

They looked at each other, smiled, and Harry said, 'I had forgotten how lovely this place is. Yes you could say we had a lovely time.'

A voice behind us, Mother Horan said, 'Tea any one?' We laughed, and all said, yes. We sat down at the table and tea and cakes and sandwiches were brought. The conversation was light. Ellen told everyone about our trip to the falls, and seeing the two moose, and the 'naughty horsey' as she put it, scared them away. Henry and Mary Ann got up, and said they should go. The children were a bit upset to see them go, but they were assured that they would see them again, maybe go to tea with them. The children accepted this with, 'When when?' to be told soon. I explained that Uncle Harry and Aunty Mary Ann had to go to work. We saw them to the door, and I hugged them both, but said nothing, because the looks on their faces told me more, and the looks they exchanged spoke more.

When Gerard arrived home later, after the children had gone to bed, Mother Horan and I told him of their visit, Mother Horan said they had been at the house about an hour, after they had put their horses in to the paddock. How could I have not noticed them? I must have been a bit pre occupied, and the paddock was quite large. I did change out of my riding trousers and boots, and put a skirt and blouse on.

November 1920

Life seemed to go on normally, Gerard and his father took time out to visit the hill people and those in the logging camps, whilst we got ready for winter by getting logs in the shed, made sure there was plenty of hay and straw for the horses and mules. We took the children into the town to get some warm material for winter coats and clothes, and we met Mary Ann who was posting a letter home, she had a few hours spare so we all went to a tea room for tea. The children had a cake, well Jarred had half of a cake with custard, with the cake mashed up and Ellen had the other half with ice cream and a hot chocolate. Jarred just had hot milk which he drank from a small cup, he did not want to drink from a feeding bottle, but he dribbled a bit. Mother Horan and I had hot muffins with tea, but Mary Ann declined anything sweet, just asking for a soda and buttered toast. I asked her if she was feeling all right, Mother Horan nearly choked on her muffin, and Mary Ann laughed nervously, 'Well I am feeling a little unwell, but I'm sure it will pass,' she smiled and continued, 'What do you think? You have been through it twice!'

Then I laughed out loud and then covered my mouth as people looked at our table. I lowered my voice, 'How long have you known?' Mary Ann also whispered, 'About two weeks after I missed my monthly…' We (adults) smiled, and I held her hand, 'I'm so happy for you, does Harry know?' She nodded, 'I told him last night, but it is early days yet, so please keep it to yourself, my job is also important, I need to be fit for work.' Mother Horan and I both nodded, I said quietly, 'Please do not worry about later, I will keep my promise, after all what are friends for?' Mary Ann smiled, and ate a piece of toast delicately, and swallowed hesitantly, and then sipped her soda. Ellen was watching us, and said, 'Are you OK Aunty Mary Ann?' Mary Ann nodded, 'I'm just not very hungry darling.'

Jarred who was on Mother Horan's lap and was happily eating and drinking, and Mother Horan was talking quietly to him, as well listening to our conversation, she just said in a whisper, 'My lips are sealed, just let us know when it is safe to say anything, after all your in laws are interested parties, and they may well pick up signs.' Mary Ann nodded, 'They are very kind and discreet, and not like other in laws. I have heard of who cannot wait for grandchildren, so I will wait until things are OK, my training is very relevant and helpful, and I do love my work.'

We finished our tea, and went our separate ways, Mary Ann went to the bus stop to go back to the hospital, we said our goodbyes and hugged Mary Ann and she knelt to kiss the children goodbye, and Jarred reached out to give her a hug and Ellen reached up and kissed her, and said, 'Love you lots Aunty Mary Ann.'

We waited until the bus arrived and Mary Ann got on the bus, and we waved to her until went out of sight. I could hardly contain myself, but had to because of the children, and Ellen was very bright and would repeat things the adults might say, so we were careful what we said when she was around. When we arrived at the house, dusk was falling, and we saw that Gerard and Father Horan were just coming out of the stables with their bags. Ellen saw them and ran to her father, who scooped her up and kissed her, and she then called to her grandfather, who also kissed her, 'How is my little grandgirl?' and she nodded and said OK.

We all went inside, and left our parcels on the table in the porch, and I took the children upstairs to take their coats off and change their shoes. It was dark by now, so the lamps were put on, we were lucky enough to have electricity instead of just gaslight. The coal fire was lit in the nursery and in our bedroom, and after settling Jarred to sleep in his bed, Ellen said she was sleepy, so she had a little lie down in her bed, as she had walked quite a way today. Riella was away for a few days, so I was happy to be a mother in all senses of the word. I left the door ajar and went downstairs to the lounge where Mother and Father Horan were sitting with Gerard and having tea with scones and cakes. Both men rose when I went into the room, and I went to Father Horan and gave him a kiss on the cheek, which was stubbly, and to my man and kissed him quickly on the mouth, and we sat down I sat with Gerard, fairly close but not exactly nestling. Mother and Father Horan sat next to each other, and he held her hand, they were very correct and discreet, but I could tell that they were devoted to each other, and this was filtered through to Gerard, as he had been shown love from his mother, and although his father was firm Father Horan gave praise when it was due, and their trips to the logging camps were always good for them and they came back content, so they seemed to be happy in each other's company.

We sat happily chatting, drinking tea, but the men were obviously hungry, and they ate all or most of what was on the plates. Mother Horan asked if they wanted any more, but they said they would wait until suppertime. We went our separate ways to our rooms, and once there, we went to the main door, so as not to disturb the children, I did look around the door to their room to see both of them sleeping peacefully, with the single low lamp glowing on the dresser by the wall. I went to our room to find Gerard taking his boots off, and then his lightweight jacket. I went to him and asked him how his trip had been, and he said, 'Just as usual, they don't always take enough care of themselves, cuts and bruises, some broken arms, we just patched them up and they just carry on. Enough of my news what have you been doing?'

I sat down on the bed next to him as he took his trousers off, and to put a fresh pair on, 'Well we went shopping today to get some material for winter clothes, and we saw Mary Ann, and had tea with the children.' He looked at me in the eye and I had half an idea what he was going to say next, 'And how is she?'

I said, 'Well she didn't eat much, some buttered toast and a soda, why?' He smiled and said, 'Oh nothing, so maybe she is?' I put my hand over his mouth and nodded, 'It's too early yet and we mustn't tempt fate, she said she hadn't told his parents yet, we must wait and be careful what we say in front of Ellen, she's getting clever and will repeat things.' Gerard took my hand away gently after kissing it, and he kissed my mouth and before we knew it we were in bed making love. Afterward, I looked up at him with the firelight playing on his lovely face, 'So you missed me a little?' I said with a little laugh, and he rested on his elbow, 'Well yes a little, and the children, oh darling, you are all worth coming home to, Mother isn't lonely any more while Dad and I are away, and he is very attentive to her, at night you are all he talks about, Mother you and the children, and dear Mary Ann, you have no idea how happy this house is with you.'

I turned away a little overcome, I said with a quivery voice, 'I have never been as happy as I have been with you all here, thank you for my life, I just wish that my mother had made a happier marriage.'

Gerard kissed me again and suggested that I write to my mother and send some photographs, perhaps to my aunt in London. I did just as he suggested, and sent a fairly bulky but flat package to my mother at my aunt's house in London. The postal clerk said that might take four weeks at least by sea mail, if the weather was not too bad and there was no other route at present, but there was talk of aeroplanes, and perhaps flying across the Atlantic Ocean, but the clerk chortled a little, I paid the postage and lived in hope that it would reach her. I went back to the house with little Ellen, and the light was beginning to fade and it was only mid afternoon, the sky looked dark and Ellen looked up to the sky and pointed, 'Mama look, snow.' Surely enough there were a few flecks of snow coming down. By the time we got back to the house the fine snow had left a thin layer of snow on the path and surrounding vegetation. I had to hold on to Ellen's little hand to stop her from running, in case she slipped and fell, but as we walked through the gate, and she saw her grandmother at the door with Jarred by her side and with Riella, Ellen finally pulled away from me and ran to the door. I threw my arms up, what will be, but she did not slip! She ran to her grandmother's arms, and Mother Horan bent down to hug her. I walked sort of quickly bearing in mind that my shoes had little grip, and I managed to get to the door and walked up to them as elegantly as I could. We all went inside, and I took off my warm coat, brushed the flakes of snow off my hair, and went to the morning room after dusting off my shoe soles. I asked what the reception of them at the door was all about. Riella smiled and said to me as I sat down, 'Mary Ann called us on the instrument, but as you were not here she said that she would call back in half an hour, that was twenty minutes ago.' I guessed that she meant the telephone.

Whilst we waited, we all had hot drinks and Riella asked if she could wait too, and Mother Horan and I both nodded, as Riella was a good friend, and she was as much a part of the family as Mary Ann is. The children were playing on a small square of carpet with some tops and small bricks. There was a warm fire going, not far from them and it was protected by a metal sort of fence called a fireguard. Jarred was just over a year old and was crawling and pulling himself up by the furniture and trying to walk. Ellen loved her little brother and was very protective. As we were drinking some tea, there was a ring, ring, ring, in the hallway and I got up first, and looked at Mother Horan who nodded, as I got to the telephone first, and lifted up the wright and took the tube shaped part to my ear, I said tentatively, 'Hello, who is calling?' The voice at the other end sounded a bit nervous, 'Hello is that Anna, this is Mary Ann,' and I replied, 'Yes dear Mary Ann it is I, Anna, I'm sorry that I was not here before.'

MaryAnn then said, 'I wanted to come over, but it is so cold, and the snow is getting heavy, I just wanted to give you my news, Harry has told his parents, so I can let you know that I am pregnant, and have been told to rest for a little, but my morning sickness is getting better.'

I nearly whooped, but this was unladylike and said, 'Oh Mary Ann that is wonderful news, congratulations, I will come to see you soon, shall I telephone first?' But she said, 'No just arrive.'

The others were quiet, and I looked at them and said, 'Mary Ann wanted me to know, and to let you know that she is pregnant, and she is resting for a little while, but her morning sickness is improving, I asked if I could visit, and she didn't mind.' The two women smiled and Riella clapped her hands, and Ellen laughed and said, 'Why you clap Riella, you happy?' Riella looked a little sheepish and she covered her face for a moment, and apologised, when she took her hands away, she couldn't help smiling, her hazel eyes a little misty, and her dark auburn hair was a little loose, so she pushed it back with her hand. Ellen looked at Riella and clapped her hands too and said, 'Aunty Mary having a baby! Jarred Aunty Mary having a baby!' and Jarred said, 'Baby baby Maryann!'

We were very happy and went back to the morning room and finished our drinks before they got cold. Riella and Mother Horan and I went with the children to their room for their afternoon sleep, and after they were settled down, left them with Riella, who sat in their room tidying. Mother Horan and I went back downstairs. We went to the lounge and sat by the fire with the shadows lengthening as it got dark. I went to the window and noticed that the snow had stopped and there was a thin layer on the ground, I turned around to Mother Horan and said, 'The snow has stopped but this is the time the snow starts, how am I going to get to Mary Ann?'

She smiled and gave a little laugh, 'Well if all else fails, you could call on the telephone!'

I smiled wryly, I had been in Canada two years and the snow was predictable, but I desperately wanted to see Mary Ann face to face, but I guessed I would have to wait, at least until Gerard got home.

Riella came back downstairs and said that the children were asleep and she was happy to hear Mary Ann's news. She helped to clear the tea things away, and went back to her room to rest but she said she would keep a listen for the children.

Gerard and Father Horan arrived home at about 7p.m. when it was quite dark. They had checked on the horses and made sure they were cosy and had enough food. Gerard came in the back door, took off his coat and Father Horan came in too. I went to greet them, Gerard was kicking off his boots after he had closed the back door, so I hugged and kissed Father Horan first, and he carried on to kiss Mother Horan, it gave me joy to see them affectionate after their years of marriage, I had been unused to it as my own parents were only civil to each other. Gerard came through and gave me a hug and a kiss, and whispered, 'Great news, will tell you at tea.' I wondered what he meant, and followed him into the lounge where Mother and Father Horan were sitting near a small table where they were drinking tea and talking quietly. I walked to the table and poured out two cups of tea and put sugar into one, and then carried them over to Gerard who was sitting on a chair at the table, and gave him the sweetened cup and sat down next to him. They all went quiet, and I said, 'So what is this great news?'

Gerard put his cup down, after taking a gulp of tea, and said, 'Mary Ann is having a baby.' Father Horan said, 'Oh that is good news.' Mother Horan gave a little laugh, 'We know, who told you?' Gerard, my Gerard, replied, 'Harry told us, he's very happy but she isn't very well at the moment, but he thinks it will pass.'

I spoke then, 'Mary Ann called earlier on the telephone, when I was out with Ellen. She called back when I got back, and she told me then, but she was told to take some time off, and rest, and then she rang off. I think I would like to see her, to help her as she helped me.' Gerard picked up on the anxiety in my voice, and said, 'I will take you and Mother, we are getting a motor car.' I looked alarmed, 'But what about the horses?'

He laughed, 'Do not worry, they are still of good use, the logging camps are only accessible with them, we will not sell them or anything like that they are too precious, besides it is getting noisy in the town and there is a lot more traffic plus the cars are a bit more closed in although we will need to wrap up warmly. The car that we are getting will take about six people and has storage space.

I listened to what Gerard senior and Gerard had to say about this new motor car, I had told of my dislike of motor cars, but they told me that this car although not new, was a more improved model and was not so noisy or smoking, and they would store in another building from the stables so it would not scare the horses! We all laughed, Mother Horan said, 'We wondered if you knew about Mary Ann, Anna is a little worried about her as am I, she is like another daughter, maybe we could visit, and later when she feels better with the children.'

The two Gerards smiled and looked at each other, Father Horan spoke, 'Well we get the car tomorrow from the car sales, and when it is checked out and we are happy to drive it, you two will learn to drive, but Gerard will use it to get to the hospital for work but the weekends will be free. I think this calls for a little celebration, I will open a bottle of sparkling wine.' I was not exactly sure that it was a good reason to celebrate, but Gerard whispered, 'I will take you to see Mary Ann as soon as possible, I know that you will want to see her, as you haven't seen her for a while, and I know how you worry and care for her.' I kissed his stubbly cheek and he moved his face to meet mine and kissed me quickly on the mouth.

We were handed wine glasses and Father Horan popped the cork and poured sparkling white wine into our glasses and I asked for a half glass as I had not eaten since lunchtime.

Later after supper and having put the children to bed after their tea, I told Riella all the news, and she was quite excited and happy, and asked if she could visit Mary Ann also, I said that if the snow was not too bad, or when the new car was in use, we could take the children, if Mary Ann was not too unwell, but if she wanted to visit on her own, did not mind as I knew they were great friends. Riella went to her room after smiling her thanks and saying goodnight.

The snow held off for about five days and Father Horan and Gerard brought the car back to the house on the Saturday with a roar and a poop, poop of the horn. The car was black with a spare wheel on the side sort of ledge and it was quite a large long car. Mother Horan and I went out to find out what the noise was. We were some way from the town up a tree lined lane which was a bit more than a mud track; it had some properly laid road, paid for by Gerard Senior's father. We quickly put coats on as it was very cold, and although it was daylight the sky was overcast with clouds. The children stood with us (Riella and mother Horan and I) and Ellen squealed, 'What that noise cart with no horses Mama?' I calmed her down by crouching down to her level and put my arms about her, 'It is called a motor car and yes it is noisy Darling, but this is progress.'

Ellen's eyes went back to her normal size as they were opened very wide, and she clung to me. Little Gerard just looked from the safety of Riella's arms and pointed and said, 'Noisy car, make Ella cry.' And he seemed unafraid, I looked at him surprised as he seemed quite happy, and he made a full sentence. Ellen heard his laugh, and she relaxed, I said with surprise, to Riella, 'He called her Ella!' and she smiled, 'Yes he manages that version, and he calls me Rella, he is coming on very quickly because we all talk to him.'

I smiled and little Gerard wriggled to get down, and my husband got out of the car and he walked towards us as did Gerard Senior and my Gerard went to his son who put his arms up to be picked up, and he lifted him up.

Gerard Senior said, 'Want a ride in it now? There is plenty of room for all of you, even Riella.'

We nodded, I with a little reserve, but the others were quite happy, and Ellen got in the back with us (Mother Horan and Riella and myself) however Jarred went with his father and grandfather and sat on his father's lap whilst Father Horan drove, the doors were closed so that we seemed less cold (note to self, bring blankets to put over our legs, very chilly). Father drove backwards after a crunching noise, to the end of the driveway and found room to turn the car around and drove forwards towards the town. There were other cars driving by, not a large amount, but enough for Father Horan to be careful when he drove out onto the street, as the steering wheel was on the left they drove on the right side of the street, I was noticing a lot more. I thought that the drive would be a short one, but then was aware that we were going towards the hospital, and lo and behold Father Horan stopped outside the apartment building where Mary Ann and Harry lived. I was a bit concerned about many of us arriving, seven in all including the children, and said so to Gerard junior, but he said, 'It's all arranged, Harry is expecting us, and you can see Mary Ann for a chat, and if she feels well enough the children and the rest of us.'

My Gerard rang the bell against the number of their apartment, and after about a minute, Harry came down and let us in, he seemed pleased to see us, he ushered us in and closed the front door, 'To keep the cold air out' and led us upstairs to the first floor apartment, and let us in to the hallway, where it was much warmer, we took our coats off, and Harry then greeted us, shaking hands with Father Gerard and my Gerard, and was embraced by Mother Horan and myself and Riella, the children wanted to greet him too, and he knelt to hug Ellen, and Jarred wanted to be picked up, so he walked into the main room which had sofas, and an armchair, and a table and chairs by the window. The kitchen was through a doorway where Mary Ann was sitting in a wooden armchair.

Mary Ann was sitting by the stove and near a fire grate which was an old oven but they were using to heat the kitchen. It seemed quite cosy, Mary Ann looked quite well, and did not look like an invalid to me, as the others sat down in the living room. I went into the kitchen to see Mary Ann who when she saw me stood up and we hugged each other and the words tumbled out, I said, 'How are you, you sounded a bit strained, I was worried for you.'

Mary Ann laughed a little, 'Oh it was that telephone thing, I had not used it before, I prefer talking face to face, I am so glad to see you all. I am getting better now as I can eat more things' she said this in a bit of a rush. I was so pleased to see her. Together we made hot drinks for everybody, and I helped Mary Ann with taking trays of hot drinks through. Once we had put the trays on the table and Harry helped with serving of the drinks. Once Mary Ann had greeted everyone, and they greeted her, they sat down, and as soon as she did Ellen got on the sofa and sat next to her and cuddled up, and little Jarred went, he almost walking and said, 'Up Mary Ann up.'

So Harry lifted him up on the sofa, and he went straight to her and hugged her and she let him sit on her knee. We all laughed, the children were certainly glad to see her.

As we sat and chatted and had some refreshments, we talked about getting the car, well the men did. I sat with Mary Ann and the children and being closer to her, asked discreetly, 'Have you written to your parents?' She shook her head, 'I have written a letter, and Harry said he would post it. I'm worried about what my mother will say. You see after she had me, she had to give up nursing and she will probably berate me for having a baby so soon. I have the feeling that she never quite got over having to stop nursing.'

I said a little firmly, 'That was twenty or so years ago, it was expected, I guess it still is, but do not worry, we will help you complete your midwifery training, I will help you with the baby as you did with me. When will you be able to go back to work, soon?' Mary Ann said, 'The doctor said he would check on me in two weeks, but I can continue my studies until then.'

I smiled and Mother Horan said, 'What are you talking about?' she was smiling.

I replied, 'Oh just catching up and starting to make plans with the baby and to help Mary Ann complete her training.'

Mother Horan smiled, and Harry sat next to Gerard and said, 'Mary Ann should be fine in a few weeks, she is anxious to get back to her training, and I do not mind if she doesn't overdo it, we are grateful for your support. My parents are a bit concerned as this is not how they would do it, so they will be reassured of all your support.'

Mother Horan said with a smile, 'You are modern ladies, when I was pregnant with Gerard, I had to give up my work as a nurse, and regretted it for a time, but I found other ways to be useful, and I am happy that I could help you Mary Ann and you Anna, these are modern times, and I will fully support both of you, and your spouses. Let us go forward together in this new world!' she said with a flourish and she raised her right hand. We all laughed happily and clapped a few times, and the children just clapped, not understanding what we were talking about. After a happy social hour, it became time for us to go. Mary Ann seemed a little brighter although a little worn and tired, so we took our leave, and Harry saw us out, saying quietly to me as he hugged me, 'Thank you, I think Mary Ann will be a little relieved and I am happy for her to continue with her training, you are a true friend.' I just smiled and kissed him on the cheek and said that we were just a telephone call away, and besides, their horses were at our house and he laughed.

December 31st 1920
New Year's Eve what a year, Mary Ann did go back to work, and at first did light duties in the maternity wards and she was in the right place, and was checked on at the clinic every two weeks. We managed to keep in touch on the telephone instrument, and I became quite used to making telephone calls to Mary Ann, knowing when she would be in. Mary Ann and Harry and his parents came on Christmas Day collected by Gerard in the motor car and they stayed overnight and went back the next day by motor car. It was still very cold, and the snow lay about, except on the streets, as when it had snowed again the horses were taken out to use the snow plough, but it was not too much, and they seemed to be happy getting some exercise as they were led out to the small paddock to have a bit of a walk around and back to their stalls. We had a quiet new year and carried on as usual.

1921 January 31st

It has still been very cold, but no more snow, but what is there on the hills and roofs and gardens stay there. I wish that it would thaw. We did go into the village at times, when taken out in the motor car. We wrap up warmly and sometimes the children come, Ellen does not really like the vehicle but Jarred is happy to sit in the front with his father and grandfather, whilst Riella and I sit in the back with Ellen and or Mother Horan who does like to come with us occasionally, as she sometimes prefer to stay at home in the warm but if we go to church, or to visit Mary Ann she happily joins us. I can understand as she is getting older, and prefers the warmer weather. I am 22 years now and like to get out whatever the weather, except when it is raining. Mary Ann continued her studies at home, and went back to the hospital before Christmas but she was given transport to go to and fro, usually Gerard or Father Horan collected her and another doctor with Harry took her back to the apartment in the evening. She was not allowed to work at night although she moaned that she needed to become a midwife. I sympathised with her as I was not working when I was pregnant with my children, but she was gaining experience with her own. Mary Ann was not quite convinced, as she said on one occasion, 'But every mother is different, they experience things differently, I need to know that.'

Mother Horan was with us at that time, and we were discussing the subject quietly whilst the men were talking medical matters. She put her arm around Mary Ann's shoulders and said, 'All in good time my dear, you are doing things that were unheard of five to ten years ago, we will support you, please be patient, there will still be babies born after you have yours, and we will help you have your baby, I am so glad that times are changing, but slowly.' Mary Ann nodded, and accepted Mother Horan's reassurance and I could see her point, I wanted to do more, but I was learning too, I didn't want to be independent; I just wanted to help, not just at home but in the community.

February 1921

The snow seems to be thawing at last, I can see gaps in the snow now, and tiny green shoots are showing through the barren ground, or at least it looked barren but nature has a way of renewing flora and fauna. We were able to walk into the town during the day when the sun shone. Ellen was walking well so could walk for the 15 minutes to the town, we had bought a pushchair (seat on wheels) which Jarred sat in, although he could walk for a little way, he could not manage the walk to the town, he walked around the house and outside to the stables, but if he went any further, he would stop, hold out his arms to be lifted up and carried. He is quite heavy now and only his father could carry him any distance and only perhaps for half a mile. He was quite happy to get into the chair, but only when he was tired, quite a little independent chap, and sometimes walked for a way and when he was tired he was helped into the chair. These trips out were fun for the children and when Mother Horan joined us with Riella, we went food shopping for small items such as bread, butter, tea and some material for clothes and looked at shoes for all of us. We stopped in a café at times for drinks and cakes which the children loved; they sometimes had hot drinks sometimes cold drinks.

Our return home was usually with Jarred asleep, as the trip out made him tired, as he tried to walk as much as he could, but he was getting stronger and walking further. Ellen did walk quite well, and when we arrived back at the house she ran upstairs, with one of us, and she sat on her bed and fell asleep, so either Riella or I took her coat off, and Riella stayed with her, and I usually arranged for Riella to have something to eat and drink in the nursery and Jarred used to have a sleep too.

April 1921
Things have been going well, and the children are flourishing. Spring thaw came by the middle of March.

Mary Ann is looking well, and she has been advised to slow down, and to take leave at the end of April. Sadly not everything has gone well, Riella had a telephone call from the doctor in the town where her mother lives to say that her mother was very ill, and this time it was serious, so she took her leave with our sympathy and good wishes for a safe journey and a good outcome. But sadly this was not to be. We received a short letter from Riella to say that her mother had died of heart failure, and that she would stay for the funeral, and asked for an advance on her wages as she did not have enough money to pay for everything. Mother and Father Horan went away and had a discussion and came back to us and announced that they were both going to the funeral and would leave almost at once, after Father Horan had made arrangements to take some leave from the hospital, go the bank, and get rail tickets, and to send a telegram to Riella to let her know that they were going. He just said to Gerard, 'Well son, you are in charge, hope you can manage, and Anna will you be okay without help?'

We assured them that we would, as I had looked after the children on my own before and I think that I could cope, and the staff such as they were, cook/housekeeper Helen, groom Nestor, who is married to Helen, and we had a lady who came in every day to help with the cleaning and the laundry and ironing and I was not afraid of getting my hands dirty. Gerard smiled at me, and also reassured his parents that he would carry on as usual and also try to see his father's patients. They were reasonably reassured, and Father

Horan went to put his coat on and Gerard did also, to take his father to town in the motor car so that his arrangements could be made quicker. I heard the motor car being started up and went to the front door and looked through the window as it went out of the drive to the town. I went back to the lounge where Mother Horan was trying to tell Ellen that she was going away for a short while, Ellen was standing in front of Mother Horan who was seated, and Ellen was looking intently at her grandmother with her hands resting on her knee, 'Why Riella?' Mother Horan gently held Ellen's head in her hands and said quietly to her, 'It's not the right time little one, Riella's lost her Mummy and she needs our help, this is a sad time for her. We need to help her with things and to bring her back in a little while. Sorry darling.'

Ellen looked sad, and tears rolled down her cheeks, 'Poor Riella tell he we love her, we want her back.'

I went over and knelt down next to them by the chair, I took out a handkerchief and dabbed at Ellen's eyes, and I noticed that Mother Horan was using her handkerchief to wipe her eyes. I put my hand on Mother Horan's and said, 'This must be a very difficult time for you, I know that Riella's mother was a good friend, please take my love and condolences to Riella, tell her to take as long as she needs.'

Mother Horan stood up as Ellen moved back and I held Ellen's hand. Mother Horan said, 'Yes, yes Riella's mother Louisa was a good friend, I want to do all that I can to help Riella at the time. I must go and pack for both of us. Would you tell Helen that we will not be here for lunch and will be away for at least a few days, and then you can work with her on the day to day running of the house. In life skills this will be your first test. We will telephone you when we are returning.'

I thanked her for the trust and promised that I would do my best. The men came back about an hour later, with the train tickets, and

Father Horan patted his breast pocket and took out an envelope, and gave Gerard some dollar bills for household expenses, Gerard tried to stop his father, as he said, 'But Dad I have my own money, we can buy our own food, and fuel for the car.'

Father took his son's hand and said, 'I know that you can do that, but you will need to pay the staff wages, if you come with me I will show you how much, and the cash that I use and the food for the horses, these are for household expenses, come with me and I will show you the details, I need you to take care of the administration of the household, this will be a test.'

Gerard nodded and just said, 'I'm sorry, I did not understand.'

Father Horan smiled a little and put his hand on Gerard's shoulder, and they walked into the study together. They were there for about twenty minutes and emerged with Gerard wearing a little frown, and Father Horan smiling. Mother Horan came downstairs carrying a small valise, with Nestor following with two small suitcases. Helen came from the kitchen, and I went over to Helen and quickly explained the situation, as she seemed to be aware of something going on as she was having coffee with Nestor when Mother Horan asked for his help. We closed the door and I went into the kitchen with Helen and Ellen. Helen and I sat at the kitchen table, and she offered me some coffee, and Ellen a drink of cold milk. Helen asked if I minded being in the kitchen, and I replied, 'I have learned to cook here, why should? Can I not be entertained by you in your place? I need your help, I have to train as a housekeeper and that includes cleaning, laundry and meals.'

Helen smiled and assured me of her assistance. Ellen was looking around her and pointed to different utensils, pots and some vegetables. She attempted to name some of the utensils, and pointed to the serving spoons, 'Big spoons, saucepans cook pots.' And then went to the vegetable racks and I went with her and she pointed to potatoes, and she said, 'po-tatoes and she correctly picked out carrots, parsnips which she called, 'p'snips' and she asked for another biscuit, which Helen gave her, by opening a tin of homemade biscuits for Ellen to take one, it had raisins in and she carefully lifted out two biscuits, and I asked her why, and she said, 'One for Jarred, he may wake soon.'

I was entranced and pleased at her generosity to share. Just then I heard a wail and it seemed to get nearer, and the kitchen door opened and Gerard came in with our son in his arms, 'He has just woken up, and so I got him up from his room, and we came down for a drink and a snack, why are you all in here?' He said as Jarred wriggled to be let down. Jarred walked to me with his arms outstretched 'Up Mommy, to table, milk, bicket please.' He made his wishes clear. And I was so happy. But Gerard did not look so happy. After Jarred was helped to sit on a chair next to Ellen, and I had given him his milk, and Ellen handed him the biscuit that she held for him. Gerard asked if Helen would mind the children whilst he wished to speak to me. I was a bit taken aback by his action, and after making a quiet retreat, I allowed myself to be led by the hand to the hallway and to the quieter small lounge in the small corner of the house. I remembered how intimate it was; it had two armchairs and a side table. Gerard shut the door behind him, and as I turned around he looked more than unhappy, and he spoke in a slow measured tone, 'What were you thinking of having drinks in the kitchen? That is the cook's space and Nestor's. They do not just come into the house unless they need or are asked to.'

I was shocked by his words, and felt a bit taken aback, and said defensively, 'I went there to discuss meals with Helen and she gave us a drink, Ellen liked to name the vegetables. What have I done wrong?' He motioned for me to sit down, and almost raised his voice, 'For all I know you will be having all your meals there, is that any way for a lady to behave, is that an example to give to our children?'

I stood up, 'I'm sorry if I did not show a very good example to our children, but would it be such a bad thing, we are not entertaining guests, why should they bring our meals to us in the dining room?'

I was becoming agitated and felt angry tears starting to sting my eyes, and sat down defeated, I could almost hear Mary Ann's old words in my ears, 'A lady does not go to the servants quarters unless she needs to consult for meals. A lady eats away from the servants.'

'What am I going to do, I cannot do this, I'm so sorry Gerard, I'm not much of a lady.'

Gerard came over to me and knelt before me, he pulled out a clean handkerchief from his inside pocket and dabbed at my eyes, 'My darling girl, I know that you have lost your mentor for a week or two, and Mary Ann is busy, I think that you may have been thinking of what Mary Ann had been trying for years to teach you, and Mother is a very good example. We have someone who comes in when we need her to wait on tables when we have guests, she will be happy to help in the kitchen. I will give you one concession, the children can eat downstairs in the dining room to save food being taken upstairs, we can make it okay for the children to use, bring their table down here. We will eat in the dining room, and we could sit together not at each end of the table, after all we are not at Three Gates!' That made me laugh a little, 'That's better, now as you will prefer to look after the children we could make a routine, and maybe we could invite a few people for a meal not necessarily a dinner, but a tea party, at the weekend and say, invite Harry and Mary Ann, for afternoon tea and you can practice your hostess skills.'

I cheered up a little and said in a quivery voice, 'Very well Gerard, I defer to you, whatever you say I will try to do.' He stood me up and put his hands around the tops of my arms, 'No please don't defer with me, I am struggling with my role, Father always used take care of these things, I cannot do this by myself, we must work together, let Gerard Junior come out of his father's shadow, I'm afraid I would rather be up at the log cabin and fending for ourselves, but we have a reputation to uphold, so let us collect the children, and take them upstairs for a nap, and let us plan for at least the next week, is that a compromise?'

I nodded and realised that he was floundering as well as me, we are both quite young, still in our twenties, we have to grow up fast and be proper adults. I shook myself and stood tall and said, 'We have to work together, I will do my part and be a hostess and I will support you as the man of the house, but next time if you wish to advise me of my conduct, please do not drag me out of the room as if we are going to the headmasters office, it is not seemly. I am your dutiful wife, but I will not be treated like a disobedient schoolgirl!' I realised that I might have been a bit outspoken but he just laughed, 'All right I agree, but I was taken aback to see you at ease with Helen in the kitchen.' But I explained that it was a short visit, and an opportunity for Ellen to see the raw ingredients before they were cooked and looked different. Gerard was interested in my explanation, and I agreed not to spend time in the kitchen more than necessary. We then went back to the kitchen and brought the children back to the main house and I quietly thanked Helen for looking after the children and asked when dinner would be ready. She said about an hour and a half, and said that she would see that it was served in the dining room. I thanked her and smiled as she carried on with her preparations. Jarred held on to his father's fingers as he insisted on walking back to the house. I went upstairs and brought down two of their small chairs and Gerard brought down a little table and we put them in the corner of the dining room, Ellen asked, 'Why our table and chairs down here Mama?'

I took her into the dining room and showed both the children where we put their table and chairs, 'We are all eating down here while Grandma and Grandpa are away, and until Riella comes back. But when we have visitors you will still be able to eat upstairs, and Helen will sit with you. We will get you new chairs and table for upstairs. And if you are very good when we have a little tea party and we have a few people to tea, you can join us for a little while.'

The children looked up at me and Ellen was a little wide eyed, Jarred just pointed to the table and chairs, and said, 'Eat there? Not up there?' and he pointed to upstairs. I knelt down and held him in my arms and nodded, Ellen just about understood, 'we eat with you sometimes, and when grown ups come, we eat with you a little while, Mama?'

I said yes, and looked up at Gerard for approval, deferring to him as the man of the house, and he nodded, 'Only for a little while, we will find someone to be with you while we have guests, someone that you know and like, when you are older you can be good little children a bit longer you will be allowed to stay with the grown ups.'

Gerard knelt down to Ellen's level and stroked her face and smiled, 'I know you will, Ellen just think of these times as sort of like the big parties we had like Mary and Harry's wedding, only not so many people, and maybe you could have a family with some other children that you get to know.'

I remember thinking that we were perhaps frightening Ellen, as she is not a baby any more but a little girl who is learning all the time, and to ask her to behave like a little lady will be very hard, but I realised that I am her role model as my mother and mother in law were mine. I don't want her not to enjoy her growing up. I also realised that her education was mainly my responsibility, as was our little boy Jarred, who was also growing fast, he is not a baby any more, but a little boy. These were changing times, and I have to take up my responsibilities, Gerard and I have had our first disagreement, almost an argument, I didn't want him to need to correct me again, how can I be myself but be correct as a lady. Oh God help me!

May 1921

I needn't have worried, the planning was exciting, as a challenge it was good, it took me back to when we organised the little entertainment during the war. I worked with Helen, who came to the dining room, and we sat down and planned the food, and I was able to help with the invitations and even wrote them, we were inviting about ten people, including Mary Ann and Harry. I had to remember Gerard and I, numbers, numbers. Gerard invited three of his doctor colleagues with their wives or fiancée's. I also had to ask Gerard about their preferences, and if there were any foods that did not agree with them, Gerard said 'allergies' – a new word, same meaning. He also invited Harry's father and mother who I had met on several occasions. I was also relieved that I did not have to dress up in evening wear, but to dress smartly. I was relieved that Mary Ann and Harry were coming as this was almost their second home, and I telephoned Mary Ann when she was not working. Mary Ann as usual asked if we needed her help. I felt not, as this was going to be a test for me as a hostess perhaps she could observe me, and give me her opinion on my progress, and she laughed, I did ask if she wished to rest, perhaps she could sit on a sofa, and just sit with the children as they might well behave a little longer with her there, and Mary Ann went quiet for a moment and then said, 'Oh I do miss Ellen and Jarred I would love to be there.'

Then there was a discussion with Gerard about decorating the dining room, and how the food would be served. I went out with the children to the town to the florist to order some flowers on the Friday morning, which they delivered on the Saturday morning, and I paid for them (that was a novelty), and then I went to the grocer's and with the list that I had drawn up with Helen, ordered the butter and eggs and cheese and a piece of ham and took a packet of coffee beans and tea. Again I paid for the items, although the shopkeeper had asked if I wished to put the items on the account that was held there, but I declined saying it was a private party and the senior Horans were away, and the shopkeeper was already aware, and said he hoped that they would not be away for long. I thanked him for his concern. This seemed to be a small place where people seemed to know everyone's business.

The children were very good, Jarred was asleep for most of the time, but Ellen held my hand, and pointed to the cans and the flowers and almost touched the bread, but I took her hand and said, 'Later, Darling.' She asked if we could go to the little café nearby, and I felt rather thirsty so I nodded, and we went into the small café and found a little table near the window and put the pushchair near to us and Jarred continued to sleep. We had a pleasant interlude there, with Ellen drinking her milkshake and I had a coffee, and I took the house key out of my handbag. Jarred had a milky drink when he woke with a start, and blinked, and just called, 'Mama we stop, drink now?' I paid for our drinks and then we went back to the house, which took about twenty minutes as Ellen started to walk slower as we got nearer to the house. Gerard was working at the hospital of course, and would not be back until later. We finally reached the house and I took the house key out of my handbag and opened the front door and Ellen just about ran in, I pushed the pushchair in and saw Ellen sitting on a chair in the hallway, falling asleep. As I shut the door, Helen came into the hallway and exclaimed, 'I heard the door Mrs Anna, I'm sorry, I should have come sooner but I was taking a cake out of the oven. Let me take the purchases for you and put them away.' I smiled, and nodded, 'It's no problem Helen, you have your job to do, as do I. Thank you so much for baking those lovely cakes. The flower, bread and groceries will be delivered tomorrow morning, but I brought the coffee beans and loose tea.'

She smiled, and took the packages through to the kitchen. I carried Jarred upstairs and Ellen followed us, holding the banister. We went in to their bedroom, and I helped Jarred out of his coat and Ellen managed to undo her buttons on her coat, and took it off. I hung their coats in their closets, and asked Ellen if she would like to take a book or a toy downstairs to read or play with. We went downstairs and went to the small lounge, after telling Helen where we were. Jarred played happily and Ellen read from her book with a little help from me.

The Sunday afternoon came only too soon, the dining room was transformed with a lovely arrangement of flowers in the centre of the table and there were four small tables around the room with little posies in water on each table. The food would not be served until people arrived, and the hot drinks. I went around the tables and checked the positioning of the flowers, the chairs, the plates on the centre table, the serviettes, the cups and saucers, Gerard came over to reassure me, and I then checked on the children who were sitting quietly on a sofa near the window where there was another table.

Soon Mary Ann, Harry and Mr and Mrs Manton arrived at the front door, Gerard had arranged for Norbert to kindly be our 'butler' for the afternoon, and he was dressed smartly; in his best suit and tie as people arrived, another 'occasional' young lady took their coats and put them on a table near the front door. Norbert escorted them into the dining room where Gerard and I greeted them. I was so pleased to see Mary Ann and Harry, and Mr and Mrs Manton at least I knew them and greeted them warmly, getting a hug from Mary Ann who looked very well and her stomach showed a neat swelling of her pregnancy, and we all chatted pleasantly for a while, and the children saw them and they got off the sofa and greeted Mary Ann, Harry and 'Unca Stanley and Aunty Mabel' who were very impressed by their behaviour, as led by Ellen who put her hand to greet, and then put both her arms out as she recognised her friends. Jarred who held Ellen's hand as they walked over, just put his arms up and said 'Hello.' Harry lifted Jarred up and Ellen after the children had greeted their favourite people next to her grand-parents and us of course, they went with Mary Ann to sit on the sofa, and Harry followed with his parents to sit nearby. They were all offered a drink of tea or coffee as they sat down. Soon the other guests arrived, and Gerard introduced them to me, and I tried to be as relaxed and gracious as possible, the doctors looked quite familiar, and I remembered two of the doctors from the graduation ceremony, and one of the lady doctors was a guest, with her husband who was another doctor. I did use a little small talk, but I was interested in what they were doing, and as they found a seat, and were offered hot drinks, I gave the signal for the food to be brought in, and then went from table to table to invite them to help themselves to the sand-wiches and scones or cakes that were laid out on the table. I was a little nervous, but gave them my sweetest smile and hoped that I was being a good hostess. I then went over to the sofa with plates, and then a plate of sandwiches and some serviettes to Mary Ann who was talking to Mrs Manton and the children were very happy. Harry was talking too with Gerard and the other doctors and Mr Manton seemed quite happy at times talking with doctors and checking to see that his wife and Mary Ann were alright. Mary Ann caught my eye and just nodded as if to say, 'You are doing fine.'

The afternoon went quickly and I went around to each table and asked if everyone was fine and if they had enough to eat or drink, sometimes they asked for the 'powder room' and I guessed that it was the lavatory, and fortunately we had two on the ground floor besides the bathroom upstairs. I directed them to these places, and returned to the dining room. Apart from some of the men standing talking, and wives or fiancées sitting down talking, the atmosphere seemed convivial. I heard the front door open and looked out to the hallway, and to my surprise Mother and Father Horan walked in with Riella, and another man who brought in their bags. My blood ran cold! What would they think? They had not telephoned to say that they were returning. I tried to get Gerard's attention, but he appeared deep in conversation with three other doctors, so I went into the hallway as Mother and Father Horan and Riella walked towards me, I stood quietly and wondered what would happen next. Mother and Father Horan went to the dining room door, and looked in, everyone seemed happy, talking among themselves, I thought that I had better explain, 'Gerard and er I thought that we might do a little entertaining and so we organised a tea party with his colleagues and their partners, just a small thing, we used our own money, or at least Gerard did, I'm sorry, had we known you were coming we would have let you know.' I almost spoke too fast, and Father Horan took my arm and walked into the room, they looked at us and carried on talking, they did acknowledge him, and he and Mother Horan looked around and at the table, all he said was, 'I'm sorry my dear, we were not able to get near a telephone and were not sure what time we would arrive. I hope there is some food left, I'm hungry, are you hungry Marie Claire, Riella?'

I heaved a sigh of relief. I asked the young lady who was filling the cups with tea to see if there was any more cake, and she went off and came back with a tray with a sponge cake and sandwiches and scones.

The guests stayed another half hour, and gradually took their leave, greeting Mother and Father Horan who had a drink and something to eat. Gerard and I stood at the door as they took their coats and said goodbye and thanked us for our hospitality, for the lovely food and hoped to see us again soon, phew! We went back to the dining room where Mother and Father Horan and Riella were sitting near Mary Ann, Harry and Mr and Mrs Manton or Stanley and Mabel as they wished me to call them. The late arrivals were chatting with our special guests and enjoying a drink. I was happy that the children were occupied and had behaved so well. But I was suddenly aware that I had been so busy being a hostess that I had not eaten or drunk and was hungry and thirsty. I sat down and breathed out slowly. The waitress came to me with a cup and saucer and offered me a drink I chose tea and she then brought me a tray of cakes and sandwiches and laid them on the table. I thanked her and she started to clear away the plates and cups and saucers from the tables. I was going to get up to help her, but Mother Horan put her hand on my arm and said, 'No my dear, let her do her job.'

Mary Ann then said, 'A lady does not clear tables, she is a hostess.' I smiled and then gave out a little laugh, 'Oh dear, I forgot for a moment, forgive.'

They all smiled and Mary Ann gave a little explanation, about how she was formerly my maid, and had been engaged to train me to be a lady and the niceties of being a hostess and conducting myself, I was a little embarrassed, but Stanley said that I had behaved like a gracious and hospitable lady, Mary Ann said that I had done very well. I was still a bit worried about the fact that we had organised a tea party without Mother and Father Horan's permission, and said so, Mother Horan spoke this time. 'Well I do not have a problem, there were no breakages, the tables are pretty and tastefully decorated, the food is excellent, and you seemed to engage with your guests I am told by Mabel, and everyone seemed to be at their ease, the only person who was not quite at her ease but managed to hide it was you. My dear Anna you have done well.'

I relaxed and smiled and thanked them. 'I am so grateful that you were here Mary Ann, Mabel and Stanley, it was good to have some familiar faces for my first test as it were.' They laughed and the children laughed too, although they did not understand what we were saying. Gerard stood with Harry, and he smiled at me. Riella asked if we would like her to take the children up to their room, as Jarred was looking a bit sleepy, I thought that was a good idea, and Mary Ann stood up slowly and said that she would like a walk, Riella carried Jarred and Mary Ann walked with Ellen after Ellen had said goodbye to Harry and his parents, and said hello to her grandparents. As they left the room, I made a mental note to talk to Riella to ask how she was and whether she felt able to look after the children. Then Harry's parents took their leave, thanking us for inviting them to the tea, I thanked them for coming as family, 'At least I knew you four, it is quite daunting to entertain strangers, but I do not actually know many people.'

They smiled and mother Horan said, 'Well, we will have to change that! I can help you meet some more people, there are other acquaintances besides the medical fraternity, there are my circle of friends, and Mabel, will you help us and be involved too?' She looked at Mrs Stanton, who smiled and nodded, 'There now we should get together for coffee and organise something.'

I must confess I was a little overwhelmed by her statement, and asked for a little time to look back on the event and look at the experience, and they laughed, good naturedly, and nodded.

Soon it was time for Mary Ann, Harry and his parents to take their leave. We saw them out and I asked Mary Ann if she was all right, she said she was, and that she was given a date when she was to finish working on the wards, and that she could continue to study at home for her exams. Harry gave me an envelope, and said quietly, 'This is from both of us, if you want to visit Mary Ann whilst she is at home, you can let yourself in, sort of a house call.' I was a bit taken aback, it felt like keys in the envelope, and I felt privileged. I showed the keys to Gerard, who told me to keep them safe, and he disappeared into the study, and came back with a key, he looked at Father Horan who nodded, and gave it to Harry. 'This is for you both, my house is your house, you are family, of course, we will let you know when we will be visiting and I'm sure you will do the same.'

Gerard then shook hands with Harry who put a hand on his shoulder, I could see that they were great friends, and there was a great affection between the two. Mary Ann hugged him too, and Mr and Mrs Stanton shook hands and kissed me on the cheek and Mother Horan's also.

After they had gone we all returned to the dining room and Mother and Father Horan recounted what happened when they went to New Brunswick for the funeral of Riella's mother. Apparently sadly, there were very few mourners apart from Riella and Mother and Father Horan and a few friends of Riella's mother. Mother and Father Horan helped Riella to move the clothes and other belongings after the funeral and burial. Riella had been very quiet during the journey back and although being assured of a home here, she just wanted to get on with looking after the children. I had noticed that she seemed subdued on her arrival, but brightened up when she saw the children and they were pleased to see her. I made a mental note to also have a talk with her to welcome her back and see if she was happy to carry on.

June 1921
Riella appeared to settle back in and the children responded well to her, and we took some trips out, to the town, to the shops, to visit Mary Ann with telephoning first, as she had begun her time off

from working, and when she was not studying, the children have been very good while visiting her, sitting quietly with her, especially Ellen, Riella chatted with her and helped Jarred. With her and with Mary Ann's permission, I made us all a drink, and after we had finished, Riella kindly did the washing up. Before we left, Mary Ann asked me quietly if I would be with her when she gives birth. I assured her, 'When the time comes I will be with you, and after as well, as I promised, after all you were there with me, so I shall be there for you, dear Mary Ann.' She hugged me, and then said her goodbyes to the others and we left.

There was a day when with Norbert's help we hitched up two of our horses to a carriage and with Mother Horan and Riella we went to Moose Falls and the pool for a walk and a picnic made by Helen. Norbert stayed with the horses who he had unhitched and were grazing. He had his own lunch. We also took a small folding chair for Mother Horan so that she did not have to get down on the ground, as she was finding it difficult to get up from there to save her any embarrassment. She walked with us for a little way, and then went back to where the horses were and talked to Norbert and petted the horses, and waited for us to return. It was so good to get out to the countryside. The horses seemed relieved to go out as well, so we went out about twice a week with a different pair to exercise them, and the other horses were let loose in the paddock with the mules, for we had bought another. The children loved to explore and Riella was very good at showing the children new plants, flowers, and they saw small animals. Riella appeared to settle back in, and she brightened up her mood, but when I asked her if she was all settled, and she assured me she was, and I asked her if she wanted to confide in me, but she seemed to close her expression and declined, I felt sad that Riella maintained her serving attitude, but left it at that, and I left the offer open.

July 1921

How time flies, in the middle of the month, we went to Harry and Mary Ann's for what is termed a 'baby shower' in Canada and America, giving of gifts for the new baby to come, clothes, bedding, a cradle, cot, feeding bottles. Harry's mother and Father were there of course, as were Mother and Father Horan, Helen our cook/ housekeeper was there too, having prepared a light tea, and with another friend served it to the guests. Mary Ann was sitting in an armchair, with her feet up at times, as she had swollen ankles, but she kept putting her feet down, and got up to walk around to talk to her guests, as she found it difficult to rest as she is quite an energetic lady, like me. I well remember my pregnancies (new phrase for me) and my ankles swelled also. Harry was very attentive, it being their first child, he is such a lovely man, and Gerard, although not with me all the time, has been very attentive to me, and although he is busy with his further studies, we have our moments of privacy, but I wish I could have another child.

Still enough of that, during the next two weeks, we visited Mary Ann as a family, with the children, but on some occasions on my own, to spend time with her, discussing the where and when she went to give birth.

One bright afternoon, the 28th actually, and the children, Riella and I were in the vegetable garden, looking at the fruit bushes, and to see how the vegetables were getting bigger, and into the greenhouse at the tomato plants, I suddenly had an urge to call Mary Ann, so excused myself as the children were engrossed in their little gardening session. I went to the hallway and picked up the tubular earpiece of the telephone and lifted up the speaker long stand part and tapped the lever at the bottom, and heard a voice on the exchange part asking me what number I required, I identified my house number and asked for Mary Ann's telephone number, three was a click and then a burring noise, which was the ringing tone, then after a few of these tones a click and a voice said, 'Mary Ann Manton speaking who is calling?' I told her it was me and said, 'I just wondered if you were all right, just to say hello.' There was a pause on the other end then, 'Well I have felt rather weird this morning, I just cannot relax, but I have also had a funny stomach, sort of cramps.'

I was a bit worried and thought back to my babies' births, everyone is different; she should not be alone, maybe if I went for a little while. 'If you like, I will come over to see you now, as soon as I can get a taxi, just me, try to relax Mary Ann dear.'

She just said, 'Thank you' and the line went dead. I went to get my coat and my handbag from our room, Gerard was very generous and gave me a small allowance, for expenses if I took the children out, and as I went downstairs I saw Mother Horan who came out of the study, who asked me why I was in my coat, 'I am going to see Mary Ann, she seemed a little strained when I spoke to her, and she seemed restless, do you have a telephone number for a taxi?'

She held my arm and reassured me, so a taxi cab was called and as I waited on the step outside of the house, she just said, 'Any problems, just call me, I was a nurse and midwife once as you know.' I thanked her for her support and hugged her just as the taxi cab pulled up through into the drive, also the children came running up with Riella close behind them, Ellen asked me, 'Are we going out Mama?' I knelt down and held both of them and said, 'Not this time darlings, Aunty Mary Ann is not very well, and I am going to see her, to help her, so please stay with Riella and Grandma until I come home.'

Riella just mouthed, 'Is it time?' and I nodded. She took both children by the hand to the door and they waved to me as I was driven off to the apartment building where Mary Ann and Harry lived. After paying for my fare, I walked to the door and took the keys that they had given me to open the street door, and after closing it, ran up the stairs to their apartment and let myself in after tapping at the door. I walked in to the hallway and called out, 'Mary Ann' and got a reply, 'I'm in here,' from the living room. I walked in there and put my bag down on the table and took off my coat. Mary Ann was walking around, fluffing up the already fluffed cushions, tidying the ornaments and pacing.

'Mary Ann what is the matter, why aren't you resting?'

She shook her head, 'I don't know, oh Ann I am scared, when the baby comes, it will hurt won't it?'

I managed to get her to sit down, and sat with her, as the tears started to roll down her cheeks. I took her hand in mine and said, 'I cannot lie Mary Ann it will hurt, but you know as a midwife that it is a movement to let the baby out, I have read up on it! And I am here, and I am not going anywhere, you are not alone anymore.'

She smiled through her tears and sat quietly for a while. I got up and made us a drink of tea, and brought the tray in and we sat down to drink and chatted for a little while and she seemed to relax, she sat for a while and then got up to excuse herself, and went to the bathroom she was there for a little while so I went there and knocked on the door and asked if she was alright, and she said, 'No, the door is not locked, come in.' So I opened the door and she looked very worried, 'Oh Anna my waters have just gone, the baby must be on its way.'

I went to her and helped her off the toilet, and flushed the full toilet. I helped her to walk to the living room and she asked me to get a towel, so I did, having a good idea where they kept things. She sat on the sofa on the towel and I suggested that she put her feet up on the sofa, and I got a sheet to put over her. I asked if I should call anyone, but she said, 'No it could be a while yet. I have not had any labour pains, just a really bad backache since this morning, I thought nothing of it, so did not want to bother Harry.'

I was still worried, so I asked if I could use her telephone she nodded, so I telephoned to my home, and spoke to Mother Horan, telling her what had happened and what I should do. She told me to keep calm, and would be over as soon as she could, and asked me to boil some water and prepare the baby clothes and get Mary Ann into a nightgown if it were possible. I asked Mary Ann where the baby clothes were, and she told me, so I brought some out and some of the new towels. Mary Ann said she was not ready to get into her nightdress yet. So I asked if I could help her, and she asked if I could rub her back, and she rolled over to her side and I massaged her back, just below her waist.

After about an hour, Mary Ann was beginning to perspire, and she started to moan, I was feeling a little out of my depth but continued to support her and reassure her. After about an hour and a half there was a ring at the street door, and I said I would see who it was. I ran down the stairs and opened the door to see Mother Horan there with not just her handbag, but a small valise. She came in and I told her what had happened, as we walked quickly upstairs, fortunately I had left the door on the latch, and shut the door as we went in. She held me back for a moment and said, 'I telephoned the hospital and spoke to Gerard, and he will tell Harry and they will bring a midwife, if she is in time.'

I was grateful once again to this wonderful kind resourceful lady. We went into the living room and I said, 'Look who is here, Mother Horan, we will be all right now.'

Mary Ann looked at us, and smiled weakly, and Mother Horan reassured her that she had not forgotten how to deliver babies, and was Mary Ann happy to stay on the sofa, or would she rather go to the bedroom, Mary Ann wasn't sure, so Mother Horan asked if she could look at the progress of her labour, and looked between her legs discreetly keeping the legs covered. She also took out a cone shaped instrument, not unlike Mary Ann's and listened to the swelling of the unborn child. She smiled at Mary Ann and assured that all was well.

Very gently we helped Mary Ann get up and go to her bedroom. We carefully and discreetly helped Mary Ann to undress and put on her nightgown. Mother Horan also produced two calico aprons for her and I to wear. Mary Ann settled onto the bed which had a long towel on, and I covered her up with a sheet. I also brought the baby clothes in, and a bowl of cold water, and a cloth to mop Mary Ann's brow. It seemed such a long time but was about two hours, by which time Mary Ann felt the desire to push, Mother Horan checked her again, and asked her a little longer, but I'm not sure Mary Ann heard her, being nearer to her head, and said, 'Please wait, a little longer, you are not open quite enough.'

Mary Ann breathed in and tried to relax, but was straining. I held her hand and she squeezed mine hard, and I prayed that it would not be long.

After another ten minutes, which seemed like an hour, Mother Horan looked again and looked to me and nodded, and I said, 'If you want to push, it's all right now.'

Poor Mary Ann, she worked so hard, if the previous few hours were hard, this was her time. I bathed her brow, and encouraged her, each time was a bit further for the baby, Mary Ann was making reasonable sound, but she never screamed.

I heard a door open outside to the apartment. There was just one knock at the door, so I went to the bedroom door and looked outside, Gerard, Harry and Father Horan were there with a young lady, who had a bag, I spoke to them all, especially to a very worried looking Harry. I beckoned the young lady in, and said to the others,

'Not long now and I'm not alone, your mother is here Gerard.' They stood there and I turned back to the bedroom and the young lady I recognised her as Doctor Helen Mackay, who said she had come as an obstetrician just in case of any problems, as apparently we had a midwife here already. I went straight back to Mary Ann who was straining and red in the face. I knelt by her and whispered, 'Harry, Gerard and Father Horan are here, and they brought Dr Helen Mackay so come on darling, just a little longer.'

Mary Ann opened her eyes, looked at me, and breathed in and gave a huge push and a grunt, and the others said, 'Baby's head is out, one more push Mary Ann.'

Mary Ann duly obliged, and she sighed. The baby was lifted gently from between her legs, and gently tilted upside down, and I watched as Mother Horan wiped the inside of its mouth and then a mewling cry came from its lips. I was holding my breath until I heard the cry, then we both (Mary Ann and I) asked was it a boy and girl.

As the doctor cut the cord, and Mother Horan wrapped it in a towel they both said, 'It's a boy! Congratulations Mary Ann.'

I started to cry, Mary Ann started to cry, happy, happy tears. They handed the baby to Mary Ann, and she opened the towel to show me her new born, and then as I was still kneeling down she whispered, 'Thank you so much Anna. I am so glad you were here.' After the doctor and Mother Horan were satisfied that Mary Ann had delivered the afterbirth, they put a sanitary dressing and under-pants on her, Mary Ann also thanked Mother Horan and Dr Helen. I thought it time to relieve the suspense of the three men outside, so I went to the door and said to Harry, 'Would you like to meet your son Harry. He is fine, no problems Mary Ann has been very good.'

They clapped and shook hands with Harry, and he came towards me, and I saw tears in his eyes, and he hugged and kissed me on the

cheek and said, 'Thank you so much Anna, just for being there.'
And he went into the bedroom as Mother Horan and Dr Helen
came out taking their aprons and gloves off, and he thanked them
too. I remembered that I was still wearing one so I took mine off
as well. Harry went into the bedroom. Father Horan thanked Dr
Mackay as she took her leave, promising to visit the next day, and
arranging to excuse Harry from his commitments for a few days
so that he could spend time with wife and new son. Father Horan
hugged his wife and they sat down on the sofa talking. Gerard came
over to me and held me gently, and said, 'How did you know she
was going into labour?' and kissed me, as I hugged him back, and
nearly collapsed, the effect of the last few hours taking its toll, he
gently led me to the other sofa and we sat down. 'I telephoned Mary
Ann and she seemed a bit strange so I offered to come over, and
when I got here, her water went so I telephoned your mother who
I guess let you know and you brought the lady doctor, who was
marvellous.'

After recovering myself, I said I thought it was time we went
home if we were not needed anymore. Gerard said that they brought
Harry and stayed to keep him company as he was a first time father,
and he was very agitated. Gerard knocked on the door of the bedroom, and asked if we could leave, and Harry came out with the
little bundle which was the baby, to show Gerard and Father Horan,
Harry was very happy and showed the little one, who was now
dressed in a nightgown and wrapped in a blanket and his eyes were
open, but he was quiet, Gerard looked at the little one, and Father
Horan looked as well, and they congratulated him, he said that
Mary Ann wanted to speak Gerard and I before we went, so we went
in to see Mary Ann sitting up in bed with a shawl around her. There
was a crib next to her by the bed with some lovely bedding. We went
up to the bed and I sat down near her and Gerard stood behind me,

she looked a little tired but bright, 'Harry and I have had a talk, and we would like you to be godparents to our little baby boy.' Gerard said, 'Thank you dear Mary Ann, my wife and I would be honoured to wouldn't we darling?' he said gently stroking my head, and I nodded, and took his hand and held it in mine. He continued, 'Have you decided on a name? I know it is a bit soon, but?'

Mary Ann said that they had talked about boys and girls names and thought of some so she said, 'We settled on Henry Stanley James, as my father's name is Henry and of course Harry's dad is Stanley.'

Harry returned to the bedroom with the baby, who was crying now, and I remember what that meant, and Harry gently handed the baby to Mary Ann who asked us to leave the room, except Harry, who saw us out, and we thanked him and took our leave. Mother Horan and I put our coats on, she put on her hat, and we picked up our bags and left. Gerard had brought the car so we got in, Mother Horan and I in the back, and Gerard and Father Horan sat in the front with Father Horan driving. It was getting dark by the time we got home, and as we went through the door, the children came down the stairs with their nightwear on and Riella close behind. She explained that the children had their tea and got ready for bed but would not settle, worrying about what had happened. I took my coat off and we went in to the dining room with the children and I told them that I went to Aunty Mary Ann who had started to have her baby and then called their grandmother, who brought her bag and helped Mary Ann to have her baby, and she telephoned the hospital and Grandpa and Daddy and Uncle Harry came with a lady doctor just in time for the baby to be born. The children were very excited, and Ellen asked, 'what did she have Mama, a boy or a girl?'

Before I could answer, Gerard and his father said together, 'It is a boy!' and they laughed. The children were excited and clapped.

Father Horan sat down near the children and called them over to him and he put arms around them, 'Your Mama has been very quiet about something, she went to your Aunty Mary Ann and stayed with her all the time she was having her baby, oh except for when she let your Grandmother in, and your Grandmother helped mothers to have their babies before your Daddy was born, and she helped Mary Ann, but again your Mama helped Aunty Mary Ann and these ladies are very special.'

Ellen and Jarred looked at Mother Horan and I and Ellen said, 'You with Aunty Mary Ann all the time, baby took that long to come?'

I nodded feeling suddenly very emotional and almost tearful, and so Mother H sat next to me, as the experience had a profound effect on me, my shoulders started to shake, and the tears flowed. Mother Horan put her arm around me, and handed me a handkerchief to mop my tears, they all looked at me, and the children hugged my knees, and looked up at me, 'Not cry Mama, it is okay you home now.'

I looked at her and smiled through my tears, 'It is all right darling, these are happy tears, when you are older you will understand, I don't know about anyone else, but I am hungry I haven't eaten since lunch.'

I felt very happy and my tears dried up. They laughed and the children yawned and Riella offered to take them to bed, and I went with to help settle them. After the children were in bed, we walked out slowly, and I thanked Riella for looking after the children for so long, she smiled and said she was happy to do so, and asked me some of what happened, and I told her what I remembered and she asked if she could visit Mary Ann, and I was happy for her to go when it was convenient for them to have visitors. Riella was looking so happy and the mask slipped a little, and she took both of my hands and said, 'Thank you so much Mrs Anna.'

I almost reached out to hug her, but her hands dropped to her side, and she walked back to her room. What a sweet girl, I thought, I am so fond of her, but she is so closed, I do not really know her, and Gerard or his parents seem to be hiding something, so I respected that, and did not pry. I returned downstairs to find them seated at the end of the table with a simple meal laid out, hot soup with bread and cold meats and salad, with hot drink. I joined them at the table, after Gerard stood up and helped me to my chair and sat down. We had a quiet meal with a little conversation. After we had eaten, we went to bed, tired but happy.

The next morning was different however, as after a slightly rest-less night, I joined Gerard and Mother and Father Horan in the smaller less formal room where we had breakfast, I heard chatter as I went, and after helping myself to cereal and a drink of tea I sat down with Gerard and his parents, I greeted them all warmly and sat with Gerard, and enquired what they were talking about. Father smiled, and then swallowed and after a nod from Mother Horan, he said quietly, 'Marie Clare was telling us about the birth of baby Henry. She was aware of how he emerged during the birth, are you happy to hear the relevant details?' I nodded and said, 'Well, yes, I was there and stayed with Mary Ann, what did I miss? I know that I was at her head and top half.' Father Horan smiled back and said, 'Well he came out face up, not face down my dear, which might explain the back pain she was experiencing.'

I was a little shocked and sounded so, 'I have read some books on childbirth and pregnancy, but there are always different experi-ences, even mine were not the same, was his back affected, is Mary Ann going to be okay?' Gerard (mine) put his hand over mine, as Mother Horan said, 'No, she appeared fine, she is young, and the baby is fine, completely intact, and his little legs and arms seemed to move quite well.'

I was a bit taken aback, thinking that the birth was sort of normal, but who am I to say what is normal? I just said, 'Does she know?' Gerard said, 'Doctor Mackay is visiting them today to check on them both, and she will explain things to them, for them to decide what to do, as this could happen again. Do not worry darling, they are in good hands.' I nodded and just hoped that Mary Ann would take the news well.

June 1921

After a few weeks, Mary Ann and Harry gave up their apartment and came to stay with baby Henry, they had a room towards the back of the house and a room adjoining as a sitting room to give them some privacy, but when they wished they joined us for meals, as did Harry's parents, who were quite amenable to the change, as Mary Ann needed a little support and should not be alone during the first few months after the birth, but it was a temporary arrangement, as Harry intended to find somewhere to live close by and Mabel came most weekends, on a Saturday afternoon, to have tea, and to see Harry, Mary Ann and little Henry, as well as us, and the children who were always happy to see them, as we didn't have many visitors. Mary Ann seemed to recover well and was a good mother, and allowed me to help with Henry at times, and I always checked with her if I was dressing him or holding him right, after all, he is not my baby. I have to admit it is nice to have Mary Ann close by, and Riella is very happy too, having another child to look after. Ellen and Jarred are inquisitive and very gentle with the little one.

Mary Ann told me that she had a discussion with Doctor Mackay and Harry shortly after Henry's birth and she with Harry decided not to have any more children, in case she had problems with other babies, poor Mary Ann, she said she could not ask her mother, and her letters from her were not very encouraging, telling her that she would have to give up all that she had worked for, and only my reassurance that she should feel safe to carry on working knowing that Riella, Mother Horan and I would take care of baby Henry when she went back to work. I felt sad that Mary Ann's mother seemed less than happy to be a grandmother, although she received a card from her father who did seem happy. What a nice man, I remember feeling that during my schooling, that he had time for everyone, as much as Mary Ann, which was more than my own father.

July 31st 1921

On a lovely sunny Sunday, we got all the horses out, and paired them up to the three carriages that we had, and went to the church. When there were fewer cars fortunately, they walked sedately, with our men driving them, and Mary Ann, Mr and Mrs Manton, Mother Horan, Riella and I, with the children of course, who were very excited to go to church in the carriages. We were met at the church by Doctor Mackay with her fiancé, and some of the doctors and nurses who worked with Harry and Mary Ann. It was a lovely service, Henry Stanley James was duly baptised, with a minimum of fuss, he cried a little, especially when the pastor handed him to Doctor Helen (later just Helen) but she cooed to him and he looked straight at her, and stopped. We then left the church and went back at a reasonable pace in the warm summer sunshine, and the horses seemed content to walk the two miles each way. They had been left on the shady side of the church, as I suggested and they moved the carriages and I smiled my thanks.

On our return, with some of the guests in cars, who left before us, and were waiting outside the house, we alighted from the carriages, and the horses had been unhitched and left loose in the paddock, where some lovely oak trees shaded in places and I noticed them skittering around, as it was such a lovely day some refreshments were served outside in the garden at the back of the house, with a shady area, mown grass, quite flat with two oak trees on one side. There were tables set out under the trees, with chairs and a pretty cloth on each table and a small arrangement of flowers on each table, there was a slight breeze, but not enough to disturb the table cloths. I had asked Mary Ann where she wished to have the christening party, and what refreshments and what area she like to have them served, so between us, Harry's mother and Mother Horan, Mary Ann and I set up the serving area, with soft drinks for the children, apart from ours there were three more, being children of the doctors. These children ranged from between two years to five years in age, and were quite well behaved, and sat with their parents, and our two, with Riella who went to greet them. Jarred is nearly 22 months old and followed his sister.

There were some alcoholic drinks also for the adults, and also coffee and tea for others. Harry and Mary Ann and Mr and Mrs Manton sat at a table together with baby Henry in his perambulator, that is, Jarred's, which we had repainted and recovered and recovered as part of our gift. There was a little muslin curtain hanging from the hood to shade him, but he could still be seen.

Mary Ann excused herself for a little while as Henry made a little cry, and we smiled as she carried him indoors for about twenty minutes. We carried on eating and drinking, with trays of sandwiches and other savouries being taken around by hired girls and a young man, who carried plates. I walked around checking to see if everyone was comfortable and greeted the guests as did Harry and Gerard. Father and mother Horan sat with Stanley and Mabel, chatting amicably and greeting people. Our children were very well behaved, and they sat at a table with Riella, and I joined them for a little while to eat and drink with them. Riella thanked me for allowing her to go to the christening and to stay a little while and I smiled and thanked her for taking care of the children on which was her day off, and we shared a smile.

Mary Ann reappeared with baby Henry carrying him with his head near her shoulder with a little muslin cloth over her shoulder, just in case he brought some milk up, which he did sometimes, as he too seemed a greedy feeder, just like my little man. She placed him back gently into the perambulator, and he appeared to go to sleep.

Shortly after, Father Horan and Stanley Manton stood up and Father Horan tapped his glass for some quiet, as people sat down, and Father welcomed everyone to his home, and formerly Mary Ann's home, then Stanley continued and asked everyone to raise their glasses to welcome baby Henry into the world, as previously the pastor had welcomed him into the church family, and to congratulate Harry and Mary Ann on the birth of their beautiful son. We all raised our glasses and duly toasted the new family.

The afternoon turned to evening and after the christening cake had been brought out, not a tier of their wedding cake, as might have been the custom, but a beautiful round blue iced cake made by Helen. Everyone commented on it and Helen was complemented before she retired to the kitchen.

All too soon people started to take their leave and go home after thanking Harry and Mary Ann for the party and the parents of Harry and Gerard. The children were inquisitive to see little Henry in his christening gown, and gently touched his hands and he being awake, held on to their fingers. This was a novelty for Jarred, but Ellen had this experience with her baby brother. Riella offered to take the children to their room and get them ready for bed and they appeared tired so I let her take them, after Ellen said thank you to Mary Ann and Harry. She took Jarred's hand and they followed Riella into the house. As the last of the guests left, there was Gerard and I with respective parents, and Mary Ann and Harry went inside with baby Henry to get him ready for bed and enjoy some special time with him. The tables were cleared and put away as we went inside for a warm drink before Mabel and Stanley went home. They are such nice people, and Ellen and Jarred are very fond of them as am I. It was such a lovely blessed happy day.

September 30th 1921
Mary Ann had a 'little operation' as she put it to cut off and tie her fallopian tubes (she showed me in a biology book exactly where they were being part of the reproductive system). I was quite worried about what she had done, but she said that they would be happy having one healthy child than risk injury to her or another baby. I have to respect their decision. Whilst she was in hospital for the four days, and then at home for a week, Riella and I looked after baby Henry, with Mabel and Stanley visiting both Mary Ann and their grandson. During these visits when Stanley was talking to Father Horan and Gerard and Harry downstairs, we were upstairs in the bedroom, Mary Ann resting on the bed, nursing Henry, after she had fed him, whilst we faced the fireplace to be discreet. We had taken little Henry to the hospital so that Mary Ann could feed him except when she had her operation, but that only took two hours until she woke up, and I was concerned about her, but Doctor Mackay performed the operation, and she was very good. I was relieved when she woke up, and sort of murmured, but after dozing for a while, she woke up, and the first thing she said was, 'What are you doing here, tell Harry I'm okay, where is my baby?' in that order, I smiled and replied, 'Why should I not be here, I have your son, he is over there, and is waking up,' and she laughed, and then winced. I went and called a nurse, who checked her bandages, and offered to give

her something for the pain, but Mary Ann only accepted it if the injection didn't make her sleepy. So she fed little Henry first, and then agreed to some pain relief, which did make her sleepy.

When Mary Ann had returned to the house, and she was convalescing, one evening after Mary Ann had fed Henry, and I took him from her for a moment, so that she could get off the bed, and walked over to the chair, and I handed him back but could not resist rubbing his back, to try to help him bring his wind up, which he gave a little burp, I had not lost my touch, and handed him back to her and she continued to wind him. She looked so happy.

Mabel watched Mary Ann with her grandson, and her eyes glazed over as she recounted her time when Harry was a baby, Harry is six months younger than Gerard, and they lived in Toronto, and Stanley was a chief cashier in a bank there, they were very happy having been married for just over a year. When Harry was four years old, they moved to Moose Falls to be an assistant manager in the bank in the town. Mabel was expecting again but apparently, she slipped the last two or three stairs from the bottom where they lived, and fell heavily and sadly lost her unborn child and could not have any more children. I felt so sad, and put my arm around and hugged her, as she dabbed her eyes. Mabel did say not to feel sorry for her, as she was proud of Harry's achievements and that he had married a lovely girl, who is very clever, and Mabel felt part of another family, ours.

Mary Ann smiled, and said that Mabel had told her after she had told Harry's parents of her decision, which she had told me about the same time. There was a knock at the door and Mother Horan brought some refreshments in helped by Helen. Mary Ann asked her to stay, and we pulled over a table for the tray of sandwiches and drinks were placed.

I told Mother Horan that Mabel had told me about how Harry was an only son, and Mother Horan told us her story, which was almost as sad as Mabel's. Apparently Gerard was born in the first year of their marriage, but after a year or two she had three miscarriages, and a stillbirth, so she had the same operation as Mary Ann in 1900 and then it was a bit more risky, but she recovered, and Gerard is the more precious. Mary Ann had placed Henry in his crib, and sat down again slowly, but she is walking around as much as possible. I felt a little overwhelmed by their personal stories and felt that Mary Ann has been very brave.

November 30th 1921

So much has happened, Harry and Mary Ann moved out, as it was only a temporary arrangement, but to only about five to ten minutes away from us, as a small house went up for sale, just down the road from us. We all helped them to move, after Harry had drawn his savings and with a little help from his father, was able to put quite a big deposit on the house, so the 'mortgage' would be quite manageable. After some redecorating and cleaning, the house was ready to move in to. The house consisted of a kitchen, small dining room, and a good sized parlour or living room, and a cloakroom or toilet with a washbasin downstairs, and upstairs were two good sized bedrooms, and a bathroom, but on the plus side, as they were further down the road the back bedroom were views of the woodland and hills. On the days that Mary Ann would work, she would bring Henry down to us for the day in his perambulator, with his feeding bottles, and we undertook to prepare the solid meals, with her guidance. But this would not happen for a few months when Mary Ann felt fit enough and was found so by the doctor and ready to leave little Henry with us.

December 30th 1921

Christmas was a wonderful time, we had a meal in the dining room with our friends including Doctor Helen, and her husband, Harry, Mary Ann with little Henry, who was sitting up now, and our children were so happy to have them with us. Stanley and Mabel Manton came too, and they all stayed overnight, fortunately as the house had nine bedrooms, of which we only used five rooms at most, and Norbert's and Helen's living room and bedroom were in a little annexe behind the house not far from the kitchen and the stables, which they kept warm, but of course it was not somewhere we would go, as it was their little home.

January 31st 1922

Riella has expressed a wish to take an extended holiday. We were sorry to let her go, but she did seem tired and I felt that she needed some rest and relaxation, so saw her off at the station, and just asked her to keep in touch, send us postcards, and she was welcome to come back whenever she was ready.

June 30th 1922

So much to do, and I have not had much time to record my thoughts, what with looking after little Henry which is a joy, and being a full time mother to my children, who are growing fast. I have been helping Ellen to learn her alphabet and numbers and to make words, and to do simple sums, sometimes with symbols, to help her to count. We received a few postcards from Riella, who travelled to New Brunswick, and then to Quebec, where she had found a position with a lady as a governess for her two young daughters aged five and seven years, as she was running short of money. She always sent her love to the children, but she never left a forwarding address.

We have had some garden parties, and even had a birthday party for Ellen, and we went to Harry and Mary Ann's for a first birthday party for Henry, which was a joy, and Mary Ann is a good hostess. She does her own cooking, but on this occasion accepted help from Helen, who made a birthday cake, and some small cakes. It was a lovely occasion, with Henry's other godmother and her husband, Doctor Mackay is expecting a baby, and she plans to continue working after baby is born. We seem to be a progressive generation.

Present day
There was a gap in the years; Sara noticed that there appeared to be a blank except for a passage of years. Sara had found time to read this episode of Anna and Mary Ann's lives when she had some spare time each day for a month and she found it hard to put it away. Sara was alternately happy and sad, their life seemed almost idyllic, but reality and sadness seemed to impinge on their lives. She felt sad that Mary Ann decided not to have any more children, but after researching history on childbirth, and anaesthesia in the 1920s she thought perhaps Mary Ann had made the right decision in the circumstances, and she wanted to continue with her career, plus bring up her baby, with the help of her best friend Anna. She looked at the journal and noticed the passage of years.

1923
So much has happened; I have been busy looking after my children and baby Henry at times which has been a joy. Gerard has been busy with his work and studies but he still finds time to spend with us and me, we have taken time out to go to the log cabin with some of our horses, and got back to basics. The children are growing well, Jarred is only four years old, but he is as tall as his sister, who is quite a little lady, and is quite well spoken, did I teach her that, or Mary

Ann? She is a little like me with the horses, and when we go to look after them or go riding, she wears her trousers bless her, she asked for some with lace up boots, quite the little cowgirl.

Jarred seems to be more interested in mechanical things and loves to go with his grandfather or father in the car. Things seem to be quite settled, I look after Henry about five days a week, during the day, and Harry and or Mary Ann collect him in the evening, and if they are a bit late, have something to eat before they go home.

1924

Still very busy, Ellen is growing up fast, we have found that the school in the town which takes younger children, it only takes about twenty minutes from the house to within the town, and I take Ellen, and sometimes Jarred comes too, he is looking forward to going to school too. They said they will have a space for him in September, in the meanwhile, I am helping him with his letters and numbers and words which he likes, just like Ellen did, which helped her to fit in and she helps the others, she really enjoys going to school and meeting the other children there and making new friends. She does not seem to have the stigma that I had, 'the girl from the big house' as Gerard's parents are well known as being caring as well as being hospitable. The mothers who collect their children are mainly resident in the town, and were a little curious about the 'English Lady' but some accepted me as I seem to have picked up the accent and do not have airs and graces as such, but am just polite, they accept me as Mrs Horan Junior and are really nice and kind, and their children seem happy and excitable but not too much.

We received a rare letter from Riella, she says she has met someone, a French trapper, and she loves him and he says they will be married. The postmark said Quebec, but again no forwarding address, poor Mother Horan seemed a little sad, as am I. Riella seems to want to follow her own 'trail' as Father Horan put it. It's not that I want her back as a nanny again but to know that she is safe and protected, I hope this Frenchman will look after her. I have prayed so hard for her safety.

31st March 1925
I think I might be pregnant, after all this time, Jarred is five and a half years now, and Ellen will be seven next birthday. I had almost given up hope of ever conceiving again. I am feeling sick for most of the morning, and my monthly bleed hasn't happened since January. I have not said anything yet, just saying that I do not have time to eat, to get Ellen to school, or am not very hungry. When Jarred and I get back from taking Ellen to school, sometimes, with little Henry, who is an amazing three years old, walking quite well now, but we take him in the pushchair. I have felt a little faint on our return, so have some tea and a piece of dry toast, and sit with the children whilst they play.

30th May 1925
I feel so happy, I spoke to Gerard, and he seems happy too. The children have been told; I'm not quite sure when it will be due, perhaps October or November. Mary Ann is quite concerned, and wants me to go to the hospital to have checks made. I was a bit wary, I did not have to have checks before, but I was somewhat younger.

30th June 1925
Tragic news, firstly, two weeks ago I started bleeding from down below, not like the monthly bleed. I was so worried, Mother Horan called Father Horan on the telephone who came home, and drove me to the hospital. Mother Horan stayed with Jarred and Helen helped her. Once we arrived at the hospital we were met by a doctor

and a nurse who went with me into the hospital and helped me onto a trolley, and covered me with a blanket. Father Horan came with me and held my hand and told me not to worry, he stayed with me and they helped me into a nightgown, and he came back in and said he had got word to Gerard, who would be coming as soon as he could get away. Then the nurse put a mask over my face, oh no! But I soon went to sleep.

I cannot remember how long I was asleep or under the 'anaesthetic' as they put it. When I woke up, Gerard was sitting next to my bed, he looked relieved that I had woken up, I felt different, and tried to sit up but it hurt so much, I have awful soreness from my navel down. Gerard gently asked me to lie back, and told me with eyes misting up, 'My darling girl, I am so sorry, you had a baby, but it could not take hold in your womb, you bled so much that they had to remove your womb, oh darling when they checked it they found an old tear from Jarred's birth, it never quite healed. Fortunately Doctor Mackay was on duty and she took charge, and did a neat repair, and she refused to remove your ovaries, she reckons they have another job. Also Mary Ann donated her blood, as you had lost so much, and she stayed with you until you were out of danger. She is taking time off to help look after the children staying with us as is Harry. I'm so, so sorry, I know you were so happy when you found you were pregnant.'

The nurse had come in, and between them, they gently propped me up, to save moving too much. I thanked her. All I could say to Gerard, 'I'm sorry I cannot give you any more children…' But I could not cry, I was just numb. I noticed that I had a drip in my arm, of saline they said. Shortly after a nurse came in and had a syringe, she said it was to ease my pain, but she could not ease the pain in my heart, but I could not cry, so numb. The injection made me feel sleepy after a while, and Gerard gently kissed my forehead as I seemed to drift away. He seemed to drift away, but I heard another voice at the door, it seemed like Mary Ann's voice, her words sounded like 'But she has no one to fight for her Gerard, please you know the alternative.'

Gerard's reply was quiet and pained, 'But you know what Anna has been through, I don't know if I can ask her, it might be too much, and I know what you have done for her, and I am so grateful.'

Mary Ann said quietly, 'It is nothing more than I would have for anyone else as I am a registered blood, but Anna means the world to me as you know.' Gerard just said he would think about it.

I think I must have gone off to sleep, and when I woke up it was daylight. Mother Horan was sitting with me. I smiled when I saw her, and she stood up and leaned over to give me a little hug, gently and a kiss, I responded, and was glad to see her. She assured me that the children were fine and missing me and sent their kisses. Father Horan came in, and I held up my hand to him which no longer had a needle in the arm, but a dressing over, he took my hand and leaned over to kiss me on the forehead. He then told me that Gerard was waiting to talk to me, and took Mother Horan's hand and they walked out together and shortly after Gerard walked in, looking very worried, he came over to me and kissed me on the forehead before he sat down, holding my hand. He asked me how I felt, and I said, 'A little better, I am hungry, how long have I been here? I have lost track of time.'

He told me three days, from when I came in, had the surgery, was sedated while my body recovered and slept off and on until that morning. Gerard seemed a bit hesitant, so I asked him about the conversation that I overheard before I went to sleep, 'Who hasn't got anyone to fight for her?'

Gerard gulped and his eyes grew misty, it seemed to be hard for him to speak, 'Well er, Riella came back two days ago, she was heavily pregnant, apparently her French trapper spent time with her and she got pregnant, and he stayed with her for a while, and said he was going to check his traps. He left her in the cabin with food and water and she survived through the winter, but when the thaw came, and he did not return, she left the cabin and came back down. She had some money to find some lodgings and food, but no one seemed to want to know a lone woman who was pregnant. She used the last of her money to get to Moose Falls a day after you came here. She was tired, hungry and broke. Mom and Dad brought her to the hospital and she gave birth to a baby girl last night, but she used up all her strength, as she heard the baby's first cry, she died.' Gerard's eyes were misty and he stopped, and gulped. I held his hand and said, 'So this child has no one to fight for her. What are the orphanages like?'

He looked at me and said, 'Pretty grim, there is not a lot of money to help them, and people are not happy to take on any more, they are not able to take on extra.'

I made up my mind, 'Let me see her, we could at least foster her. Oh Gerard, you know I am not good at feeling sorry for myself. Please I want to do this, for Riella, she has done so much for us.' He just nodded, and could not meet my gaze, and went out.

After about half an hour, I heard a little wail, and Mary Ann and Gerard walked into the room with a tiny bundle which was making a noise, Gerard held back as Mary Ann placed the little bundle into my arms, she looked at me as I mouthed, 'Thank you' and she smiled and kissed me on the cheek, and they both left. I opened the blanket and looked at this scrap of life, she had a head of dark downy hair and a slightly olive skin, she looked a lot like Riella except for the nose and fingers, which were different to hers. I looked at the little one, as she cried, and finally the tears came, great gulping sobs, as my chest heaved, the little one looked at me as I grieved for my lost baby, the future of no babies and for my dear lost Riella. Slowly the tears subsided, and the little one quietened down and I felt a love that was from a deep well and did not affect the love I had for my other dear ones. Little did I know the support I would have from an unexpected source.

Mary Ann and Gerard returned after half an hour, and she went to take the little one back, but I asked if she had been fed, Mary Ann said only once, but she did not take much. So I asked for a bottle to see if she would take a feed from me. So Mary Ann went away and came back with a small feeding bottle and I gently placed the teat near the little one's mouth, and she opened her mouth and started to suckle a little, and tentatively carried on until she had taken about half, and stopped, so I put the bottle down and turned her to rub her back. They looked at me and I said, 'It's not just my decision, the children need to know, the whole story, can you bring them in, I want to see them, I have missed them.'

They brought a crib in, and Mary Ann gently took the baby from me, and placed the now sleeping baby into it and covered her. Gerard looked at me and gave a watery smile, and said he would bring the children. After about two hours, when I was given another bottle to feed the baby and she took it. Mary Ann came in for five minutes and said they were on their way. I smiled and thanked her for her donation, meaning the blood, the most precious gift she could give, I have part of her inside, making me strong. She just said that it was the best thing she could do, and would do it again.

After about two hours, I heard a commotion in the corridor as two boisterous children came bounding in, followed by their father, who asked them to calm down, and they walked a bit slower towards me, I asked Gerard 'Do they know about my operation?' and he nodded.

Ellen came up to the bed, and said, 'How are you Mama? Why are we here, grandma said children are not allowed but you wanted to see us' and she took my hand. I so wished that I could get up, I hate using the bedpan. Jarred stayed back a little, and held his father's hand. He then said, 'Who is in the crib Mama? You not able to have babies now.'

I asked if I could be alone with them for a moment, so Mother and Father Horan went out with Gerard, who gently led Jarred over to Ellen who took his hand. I explained to them gently as I could about how Riella had come back, and had a baby, but could not look after as she was too weak to stay with us and died. I said her baby was in the cot, so they looked at her in the cot, as she stirred and opened her eyes and looked around. Before I could ask that question, Ellen said, 'Can she come home to live with us Mama, Henry keeps on going home, we want a baby to keep.' Jarred nodded and said, 'Yes Mama, she could be our special sister.'

I almost cried, and called the others in, and went to sit up, and Gerard moved quickly to stop me, but the soreness is going. I told him what the children had said, and he smiled, and told them yes, she could come home with us. He lifted each one of the children so that I could kiss them goodbye, and he kissed me too, and said he would be back later. The children skipped out, how I have missed them.

Shortly after Mother Horan came in and she looked drawn, and a little shaken. I asked her if the children had been tiring her out, but she shook her head. She said they had all been worried for me, and that even prayers had been said for me at church, this shook me. I didn't realise how ill I had been, but she told me that many people in the town had come to like me, not just respect, but liked me.

Then Mother Horan started to cry, and I held out my hand to her cheek, and she held it. Through her tears she said, 'I am so thankful that you have taken this child, especially since you had such a difficult time and losing your chance to have any more children.'

I told her what I had heard about my womb that had occurred when I had Jarred, when they used the forceps. She still looked distressed, so I asked her to ring the bell, and when the nurse came in, asked if we could have a drink and I felt rather hungry. The nurse smiled, and I also asked if I could get up and sit in a chair, so she said she would ask. Shortly after two nurses came back and they moved the armchair over and gently helped me up, ooh my legs were a bit wobbly, but with their help, I walked a step or two to the chair, and they put a blanket over my legs, and went away, and came back with a tray with two cups and saucers, then left. Mother Horan poured out the tea and handed me a cup. This seemed to help her to compose herself. I asked her why she was so concerned about the baby, as I had been told that Riella was her best friend's daughter. She gulped and nearly choked, and I leaned over and tried to pat her back, but she put her cup down and said, 'Not my best friend, although I loved her dearly, she was my sister, Riella was my niece.'

It was my turn to be shocked and I almost choked, but recovered and asked, 'Why didn't Riella tell us?'

Mother Horan continued, 'It was not my choice, Riella insisted that she did not want any favours, she wanted to earn her pay, but she did love the children. My sister only had Riella, and her husband died when Riella was three, and he left a small bequest and the house, but by the time Riella was about 18 years, when she came to us to work, the money that she earned mostly went to help her mother. So when her mother died, Gerard senior and I were able to help her, which was the thing we wanted to do. Then she came back to repay us, but what she did not take in wages we saved for her. When Riella went away, we were sad too, but she was very proud, and now we have lost her, but at least she came back,' and she started to cry again. At least as I was sitting with her I could put my hand on hers and she held it, I asked if Gerard knew, and she said, 'I just said that Riella was the daughter of a distant cousin.' I thanked her, and said, 'Poor Riella, I really wanted to befriend her, but she kept herself to herself, and was very deferential, I struggle to deal with the class system, I have managed to be dignified when it called for me to be so, but I do not like the divide.'

She nodded, 'I know but you have learned to adapt, my dear girl, please stop calling me Mother Horan, what do you call your mother?' I was a little taken aback, 'Err Mama, why?' She replied, 'then will you call me mother, it is less formal, and I love you like a mother.' I nodded and said as long as Gerard didn't mind, but she told me that he used to call her Mommy, then mom, so I started to call her mother, and leaned forward and kissed her on the cheek, and winced, she made me sit back and called a nurse. A nurse arrived, and Mother (Horan) told her that I might be in pain, and I asked the nurse to put me back to bed. She got me to stand up for a moment, and got me to lie on the bed for a moment whilst she checked the dressing and my wound. I waited whilst she gently removed the gauze and checked the scar, which Mother H told me went from my navel to just above my pubis. She said that stitching was neat, and the line looked red, but seemed to be healing well. The nurse cleaned it gently, which smarted, and I was glad when she had finished. She put new dressings on, and bandaged it securely.

The nurse looked stern for a moment and said to be careful, we laughed and just then the baby started crying. The nurse checked her, and she was wet, so changed her napkin with a spare one, and the baby continued crying, so she said she would get a bottle of milk. She handed the baby to Mother H who sat down whilst holding her, and looked at her little great niece. I said, 'We need to give her a name, what was your sister's name?'

Mother H looked at me with a soft smile, now, 'Louisa.' I said 'Perhaps we should call her Louisa, Marie Ella, how does that sound?' Mother H smiled and said 'Oh yes, that would be lovely, how do you like the name Louisa little one?' she addressed the baby, who looked at her and gurgled. Then the nurse came in with a feeding bottle with a small amount of milk in. Mother handed her to me and I cradled her gently and placed the teat to her mouth and she drank slowly, but surely.

I looked at Mother H and said quietly, 'Riella may not have known how much she was loved, but that love will be given to her daughter, and she will feel part of a family.' We both smiled, and I thanked God silently for giving me a different chance to look after and bring up a baby, we would heal each other, and the children, who seemed to like having a sibling, and to play with her.

20th July 1925

After two weeks in hospital, which could have been boring were it not for me being able to take care of Louisa as we decided to call her, and registered her birth with Riella's name on it, and arranged to adopt her, which would take a little time, but the lawyer saw no problem in processing the papers.

I was allowed to go home with Louisa, and I have been getting up and walking around the room and then down the corridor with a nurse with me and I had a course of exercises to help me strengthen my stomach muscles, this seemed quite new but I am glad as I want to get fit again, to be able to get up on a horse again, not just run up the stairs, ha I can just walk at the moment.

31st July 1925

We laid Riella to rest yesterday, after her funeral at the church they (Mother and Father H) went with the coffin to New Brunswick and buried her next to her mother. The children went to the church and were very subdued and I took Louisa as well, and as they carried the

179

coffin out, I whispered to Riella, wherever she might be, that we would take care of her child and would love her.

When Mother and Father H went off, we returned to the house, and entertained the twenty or so mourners who went to pay their respects. They were interested in the baby, and praised us for taking her on, but they were assured that it was not a chore, we loved her and she is family. I did not move around very much, being still convalescent, but I am feeling better each day.

30th August 1925

At last, I feel so much better, my scar has healed, and I am able to do as much as I did before. I still feel a bit odd every four weeks or so, and have odd pains, but sometimes it is a relief not to have monthly bleeds. Gerard is very loving, and we have become intimate again, and he assures me that I am as attractive to him as ever.

The adoption of Louisa has been finalised, so we arranged to have her christened, on a lovely Sunday afternoon, and again used the horses to take us to church and Louisa Marie Ella Horan was duly baptized, and her godparents were Stanley and Mabel and Dr Helen and her husband who of course brought their little boy along. The reception afterwards was a happy affair, after all the sadness that we have been through; having Louisa was a bright light in a dark cavern.

I wrote to my mother and told her all that had happened and she was most gracious and sent me her love and good wishes and assured me that I had done the right thing for me, and not to regret it for a moment. I showed the letter to Mother H and she hugged me and said I have a very caring and understanding mama.

10th September 1925

Louisa seemed a little slow to put on weight, and she has not been able to keep all her milk down. I told Dr Helen who visited us and observed Louisa when I gave her another feed, and I was sitting in our bedroom during the day, away from the children, again after several days, she started to feed, but was only able to drink half, and then she vomited, and she cried, a hungry cry, and I started to cry, with frustration, I am so sad that I cannot feed her myself, I guessed that the cow's milk might have not been good for her or 'unpalatable' as Dr Helen put it. She took a bottle from her bag and it held a white milky coloured fluid, she told me it was goat's milk, which she had found that with some weaker babies seemed to be able to accept this milk when some mothers did not have enough milk. So Mother H took it downstairs, and heated it up and brought it back in a feeding bottle, and I tentatively put the teat to her mouth, and she took a suckle, and I could almost see her swallow, and waited for a repulse of the fluid, but she relaxed and finished her feed. Tears ran down my cheeks tears of relief, Mother H was also in tears, Doctor Helen seemed relieved and she rested a hand on my shoulder, and said, 'It may well be her natural father had an intolerance to cow's milk, or his mother was unable to feed him. Do not worry, I suggest you buy a nanny goat or two, with a kid, and then you could get your own milk, and perhaps your man Mr Norbert could stay in the stables, they seem to get on well with horses.'

September 15th 1925
Oh Joy, Father H purchased two nanny goats with their kids from a farmer he heard of in a town further down the railway line near New Brunswick, so he and Gerard went there on the train and came back the next day with two nanny goats and their kids, one of which was a nanny kid and a billy kid (female and male apparently). They got someone with a truck from the station and placed the four creatures in the back, with Gerard sitting in the back, to make sure the goats were not unduly upset or escaped. They arrived back late morning,

and with Norbert's help, lifted them from the truck, and Gerard and Father H took the goats with their kids to the back of the house to the stables. The children and I followed them, as we heard their arrival, Mother H was inside with Louisa in the library, and Louisa was asleep, for the moment. The children were very curious, not having seen goats before, and Henry who now three years old was spending the day with us. Ellen and Gerard held his hand as they led him gently to the stables. The kids were quite skittish once let down, as they were still little. Father H explained that the nanny goats had to have babies to produce milk, and that we would milk the nanny goats for some milk for Louisa so that she would grow strong, as she could not drink cow's milk and I could not feed her as I did them. The nanny goats were a bit skittish too, so they were let into the paddock with the horses who sniffed them and nuzzled them and then licked them, and they seemed to be accepted, and they remained as a group, which was lovely to see. Louisa has settled down and is able to drink the goat's milk and the children have got some new 'pets'.

October 20th 1925

I have been a bit worried about how Gerard is reacting to my surgery and taking on Riella's baby. I have felt that he might have been 'press ganged' into keeping the baby with children eager to take her home, and Mother H revealing Riella's relationship with the family. I was worried that he was not happy with the situation and just avoiding spending time with Louisa.

When we were alone after supper one evening and Father and Mother H had gone to bed, as he was a little tired and he had worked the weekend as an on call doctor at the hospital and I think actually that he wanted to spend some time with his wife which was lovely and I marvelled at the love that was there after about thirty five years of marriage I hope that we still have that after so long. But I digress, I went and sat next to Gerard after bringing him a cup of coffee and asked him how his studies were going, his research into shell shock of post traumatic stress, and he said that he was busy with the general surgery and had learned a lot, and became experienced, and his studies into the after effects of shell shock, and other reports from various doctors who did not see the young men as cowards. When he finished, and sipped his coffee, I broached the subject finally, after having a gulp of coffee and asked Gerard if he was happy with our family at the moment. He asked me to clarify, and I said, 'You have been so supportive, and I know that you had a difficult decision to make with Jarred and my last surgery, I am so grateful but I feel that you have been pulled along by events, and I'm not sure if you really wanted to take on Louisa as ours, please darling, are you happy with the situation?'

He gulped and I could see him fighting back tears, so I held his hand and his arm as he finally let go, and after a sob or two, when I held him tight, and he swallowed, 'I was afraid that I was going to lose, we were going to lose you. When Doctor Helen told me you were bleeding heavily, and that she had cut into your womb, and she said that any baby that you might have, could not stay as there was a scarring at the lower part, and it had opened up and caused the bleeding, and she thought that the forceps might have been pushed too far. The only way to stop the bleeding was to remove your womb, and you had already lost a lot of blood, so when Mary Ann heard that, as she was in the waiting room, she rolled up her sleeve, and said she had roughly the same blood group, so she went with another nurse. Harry was there too, so he sat with me and reassured me. I remember praying that you would pull through.'

I held him close, oh how he had suffered. Gerard carried on, 'Whilst Mary Ann sat with you, I went home to find Riella there, heavily pregnant, in quite a state, she looked ill, and Mom said that she had come to us as a last resort and half-starved and she had started labour. So we took her to the hospital and Mom took her to the maternity ward to give birth, and you had woken up and Mary Ann left, and I wouldn't have let anyone else do it.'

He stopped for a minute, and drank some more coffee, 'When Mary Ann told me that Riella had died, I well, it was another upset, she was a nice girl, young woman, and the children loved her, I was torn, and I didn't realise that you had heard.'

I still held his hand and he continued, 'Mom was very upset, and Dad was very quiet, and consoled Mom. I swear I did not know Riella was a relative, which was kept from me too.' I said quietly, 'Your mother told me that Riella had requested that we did not know, she didn't want any favours, and I am sorry, I liked her so much, but she chose not to confide in me.'

Gerard kissed my hand, as he continued, much more confidently, 'Well I was a bit upset, as I had no brothers or sisters, and only met Harry when I started school. It would have been nice to have a cousin as a playmate, as Dad was an only child. I am happy that we took on Louisa especially after Ellen said about having another baby in the house. I'm also glad that we got the goats, they are such quirky creatures. I just haven't had a lot of time to be a father to the children, I have been so busy, and well you just seem to be able to rise above things.'

I felt so ashamed, I had not realised until now how much the events of the last three months had affected him, until I asked him now. I hugged him and thanked him for being so generous and kind and going to the trouble of getting the goats. Just then as we usually left door open, we heard a cry, and it was not Ellen, or Jarred, it was Louisa, so I went upstairs and through our bedroom door to the cot, where a very hungry and wide awake Louisa was. Gerard had followed me just as I lifted Louisa out of the cot, and he had brought in a bottle of goat's milk, and he put it in the little saucepan which we had some water in and it was suspended, over the fire from a hook. He held his arms out to hold Louisa, whom I had wrapped in a shawl, and placed her gently in his arms. She looked at him with a surprised look and whimpered a bit, but Gerard whispered to her, telling her she was loved and that she will be alright. I felt a little glow, after all she was kin to him and I watched as the water came to the boil, and waited a little before lifting the bottle out very carefully, and used a muslin cloth to hold it, and used a thick cloth to remove the saucepan from the fire. I shook the bottle as I had been taught, after putting a teat on the bottle, and put a few drops on my wrist and it seemed a little hot, so waited a little longer, and the milk was just right, and Gerard held out his hand to take the bottle, he nodded, and I placed a towel over his shoulder, and a little bib under Louisa's chin, and after adjusting her position, he offered her the bottle, and she took it hungrily, and drank well. After she had finished, I offered to rub her back, but he wanted to try, so he lifted her to his shoulder and rubbed her back gently, and was rewarded with a large burp, and another and she fell asleep on his shoulder. I was so happy, and he smiled and said, 'I always wondered what it felt like to feed a baby, now I know, you always did that. I feel kind of modern, how many men can say that?'

I smiled and as we gently laid Louisa back in her cot, 'Not many, they might say that it was women's work, but you have always been a good father, not like some I have been aware of.'

October 31st 1925
Mother H finally felt able to check through Riella's bag with her few possessions, and found to our relief a marriage certificate between her and Philippe Le Duc and sadly a pawn ticket for a gold wedding

ring for the amount of three dollars, oh she must have been desperate, and we shed a few tears that she had such a hard time, but I respected her choice. We tried to find out what happened to her husband, but it was difficult with him being a trapper. Father H contacted the police department in New Brunswick as that was where her last port of call was and they contacted the Mounted Police who patrolled the mountain and trapping region, but no news was forthcoming. Louisa thrived, slowly but surely, she was such a tiny baby, and I wondered if she was a little premature, but I was told that it might have been that Riella might not have had a good diet before she came home. I managed to put aside my sadness for such a nice kind young woman and concentrated on helping her daughter thrive. The children have been very good, and growing up fast. Ellen chooses what she will wear, and dresses and undresses on her own. She allows me to style her hair, but she tells me how she wants me to style it. Quite the young lady! Jarred still needs a little help with his boots, not because of his arm, which is not bad, but because of the laces. I think that he will manage soon. They love having a baby sister, and still like having Henry visiting most days, and as Jarred has started school since September so I have been taking both my other children and Louisa to school, when it is still fine, I take Henry too in the pushchair which he loves, and I am happy to be able to, as I have been building up my strength since my surgery, and even Mary Ann thinks any exercise is good. I am still not allowed to ride any of the horses yet, as it is four months since my surgery, and although I do not have monthly bleeds, I still have symptoms that I had before my bleeds. I have to go back to the hospital every month to be checked on, and my scar has healed very well apparently and Doctor Helen and her colleagues seem pleased with my progress and I should be able to ride again next year, and I seem to have no ill effects, and it has been good to meet the other mothers at school again. Sometimes if Mary Ann has a day off in the week, we go together to the school, her with Henry and I take Louisa to give her a little air, to give Mother H a little rest as she is very helpful with Louisa as she loves her so much as we all do. Mother H likes to be involved with all the children's daily routine, and she gives Louisa her morning feed whilst I help the children get ready for school, and it is such a lovely arrangement. Louisa has also started on light solids, like pureed apple and started trying pureed carrot and potato. Helen is so good, she takes some of what we have, and puts it through a sieve, and we have offered Louisa tiny portions, just an egg cup full at first and after she spat it out at first, so we added goat's milk to the apple, and she ate, and seemed to like it. Ellen is so attentive, and asked if she could give Louisa a few spoonfuls, so whilst I held Louisa, Ellen offered the spoon and Louisa looked at her and the spoonful of food and she opened her little mouth and Ellen gently placed the spoon into her mouth, and spoke to her, and gently fed Louisa, it would seem that Ellen had been watching me and Mother H and got the action just right.

31st December 1925

Another year over, so much has happened, not all of it good, in fact not much good at all. We lost a good friend, I lost the ability to have children, and in balance perhaps taking in her baby as our own, in a sense she is being family. I have become fitter and stronger and Gerard is making good progress with his studies and research, and he spends a lot of his spare time with us and his parents. We had a lovely Christmas Day, with Mary Ann and Harry with Henry, who is growing fast, and loves spending time with us when his parents are working. Stanley and Mabel joined us again, they are really good friends, and they dote on all the children from their own grandchild and especially Louisa as they see her as another grandchild.

I remember coming home with Mother H a few days before Christmas and could hear music, and I thought that was the gramophone, which was in the large room which we used on special occasions and head a little dance, but then heard a strange voice and I wondered if Gerard or Father H had a guest. We both looked at each other with puzzled looks, and found Father H, Gerard and the children in the library listening to sound coming from a brown arched shaped box with some mesh for a window and two knobs, and a clear oblong plastic covered white strip a little like a ruler with numbers and names on. I asked what they were listening to, and Father H laughed, and Ellen said, 'Mama it is a wireless thing.'

Gerard stood and beckoned us both in, and Father H did the same and he escorted Mother to the sofa next to him, and Gerard did the same to me. As we sat down, the men brought us a drink of tea, and Gerard explained to us the workings of a radio, and where the music and speakers came from, apparently at present most of the programmes came from the United States of America, but the shop where they bought the radio said that Canadian radio stations would start after a while, but we would be able to get world news than perhaps buying a newspaper. Whilst the men were explaining the principles of the radio we were getting requests to 'shush' by the children. Well they seemed to like the instrument.

1st January 1926

We stayed up to see the New Year in, after the children had been persuaded to go to bed after 8 p.m. We listened to the countdown to the New Year on the radio, and had a drink of wine to toast the New Year. We kept Louisa with us, first in case she woke up and needed a drink. Whilst we had our drinks we had a look outside the window out to the side of the house, it was eerily quiet, with the usual blanket of snow, and the empty corral, as the horses and goats were inside the stable, but the horses would be hitched up to the snow plough to help clear the drive and streets. We went to bed at about 1 a.m. after again wishing each other Happy New Year, and I carried a sleeping Louisa up with us to bed, she stirred a little when we laid her in the cot, but did not wake until 4 a.m. and I stirred, and put on the little bedside lamp on and sort of stumbled over to her, and she looked at me as I lifted her up and checked her napkin, which was a little wet, and placed her on the chest of drawers, which had a towel on and all her powders and creams and clean napkins and clothes in. After changing her napkin and cleaning her, and made her comfortable, I picked her up and whispered to her all the time, reassuring her, telling her she is beautiful, which she is, that she is loved, which she is, by all of us in this house, and Mary Ann and Harry and Henry too. She gurgled a little and went to sleep, I gave her a little kiss on her forehead, she said, 'Mama, Dada, mm.' I nearly cried, but did not want to startle her, and covered her up as she settled down to sleep. I went back to bed and just before I turned out the light, Gerard stirred, and he opened his eyes and looked at me sleepily, 'Did Louisa wake up?' I said, 'Yes, but she spoke two words, Dada, Mama.' He smiled and said he was sorry that he missed that, and then I put the light out, and I felt a bit cold, so I snuggled up to him, and he held me as we fell asleep.

March 1926

Louisa is growing well, she is making more words, as Ellen and Jarred call their grandparents and father by their name for them, she listens and follows, later Ellen asked if Louisa could sleep with them so that she wouldn't be lonely at night how sweet and loving. There was already a little bed in their room for when Henry stayed over and when we put the cot in there it seemed like a dormitory, but the children were so happy, and there is still room for them to move around, and us, and it seems to work well, and Louisa seems to have settled down. She still has goat's milk and does not tolerate any other milk.

The children are doing well at school, and I understand why they wanted another baby as well as I did, it would seem that most of the children in their classes have younger brothers or sisters.

(There seemed to be a gap in the years with just a noting of years beginning and years end, with just a short note of what happened during these years, as if things happened with a routine and they seemed settled.)

1927

All has been well. The children are doing very well at school, and their examination marks are good. Ellen seems interested in sewing and dressmaking, and she likes to help look after the horses and the goats, even attempting to milk the nanny goats, and the kids are not kids of course but grown up and she loves them. Henry spends time with us and although he is about six years old he seems very interested in animals, and spends time with Ellen and they help to clean out the stables to groom the horses, and he asks Norbert many questions about his knowledge of horses, and he found an injured bird which he brought to Norbert, it had broken its wing, and sadly it died, and Henry cried, but Norbert explained that it might have died of shock, but this did not put Henry off, bless him, he and Ellen asked for books on the care of animals, is this a sign that he may want to look after animals not humans? We will see.

1928

I do not seem to have a lot of time to write, but when did I? Life goes well our children are so bright, Louisa is happy, she feels loved, protected and wanted. I do hope that this remains so. Sadly one of the mules died, Henry and Ellen were very upset and the veterinary surgeon who came just before she died said that was old age and she was probably tired. He gave her an injection to make her comfortable and she lay down and went to sleep and just faded away and died peacefully in her sleep. Both Ellen and Henry stayed with her, and Harry and Gerard took it in turns to be with them, as she died late at night, and they didn't want the children to be on their own when she died. They buried her in the wood at the back of the house, and once they put her body in the ground and covered it and put a little cross with her name on (Clover) and had a little funeral.

Henry and Ellen asked if we could have another mule, but we were not able to find one, and as they were not used so much they would have to look after the one we still had after all he would be lonely. So they took him out for a walk on Sundays with us as we rode the horses to Moose Falls Lake for picnics, and the children either rode on the mule with the picnic on his sides or they rode with us. Jarred did not mind coming out with us, but seems more interested in the motor car or the working of the wireless radio, which was moved to the lounge. I'm surprised he hasn't taken it apart, but when he was twiddling with the knobs on the front, Father H walked in and asked him abruptly what he was doing, I was in the library looking at a geography book and heard a voice piping up, 'Nothing Grandpa I was just looking for another station.'

I walked to the lounge and just stood by the door, and Jarred got a little telling off, which he may have deserved, but Father H explained to an eight year old that the wireless was a delicate instrument and that Jarred should not 'mess about with it' on his own. But if he was that interested he, his Grandpa would show him but he was not to play with it on his own, he needed to ask his father or him if he wanted to use it. I could see Jarred smiling and promised to do that. I walked in after the conversation and Jarred stepped away from the radio, and I asked innocently what was going on and Father H said with a twinkle in his eye about Jarred's interest in radios and mechanical things. I smiled and accepted what Jarred was forming a preference for mechanical things and he was also making models, with paper and glue with supervision when he used scissors so that he did not cut himself. I wish that someone could make scissors that were not so sharp that would cut paper not fingers. He has come home with some lovely models and he is good at craft and he can be found sometimes in the paddock on the fence looking at the horses and later with a sketchbook and he seems to be good at drawing the horses, and has no problem with his hand. I wonder where he gets this talent from, I mentioned to Gerard one evening and he laughed and brought my sketchbook from our bedroom. I was a little embarrassed, but he praised me for my unknown talent, and I laughed and told him that I had not felt free or comfortable to sketch until I came here. Ellen celebrated her 10th birthday and we had a garden party which she asked for and she invited her class friends, and of course their parents, and Harry, Mary Ann with Henry and Stanley and Mabel, and we all had a really good time, so many sandwiches, jellies and cakes and soda pop drink were consumed by the children and their parents, who numbered in all about fifty; twenty class friends and most of their parents, phew! How did we organise that, but between Mother H, Mary Ann, Helen and I the parents had either cold drinks or tea or coffee.

Ellen was a very lucky young lady, receiving loads of birthday presents, including a saddle from Gerard and I, and riding boots from her grandparents, she did not ask for a pony, as she wanted to ride one of our horses. I left my twenties, and became 30 years old in June also, but we just had a small dinner party. Life seems wonderful at the moment I am so happy.

1929

Life still goes well; the children are doing well at school. Louisa is very inquisitive and I try to answer her questions, and encourage her to learn, and I have been helping her with her letters and numbers, and she is a quick learner. Whilst the children are at school, we sometimes go on walks, and she comes with Mother H to the town for a look around the shops and to the café for tea and cakes and soda for Louisa. She has responded well to us and seems to feel part of the family. I could say it's the least I could do, but that would be patronising, we wanted to have her as part of our family, she is a relative, and the children accept as a sister in the true sense.

Theirs has been a great decade; sometimes things have been difficult, but we have overcome them, thank God. He has been with us somehow throughout the good and not good times. I'm almost afraid to leave this decade. I wonder what the 1930s hold for us. I have been writing quite frequently to my mother, she loves receiving our news and photographs of the children and us. But her letters seem a bit flat, as if her life is difficult, she seems to have spent time with my aunt, and when she goes back to Three Gates, she spends a lot of time on her own, and she does not really mention my father, who apparently spends a lot of time drinking or going to expensive restaurants. She does not go to the village very much. I understand that she has a small income which was left to her from my grandfather, which my father was not able to access, so she has a little independence. Oh I have missed her so much, I hope that my letters cheer her up a little.

1930 March

Things are not right in the world, even here in Canada in some of the urban areas. The men are trying to keep it from me, but I hear snippets on the radio, and sometimes when I take a discarded newspaper to read on the front pages. Last year there were rumours about investments, some people falling on hard times. When I have gone into the lounge when there is a news programme or bulletin, when Mother H walk in and someone is talking about the news, they quickly turn the radio off or change the subject. It is a little off putting or even irritating. I heard the comment, 'Don't want to worry the ladies.' That did annoy me, I have finally come to the realisation that there are things going on outside this lovely town of Moose Falls, and from what I can piece together by looking at the boring pages, the financial pages with what are called share prices, and headlines 'shares fall'. What can this mean?

April 1930

I finally summoned the courage to ask Gerard about what I had read, and he took me to the library where Father H was listening to another radio. When a news bulletin was being broadcast, he got up to turn it off, and only asked if he would turn it off to talk to me about the shares and banking situation, and to explain about mortgages. Father H asked me to sit down and offered me a drink, and I asked if I needed an alcoholic drink to steady my nerves, and he laughed, and I saw a tray with tea and cups and saucers and I accepted a cup of tea.

At reasonable length he explained about investments, and shares and mortgages. He explained so carefully that I understood. That some people bought shares in different companies and the shares went up and some people sold at high prices but then the prices went down, and in 1929 the stock markets crashed and people lost a lot of money, mortgages, borrowing to buy houses. People lost their lives by killing themselves. People lost their jobs; this is just a beginning there are going to be hard times ahead for people. But then he made a very interesting statement, 'My dear Anna and Gerard, for one thing I do not have a mortgage, my father left us the house, he did not believe in stock and shares, as such but he saved his money in a good bank, I have found that unfortunately the banks invest these moneys and we appear to have lost about half, but the other money is left on deposit which pay a modest amount of interest, and is still intact. I have not touched that money as I have been working, and my salary pays our bills. I may still have to work a bit longer. Sadly not all have been fortunate as us. Gerard also has a salary which he uses to help pay the bills. Harry and Mary Ann work long hours for moderate salaries, as some people struggle to pay their hospital bills. Also things are becoming harder to get hold of, we will have to make do and mend, and as we have more than some, we look after Henry and we will have him overnight more often, and be as charitable as possible.'

I was shocked and saddened about the effects of investments and stocks and shares and the fall of the stock market last year. I was allowed to read the newspapers, and they sometimes made grim reading.

November 1930

Things have got no better, sadly Harry's parents moved in with Harry and Mary Ann as his branch of the bank closed and although the younger employees found positions elsewhere to larger branches, Stanley was deemed too old and he lost his position, and only had a small pension, so he could not pay his mortgage, so he lost his home, which after it was sold left only a small amount of money which he put to his pension, poor Stanley and Mabel. Just as well we are only ten minutes away.

December 31st 1930

Christmas was a subdued affair; fortunately we were able to entertain friends and family, as well as helping the Christmas party at the school. I feel so blessed and as before during the First World War I wanted to help others and thankfully I can, with Mother and Father H's blessing. We are growing some of our vegetables as we have done for years, but try to help the shopkeepers by buying fruit and vegetables from our local grocers and also any surplus vegetables to the shop to help them and accept a token amount in return so that they can sell the produce a little cheaper, to help the townspeople afford to feed their families. We are not giving charity as such we just want to help, like in the prayer 'to give and not to count the cost, to labour and not to ask for any reward'. Sometimes I have offered to help in the grocer's shop, for a short while to give him an hour or two, and in the process am able to improve on my weights and measures and to do the calculations of what they spend, fortunately it is in dollars and cents not pounds shillings and pence. It seems so long ago, but I only had shillings and pence pocket money. I am enjoying my learning. This little voluntary stint lasted for a few months, when they found a young girl who was fourteen years old who needed a job, so as the shopkeeper wanted to employ her for half days during the week, as after a little training from the owner and myself, the girl became proficient in weights and measures, calculation and giving the right change (very important) I did say to the shopkeeper if she had any problems, or needed any help to let us know. She thanked me and I made my way home, a little sad but happy. Mother H looked after Louisa whilst I was out but she started school last September, and she seems to have settled in well, but her slightly darker skin was a little problem as the other children were paler skinned, as are Ellen, Jarred and Henry, but our children accepted her as they loved her, and I did not want to get her confused or frightened, as although I have told her that we adopted her, she is family, but I'm not sure that she understands quite, but she is getting older and wiser and outside where people can be cruel and unkind without meaning to be. We have to help her understand, and the children will protect her, as they have undertaken to take her to school and back home, and they are so good, they do not stop anywhere on their way home. If they wish to meet their friends out of school, they meet at the weekends on Saturdays. Ellen is 13 ½ years old, and Jarred is 12 years old, and they are quite grown up, and Henry is 9 ½ years old but he is quite tall like his father. We seem to have quite a close knit family who are growing up fast.

(There was a jump in the years.)

March 31st 1932
Things get no better, Mary Ann and Harry are working hard at the hospital but they do not seem to earn very much more and they really need a bigger house as Harry's parents live with them and they really only have two bedrooms, with a little room off Harry and Mary Ann's bedroom which was a 'dressing room'. Henry is happy there, but he does not have a lot of room, only a chest of drawers and a chair. He has to go through his parent's room to go to the bathroom and out to downstairs, being only nine years old he was not too worried at the time, as Mary Ann usually prompted him to get up and go to bed, but she and Harry fretted that they would need more space as he got older. They wanted to move, but there was nothing for sale which they could afford, and moving further away was not an option as they were so settled at the hospital, and though their salaries were very good they were doing good work and would find it difficult to find work elsewhere. The Depression is getting to everyone. We try to economise, and to help where we

can, and not be extravagant. Gerard and Father H go on their six monthly visits to the logging camps on horseback, taking extra provisions and using the mule, who is still fit enough for the work. Father H is not getting any younger, and he always looks tired when they return, but he insists that he has to go to help the poor people up there, whilst he can.

May 1st 1932

Well, Mary Ann, Harry and Henry with Stanley and Mabel have moved in with us. Harry decided that the house was not big enough for them anymore, and after discussing with Gerard and Father and Mother H they decided to rent their house, which would pay the mortgage and we were all under the same roof, and the arrangement seemed to work. We had enough rooms, and Henry shared a room with Jarred, which they both loved, and Ellen shared a room with Louisa, which seemed right as they were all growing up.

Whilst Gerard and Father H went on their visits, Mother H had company of her own generation, which was good for her when I went out on occasions shopping, or even spent time with Mary Ann on her precious days off, when we could catch up and relax.

June 1932

I cannot believe it! Gerard is 40 years old, what a milestone, he joked and said he is getting old, but I cannot see it, his hair is still golden brown, as he was when I first met him, but not too slim, and there are a few lines around his beautiful green eyes, but they are laughter lines, and I ask him not to frown, and he laughs and hugs me. My hair has been cut shorter in the last five years, but not too short, it is almost shoulder length not the bob which appeared stylish in the 1920s and I still pin it up to keep it tidy. We have a bit of a house full, but we all seem to get on. Jarred and Henry get on so well together, and after a few late nights and games of pillow fights, which their fathers put a stop to, they settled, and sometimes together at a table in their room doing their homework, or reading, or spending time with the horses either making sure they have enough food, or grooming them or clearing out, they also looked after the goats who have grown older, including the billy kid which is now a billy goat of course. And the jenny goat which had grown and as nature continued was mated and had a kid of her own, so we still have milk, which her kid had some, and so did Louisa, sometimes as a drink or as cheese, which Helen made, and we all enjoyed. We were not exactly self sufficient, but tried.

I have to record that Mary Ann qualified as a midwife in 1925, and besides nursing at the hospital, she did home deliveries, sometimes by herself, but only straight forward ones. She knew the difference and had become very expert in her ministrations and had a very good reputation. Harry and Gerard did not talk about their work in my hearing, but sometimes could just overhear them with Father H and Stanley talking about medical matters after supper when they went to the library to have coffee and sometimes a little brandy. Mother H, Mabel, sometimes Mary Ann and I went to the lounge where we had our after dinner coffee, and listened to the radio sometimes. I sometimes went upstairs to make sure that Louisa was all right, and to see that she had got ready for bed, as Ellen spent time downstairs doing her homework or studies, and went to bed about an hour later, and their room was still next to ours. Louisa was very good, and I always made sure that I read her a bedtime story and tucked her in for the night. I quite liked our little time together, and hoped that she felt loved and treasured. After she had settled down for the night, I joined the ladies for supper or to listen to the radio with the men, and I have learned to play some card games, much to Mary Ann's amusement. She feels that I am turning into a lady at last, and I replied that I had some good role models and we all laughed.

September 1932
Ellen has seemed a little moody and a little out of sorts, and she has become quite irritable at times with Louisa who does not understand and seems to think that Ellen does not like her anymore, and I have a tearful child who feels abandoned, and a tearful daughter and what is happening to her. I managed to pacify Louisa and tried to explain that Ellen did not mean to be unkind, and I tried to talk to Ellen who was still a bit moody and said that there was nothing wrong with her, she just wanted to be on her own, so I left her alone for a little while, but was somewhat worried. I was right to be worried, as about three days later early in the morning I heard Ellen call out to me from the bathroom of the room next to ours, and went to the girls' room with the connecting door, which we had stopped using and went quickly to the bathroom, but not before noticing Louisa sitting upright in bed, and her eyes were wide open with fear. I knocked on the door just in case it was locked, but it was not. Ellen was still sitting on the toilet, sobbing, and her eyes were wide with fear also.

I went to her and knelt down in front of her and asked what was wrong. 'Mama I think I'm dying,' she said through sobs. I asked her why and she said, 'I'm bleeding just like you did when you went to hospital!' I asked her from where she was bleeding, and she said from the middle underneath, and she was hurting, she showed where, which was in the middle to the top of her abdomen, and it was nothing like stomach aches before. I breathed a sigh of relief, and said I knew what was going on. I went to the cupboard which I had used, and found an unopened package of sanitary items which I had stored but of course not used since my surgery in 1925. I just hoped that they would not too big, as Ellen was a good six inches shorter than myself. I also went to our bedroom and rummaged in my stocking drawer for a little belt with hooks hanging from the belt on elastic. I noticed that Gerard was sitting up in bed, and I whispered, 'Our daughter is on the road to be a woman.'

He said, 'Should I worry?' I replied, 'Not if I can help it, Mary Ann and I will give her a little talk.'

I returned to the bathroom when Ellen was still sitting on the toilet not crying, but still frightened. I turned the taps on in the bath, and got some towels and asked if her bleeding had stopped for a moment, she nodded, so I asked her to have a bath and I would help to put on a sanitary item and if she had any more pain, that we could give her some pain relief. I went to the bathroom door to tell Louisa that Ellen was all right, and what was happening to her was natural for a young lady. Louisa asked if she could get up and I asked her if she could wait a little longer unless she wanted to use the toilet, to go out to use one on the landing, which she did. Ellen had stood up and I flushed the toilet. Ellen was a little embarrassed but I explained that I had bathed her for many years before she chose to bathe herself. Ellen seemed content to soap herself and she allowed me to wash her back. Ellen stood up and I held up a towel for her as she stepped out, on to a towel and she dried herself, and before I left her to dress after explaining how to fit the sanitary to the belt, I noticed that her chest was not so flat anymore but she had budding breasts. Ellen went downstairs and sat quietly in the dining room and after I had washed and dressed, and helped Louisa, joined her downstairs, where Mother H and Mary Ann were sitting with her. I spoke quietly to Mary Ann and Mother H and Mary Ann went to get her bag, and Mother H tried to encourage her to eat a little, before Mary Ann came back with her bag, and took a flat package out and emptied a powder in a small amount of water and stirred it and handed it to Ellen, telling her that it would ease her pain. Ellen looked at me and her grandmother and we both nodded, so she sipped it and screwed her nose up, and then swallowed it quickly and drank some milk. She then asked me, 'What is happening to me Mama? If I am not dying, how is this natural?'

I reassured her and apart from telling her that her body is changing, promised to explain some things and Mary Ann would go into a little more detail that she would understand, after breakfast. Louisa then ran in after finishing dressing and went to Ellen who hugged her and Louisa asked her if she was all right, and Ellen said, 'Well yes a little better, I'm so sorry that I have been so horrible to you, I love you very much.'

Louisa seemed very happy and she joined us at the table after being helped to get some breakfast as she is not quite tall enough to reach the sideboard where the breakfast food was laid out. We had a lovely meal, and as the men arrived into the breakfast room, Gerard, Father H, Jarred, Harry and Stanley with Mabel, we had just finished and Ellen, Mary Ann and I left the room after greeting her father and grandfather and the rest of the family and we went to the small lounge, and whilst Mary Ann went to get some books, Ellen said to me, 'Mama what is happening to me? I was worried because Grandma told me that you were bleeding down there and you nearly died, and I was really worried.'

I reassured her that as I was a married woman and it was for a different reason, and I still get the same feelings now, and get moody, but I do not have a bleed any more. She then asked me when it happened to me, who did I talk to and I recall that my mother was not very approachable, so I confided to Mary Ann who explained what was happening to me, and was able to acquire some sanitary equipment and I eventually told my mother, who was happy to help me, when I needed some time alone. But I was naïve about having babies, and she appeared to be more knowledgeable, coming from the village as they talked about these things more than where I lived. Also we were not told about procreation in those days. But I didn't go into how she came about, she's too young for that information. Between us, Mary Ann and I explained with some pictures what happened every 28 days. She did say other girls in her class seemed to be a bit moody at times, and were sometimes absent from school once in a while, but would seem that their teacher being a lady was understanding, and the young lads were unaware at the moment. As Mary Ann and I have sons, we have been noticing changes in their voices, which first seemed to crack, and seemed croaky, and then lower. We left their education to their fathers.

31st December 1932
Oh, what a year, our children are growing fast, even Louisa, who is turning into a very pretty girl, who although the youngest appears to have a good head on her shoulders who is eager to learn, has got good marks in her class, appears to be popular, and has made friends with her class friends, and is loved and protected by her brother and sister and Henry, who spend time with her when she goes to the goats and helps to groom and clear out the horses in the stable, she seems to have an affection for the horses as I do. Christmas was a modest affair, as I was aware that a lot of people in the town did not have a lot of money, so instead we donated money and toys some old, some new, and some clothes which had been laundered and ironed, so that the church could arrange a little Christmas party for all the children in the town and nearby villages who arrived in an assortment of trucks, old cars and on foot. Some of the children looked a bit thin, and their boots looked a bit worn, and they looked cold. We gave them a good meal and a drink, and a little present, and they were all given gloves and scarves some of which we had

knitted, Mother H, Mabel, Mary Ann and I. I was a little concerned that their less well-off parents would possibly say it was charity, but Mother H said the Pastor's wife had said it was sharing what good things we had, and the Pastor quoted from the Bible about when some people asked Jesus when did they give things to him, or give him clothes and he said when they gave to the poor man or the prisoner that they were doing it for Him, I begun to understand, and our poorer friends understood too, and they accepted with good grace. This was another lesson I learned, and I felt better.

We had a quiet Christmas with just the family, all who lived with us, except that Mary Ann was called out to deliver a baby to a lady at the edge of town, and Harry went with her in the family car, and this was dawn on Christmas morning, and we waited to have dinner until they came back, which was after dark about 6 p.m. and when they came back Mary Ann looked a little tired but happy. She told us that the birth was uncomplicated, but it was the first birth for the mother, and she was quite young, and it took a while and she was glad that Harry was there, as the father was a bit anxious, so he reassured him, and Mary Ann and the grandmother attended the mother. When the child was born, it came out the right way and cried fairly quickly and finally she said it was a boy. We all laughed. The parents were very happy and wanted them to stay to toast the birth, before Harry and Mary Ann took their leave.

We were relieved that everything went well, and I voiced the fact that Harry was there in case of any complications, and he laughed and said, 'Well if there were any, Mary Ann would call me, but I am not an obstetrician, and Mary Ann is more than capable,' and he hugged her. We all clapped, and Helen knocked on the door to say that supper was ready if we would like to go to the dining room. How formal! But when we went through to the table it was so beautifully decorated, although we ladies laid out the cutlery and glasses,

Norbert had brought in some holly and a tree and the children had helped him decorate it, and there were presents piled underneath. Helen and Norbert took their leave, after receiving their Christmas presents to eat their own meal.

Father H sat at the head of the table and carved the turkey, and we helped ourselves to vegetables and gravy. It was a lovely meal, and when we cleared the table we managed a small amount of Christmas pudding with brandy butter or, for me, vanilla custard as I do not like brandy. After supper, we had coffee, and cold drinks for the children, Ellen took charge of distributing of presents, and Louisa was asked to take them around. The presents were wrapped in brown paper with ribbons and we were asked politely not to tear the paper, so that it could be used again, which we duly obliged.

The grandparents were given their presents first, and of course Louisa received kisses from them as she handed out their piles of parcels, which made her smile and she gave a little curtsey after giving them their gifts. Then the parents received theirs, and I had about six packages, and I hugged Louisa as well as kiss her in thanks. The children received theirs last, and Louisa was a little disappointed that she only had a small pile of presents, and Father H called her over to him and sat her on his knee. He said, 'Well my little lady, there is another present which we could not wrap, because we could not wrap I, because it would not stay still, Jarred will you get it for me.'

She looked puzzled and Jarred went out through the door and came in with a basket with a blanket covering something which was moving and making a funny muffled noise. He went to Father H and he pulled the blanket to reveal a small bundle of fur, which was a puppy of indeterminate breed. My eyes were starting to fill. 'This little fellow was the last in the litter and the farmer said he was the littlest and he could not afford to keep him, so I asked if we could have him once he was weaned. I know you like the goats but you cannot take them for walks. We will help to take care of him when you are at school, but you will need to be the main person to look after him, will you do that?'

Louisa slipped off his knee, and hugged Father H 'Oh yes Grandpa, I will, thank you oh this is the best thing, look everybody!' She lifted the puppy which was a fluffy brown and white colour, and held him to her chest and took this little wriggling creature to everyone to pet, even Mabel stroked the little thing, and did not flinch, well she visited the horses to pet them and give them treats, because I saw her.

I held the little chap and stroked his sweet downy head, and I knew what I would do at her age if it was mine, but of course would not be allowed to. Just as I thought when it was time for Louisa to go to bed, she begged us to take the puppy with her, I waited for what Gerard, would say, and he asked Ellen if she minded, Ellen said, 'Well I do not mind, as long as he does not wee on my clothes or my bed. He is so sweet. Let's go and make up a bed for him, oh, and keep your shoes out of the way, I believe puppies like to chew something whilst they are teething. Isn't that right Henry?' Henry nodded, so all three went up with Louisa to settle the puppy and her to bed. When they came down after about half an hour, I went up to check on her, and found a box with a blanket in, and some food in a dish, but no puppy, ah Louisa was fast asleep with the puppy on the bed over the covers next to her both fast asleep. I gently lifted the little fellow and after giving him a little stroke, laid him in the box, and covered him and tiptoed out. Just what I would have wanted, ah life seemed good.

I returned to the dining room as they were raising their glasses in a toast, I was handed a glass of sherry and the toast was to the new baby and to our blessings including the four legged one upstairs.

When I finally opened my presents, which were gloves, scarves earrings and some notebooks from Gerard, which he had written on the label, 'For you to continue your journal' I smiled my thanks and knew that he understood what I was doing in my spare time.

March 1933

I am a little worried about Stanley. Mother and Father H are not saying much but he seems to spend a lot of time on his own, and he started taking 'Scuffy' which Louisa christened him out for walks. The puppy had grown into a perfect miniature brown and white sheep dog, and he seemed a very friendly if boisterous dog, and he seemed to rush around the house, and on the uncarpeted floors, in the hallway and passages, he slid to a stop when called so hence 'Scuff'. Whilst Louisa was at school on the warm sunny days Stanley used to put his coat and 'pork pie' hat on and said he was going to take the puppy for a walk for exercise for both of them, I noticed that Stanley was going out first after lunch most days, with Scuffy and the dog seemed happy to go out. Stanley had found a dog lead in the hardware store and a collar which Scuffy wore all the time and he seemed very excited when Stanley took his lead from a hook from the door. Stanley used to talk to Scuffy as they went towards the woods, and Scuffy seemed to perk up his ears as they went along.

I spoke to Gerard about my concerns, as I had noticed that Stanley looked a bit lost and seemed not to make any conversation during mealtimes when Gerard, Harry and sometimes Father H talked about their days' activities or some things about the hospital, Stanley seemed unable to contribute, and when they went to the library after supper for coffee and drinks, Stanley used to excuse himself after about twenty minutes and joined us in the lounge to listen to the wireless with us, and sat reading a newspaper, and after the children went to bed, he offered to let Scuffy out for a little run

207

in the garden before the puppy went to bed with the girls. Scuffy was quite good with the goats, and when he went into the pen with the goats, he just wanted to round them up, but never worried them or upset them, and Stanley seemed to be able to train him to behave, which Louisa was happy about.

I spoke to Gerard about my concerns about him again, one night as we were getting ready for bed, and Gerard agreed that Stanley seemed a bit lost as perhaps since he had lost his position as manager of the local bank and then his house, Father offering for him to come and live with us, that maybe Stanley had lost his independence, and ability to provide for his family, might make him feel that he has nothing to offer. I told Gerard that I felt sad, and did not realise how it might affect a man so much, but Stanley still had a pension. But Gerard said that Stanley had nothing to pass on to his son, and Harry had confided to Gerard that he had told his father that it was not a problem, but Stanley just left the conversation without another word. I just mentioned that I was glad that Stanley was taking Scuffy for walks, and training him a little and that Scuffy really took to him, and showed a liking for this proud dapper man.

June 1933
The summer is very much here and we had some garden parties on a small scale for Ellen's birthday and mine, it was just nice to have some friends around for a modest tea party. On one occasion Stanley stayed for about an hour and then he took his leave and said that he would take Scuffy for a walk as the little dog, but he is not so little now, seemed a bit excitable around the children, and he asked Louisa if she minded and she very sweetly said no, but please do not go far as it was very warm, and he promised. So we watched Stanley with Scuffy on a lead, Stanley wearing a white sunhat walking briskly down the lane. After about an hour when it was very hot

and people were sitting in the shade fanning themselves, there was no sign of Scuffy. I was concerned, but after two hours I did get worried. Shortly after two and a half hours had gone by there was a yapping in the distance and then Scuffy came dashing back but no Stanley, we thought that Scuffy had slipped off his collar and run off, but there was no sign of Stanley. Scuffy jumped up and down and barked and Gerard and Father H called him and he still barked, and jumped up. Norbert was around and he suggested that Scuffy was trying to tell us something. Gerard knelt down and Scuffy licked his face and then ran towards the lane, 'Is there something wrong Scuffy? Where is Stanley?' the dog may not have understood but he seemed to want the men to follow him. Father H got the car out and Gerard and Norbert went on foot, following the dog who according to Gerard led them to the woods, Father H followed in the car and as a precaution took his medical bag. The dog led them running back and forth to make sure they were following him. When Scuffy got there where Stanley was he sat down by Stanley and whined, trying to lick Stanley's face, and when Gerard and Norbert arrived, he said, 'Well done boy, thanks' very quietly.

As soon as they got to Stanley Gerard knelt down and after praising Scuffy, checked Stanley by opening his shirt, taking his pulse, and asking Stanley questions about how he felt. Father H arrived after driving the car as close as possible to the forest, which was about 50 yards away. He brought his bag with him and opened it and Gerard took out the stethoscope, and after checking Stanley's vital signs, thought that it might be a heart attack, and gave him a capsule to place under his tongue, and then Gerard and Norbert went to the car and found a longish board and blankets to help Stanley to be put on a makeshift stretcher to take him back to the car, and to the hospital. Stanley was not a thin man but was not really fat, so between the three of them, they managed to move Stanley on the stretcher and to lift him up and move him to the car. Gerard sat in the back next to Stanley who was propped up long ways in the car and he covered him with a blanket. Norbert sat in the front. Apparently they took Stanley straight to the hospital and Father H went with him after he was gently helped on to a trolley and taken straight into the hospital. Gerard and Norbert returned with Scuffy, who had sat patiently in the car and did not bark, but just looked out until they got back into the car. By the time they arrived back, some of the children and their parents and other guests took their leave.

Gerard left the car in the drive and after Norbert went to his rooms, after being thanked for his help. Norbert just shook his head and said he was glad to help. Gerard went to Harry and gently took Mabel by the arm and took them inside to break the news gently to them. Mary Ann looked at me and I shrugged my shoulders. Louisa was pleased to see Scuffy back and made a big fuss of him and petted him as we all did. There were only a few guests left, and they took their leave and asked for news of Stanley.

After about half an hour Gerard, Harry and Mabel came out, and Harry had a small valise, and Gerard had a small bone for Scuffy and the little dog came to him when he called, and Gerard gave him the bone and made a big fuss of him and said, 'This is a very clever little dog, Stanley didn't feel very well, and he couldn't walk any further, so he sent Scuffy back for help, which he did. Stanley is not very well so we took him to hospital and Dad is with him, so Harry and Mabel and I are going to see what is going on. We will telephone you later to let you know what is happening to him. Make a big fuss of this little fellow and be thankful that Stanley has such a good friend in Scuffy.'

We smiled ruefully, and hugged Mabel and Harry and Gerard before they got into the car to go to the hospital. We, the ladies and children went into the house with our hero dog, after clearing up the tables and chairs and put them into the outhouse. The air was a bit subdued, and Henry now 11 years old and Louisa soon to be 8 years old, were a bit upset, as Stanley being a grandfather figure and Henry's grandpa and they loved him dearly. Louisa understood about Scuffy's part in the 'rescue' and she fussed the little dog who wagged his tail, but whined a little as he seemed to be missing his best friend, apart from Louisa, and we explained that to Louisa. She asked what she could do, as children were not allowed to visit the patients in the hospital, except in my case; the rules were relaxed as I wanted them to meet Louisa. I suggested that she wrote him a little note to wish him well with a picture, and Henry said that he would too. Ellen and Jarred sat with them and wrote their own notes too, as they really liked Stanley also. Mother H, Mary Ann and I sat quietly, quite unable almost to make small talk. Mary Ann left the room for a moment, and I looked to Mother H who nodded, so I followed her. Mary Ann was sitting on a bench in the hallway, looking out of the window, and I could see that she was crying. I sat next to her, and offered her my kerchief, and put my arm around her shoulders. Mary Ann leaned towards me, and I could feel her shaking, and the tears rolled down her face. 'He has been like another father to me, Harry said he seemed strained and stressed, and Stanley felt useful taking Scuffy out for walks, he loved to go out, oh Anna, what has happened? Thank God Scuffy came back for us.'

I agreed with her, and said I thought that Stanley is a proud man, and the loss of his position and everything that has been going on in country has made him feel worse. Mary Ann agreed, and we both sat there with me still holding her by the arm then she composed herself. We were not aware of the passing of time until the large clock in the hall (we would have called it a grandfather clock) chimed eight p.m. We both jumped and when the telephone rang, a long ring and then continued with short rings, I was going to answer it but

Mother H came out quickly and picked up the earpiece and spoke into the speaker. She was followed by the children and Scuffy, who barked but Ellen who was nearest to him crouched down and called him to her and he did and she 'shushed' him and he obligingly went at least quieter.

Mother H listened to the caller, and she said it was Father H. She listened quietly as we all watched her face, but she just murmured, 'Yes, Yes, all right, thank you my dear, give him our best' and placed the earpiece back on to its rest. She motioned for us all to go to the lounge, taking Louisa by the hand, and Scuffy followed us, a little skippy, but Ellen reached for his collar, and she gently led him in, and he sat at the children's feet, who sat together on a sofa, and Mary Ann and I sat near Mother H who had sat on an armchair, with Louisa sitting on the floor at her feet. She cleared her throat and said, 'Well your grandfather Gerard senior called to say that doctors believe that Stanley had a mild heart attack and it was very lucky that he was found so soon, any later and it could have been more serious. They are keeping him in hospital and they have put him in a sort of tent to help him get more oxygen, and they are keeping him under observation, that is to see what effect this has had on his body, so he will have to rest, and when he comes home he will need to convalesce, that is not to do too much for a while. From what I remember from what Mabel told me, he worked long hours at the bank and did not have a lot of exercise, so maybe the walks were a little much. Please do not worry, it was something that he wanted to do, to feel useful, and someone benefitted from that, that little dog there, who may well have saved his life.'

Scuffy's ears pricked up, and she said to the little dog, 'Yes you Scuffy well done,' and Scuffy went over to her, in his springy way to be rewarded with a loving stroke from Mother H and he sat down with Louisa and he licked her hand.

Mother H continued, 'Apparently Stanley has had something to help him sleep, and Mabel and Harry will stay with him overnight, because she would leave him once he went to a room, but Gerard and Grandpa will be coming home soon, so you young ones should go to bed especially you Louisa. Perhaps you could pray for the recovery of Stanley, he could do with some help, we all could, and for the poor people who are less well off than us.'

The children stood up, still very quiet, and they all went to Mother H to kiss her goodnight, Henry included, and Ellen went up with Louisa, with Scuffy following up with them. I said I would be up shortly to check the girls and boys.

Mother H asked if Mary Ann was all right, and she nodded, but excused herself to wash her face. Mother H said to me as Mary Ann went upstairs, 'She's very lucky to have a friend like you to have someone to confide in.' I replied that I was the lucky one and Mother H smiled, and I went to the kitchen to ask if it was possible to have some coffee, and Helen with some help said that she would be happy to send some in, and asked after Stanley, and I told her what I knew, and told her if she didn't already know the part that Norbert and Scuffy had played.

I returned to the lounge where they were listening to a radio programme, and then the news. As usual it was not very good. Helen came in with the girl who helped with the cooking and catering, with a tray of coffee, and some sandwiches and she asked if we needed her anymore, and we thanked her and Mother H told her to go home, and we would manage. After drinking some coffee, and had a bite to eat, I heard a call from upstairs, 'Mama,' called Ellen, 'Louisa wants a bedtime story, and can I stay up a bit longer?' I went upstairs to find Ellen in her nightgown and wrap and Louisa was in bed, with Scuffy sitting in his bed with his tail wagging. I said to Ellen, 'Well you had better put a coat on, Scuffy probably needs a little run out in the garden before you go to bed and I will see you downstairs.'

I turned the small light on as Scuffy and Ellen went downstairs. I told Louisa another fairy story, and she settled down to sleep after we had our usual little prayer for our house, especially Stanley, and for the poor. She settled down, and as I went to the door, Ellen came back with Scuffy, who was a little slower, and Ellen said that he had run around the garden, and then stopped for a moment to 'do his business' and then came in. He settled in his bed, and I gently stroked his head. Ellen followed me down and went to the lounge and she had a drink of milk and a sandwich. She then said good-night to all of us, and I reminded her to clean her teeth.

Gerard, Harry and Father returned at about 10.30 p.m. and they told us about when they found Stanley in the woods, and when he was taken to the hospital, where Father H remained with him whilst the doctors examined him. Stanley was a bit incoherent by then, but from what Gerard had managed to work out from his questions to Stanley and the signs, and his pulse and heartbeat, he felt that it was a mild heart attack, and he would need to be observed and hopefully he would recover but will need a lot of rest. Mabel was going to stay at the hospital as she felt it was her duty, and she wanted to. We all commented on her devotion to Stanley, and Harry said that his parents were always a loving couple but didn't always seem to show it, he felt really blessed.

July 1933

Stanley came home at the end of June, he walked from the car with Henry and Jarred walking either side of him, holding him gently by the arm as he walked the few steps to the front door and it was open so they walked inside, he seemed a little unsteady, but once he had walked through the door, Stanley felt able to walk on his own, slowly but surely, to the waiting group of us in the hallway, all the family were there except for Father H, Gerard and Harry who brought him home in the motor car. Scuffy was sitting quietly in his basket in the hallway, with Louisa sitting next to him with her hand on his collar, and stroking his head. We were all so pleased to see him, and as he walked towards us and greeted us one by one starting with Mabel, and Mother H and the rest of us. We then went into the library, and as it was late morning, we all had some refreshment, coffee for us, and some biscuits and the children had soft drinks. Scuffy was so pleased to see Stanley, and he rushed to see him once he had sat on a sofa with Mabel. Scuffy went to Stanley, and put his paws on Stanley's knees, and Stanley made a great fuss of Scuffy and he would have liked to climb on Stanley's lap, but he was being trained not to do that, but Mabel made room and patted the sofa between them and Scuffy hopped up on to the sofa, and laid his head on Stanley's lap and Mabel stroked his coat, we were a bit shocked, but Stanley said it was a special occasion, and he was very grateful to Scuffy, so we all laughed and let go, this time.

August 1933

After a short convalescence, Stanley reluctantly rested for most of the day, in the garden at times, in the shade of the trees. He became quite frustrated with only being able or allowed to walk out of the house and around the garden at a leisurely pace, and to sit at a table reading the newspaper or in the library on a few rainy days reading one of the books that were there. Father H noticed Stanley's frustration so he asked for Stanley's help with the family accounts, as Father H felt he was needing another person to keep track of the money going in and out of the finances as there were more people living in the house and contributing to the running costs, and Father H was finding it difficult to make sure that the books balanced and to do his work at the hospital. After a few hours of Father H showing Stanley the books that he kept and the incomes received, Stanley grasped the situation and after a few days and weeks, Gerard told me that Stanley looked happier and more relaxed and Father H seemed more relieved. Gerard also told me in confidence that Father H offered Stanley a small fee for taking over the accounts, but he refused, saying that it was good to feel useful.

I was so happy, and as Stanley's health improved, he started to take little walks with his little friend Scuffy and sometimes with Mother H, Mabel or myself, and Louisa at times, as I loved to go walking. We always took one of the horses, led by the reins, so that each one had some exercise, and if Stanley felt a bit tired he could ride back on the horse, and as we had given Stanley's horse a home this was a pleasurable activity. We did also take another one or two horses, and a picnic, so that we could ride the horses once outside the town to Moose Falls Lake, and had a picnic which was a lovely way to spend an afternoon with Scuffy rushing around and occasionally take a dip in the lake for a swim, he was a good little swimmer, but did not go too far. Stanley did still have to take his medication, when he felt some pain, or get breathless, but he seemed more relaxed and did not exert himself.

Life seemed to carry on well enough, and I still continued to read the newspapers, and listen to the wireless news, and the financial situations did not seem to get any better. The logging camps slowed down as the trees had been over cut and there was a direct result of that as there was erosion and no water could settle when it rained and the word dustbowl became used a lot, and the plight of the families as the men lost their occupations. We seemed to be sheltered well, as the forest near us and the rocky lake had not been affected, I felt really sad for the people across the country who were affected.

We seem to be getting to some normality, and I have found time to write to my mother who asked me last time to send letters to London to my aunt, who sends the letters on to my mother. Mary Ann corresponds with her mother, who seems unhappy and quite jaded, I feel sorry for Mary Ann's father whom she says is not very happy. He seemed such a nice man, he was always kind to me, unlike my father, and I remembered I enjoyed studying Geography although it was not a ladylike subject, and I continued to look at maps, and the information of land masses and I have found to my astonishment at first how small Great Britain is, and how big the North Americas are, especially Canada, and how provincial I was, preferring to stay in a small town, but I have ventured out at times further even to New Brunswick, with Gerard, Father and Mother H and the children to visit Riella's and her mother's graves to pay our respects. Louisa was a little confused at first, although I did try to explain to her when she was old enough that she was adopted, but still a relative, but she did not quite understand, and she was and is still too young to be told about the circumstances she came into the world, and how she came home with us.

I was glad that we did go because when we visited the graves I saw that Riella's full name was Marie Ella, so Louisa bore her mother's full name and that made me feel better and that Louisa would grow up within a loving family, her family.

December 31st 1933
Another year gone, not all good, but we are stronger and more resilient for what life may throw at us. Christmas was a quiet subdued affair, and we again had a little part for the poorer members of our town, giving the children some warm clothes, shoes, some second hand, but good quality, and a warm meal and some food parcels this

time to help them into the new year. Our own celebrations were low key and quiet, but we entertained Dr Helen, her husband and little boy, which was lovely because they announced that they were moving away in the New Year to the United States of America where her husband had been offered a very good position at a university hospital, and she might take up a position there also. We were sad to see them go, but grateful for their expertise whilst they were here, especially Dr Helen as she had been a great help in a time of need about eight years ago, I for one would not have survived but for her and dear Mary Ann of course.

January 31st 1934
Although the snows are still here the roads are passable, thanks in part to our wonderful horses who when their halters and the collars for helping to tow the snow plough, they became quite excited and skittish, for they loved the exercise and they walked almost sure footed through the snow, pulling the heavy plough and leaving a clear path and some men following with some salt.

As the school term started, sometimes we walked to town with the children, although it was only Louisa who needed escorting now. Jarred was 14 years old and the next year he would graduate, and we wanted to know what he would like to study. He said that he wanted to work with machines, maybe motor cars, or aeroplanes, I was horrified, they are or could be quite dangerous. Ellen wanted to either be a dressmaker or teacher. Henry made his ambitions quite clear, he wanted to be an animal doctor, or veterinary surgeon.

May 1934
Mary Ann has had some sad news, she had a letter from her father, to say that her mother had been ill for some time, after having a fall, and she did not recover well, and apparently took too much

medication, and she did not wake up one morning, and after being taken to the hospital did not survive and died. Apparently she had a weak heart and it just stopped beating. So sad, and Mary Ann was a bit subdued, but when I offered my condolences she just said, 'Well she is at peace now. Mother said she always felt that was second best, although Father was very kind and attentive to her, she was unhappy to give up being a nurse, but she didn't mind being a schoolmaster's wife, it gave her some position in the village, I do feel sorry for my father though, he was a good husband.'

We sent a letter of condolence to Henry Silvester and a cheque either for flowers or a headstone. It was rather difficult to decide what to suggest to send. I also wrote to my mother again to the London address, but guessed that she might be aware of the situation as we lived in a small town.

April 1934
I received a letter back from my mother, who said that she returned to Three Gates for a few weeks, and was aware of Mary Ann's mother dying, and attended the funeral which was very quiet, with a few villagers paying their respects. I told Mary Ann and she was touched by my mother's action, but did not mention the subject after that, so I did not mention it any more. Life seemed to go on with little change. Stanley seemed to enjoy his role as banker and auditor, and Father H seemed relieved that the responsibility of managing the household income and expenses which was the only drawback of having four couples, and four children. This arrangement seemed to suit both of them, and Stanley seemed less unhappy and happy to take on a role in the household. He still took Scuffy out for walks but he was always joined by one of us, and we took a horse or two for their exercise, as we took a quiet route to the woods, and if Stanley felt a little tired or breathless, he was helped on to a horse,

and he rode back with Scuffy running back and forth but not going too far. We spent many a happy afternoon going for walks, and Mabel came sometimes, and she would also ride back on a horse, and we also took a picnic, and sat by the lake which is near a river which ran down from the hills, which the loggers used to float their logs down, but I was never in a position to see them.

The children were growing up fast, not really children any more, except for Louisa, now nearly eight years old, and very pretty with her dark hair, slim build, and delicate features, with her dark brown eyes, and her slightly tanned complexion, despite not looking like Ellen and Jarred or Henry, they being of a fairer complexion, but they all loved her as their own, and protected her and Ellen looked after her in the mornings when she got up, although I used to get up in good time to make sure that they were up, and Gerard and I used the bathroom a little further down the landing, as we had three bathrooms, some en-suite, and the other one was with Mother and Father H's room. The bedroom that Ellen and Louisa were sleeping in which was used as a nursery, was apparently a dressing room, as it did not actually have any windows although the bathroom did. This arrangement worked well, if we rose from our beds in good time, that is Mary Ann, Harry, Stanley and Mabel and us of course. We had arranged times when we might use the bathroom and tried to accommodate each other. There were times of course that during the night Gerard and I would use the bathroom next to our room as we had another door to go in, and in that case would lock the other door, to go in and in that case we might actually use that bathroom, in the case that Gerard had returned from the logging camps with Father H to have a well- deserved bath and shave. But I digress, I am a little worried still about Stanley, he tries not to show it but he is slowing down, and he does try to do a little too much, and he does love his morning or afternoon walks out. If no one is about he will put his hat on call Scuffy and go out. Luckily, someone notices the yap of Scuffy as he goes out and either Mary Ann or I if she is not in, make as to go out also, and sometimes take a horse as well, we do not always saddle him or her up, just taking a bridle and a lead rein, and of course any horse that goes out is quite happy to do so. So far we have kept up with him, and he accepts the company, although I think that he knows what we are doing, and both Mary Ann and I have heard many a sigh when we catch up with him. Scuffy is quite a biggish dog now, and he may pull on his lead, so we need to be aware of that.

June 1934
Ellen is due to graduate from school, she seems to be set on a career not content with staying home and being a lady. How modern we are. Ellen said that she would like to be a teacher, and she is very bright, and has been very studious and has got good 'grades'. She has applied for a scholarship and has an appointment for an entrance examination to a nearby college; at least it is three miles away. She has been helping at Sunday school and enjoys spending time with the children and is very good at art and craft. She also loves animals, and still helps with the horses and goats. Jarred seems more inter-ested in machines, including the motor car, and he likes to make things like model cars and aeroplanes. He is nearly 15 years old and really wishes to learn to drive, but fortunately father and grandfather absolutely refused, saying he is too young at present, so he asked if he might have a bicycle, and he was told he could, but he would have to work for it, and if he had any money to put towards it; our children are learning the value of things, despite the fact that our family are reasonably comfortably situated, other people may resent that they can have anything that they want, when they want.

Henry has expressed a wish to work with animals as an ani-mal doctor or veterinary surgeon, which is a change from looking after people, but he does love animals, and spends lots of his time with the horses and goats, and when the farrier comes to check the horses, and when Norbert or the veterinary surgeon visits the animals. Mary Ann and Harry were a bit taken aback at first, but have started looking at training, with the veterinary surgeons involvement, and he has kindly allowed Henry to go with him on his visits when Henry is free.

August 1934

Wonderful news, Ellen duly attended her entrance examination, and she gained very high marks on all subjects and she has been offered a place at the college for a teacher training course, and was offered a scholarship, but when Father and Gerard heard, they went to the bursar, and even though I was not aware, between them, they paid for her two year tuition, so that a less well-off student might be able to have the opportunity of having the course also. When we heard, Ellen was a little surprised, but her father and grandfather explained that she needed to earn her place, not just to be able to attend, she needed to attain a good standard from the beginning and she understood and tearfully hugged father and grandfather together, thanking them for their kindness and belief in her.

We all attended her graduation at the school which she had attended all her school life. She looked so pretty with her shoulder length hair swept up into a chignon, and some pretty combs in her hair, and with a pretty summer dress with a shorter skirt, about calf length with a belt, she chose a sky blue, with cap sleeves and she wore a pair of shoes that she felt comfortable in, but they were polished up, being a beige colour. Father and Mother H gave her a lovely corsage which Norbert took from the garden of roses, small ones with ribbon over the thorns. As it was a Sunday, we brought the carriages, giving them a wash and clean, and hitched the horses up to two of them, with Henry and Jarred riding the other two, and so almost all of the horses had a walk out. Ellen wanted to ride a horse there but I explained that she would look a little unlady-like with her pretty dress. She reluctantly agreed, and so we had a lovely time, just like years ago, when we used the horses to take us to town and to the hospital. Norbert drove one of the carriages, and Gerard drove one of the others. Louisa was desperate to take Scuffy, but we explained that it was not possible to take a dog into the hall as he might disrupt the proceedings, but Norbert offered to look after Scuffy and if he needed, to take him for a little walk. So that is what happened, and whilst we were standing in the shade, and Norbert stood apart with Scuffy who apparently got a bit anxious so he walked the dog up and down the schoolyard, and back to the horses, who seemed calm enough.

The graduation went very well, and a young man stood up to speak, the 'valedictorian' as it was called, and the young ladies and gentlemen were called one by one. When Ellen went up to collect her scroll, we all clapped the loudest, and she seemed quite touched as she walked back down. After a short while she stood up to make a short speech before we made our way out after saying goodbye to her teacher and she wished them well in the next stage of their lives.

Just before we left, Ellen and her class friends gave her a small present, one was a book with all their signatures in and a short note, and a boxed pen and pencil with their love and thanks. I felt so emotional, my little girl was almost grown up, and she was going to do something with her life, not like me, but Mother H would tell me otherwise.

When we arrived back to the house after relieving Norbert of his looking after Scuffy who had become anxious, and was pleased to see us, well so did Norbert. We made our goodbyes to the other parents and children. On arrival home, we took the horses to the stables after unhitching them and brushed them down, and made sure that they had something to drink, and to eat, and let them go free into the corral if they wanted to. We then went to the lounge where a small but tasty buffet was set out with a lovely cake with 'Well done Ellen' in pink icing. It was a lovely ending to a lovely day.

August 1934

Oh dear, Ellen will need transport to her college, and she is considered too young to drive a motor car, although some young men are allowed to drive at her age, so Gerard has bought a used two seater car with a little seat in the back called a 'rumble seat' which I have been given and must learn to drive, although I would rather take a taxi cab or an omnibus to the destination, or even ride a hose, but this is not to be! My first lessons involved learning about starting the vehicle, which pedals to push, and which is the brake, very important to stop, and the steering wheel and is on the left of the motor car and people drive on the right and as I recall about 18 years ago, in England, that the cars had steering wheels on the right hand side. But I must persevere for Ellen's sake.

August 30th 1934

Oh, what a month! I have been expected to go out in the motor nearly every day, either with Father H or Gerard, or Harry, who have all been very patient. I must say, when they even made me drive the family car down the drive, which seemed a nightmare, it is so heavy to steer and to drive, I have become a little more confident to drive the smaller car. I of course had to apply for a driver's licence, to be able to drive out on the roads. Father H and Gerard encouraged me to go to the town, and although there are no such things as driving tests as such, but I think that this will come, as in the bigger towns and cities where there are more cars, so that people might be aware of other drivers, they asked one of the policemen to go out with me, with Gerard sitting in the back seat, where he could not prompt me. I was so nervous! But after about one hour at times driving on the back roads, carefully, and he asked me to stop at a crossroads, and I looked left and right, and he just told me to proceed when I thought it was safe to go, so I did after a few cars had gone by. Well, to be short, the nice policeman told me after I had arrived back at the office, and stopped, put the vehicle safely in place and he asked me a few questions, we got out, and Gerard got out of the back seat, and the officer told us both that he thought that I was a safe enough driver to go out on my own, and he wrote a statement to that effect, which I placed with my driver's licence. He shook both our hands, and said that he actually enjoyed the journey, but that I could drive a little faster, and we all laughed. Gerard was so pleased with me, but I was shaking and I asked him to drive us back, which he did. Wow! For want of a better word, that was very hard, but I would still prefer to ride a horse, if I had a choice.

When we arrived back at the house, everyone was waiting outside for us, and when Gerard stopped the car near to the front door I was still reeling from my experience of being put through my 'paces' by the police officer in the town, and I just sat in my seat. Gerard walked around the car and he opened the door to me and extended his hand to me, so I alighted from the motor car and allowed myself to be led to the front door to the waiting family of Mother and Father H, Mary Ann, Harry, Stanley and Mabel and the children.

Gerard let my arm loose, but put his arm around my waist, he stood up straight and said, 'Well despite Anna's expression she has been approved as a safe driver, and has a written statement to say so. I am so proud of my beautiful wife!'

I became a little emotional at that point and lowered my head and took out a handkerchief and dabbed at my eyes, but I also reached for the piece of paper written by the police officer with my driver's licence and Gerard held it up, and showed it to his father and mother and the rest of the family, who clapped and hugged me each in turn and I felt that I had to say something, 'I did this because I was needed to drive Ellen to college, and I am happy to do so,' but I finished, 'but I would rather ride a horse, but we might wear them out going back and forth twice a day, five days a week!' and we all laughed and went inside to a set out tea to celebrate, and I asked why, in case I did not do well, and Father H said that he could see no reason to think otherwise.

September 1934

September has come only too soon and I did not feel very confident to drive on my own, so if I drove the little car out, I always had a passenger, whether it be another driver, Gerard, Father H or Stanley, Mother H or Mabel, who was very happy to go out, and she chatted away while we were on a clear road, and this seemed to calm me and I gained my confidence, and after I had taken Ellen to the college a few times I became accustomed to the journey, I still took a passenger for either the journey there or back just for the company, and at times when there was not always a person ready to come or an adult, Louisa would ask to come and she put the lead on Scuffy's collar and he came also, and he was sitting next to Louisa with his tail wagging and barking at times, at a passerby, but it was a happy yap. Ellen did not seem to mind when we arrived to collect her, and her fellow students were quite impressed or not (I'm not sure), but she just got in the car and greeted us as usual. But when I asked her shortly before she went to bed after doing some studying, what her fellow students thought of my taking her and collecting her from college, she said that they were a little envious that (a) her mother was driving, and (b) she had company to and from home. Sometimes she asked if I could take an extra passenger or two, and if Mabel or Mother H were in the car, they sat in the back and they sat still for a little while, but then seemed to relax and call to Ellen and she looked behind her and she smiled and turned back and said that they were happy and they liked the way I drove. I relaxed and stopped when they wanted to get out, and they went to my side of the motor car, and I wound down the window, and they thanked me, one who was a young lady and a young man who were quite well dressed, and very polite. Ellen did say that young man had gained good marks in his entrance exam, and was not able to pay for his tuition fees, but he had an unexpected offer of a scholarship, and we both felt that had been passed from Ellen's as she had hers paid by her father and grandfather and as she has been brought up as a lady but to be gracious and loved, she seemed happy that someone less fortunate than herself could be able to take advantage of such a good education at the college which had a very good reputation. She is quite grown up now, and helps with keeping her bed tidy and the room that she shares with Louisa, and encourages Louisa to do so also. She also helps Louisa with homework, not by doing it for her, but talking the subject through and explaining anything that Louisa does not quite understand. The boys sometimes cheek Ellen when she is sitting with her and doing her own studies. If Mary Ann or Gerard or I see them doing this, they are asked if they have any homework, which they sheepishly say yes, so they are despatched to another room to settle down and ask them to get on with it, unless they would like to be shopkeepers or assistants instead of working towards what they wanted to do. After a while if one of us adults looked around the door, they just got a look from one of us, and they went quietly to do their studying. They soon understood that once they had finished their studies they were at liberty to relax.

November 1934

I can hardly put pen to paper, I am so sad, when things seemed to go on so well, one of our number was not so well. Dear Stanley has died! I am able to put my thoughts down now, before I let things move on. One lovely autumn afternoon in late October, it was a Sunday, and we were in the garden, well Mary Ann and I were brushing away some leaves from the grass in the orchard, and then we went into the house. I could hear a yapping and then a whining noise and Louisa came out from the library running and she called to me, 'Mama, Mama Uncle Stanley fell asleep, but he isn't waking up!' We followed her in and saw Stanley slumped on the sofa, and his newspaper had slipped on to the floor, and Scuffy sitting near him whining. Mary Ann went over to Stanley and touched his face and lifted his wrist, she told Louisa to get Father H or Gerard or Harry, and she ran out, but Scuffy stayed with Stanley, who was still motionless. I looked at her, and she looked back at me and shook her head. Scuffy seemed to know that he had lost a friend, and I knelt down next to him, and held the dog close, and rubbed his neck.

After a few minutes, Gerard came in, being pulled by the hand by Louisa and with Harry following, with a medical bag. Gerard asked me to move, and I took Scuffy with me to another sofa, and Mary Ann and I sat together with Louisa and held hands. I tried to maintain my composure and not to give way to my emotions for Louisa and Mary Ann's sake, and Scuffy was very quiet now. When Gerard stood, he whispered to Harry whose shoulders began to shake, and he just motioned to us to leave the room, as he put his arm around Harry's shoulders. We walked out slowly, just as Mother H came to the door, I said to her in a shaky voice, 'Could you please find Mabel, and take her to the lounge,' and she nodded. Just placing a hand on Mary Ann's shoulder, and stroking Scuffy, who followed us, and we went to the little lounge, and as we all sat down Mary

Ann started to weep, and I held her and Louisa who was crying also. Scuffy sat near us and Louisa held him and crying softly, he was whining and I felt the tears rolling down my cheeks unchecked. We had lost a great friend; he had been like an uncle to me.

It seemed like hours before Mother H came into us, and she had found Mabel in the garden, with the boys who were attending to the horses, and Mabel and Henry went to the lounge, and Jarred was very strong and composed, and supported Henry as he went to his father. Ellen was upstairs, and came as the usual noisy household was suddenly very quiet, and she saw Mother H and Mabel and guessed that something bad had happened. Father H arrived home from a visit and called another doctor to verify the cause of death.

Ellen came in to us in a little while, her eyes a little red, and said that tea was set in the dining room, and she hugged Mary Ann, and Louisa, and knelt down to fuss and hug Scuffy who raised the alarm. We went to the dining room where tea was set, but none of us felt like eating. Henry and Jarred were there, and Henry went to his mother, and hugged her and held her tight. Mabel was sitting quietly at the end of the table, and was holding a cup of tea, but was not drinking. Mary Ann went to her and held her tight, but she had no tears left, and then she sat next to her mother-in-law, and they talked quietly, and drank some tea. Jarred sat with us but we were close to the others. We all sat there quietly, and Scuffy for once sat quietly as if he sensed the solemnity of the occasion.

After a while, we heard the front door close, and Father H asked us all to remain where we were, as apparently Stanley's body was being removed to be taken to the hospital mortuary, but did not say more as he did not wish to upset Mabel further. Harry then came in with Gerard, and he also went to sit with his family, we in turn went to Harry and gave him a little hug, as no words seemed possible. We were all very shocked as it had appeared to be so sudden.

No one seemed to sleep much that night, and Louisa begged for Scuffy to sleep on her bed that night, so that she wouldn't be lonely, and we agreed. Gerard and I sat by a small fire in the grate in the bedroom, as he told me what had happened after we left the room. It would seem that Stanley's heart condition had deteriorated despite his taking his medication, and that he had put on some weight. Stanley had done some walking for exercise, but might have got a little worried about the accounts, if we were paying our way, he just wasn't sure. If Scuffy had not been there, Stanley might not have been discovered for some time. That dog is a very clever little chap, and I agreed. Gerard had helped Harry place Stanley's legs up on the sofa, and then covered him up with a throw. Father H arrived back and he telephoned for the local general practitioner doctor to certify death, and they were quite sure of the cause, his heart just gave out, Gerard said he was very sad also, as Stanley was the nearest thing to an uncle, and I said the same for myself.

The funeral was a solemn affair and we borrowed the horse drawn hearse, with our horses, and used the carriages again, with all of our horses. It was early autumn and the leaves were russet, those which hadn't fallen. When we arrived at the church, there were quite a few people there to show their respects and condolences. Mabel travelled in the first carriage with Father and Mother H, and Harry with Mary Ann. Henry travelled in the second carriage with us, that is Gerard, who sat up front and Henry sat next to him, Ellen, Louisa, Jarred and myself. We were all in black of course, as was the custom and even Louisa wore a black hat. Scuffy came with us, sitting on the floor, with a black lead and a black scarf around his neck. Scuffy had grown into a very handsome dog, with a smooth long brown and white coat, and brown ears that perked up at any sound. He was very, very well behaved, as if he knew the occasion was solemn. We alighted from the carriages and Henry walked forward and joined his parents and grandmother who went into the church. Henry is now twelve years old, and quite tall for his age, but he looked very young with his dark brown hair, just like Harry's in a neat style, he is such a nice young man, and walks very well. He stood close to Mary Ann and Harry, and Mary Ann took his hand. We joined Mother and Father H, and left Norbert and a groom from the undertakers to look after the horses. Gerard and Father H saw us to our seats and then went outside again and then the undertakers placed a table at the front of church, and the pastor asked us to stand, and then the coffin was brought in and I was overwhelmed that Father H, Gerard, Harry with a former colleague of Stanley's from the bank, carried the coffin in, led by the undertaker.

It was a beautiful service and Father H, a former colleague and Harry stood up to give a 'eulogy'. But when Harry started to speak, he started well, but his voice broke, and Gerard got up, stood next to him, and Harry handed the sheet of paper to him, and Gerard continued to read what Harry wanted to say. I felt so proud, and again overwhelmed, as I could see how close they were and how Gerard was as ready to support Harry, as I was to support Mary Ann. It was this warmth and love that helped to sustain our family during such a sad time. After the service, we all filed out to the graveside in the cemetery behind the church, with Mabel and Harry, Mary Ann and Henry leading the mourners with Mother and Father H, Gerard, Jarred, Ellen, Louisa and myself, with Scuffy who sat quietly with us in the church, and his ears were down, even he was sad. After some words from the burial part of the service, and throwing handfuls of soil over the coffin, we walked back to the church and into the carriages and the horses which pulled the hearse were taken to the undertakers, unhitched, and Gerard and Harry rode them back to the house, to meet the people who attended the funeral. After we unhitched the hoses and took them to the barn and for food and drink, and settled them down and brushed each one, and gave them an apple each. Ellen, Henry, Jarred and Norbert and I had that task which we enjoyed doing.

We then went into the house, removed our hats and gloves, and joined the others in the lounge where Mother and Father H, Mabel and Mary Ann were welcoming the guests, who wished to pay their respects, and to greet the family. There were extra chairs set around the room, and there was a long table set with food to be eaten buffet style, and guests were invited to queue up to help themselves, which they did slowly and orderly. Mabel remained seated, and Harry (who had arrived a little later from the undertakers with Gerard and had brought the horses back to the stable) took a plate of food to her, but she looked a little pale, and her eyes were red, and she looked tired, which was understandable as she had lost her husband whom had been married for over forty years and was obviously struggling to adjust to being on her own, although Harry and Mary Ann and Henry were with her, they were also feeling the loss of such a good man. Once people had sat down and eaten, and were settled, and they had small tables near them, Father H stood up which just filled the room, 'I should like to welcome you to our house, unfortunately on a sad occasion. On behalf of Mabel, Harry, Mary Ann, Henry my wife and family, I should like to say a few words about my good friend Stanley, whom I had known for many years shortly after our sons had started school. He was my bank manager, and my good friend, and we had met socially before his good son Harry met our dear Mary Ann, and they married. It was my pleasure and joy to host their wedding from here. As we all know, the depression has hit people hard, and others very badly. Stanley had lost his position and sadly his home, and then eventually was offered to move in with us, and I was happy to do so as he had become a very good friend, as good as a brother.' He stopped for a moment and took out a kerchief and blew his nose, he took off his spectacles for a moment, as he was reading from a piece of folded paper. He continued, 'Stanley will be remembered as a genial kind man, who was good at his position and was retired early when the branch of his bank closed down and moved to the city. Stanley did not quite recover from this blow. He will be sadly missed. I would invite you to raise your glasses to Stanley Manton a good man and a good friend.'

Most of the assembled guests stood up and raised their glasses and repeated what Father H had proposed. Gradually people took their leave, and they said goodbye to Mabel, Harry and Mary Ann and Henry and Father and Mother H.

December 31st 1934

Christmas was a quiet, almost sober time, with no one feeling very much like celebrating. Stanley has left a void which is quite strong. Even the children were subdued, and were not very enthusiastic about any presents, but would rather give to those less fortunate than they, and asked for token small presents. On Christmas day they just almost carried on as usual doing their chores, looking after the horses and the goats. We did go to church on Christmas Day, and gave a little more in the collection as it was passed around. We went in the motor car, the large one, and wrapped up warmly. It was a bitterly cold day, but we were used to the cold now.

This last year was not a great year, with only Ellen's graduation, and my learning to drive, being some bright points in an otherwise difficult and sad year. I hope that nest year will be a little better, I pray so.

April 1935

Things seemed to have been a little better except that Mabel announced in February that she was going to stay with her sister on the other side of Montreal, a three hour journey away, she said that although we had been very kind and helpful to her, she wished to spend a little time with her sister quietly recovering, and Stanley had made sure that she was well provided for, and she had a good income, and he had left some money to Harry, which after having paid for funeral expenses, and a double plot so that Mabel was provided for, there was a reasonable amount left, which Harry left on deposit in the bank for Henry.

I felt a little lost myself, but I have my wonderful husband and children but whilst they were away, I spent time with Mother H, and Mary Ann when she was not working. I wrote to my mother telling her of what had happened about once a month, and she would correspond about once a month.

At the end of March I received a letter from my mother which made feel a little happier for her than I had for many years, almost all the time we had been here.

28th February,
Three Gates House, Sussex

My Dearest Anna,
I have to tell you that your father has died. Apparently he had cirrhosis of the liver, having overindulged on drinking and eating. I am afraid that there is no inheritance, as he mortgaged the house up to the hilt, and after realising any assets that he might have had was not sufficient, and the bank foreclosed on the loan and the house is closed pending a possible buyer or redemption of the mortgage, unfortunately I do not, or never have had that kind of money or assets, as your father had complete control of the house, and any inheritance I might have had, such was the way of things. But please do not worry, I moved the rest of my belongings out, and after the funeral, a sad affair, as only the undertakers and I attended, and there

was enough money to pay for that. I still have a small income from my grandfather, and your aunt has been most accommodating, as she has been all these years.

All my love to you all,

Eleonor Clarkson.

I showed the letter to Mother H who said, 'You could go back now, he has gone.' I smiled at her and said, 'Well, it is a relief, but I would be going back on my own, if I did, the children only know this house as their home. I shall write to my Mama and send her some money, but my home is here.' She smiled and I also told Gerard and Mary Ann. I can now sort of understand how she reacted after hearing that her mother had died.

September 1935

My life has changed in a very dramatic way. I was so sure that my situation and identity was sure, I am just about adjusting to the change. It all started with a letter from my mother the contents of which stunned me beyond all I have heard from her before.

August 31st 1935
Schoolmasters House,
Three Gates, Sussex

My dearest Anna,
By the time you receive this letter I shall be married to Henry Silvester. This may come as a shock to you, but I am very happy, at last. I gave a letter to Gerard before you left with strict instructions not a request, to give it to you only when I felt that the time was right. Tell Gerard that now is the right time. My darling daughter, please do not think badly of me. Whatever I did was to protect you.

Your loving mother

I was sitting the lounge, and we were just about to have some morning coffee, Gerard had a precious day off, he was sitting near me and I asked him, 'Did my mother give you a letter before we left England?' He gulped and nodded, 'Well this letter from my mother says that now is the right time, she says that she has married the schoolmaster Henry Silvester, I do not understand.'

Gerard got up quickly and went upstairs and after a short time returned with a plain but very expensive envelope, which had faded a little over time. He handed it to me, and said, 'Do you want to be alone, I think that it might be very important, as your mother made me promise to keep it very safe until she said it was time.'

He took my hand and escorted me to the little lounge on the side of the hall, and I sat down. He gave me a little look of love and closed the door, with the letter on the table; I picked it up with shaking hands and opened the envelope with trepidation. What I read tore my composure apart. There were two sheets of paper with my mother's beautiful handwriting.

November 1918
My dearest Anna,

There is more to the story that I told you when you were determined to keep your baby. If you recall I told you that I fell in love with a young man who was not a suitable husband for me, and that I was set to marry Cecil Clarkson, who had money and some position. I told you that I was heartbroken but did as I was told. Shortly before the wedding, a few days I went to the young man and spent time with him the night to be exact and we slept together if you understand what I mean. I went to the next town after and took a train journey back to the village, and took a taxi to the house, saying that I had been to London, I had a valise with a change of clothes, and my parents accepted my explanation, and of course I went through with the marriage, and your father was so drunk afterwards that when I did 'my duty' he was not aware of anything, and when you were born you looked like me, and you were accepted. As you know two years later Ellen was born and we then lived separate lives. I am so sorry to let you know this way; I hope you understand I am so proud of you for being determined to keep your daughter. The young man's name was Henry Silvester. Please forgive me darling, but just look back and you may understand.

Your loving Mother, always.

My blood ran cold; I had lived a lie all my life. I sat there and began to understand why I felt different, and found it so hard to be a 'lady', how I wanted to be useful, but it was not allowed, I also felt ashamed. Mary Ann was born to the schoolmaster and his wife and came to be in service, to me. I felt that she would never forgive me. I do not know how long I sat there, until a little knock at the door, and I jumped and said, 'Yes.'

Mother H opened to the door and asked if I was all right, and I burst into tears, 'I do not know, this letter, Mary Ann is my sister! Well half-sister.' She just said, 'I know my dear.'

I looked at her as she sat next to me, and held my hand, 'How do you know, did Gerard tell you, does everyone know?' She shook her head, 'No my dear, wasn't the letter sealed? No I knew when Mary Ann donated blood for your transfusion, and you recovered better than you might have, as a nurse I know that the match was better than we could have hoped for. Only a sibling with that kind of match could have had a positive reaction like that.' I nodded, 'But she never said.'

Mother H replied gently, 'How could she, you were so precious, and she did it to protect you, after look at what Mr Clarkson did to you. I think that you should be grateful that she did not, in case of the consequences. But you are a strong woman, and you get that from your mother.' I dried my eyes, but then said, 'How can I face Mary Ann? She has a letter as well does she not?' Mother H nodded, 'You will show her your letter, and work it out for yourselves.'

I thanked her, and said that I would go to our room, to collect my thoughts, and asked her to let Mary Ann know where I would be. I went to our bedroom unable to talk to anyone else, and sat on a chair by an open window, it all made some sense, how Mary Ann became my personal maid, how she was able to come with us to Canada, what a sacrifice my mother and our father made to let us go, did Mr Silvester know that he was my father?

I heard a little noise after the front door opened and closed, as Mary Ann arrived, and she was given her mail. I heard footsteps up the stairs, a door slam, then quiet. It seemed a long time before there was a knock at the door, and a very confused almost angry looking Mary Ann walk in, with her letter and another two pieces of paper.

She stood in the middle of the room, and said almost defiantly, 'Why has my father and your mother got married? They have come from different backgrounds?' I could hardly look her in the eye, 'I'm so sorry Mary Ann, I have a letter from my mother, I think that it will explain something.'

She walked slowly across the room, and took my mother's confession, and said, 'Do you want me to read this? It is addressed to you.' I said shakily, 'Please do it affects you too,' and looked away.

She stood a little away from me as she read the contents slowly, and said, 'Oh My God' and looked at me, I burst into tears, again. 'I'm so sorry, Mary Ann you were my servant, and I did not deserve to be there.'

Mary Ann laughed, 'Oh yes, you did and it makes so much sense, that is why I was sent to be a ladies' maid not a kitchen maid! They wanted us to be together, and to let me come here with you, I would not have met Harry or had a career, oh and everything.' I could not believe what I was hearing, 'But you were my mentor, to make me a lady!'

She laughed again, 'And you were such hard work, but it was all worth it dear Anna, you are a lady, with many accomplishments. Let me tell you, I always wished I had a mother like yours, and she was so gracious and kind and I think that I loved her as one.'

I laughed this time, 'Well, I always wished that your father could be mine. He was so kind and helpful and if I needed to talk to someone he was there, so yes any love I may have had for a father it was and is for him.'

Then the tears, happy tears came as we hugged each other, as equals, sisters, God is good to us. After a little while, we recovered our decorum, and I asked Mary Ann what the two pieces of paper were, and she showed me, they were baptism certificates, a little delicate so we opened them carefully. They stated that we were christened in the same church, me in 1898 in the September, and Mary Ann in September 1899, with twelve months between our christenings with Mary Ann being born in late May of that year, so there was about eleven months between us. But it was the godparents that stood out for me, as Henry Silvester was and is my godfather, and my mother was one of her godparents, oh that was so cheering, but I would think it was very difficult for them to be no more than interested parties.

After we had washed our faces in the bathroom, and adjusted our hair, and tidied ourselves up, and Mary Ann had changed into a day dress, we walked downstairs arm in arm, and laughing a little. We walked into the lounge, and everyone stood up, as the children were now, Father H said, 'Well what has happened? You appeared quite shocked!'

Mary Ann and I looked at each other, and we said together, 'We are sisters, our parents wrote to say that they have married.'

They clapped and Harry said, 'At last, we all thought that you were!' I was a bit taken aback, 'But how, after we were not aware ourselves until today.'

Gerard said to us as he walked towards us with Harry, 'Well, it was when Mary Ann donated her blood after your operation, you recovered better than you might have done, and you are both so devoted and attuned to each other.'

Harry came to me and hugged me tight, 'My sister in law, hey I am so happy at last to greet you as such, and he kissed me on the cheek.'

Gerard hugged Mary Ann and said the same to her, and the children were so happy, and Jarred said, 'My Auntie and Uncle, we are cousins,' and the boys jumped up and down. Mother and Father H were very happy and Father H said, 'Well I think that this calls for a celebration, I will find a bottle of champagne, to toast you and your parents and that they have now brought you together.' And he went out to the cellar. One person who didn't seem so happy was Louisa, who looked a little confused and lost, so I went and sat next to and held her close, 'What is wrong Louisa, are you not happy for us? Nothing has changed.'

She squirmed a little, and said, 'But what does it mean to me, you adopted me, I do not have a family.' I held her close and said, 'But these are your family, let me explain, your Mama was Gerard's cousin, but we did not know, Grandma Marie Claire was your Mama's aunt, and sister to Louisa who was your mama's mama. So Ellen and Jarred are your second cousins, so they are related to you, and to Father Gerard, you are as much family to us as Mary Ann is to me. We all love you very much, and so far as I am concerned you are my daughter, I could not have loved you more.' Louisa hugged me, and I kissed her forehead, and Scuffy who was sitting quietly started to yap and jump a little, and Louisa went over to the children who hugged her in turn, and she joined with the family and she asked Mary Ann if anything had changed, and Mary Ann said, 'I am sure not, I am still your proper auntie,' which she explained about adopting a friend as an aunt.

After Father H brought in a bottle of champagne, and Harry and Gerard brought out glasses, all except for Henry and Louisa had some champagne but they had glasses of soda, and we lifted our glasses to the newlyweds, and to a happy future. A few days later Mary Ann and I sent a telegram to the village in Sussex, which said, 'Wishing you every happiness all understood, love from your daughters Anna and Mary Ann.'

We felt so much happier when we sent that telegram, and also sent by mail a cheque from all of us towards a present, and between us, Mary Ann and I thanking them for giving us the chance to go to Canada.

Later Gerard told me something that warmed my heart, he had met Henry Silvester in the village and had told him that he was working at Three Gates as a medic, and Henry had asked after Mary Ann and I, and then asked if he had made my acquaintance, which he said when he could see me, and Henry said, 'That's good, she needs a friend.' Which in hindsight showed that he cared. I was amazed but Gerard said he had been thinking back, and a lot of things made sense. He also said, 'But do not think for a minute that you were then and now not a lady, after all you are a daughter of a lady, you just had a very caring nature as well, which you were not able to use then, but have since. I hate to say it, but Cecil was a bit of an upstart as my father would put it!'

I laughed and thanked him for the memory.

3rd October 1935

I am so sad again, we have lost another friend. We received a telegram from Montreal where Mabel had gone to stay with her sister. Mother H and I were in the house alone with just Scuffy, who wanted to go for a walk as Louisa was at school. I was just going to get my coat and his lead, when there was a knock at the door and Mother H signed for a telegram which was addressed to Harry. Then she asked me to take her to the hospital to give it to Harry, and I said that I was not exactly sure of the directions, could we not get a taxi cab, but she assured me that she knew the way and would direct me. So I put Scuffy's lead on, took the motor car keys, and Mother H put on her coat and hat, and put the telegram into her bag and left word with Helen that we might be away for a while. Mother H and I with Scuffy went to the car. I was confident to start the car, turn it around, and when we all were inside set off to the hospital. Mother H held Scuffy's lead as he sat quietly next to her as she directed me through the main part of the town as it was late morning, there were some cars around, but I just drove confidently and carefully and followed her directions. After about twenty minutes, we arrived at the entrance of the hospital, and I parked in a space near the entrance, and Mother H went into the hospital, after handing Scuffy's lead to me and stroking his head, and said, 'Stay, Scuffy, you cannot go in with me.' He whined a little but when I patted the space next to me, he moved over onto the seat. Scuffy sat patiently with me, as I watched people toing and froing into the hospital. What seemed an hour, but when I looked at my wristwatch (a present from Gerard for my birthday) it was only about twenty minutes, Mother H came out, followed by Harry, and Father H and Gerard. They waved to us and went to the family car and Mother H came back to my motor car and got in. I asked her what was going on and she said that she would explain when we arrived home. Intrigued but wishing to stay calm, I reversed the car and drove back to the house, with only a little prompting of directions this time, and when we arrived back at the house and I had placed the car in a safe position behind the house, we went back into the house, stopping for a moment near a tree as Scuffy wished to relieve himself. He seemed a little frustrated as he hadn't had a proper walk, but as a very obedient chap he went into the house and as I took off his lead, and my coat, he followed us obediently into the lounge.

There were voices coming from the study and Mother H motioned for me to sit down as she sat down next to me on the sofa. I asked her again what was the urgency and she told me that Harry's mother Mabel had died, and asked for him to contact his aunt and to make arrangements, to bring her body back for burial. I felt so sad, and Mother H said that she had no details, and it was possible that Harry was going to call his aunt as he needed to make arrangements for her funeral. I was so numb it was such a shock, and so numb that my emotions were not engaged. Father H came in to us, and came to me and gave a little kiss on the cheek and thanked me for taking Mother H to the hospital, and he sat with Mother H and held her hand after we had sat down again. 'I'm afraid Mabel did not get over losing Stanley, he was very much her other half. She went into a decline and did not want to eat, and her health deteriorated and sort of lost the will to live. As you may well expect, Harry is very upset, but our boy Gerard is there to support him, and he will go with Harry to collect her body, apparently she has already got a burial plot next to Stanley, and they just need to take a coffin. Harry and Gerard are taking a leave of absence, and they are going today. I am going to arrange the funeral as Stanley left me the money for that.' He looked at Mother H and she laid her head on his shoulder and he held her tight. Gerard came into the lounge then and I stood up as he came to me. 'I guess Dad has told you, Harry is going to pack a bag, and I am going with him, we will go shortly. Dad will you take us to the station?' he said to his father. He looked at me and said, 'You may need to be here when the children come home, and Mary Ann is coming back in a cab, so that you can explain to them Anna, will you be all right?' he asked with a solemn look on his face. I nodded and I held his arm for a moment. Gerard left the room with his father, and Mother H and I went to the kitchen to ask Helen if she would prepare a packed lunch for Gerard and Harry as they might need to wait before they could get refreshments. Mother H and I waited at the front door to see them out, with a bag with their sandwiches in. Gerard and Harry came downstairs almost together, with small suitcases. Father H gave them an envelope of money for their expenses, which Harry said that he would pay him back but Father H just said 'What are friends for, when this all over, we can reckon up, just go my boy, with our best wishes, let us know when you are returning and I can arrange things this end. Harry please consider us as your family and we are here to support you. Son, take care of your good pal.'

Harry could hardly speak, but just shook hands with his father, kissed his mother good-bye, and kissed me also whispering, 'Look after them Darling, they are going to need a lot of support' meaning Mary Ann and Henry. I nodded, and hugged Harry, as did Mother H before we saw them off.

Mary Ann arrived later in the afternoon as did the children, and I collected Ellen, with Mary Ann and we talked during the journey, it was good to be together. Mary Ann, like me, was numb and a little sad. I expect that it would affect us more once they brought her body back. It was getting a little dark when we travelled back, and I put the 'headlamps' on to show our way back, Ellen chatted away about her day at college. When we arrived back, and went into the house, Henry was the first to greet Mary Ann, 'Mama, where is Dad and

Uncle Gerard, Aunt Marie said when you get back she would tell us all.' Ellen was intrigued, so I said that she should take her college bag up to her room and join us for tea in the dining room and Mother H would explain why their fathers had gone away so suddenly.

Louisa was with Jarred and Scuffy was sitting near her. Tea was laid out on the table, with hot soup, sandwiches and some fruit cake, with tea and cold drinks. As there were no men at the table, and she asked us to bow our heads for a short prayer, we were used to doing this when we sat down for main meals, but only when we were all there, she said, 'I feel that we need to say grace and together pray for our men. Dear Lord, we thank you for our food, for those do not have enough to eat. We would also ask you to take care of Gerard and Harry as they make their train journey to Montreal, keep them safe. Amen.' And we all said 'Amen'.

As we passed the sandwiches around, and I stood up to serve the soup, Mother H explained why Gerard and Harry had gone away to Harry's aunt as his mother had died. Henry went very quiet, and Jarred who was sitting next to him, touched his arm, and Henry didn't flinch as I thought he might, but just bowed his, Jarred said, 'I'm so sorry Henry, Dad will look after your Dad, and I will look after you if you will let me, that's what friends are for.' Henry looked at Jarred, and just said, 'Thanks coz.'

Louisa picked up on the mood around the table, and said in a quivery voice to Mary Ann, 'Has she gone to be with Uncle Stanley? Cos she was lonely.' Mary Ann brushed away a tear and hugged Louisa, who put it so simply, and said, 'Yes I would hope so.' Ellen was sitting between Mother H and I and she also brushed away a tear, 'Oh Loulou, your simple faith is so reassuring, yes we all want to believe that.'

Father H arrived back about fifteen minutes after we had started eating and he said that he had seen Gerard and Harry off on the train, which takes about three hours to reach their destination, and there was a small buffet car on the train, but they only had sold snacks and hot drinks, so the packet of sandwiches and cake would keep them fed until they arrived. He joined us at the side of the table next to Mother H and I went to ask for more hot soup. He explained a little more, and reassured Mary Ann that he would contact the undertakers the next day as well as the pastor. Scuffy had been sitting in his basket even though we were eating, but he was given his supper then, and he wagged his tail when Father H arrived home. When we cleared the table and the kitchen help took the plates out, we went to the lounge and listened to the news. After about 7 p.m. Louisa went up to bed, and I went up with her, and Ellen went to the library to study or try to, but after half an hour, she came back to the library and said that she couldn't concentrate, so asked if she could read her workbook in the lounge as she didn't want to be on her own. I sat with Mary Ann and we chatted quietly, and the boys went upstairs quietly for once and they did their homework. Mary Ann and I talked for a while, and then we went to our respective bedrooms, after saying goodnight to Mother and Father H who hugged and kissed us both. We looked in on our boys who were about to get into bed, and said 'Goodnight' to them and then checked on Louisa, and Ellen who was about to go to bed, and kissed them goodnight, and Scuffy had settled into his basket, after Ellen had taken him for his night time trip out into the garden. We sat in Gerard's and my room with a glass of hot milk, and sat on the sofa, Mary Ann relaxed and seemed to let go, and she started to cry, and I held her close, and I could feel tears pricking my eyelids, and we sat together crying silently. After Mary Ann's tears had subsided, she and I went to the bathroom and washed our faces. We both felt that we could not sleep alone that night, so I suggested that she might sleep in our room perhaps in our bed, and she suggested top to toe, and I thought that might be a good idea, as we would feel that we were not alone. So she went to their room and got ready for bed, and I had put one set of pillows down the opposite ends of the bed, after untucking the bottom end and putting a hot water bottle each end. I also put some more wood and coal on the fire to fire it up a little. I had just put my nightgown on and a wrap and there was a knock at the door, I said 'come in' as there was a hesitation and Mother H came in with two glasses of hot milk on a tray, she said that she saw Mary Ann who said that she was going to spend the night in our room, and she saw how the bed was arranged, and laughed and confided that she and her sister Louisa slept like that when they stayed away from home before they both married, as they shared a room at home. She understood that this was not possible for us before, and saw no harm in it. As Mary Ann knocked and came in, and greeted Mother H I confided that I had not shared a room at home, and felt lonely until Mary Ann came. Mary Ann gave a little shy smile, and Mother H kissed us both goodnight, and left the room. I thanked Mary Ann as we drank our hot milk, and she thanked me back. We chatted for a while before we settled down to sleep, but sleep did not come easily, Mary Ann started to cry quietly, and I sat up, and went to her end and asked her what was the matter, she told me that although her mother's death did not affect her unduly, she felt very sad for Mabel, and for her loneliness, and for Harry as he and Gerard went to collect her body and her effects. I thought, let convention go for tonight, and told her to move her pillows back next to mine, and she did, and I tucked the sheets etc. back in and settled her next to me, and said that it was better if our heads were the same end, and she laughed a little through her tears, I stroked her head until she settled, and turned over to sleep; after Gerard's alarm clock, I was getting up earlier in the morning! We slept side by side for two nights, which on the second night passed by a little more peacefully as we gained strength from each other, and this helped for us to reassure the children, especially Henry who missed his father, although Father H was happy to chat to him if he or Jarred needed any reassurance or to answer any questions they might ask.

Father H was true to his word and made arrangements with the undertakers and the pastor. Gerard and Harry contacted him to say when they would arrive with Mabel's coffin. They were met at the station by Father H and the undertakers who took the coffin from the guard's van with dignity and ceremony, to place in a special car which was used as a hearse and once inside, took the coffin to their chapel of rest. Father H took Gerard and Harry back to the house with all of Mabel's effects, her clothes, books and papers. Harry appeared to be very subdued, and so did Gerard, and he told me that Harry, once they arrived at his aunt's house and they settled down for the night, he became very upset, so they shared a room, apparently it had two beds in, and they sat up half the night talking about their childhood, and how Harry's mother had been such a lovely kind lady. After hearing this I confided that Mary Ann and I did the same, as I felt lonely and so did she, and we both missed our men, and he smiled and said he was happy that as sisters and equals, we could give that support at last, and I was glad that he accompanied Harry as they were best friends and as close as brothers.

Mary Ann and I were to have our men back, and although Harry still seemed a little withdrawn, Mary Ann showed him such gentle love and support he seemed to feel part of a loving family, and gained strength from all of us.

1 November 1935
Mabel's funeral was a solemn affair; we used Stanley's old horse who was still fit and well, and Father H's horse to pull the horse drawn hearse and we went in the two cars, and Gerard and Harry

rode the two horses to the undertakers where they were hitched to the carriage with dark ribbons on their bridles behind their heads. Gerard and Harry walked with the hearse and the undertakers the short distance to the church, and as we were waiting outside as the hearse arrived, we took our places at the front of the church, we were touched to see how many people came to pay their respects, as it was less than a year since Stanley had died. The service was emotional again, with all of us dabbing our eyes, and again Gerard helped Harry with the eulogy. Harry's aunt had made the journey with her son, and we accommodated them at the house for the few days that they stayed.

After the funeral Gerard and Harry went back with the hearse and rode them back and they returned the horses to the stable, and joined us with our guests from the funeral who were about 20 in all, in the dining room where a buffet was laid out. Father H again stood up and gave a little speech remembering Mabel. We all sat together this time, the children mixed together as a family and no one saw anything wrong with this, and Father H just said that as my mother and Mary Ann's father had married, that made us a united family without going into details, which cheered us a little, as we all felt the loss of such a lovely gentle lady.

December 31st 1935
As I look back on this year there have been some bright moments, with Ellen graduating, and my learning to drive (against my wishes) and Ellen starting at college, but it has been sadly overshadowed by the deaths of Harry's parents who were friends and godparents to Louisa, and we loved and missed them. Christmas was a subdued affair, we gave clothes and gifts and food for the poor, and went to church, giving thanks for our being fed and warm, and for our families. I wonder what next year holds. Strange, but I miss Mama and

Henry Silvester, my real father, but I cannot give him that name. I will have to think what I can call him. I did of course write to Mother and recounted the events, and also sent a note from Mary Ann, and sent some money for Christmas.

1936 January 31st
The winter snow had arrived in December and our lovely horses were put to work clearing the snow, two at a time going down either side of the street at the end of our drive and they were sure footed as usual and happy to be working, we used all the horses, except for Stanley's horse, who was quite elderly now, and Father H's horse who was almost as old as Stanley's horse, but could still be ridden, and he (the horse Jasper) was a little unhappy as was Stanley's horse (Joseph) but they were led out to the corral which had been swept and cleared and hay put in a corner, so that they could move around and exercise, with one of us checking on them. I did think of putting something over their backs, and spoke to Norbert, and he suggested that we sew ties on to a blanket to go around their necks and under their middles, but he said that their coats were thick enough, but agreed to help me as they were not moving around very much. What a lovely helpful man he is. Both he and Helen are so good to us. Helen has a young lady who comes in to help in the kitchen and another lady who does the cleaning as we are a busy household.

Gerard has mentioned that he and Father H will be going up to the logging camp, such as it is, to check on the families there and the people who live in the cabins there, in the spring, once the snows have gone. I told him that was a generous thing to do, but couldn't he go with Harry, as I had noticed Father H looking a bit more tired than usual, although he had cut down his days at the hospital, and had taken more of a consulting role, and he told me that he had also suggested something like that to his father only to be told that

Father H was still fit and in fine health to go, so dropped the subject, so all I could ask that he take good care of his father, which he said that he always would, and I also suggested that he take one of the younger horses besides Jasper, just in case, and when he asked why, I said that they could alternate riding horses, as Jasper was getting older, and he said that he would, although he was sure that Father H would only ride Jasper as they were such great friends, and I could understand that.

March 31st 1936
True to their word, Gerard and Father H went off a week ago, and I have been concerned about them every night, and prayed for their safety and wellbeing, only God can help them now, why do I feel like this? On a brighter note, Henry is still intent on being an animal doctor, and spends a lot of time with the horses and goats, of which one nanny goat is 'pregnant' and he and Norbert thinks that one of the mares, which Father H bought about 18 years ago, night be in foal, and he thinks that Jasper might be the father, as he thinks that Jasper had been very 'attentive' as he put it (Henry) with her and Norbert, who knows so much about horses thinks so too, so we will look after her.

April 30th 1936
My heart is broken; I have lost a wonderful lovely man, who has been like a father to me all these years. I have to put pen to paper before I forget, but how can I? Gerard and Father H were late coming back from their visit to the logging camp, and Father H was riding the younger horse, and Gerard was leading Jasper slowly, as Jasper was limping, and even Gerard looked tired. We led the horses into the barn, and Father H got off the horse then, and settled the young horse after removing the saddle and gave her a rub down and some

food. Henry and Norbert looked after Jasper, but Father H refused to leave his beloved friend, and sat on a bale of hay, and insisted having his refreshments there, such devotion! Even Mother H couldn't persuade him, so we made a bed up for him next to Jasper's stall. By the time this had happened, Jasper was breathing heavily, and in obvious pain, Norbert had called the veterinary surgeon who arrived about two hours after they had arrived home, he checked Jasper's fetlock, a bone in his leg. He gave Jasper an injection to ease his pain, but confided that due to Jasper's age, about 40 years old, that his body might not be able to heal. He said that he would call back the next day to see how Jasper was. Father H refused to go indoors, so one of us stayed with them, Henry, Jarred and Gerard and I with Ellen staying for a few hours when she arrived back from college. Sadly Jasper did not improve, and when the veterinary surgeon visited the next day, he thought so as well, and felt it kindest to put him down, but we all asked him to give Jasper an injection instead of a bullet, so he gave Jasper an injection to make him sleepy, so he lay down on his side, and then gave him another injection to make him comfortable, but would eventually just die quietly in his sleep. The first injection took about five minutes, when he wobbled a bit and then went down, and after about another five minutes, the veterinary surgeon gave him another injection and Jasper just faded away, and after about two hours his great heart stopped and he died, to our great sadness, as one by one we said goodbye to this wonderful old horse. Finally after they covered up Jasper's body and Father was persuaded to get up with help and go indoors at last, as Norbert and the boys removed dear Jasper's body and buried him next to the old mule.

Once inside, Father H was helped upstairs to his and Mother H's room, and helped to bed where he stayed for the rest of the day. Gerard told me after supper what had happened to Jasper and father

H. They were returning from the cabin and coming home, when Jasper stumbled and nearly went down, and Father H got off his back quickly and found that Jasper had gone lame, possibly broken a bone in his fetlock, so could walk but not bear a person, so Father H and Gerard took turns to ride the younger horse and Jasper carried their saddlebags. So this made them twelve hours later, as they made slower progress to get back. So only half of my prayer was answered, or maybe it was, they got back safely, but we lost a great four legged friend, and we all felt the loss. But more was to come, as Father H developed a cold which went on to his chest, and Harry ministered to him, and the local doctor to get a second opinion, and the GP diagnosed pneumonia, and that perhaps Father H would not be able to overcome it. He was prescribed some medication which would ease the symptoms, and he visited at least twice a day to see his old friend Gerard senior. Sadly Father H did not get any better and the doctor, George Henderson, said that it was just a matter of time, and Father H seemed to know that too. He called us all to the bedroom, after speaking to Norbert and Helen, with Helen in tears, and Norbert blowing his nose, and they did not look us in the eye as they walked past us. We all went into the bedroom and Mother H sat beside him on the bed, and we sat on the sofa by the side, and chairs near the bed. Father H looked so ill, he was propped up on two pillows, and he seemed to be breathing heavily. He started by talking to Mother H, 'My darling Marie Claire, thank you for being such a wonderful loving wife, and for giving me our son, I am sorry that I have not always been around to spend as much time as I could with you, but believe me that I love you, and only you, please try not to grieve too much for me, I will wait for you,' and she leaned over and kissed him, holding him tightly for a moment, and she sat on the other side of the bed, dabbing her eyes, as he then called Gerard over to him, and Gerard knelt beside him by the bed, and he said, 'Son, I am so proud of you, what you have done, what you have achieved, and your wonderful children, I just ask you to look after your mother,' Gerard nodded, and assured him that he would, and then Father H called me over, and I knelt next to Gerard, who was struggling to keep his composure. Father H said to me, 'My dear Anna, you have been a joy to me, thank you for giving us our lovely grandchildren and for Louisa, you have become a well presented lady. I know that you love the horses as I do so I am leaving them to you, as I know that you will take care of their welfare.' I shook my head, and thanked him and promised to take care of them.

He then spoke to Harry and Mary Ann, telling them how happy he was to have them so close to us, and them part of the family under his roof, he felt them his children by adoption, and they thanked him. The children went forward to kiss him, even Henry who loved him dearly, and he was also charged to take care of the horses, and he nodded, poor Henry, he is only nearly 13 years old, and he was in tears. Harry went to Gerard as we sat down for a little, and they left the room, as Gerard's shoulders started to shake, and Harry put his arm around Gerard's shoulders, and both Mary Ann and I looked at Mother H who nodded, as she went back to his side as he went to sleep.

Mary Ann and I went outside with the children, who were all in tears, especially Louisa, the door opened, and Mother H asked if Scuffy could be brought, as Father H just called for Scuffy, so we called his name, as he was on the landing, and he went to Mother H and he was so good, he went quietly with Mother H and stayed there in the room with them. We went downstairs, and to the lounge, where tea had been laid out, Harry and Gerard sat together at the table, talking quietly, Louisa ran to Gerard, and gave him a hug, and he looked at me over her head, and his eyes were red, but dry. Henry sat next to his father after giving Gerard a little hug too, Ellen sat down with us, and she was also very quiet, Henry sat with Jarred and they talked quietly, all of us feeling the impending loss of a charismatic loving caring man. We were not able to eat very much as our emotions were in turmoil.

No one slept very much that night, our husbands stayed downstairs, our sons went to their room, but just lay on their beds, looking at the ceiling, with a little light on, as Mary Ann and I looked in to say 'Goodnight'. We also checked on Ellen and Louisa, and whilst Louisa drifted into a fitful sleep, Ellen sat in a corner, reading a book near a bedside light. Mary Ann and I sat in the little lounge chatting, remembering our time here, and the good memories that we had.

The next morning we woke up from our fitful dozes on the chairs in the library where we went later, and went up to Mother H's room, and gently knocked on the door, and there was a little yap, and Mother H came and let us in. Scuffy was sitting quietly next to the bed, and Mother H beckoned us in. She told us that Scuffy had kept her company during the night, as she could not sleep, and Father H was sleeping fairly peacefully.

I arranged for her to have some breakfast on a tray, and as Mary Ann stayed with her, took Scuffy down for his food, but Louisa came out of the bedroom, and called him, and he ran to her and went downstairs with her.

Sadly Father H did not wake up but died in his sleep about 11 p.m. in the evening of the next day, after he spoke to us.

Gerard for a while was a broken man, and Harry was such strength, giving back the love that Gerard had shown him when his parents had died. I was able to give Gerard some comfort after a while, and when we slept together again, he cried in his sleep at times, and I just held him, and we grieved together. I wrote to my mother and Henry to tell them the sad news, and two weeks later received a telegram offering their love and condolences to all of us.

The funeral was an emotional affair, we knew that Father H had touched many lives, and even though they might not be able to leave their posts perhaps like us drivers or shopkeepers, but as the funeral hearse was driven through the town, people stopped and men doffed their hats, and ladies bowed their heads, as the cortege slowly made its way to the church, which was packed with members of the community. Mother H, Mary Ann and with Ellen and Louisa sat in the carriage, with Norbert driving the carriage with, on this occasion, Helen sitting up front with him. We all wore hats, even Louisa who really did not like wearing hats, but as she loved him, she agreed, what a brave little ten year old. Scuffy was with us too, and he was very subdued, picking up on the sadness of the occasion. Mother H had asked that we meet at the undertakers and make our progress through the town for people if they wanted to pay their respects. When we arrived at the church we all went in, even Norbert and Helen, whilst the undertakers took care of the horses. Jarred, Henry, Harry and Gerard travelled with the hearse, the boys walking and Gerard and Harry sat up on the hearse. When they brought the coffin in, Gerard, Harry and Jarred, with an undertaker, carried it and brought it to the front. Henry walked behind and then sat with Mary Ann. Gerard and Harry sat on the other side. Mary Ann and I sat either side of Mother H who was being very sedate, and she wore a black net veil to hide the redness of her eyes. We had all shed tears, even Gerard and Harry, and the pastor's voice broke a little, such was the standing of Gerard senior in the community.

When it came for the eulogies Gerard went up to the lectern, and Harry went up to stand by him, with his own little speech, and Gerard started to speak, but after about two paragraphs, he faltered and his voice went, and good friend that he had always been dear

Harry and Gerard allowed him to read on, and regained his composure. Poor dear Gerard, this has taken him to very much a difficult phase, I wonder if he will recover, I know now how strong the relationship between him and his father, and that last fateful journey to Moose Falls and up to the mountain was to be their last. Harry finished Gerard's speech, and his own, the funeral service carried on, and in the conclusion, the pastor said that Gerard senior had asked to have his body cremated, not buried as was normal. So instead of the procession to the graveyard, it would be to the railway station, where the coffin would be transported to the crematoria, and the pastor and Harry and Gerard would go there to do the committal, so we all filed out, and followed the hearse to the railway station, and as the train came in, the coffin was loaded into the guard's van and placed on trestles, and Gerard and Harry took their leave with Mother H and us, and Jarred and Henry went back to the undertaker's, and rode the two horses back to the house, arriving about half an hour after us. We had already unhitched the horses and let them run in the corral, it being late spring when everything was in bloom, but we didn't feel very spring like. We all went indoors and made ready to receive our guests, who were many, and Mother H sat on a sofa, and had removed her hat and veil, and there about 50 people attending, this appeared to be about half of the church congregation. Jarred being only sixteen and a half years old was a very good host, and he greeted the guests as they came in and they were offered seating around the lounge, with a large table filled with plates of sandwiches and pastries and cakes. Although Helen and Norbert went with us to the funeral, which was right and fair, she had engaged about six young ladies, and six young men to wait on the guests with drinks and food, and Helen had quickly left the carriage on our arrival and went in the back door to check on the arrangements.

Ellen, Louisa, Mary Ann and I spent time with Mother H and circulating to talk to the guests. After a while, when people had settled and eaten, the local GP stood up and gave a little speech on how long he had known Gerard senior. For a long time, in fact they had been to medical school together, and qualified, but went different ways with Gerard senior was a philanthropic man, giving of his time to minister to people who could not pay for his services, and of his love of horses, when in 1919 he bought two horses who would have been set loose as their owners had not reclaimed them, and the two recent horses were also 'rescued'. He had also offered to give a home to Stanley and Mabel Manton, and Harry, Mary Ann and Henry, because he cared. He finished by saying that he would miss the older man, and everyone murmured in assent. I asked as a mere woman, to say something, and people laughed good naturedly. I looked at Mother H who nodded, and I stood by the fireplace. 'When I arrived here from England with Gerard junior and my friend, now 'stepsister" and smiled at Mary Ann, who smiled, 'Gerard's father welcomed me with open arms, he became more of a father to me than my own father, Mr Clarkson. I have been and am eternally grateful for the kindness and love that he has shown me, our children and Mary Ann. I will miss him. Thank you,' as my voice broke.

There was a little wave of applause. 'In the absence of my husband, I would ask that you would raise your glasses to a wonderful kind man, husband, father and father in law and friend.' I finished as everyone stood and raised their glasses to a wonderful old man. I sat down next to Mother H who grasped my hand and thanked me, with tears in her eyes. I just sat there amazed by my temerity.

After about another hour, after people paid their respects to Mother H who thanked them graciously, and said goodbye to the children, and as I stood by the door to say goodbye, some of them after shaking me by the hand, said things like, 'Nice speech,' 'Well done Mrs Horan,' 'Thank you for having us,' 'Anything we can do?'

As they had all left, we returned to the lounge, as the waitresses and waiters had finished clearing away the plates, glasses and food. I asked Mother H about their payment, and was told that Gerard had already taken care of that, they had already been paid. I thanked her, and she said that she was feeling rather tired, and would retire to her room for a little rest. I asked her if she needed any help and she replied that no, she just wanted to have a rest and would see us later. So we respected that, and as she walked slowly out of the room, we noticed that she looked a little older and diminished.

We let Scuffy in from the garden where he was happily playing with the goats, gently, and when he saw Louisa and Ellen, he ran to the gate and was let out, and went back into the house for something to eat and drink, and he settled in the library with Louisa as she listened to a program on the wireless set, and we changed into day clothes, but with darker colours, and went downstairs to join Louisa in the library. Louisa was then sent upstairs to change out of her dark clothes, to some brighter ones. When she returned, Jarred, Henry and Ellen asked if they could attend to the horses, and I went with them, to occupy myself. Mary Ann joined us and between us five, we groomed the horses, made sure they had some food and Jarred and Henry helped to milk the goats, of which there were now three nanny goats, one nanny kid, and two billy kids who were only a few weeks old. This kept us occupied for a pleasant hour, and as we finished our chores we went indoors, and went to the downstairs cloakroom, and one by one we washed our hands, and changed our shoes. As we emerged into the hallway the telephone rang, and Mary Ann motioned for me to answer it, and so I did, 'Anna Horan, Horan house, who is calling.'

The voice on the other end was Harry's, who said, 'Hello Anna, we arrived half an hour ago, and we are about to go into the crematorium. I am in the manager's office. We will go through the committal and return home. If we telephone could you collect us from the station dear Anna, it should still be light, and one of us will drive back.'

I said that I would be happy to, but I would take Ellen with me to help with directions, and he laughed, he knew that I still would not drive out on my own. I asked to speak to Gerard, and he passed the telephone to him, and he said hello, with a slightly strained voice, and I asked him if he was all right, he said yes, but was glad that Harry was with him, he then said that Harry wanted to say a few words to Mary Ann so I passed the earpiece to Mary Ann so that she could speak to Harry, and after a few words, she put the telephone down, and then hugged me. We got another call about three hours later to say that they were at the station. I asked Mary Ann if she was ready to come with me, and she nodded and went to get her coat, and then Jarred said he knew the way and wanted to come, and Louisa said that she wanted to come, and so did Scuffy, who yapped and wagged his tail. I took a deep breath and said that I was taking the small car and there were only two spare seats, but Jarred suggested that I used the family car, and we could all go, but I tried to say that I was not happy driving the large car, and Jarred said, 'Don't worry Mom, I will sit with you, I will help you,' and when I asked why, he replied a bit sheepishly, 'Well Dad let me learn the controls, and drive it around a bit.' And when I asked him how far was a bit, he replied, 'Oh just down the back roads and never on my own, I want to get a driver's license but he said I had to wait until I was 17' as he looked at me pleadingly. I looked at Ellen, who instead of being annoyed, tried to stifle I just said, 'Anyone else want to go along as well?' and she smiled and said, 'No Mama, I will stay with

Grandma in case she needs anything. Good luck Mama.' I went over to her and hugged my beautiful daughter, who looks so much like her father, and she waved to us as we left.

I just said, 'Well we had better get going, your fathers are waiting at the station,' as I took the family car keys, and five of us plus a very excited dog, went to the yard and got into the car, with Jarred sitting next to me, with Henry, and Mary Ann, Louisa and Scuffy in the back as Jarred patiently coached me to manoeuvre the car which seemed to be about three times bigger than my little car. As I turned the car around and safely drove down the drive, I remembered the way to the town, and it was still quite light and there was little traffic. I remembered thinking how glad I was that I did not consume any alcohol. Jarred just helped me with my positioning and I remember also too that steering was harder. I was concentrating very hard, and Jarred was talking quietly to me for such a young man, he is very assured. After what seemed ages, but only about 15 minutes we arrived at the station, where Gerard and Harry were waiting. As I brought the car to a stop, and switched the engine off, Jarred hugged me and told me I did very well, and I thanked him. I just sat there for a moment, my head reeling, another lesson learned. Gerard opened the door and he took my hand, and I turned and stood up and clung to him, as he hugged me and said, 'Well done Darling, but why did you bring the family car? I thought that you didn't like driving it.'

I shuddered and then said, 'Well our children wanted to come, and there wasn't enough room in my car so Jarred suggested I use this car, and he sat next to me and er helped me to manoeuvre. Oh and by the way, you didn't tell me that you were giving him driving lessons' I finished, looking him in the eyes. Gerard smiled, 'Well, he is eager and he has only been driving on the back roads, and totally supervised.'

Mary Ann had got out of the car to embrace Harry, as did Henry. Jarred however stayed in the car and had actually moved over to the driver's seat, and pleaded with his father to drive, but he was told, 'Only when you are 17 when you get your driver's license, and only on the back roads, until then, move over son.' Jarred reluctantly moved over and Harry got in next to him, and Henry and I joined Mary Ann and Louisa with Scuffy in the back of the car, and Gerard drove us back. Mary Ann squeezed my hand and said, 'Well done, you drove very well, we felt very safe dear, didn't we Louisa?' who nodded, as I relaxed in the back, and just thanked God that we didn't have an accident. We arrived home with no problem and once the car was parked around the back and we all went into the house, I went to the kitchen to ask for a tray of food for Gerard and Harry and some fresh coffee. I went back to the lounge and Ellen was there waiting for us, and said that she had checked on Mother H whilst we were out and she was asleep, so remained on a chair on the landing reading a book until we returned home, about an hour later, when she met us downstairs. Gerard and Harry went upstairs to change from their dark suits, and returned later in light grey suits, with Gerard wearing a black armband. We all drank coffee, that is except for Jarred, Henry and Louisa who had tea or hot chocolate. Gerard recounted the journey to the crematorium, which was a new experience, but was his father's wishes. Apparently the 'ashes' or remains would be returned by rail and special messenger in a sealed container. He said it was interesting and quite tasteful, and mentioned that Hindus and other different religions used this practice, and his father had said that the body is just a shell, once the soul has left it. He did say this after Louisa went to bed as he did not wish to frighten or distress her.

July 15th 1936

Things slowly returned to normal, but there did not seem to be a normal way anymore, there was someone or something missing, and I waited for about four weeks, and it was as if we were waiting for someone to come back, but he didn't, dear Father had gone, and we all felt it. We all carried on as much as we could, but we couldn't. Gerard was very quiet, except to make small talk with us, and after about six weeks, I asked Gerard as we were getting set to go to bed, and I asked him if he was all right, could I help him, would he just talk to me, and he took my hand and sat me down next to him, and held both my hands and looked at me, and said, quietly, 'I'm sorry I've been so distant, I had a lot on my mind, not least sorting Dad's will. Did you know that he left you five thousand dollars, as well as the horses?' I shook my head, and he continued, 'He left the house to me, and after a bequest to Mom making her secure and independent, and to Norbert and Helen for their future there is quite a lot of money. But darling Anna, it is not the same, the heart has gone out of this house, Dad was the mainstay, he held everything together, and I'd give everything to have him back, he should have retired at least three years ago. But he wouldn't. There is something else, things are going on in Europe, bad things, and I want to be nearer to England. We are going back, I want to take you back to Sussex, and see if the house is still needing a buyer to get your inheritance back.'

At this I burst into tears, partly because I wanted to go back, but to Three Gates? 'You say the heart has gone out of this house, but three Gates had no heart, it was a lonely place,' I said through my tears. He held me close, 'Then we will put a heart into that place, change the name even. Oh and I have had an offer on the house, some developers are very interested, and they are interested in buying the horses' he said casually, and at this, I started, and said vehemently, 'The horses are not for sale, and we are taking them with us, I have the money now. They can buy some horses from the livery stable, after all, he doesn't have many people hiring them, they would benefit from having a secure home and Norbert could help with them.' Gerard laughed and I knew that he was just checking where my loyalties were. He said that he would send a telegram to my father, Henry, to find out the situation with the house, and I said that I would send my mother a telegram also and then write to give details of our return.

Gerard spoke to Mother H who after some thought told us both that she didn't mind going, as long as we took her husband's ashes, that was no problem, and when I told her that I had insisted on taking the horses, she suggested that we might leave Stanley's old horse, and perhaps the mule, and I agreed, hugging her in the process, and she whispered, 'It is a good thing to go home now,' although I insisted that this was my home for nearly 18 years, but I would like to see my mother again, and I had issues with the house, but she said almost what Gerard said, 'The heart of the house is the people in it, and your mother loves you,' and I nodded. Gerard had also asked Harry and Mary Ann who both seemed happy about the idea, so we told the assembled children of the big move, and Louisa asked, 'Where is England Mama?' and Ellen got an atlas from the library and opened the page of the world, and showed her where the British Isles were. Louisa thought that it was such a long way, and I agreed with her and told them of our journey out, but said that was because we landed in Hudson Bay, and showed her where we landed. I proposed that we go to New York Harbour by train and sail from there, which would shorten the sea voyage by a few days, but would be nearer. They asked Gerard and Harry when we would be leaving, and they said when school is finished for the summer, and meanwhile we would get passports from the Canadian ones for Harry,

Henry, Jarred, and Louisa and Mother H and British ones for Mary Ann and I as we still had our birth certificates. It worked out that Ellen would be on my passport, and Jarred on Gerard's passport, and Henry on Harry's passport also, such was the way of things, but it meant that we could go into the USA and then to England. We also had to arrange paperwork for the horses, each one, and for four goats. Harry and Mary Ann sold their house to Norbert and Helen, who with their savings and gift of money and pension from Father H were more than able to pay the asking price for the house, and had been engaged to work as cook and groom to the new owners. Mary Ann and Harry were enthusiastic to come with us, and also asked for their horses to be included, especially as it was Mary Ann's horse was in foal, and Henry was studying animal welfare as well as his regular subjects, and the veterinary surgeon had lent him some books on the subject of horses, we are so proud of him. I am also very impressed with Ellen's progress at the college, but wondered how she would fare when we get back to England, but I am getting ahead of myself. She has taken some examinations and she will have final reports to take with her.

I have had a conversation with Mother H to see what her feelings are about leaving the house as she has been very quiet and diminished. I asked her over coffee one morning how she was coping with her loss, and she looked at me with sad eyes, and said, 'Well you know we were devoted to each other, and spent as much time together, and he held us all together, he was the glue as it were. Now all we have are memories. My dear sweet daughter in law, your coming here with Mary Ann has made us so happy. I will miss the house, but it is emptier without him. It is time to go, there is nothing to keep me here, my sister is gone, so has Riella, but we have Louisa, and my husband's ashes will come with me, I do so wish to meet your mother, she seems quite a lady, and she let you go, now it is time for you to go back.' I went to her and burst into tears, and hugged her close, how generous this lady is. I do love her so, and realised how much I love my mother.

August 20th 1936
There was a little hiccup before we started to pack things up, Louisa went missing with Scuffy; I noticed the house was quiet, without the usual yapping barks we heard every so often, either in the house or in the garden or the orchard, or anywhere. Ellen came downstairs quickly and said that some of Louisa's clothes were missing, and her moneybox was empty, 'She's run off Mama, I found this note,' which she handed to me which read, 'Dear Mama, I am not going without Scuffy, I will seek my fortune with him, Louisa.'

If I were not so worried, I would have laughed, but where could she be? I took the little car with Mother H and Jarred and Henry went to the railway station with Norbert who drove the car, just to see where she might have gone. We had no idea how long she had gone. After about half an hour, Mother H pointed towards a seat near the bus stop, where a small girl with a brown and white dog were sitting, the little girl tried to look inconspicuous, but the dog yapp was Louisa who tried to keep the dog back. I pulled up to the stop and Mother H opened the door, and Scuffy pulled away from her, and jumped into the car with Mother H who made a big fuss of him. I walked around to Louisa and sat with her, and put my hand out to her, 'What is wrong Louisa? Why did you feel that you had to run away?'

She looked ahead and said, 'Well I heard you say what are going to do about Scuffy? I thought you were going to have him put to sleep, and I don't want to go without him.' I held her close, and said, 'Oh my poor little love, I was asking your Dad what we needed to take him to England, in case he might take an illness with him, so we talked to the veterinary surgeon, and he suggested that we spoke to the British Consulate, who advised us to keep him away from other people and animals on the voyage except ours of course, and when we get to England for about six months, and that would be fine. Do you think we would leave this wonderful chap behind? We are taking some goats, and they are not pets.' Louisa said, 'But I have given them names, sorry Mama, I was so afraid.' I hugged her and we got back into the car, with her bundle of clothes, and went to near the station where the others were waiting and went back to the house.

September 6th 1936

The time finally arrived for us to leave; we loaded up the wagons with most of the luggage and pictures and some heirlooms which Gerard did not want to leave behind. Such a lot of things have accumulated over the last 18 years. We also put the four goats that we were taking into one of the carts. There was an emotional farewell with Norbert and Helen, who gave us some food for the horses. We hugged them goodbye for the first and only time, as we also said goodbye to Peapot, yes Peapot the mule, and Hector, Stanley's old horse; they would be company for each other in their old age. Some of us climbed up on to the fronts of the carts, except for Mother H who was driven by Ellen, yes my Ellen with Harry making sure that she drove safely, my children were growing up, and Louisa sat in the seat in the back with Scuffy who sat quietly with just his head showing over the top. We went slowly with the horses, as four were pulling the two carts, and three other were ridden by Henry and I with Mary Ann. Gerard took the first cart, and Jarred drove the other cart, it was quite a procession, with the car going on ahead and as we took one last look at the house, we turned out of the lane towards the town, and towards the station, as we left the lane, I could see a large lorry and two cars going into the drive, and I turned my head around and faced ahead brushing a tear from my eyes.

We made our way steadily to the station and could hear a rumble which was not the train, but as we got nearer I could see that most of the townspeople were there, partly to help us load up, but mainly to see us off. A great cheer went up as we went towards the station, and after we had unloaded the luggage, and boxes, we unhitched the horses, and slowly and gently led them up the ramp into the truck at the back of the train, and tethered them, with the goats in a little stall. Henry and Jarred had agreed to stay with them until we reached New York Harbour, and then when we boarded the ship there would be a rotation of people to look after them. I made sure that they had enough food and drink for the journey, which would take nearly six hours. They left the door slightly open after the ramp had been pulled up. I then joined the rest of the family as we made our goodbyes to as many as possible, and then joined the others in a carriage on the train, as the guard called, 'All aboard!' and we stood at the window waving to all, as the train slowly pulled away from Moose Falls, and gathered speed.

I sat down on one of the seats next to Mother H who was still looking out of the window, facing back, and we took a last look at the scenery of the town, and I lost myself in the memories of the last 18 years, when I arrived as a young bride, just over 20 years old, with a young baby, and expecting another to a strange town, with a different culture, which I adjusted to with Mary Ann and Mother H's help, to be a 'lady' but also to be able to do more than just be a hostess. I could still be useful, and I have taught Ellen to read, and Jarred when he let me, but Jarred is bright and he also asked for Ellen's help. I had taught Louisa to read. I was also able to help in the town, with volunteering to help in the grocer's shop in the town. I also remember the holidays that we spent in the log cabin, lovely, almost frontier, self-sufficient times. How I miss the falls in the forest, all of this...

I felt a tap on my arm as Mother H asked me if I was all right, and I felt that my cheeks were wet, Oh, I didn't notice that I was crying, and she gave me a handkerchief to dry my tears, I told her that I was remembering my time at Moose Falls with affection, and she said, 'I did also, I am happy that your enjoyed your time there, as I did and I came here forty five years ago, just before I had Gerard. But we must look ahead to our new life, and it would seem to be a challenge from what Gerard tells me.'

I agreed and smiled as we looked forward and turned around to face the direction we were travelling. After about two hours, we stopped at a station along the way to take on water for the engine, so we (Gerard, Harry, Mary Ann and I) alighted from the train to stretch our legs, leaving Mother H and Louisa with Scuffy, who remained on the train. Louisa wanted to join us, but I explained that she needed to stay with Mother H to keep her company with Scuffy, and she reluctantly agreed. Ellen asked if she could take a turn with looking after the horses, so we all went to the back of the train, and knocked on the sliding door and Jarred opened it and looked out, Henry joined him and they asked why the train had stopped, and explained about the taking on of water, they said that the horses had started a little, but seemed calm, as this was the first time that they had travelled in a carriage. I asked if they needed relieving or more help as Ellen was offering to go up to the carriage, and neither boy wanted to leave the horses but were happy if Ellen joined them and she climbed up into the carriage with help from her brother, and fortunately she was wearing trousers. I looked into the carriage which was shaded, but there were small windows at the side so they could see some scenery as they went along. They seemed content enough, and the goats were lying down, seemingly asleep. I called to the horses, who turned their heads to me as did Mary Ann and they raised their heads and snorted one by one. Ellen went over to them and stroked their muzzles and assured that they were fine, and would be happy to stay with them for the rest of the journey if she could have something to eat and drink with the boys. I thanked her and Gerard said that he would arrange for some refreshments and we went back to the carriage, and after Gerard had asked for sandwiches and drinks, which he took to the truck at the back with Harry. Mary Ann and I went back to our seats, and Gerard and Harry came back and joined us. Shortly after the train started to move and slowly picked up speed. They asked if we were hungry, and Mother H, Louisa and I said that we were, so they went to the dining car and before long, a table was brought through by two waiters, and then trays of food and drink brought through with cloths, serviettes and cutlery and crockery. I was surprised at the gesture, but Gerard said after they had left that as we could not go to the dining car because of our dog, they would bring the dining car to us, and he patted his inside pocket, and I guessed that he paid more than he might have, and I just smiled and thanked him very much, and started to eat, and noticed that Scuffy was licking his lips and looking very appealing, so filled a plate with some titbits and went to him where he was sitting very meekly next to Louisa, and put the plate down in front of him, and instead of eating fast as he usually did, but sniffed it, and took a piece, bit by and ate it, and we laughed. The journey continued, stopping once again for water, and we checked on the children and horses and goats, who were settled and fine and the children were quite happy.

The long journey came to an end with the train arriving at a stop for the New York Harbour, a short distance from the ship that we were due to board for our journey home. We alighted from the train with our belongings, and papers, tickets, passports, and of course the 'animals' firstly the goats, who were a bit skippy, and needed a little calming down, fortunately they had little harnesses which helped to control them, and they calmed down quickly. The horses were fine, being led out and down the ramp one by one, still with their halters, and they were reasonably well behaved, as they came into the light they started a little, but as we all took a horse each except for Louisa and Mother H, who were looking after Scuffy and Mother H carried the tickets and passports and paperwork. We all went into a large building to register for our voyage, there were no other people there at the time, as we had arrived very early, which was good as we had a lot of luggage, and what was termed as 'livestock' our lovely horses, 'livestock' but it is just a term.

There was apparently a veterinary surgeon who checked the goats to see if they were healthy and fit to travel, and he mentioned that one of the nanny goats was pregnant, as was one of the mares, which we were aware of. Henry asked the veterinary surgeon when the mare might foal, and he thought that about four weeks, if the voyage was reasonably smooth, and he asked Henry what his interest was, and he said that he wanted to be a veterinary surgeon and had been doing a course of study which included animal husbandry. The veterinary surgeon wished him luck, as to all of us on our journey with our precious cargo.

We had our paperwork checked, passports checked, tickets registered and changed some of our money into US dollars, and some to English money at the purser's office in the building before we had our luggage loaded, and went up a lower ramp to a special area that we had requested with a small sort of stable area for the horses and goats where they would travel during the voyage. There were several bales of hay, and a water trough and places to tether the horses. Henry said that he would stay with the horses and goats whilst we found our cabins, and unpacked for the voyage. I thanked Henry, and said to the others that someone or two should keep company with the horses during the voyage, or I would stay with them for the duration, but they all assured me that they would take their turn, even Louisa and Mother H. I was overwhelmed and thanked them and before we went up to our cabins, Mother H asked us to bow our heads for a prayer for the journey, 'Dear Lord, please protect us all on this journey over the ocean to new life, be with us on the smooth days and the not so smooth days, give the captain a straight course, Amen.'

My eyes filled as we all repeated Amen. How strong is this lady's faith, she voiced what I had been praying at the start of our journey.

September 15th 1936
The journey started well enough, we went to our cabins and unpacked some clothes for the voyage, and true to everyone's word there were at least two people with the horses all the time, every day, taking their meals with them, sometimes walking them up and down in the limited space so that they had a little exercise. In the evenings, we would sit with them having a meal, and singing to them. We also milked the nanny goats, for Louisa. Our days went smoothly until one day, halfway through our journey, we noticed dark clouds on the horizon and we seemed to be going towards it, and there seemed to be no way around. I voiced my concerns to Gerard, who asked the purser if this was going to be a bad storm, and he said that it might be, so as we went towards it, I told Gerard that I was going down to the horses, and he said that he would bring the others down. I went as quickly as I could below, and warned Ellen and Henry who were there that we were going towards bad weather, so the rest of the family were coming down to help with the horses. I checked the goats, who were a bit skittish as usual, and they seemed all right. I went to each of the horses and petted each one, and checked the mare who was in foal and checked her. And

Henry said that she was getting on well. After about an hour the ship seemed to move up and down a bit more and we could hear the wind. By that time all the family had joined us and went to each horse, even Louisa came with Scuffy, whose ears were down, even he was a bit wary.

The ship started to heave, and I was getting worried, the horses dropped to their knees, and Henry said this was a safe move, and it might be a reflex, but their eyes started to open wide with fear. As I knelt down near one of the horses, a palomino, I started to pray, I did not realise that I was praying out loud, 'Please Lord, your son asked the storm to be still, we are at your mercy, have I done the wrong thing? I fear for these horses, it is my fault, I have done the wrong thing to bring them with us, I'm sorry,' and I wept as I heard some guns being cocked, and waited for the report as the horses whinnied, but then I heard someone start singing the hymn 'For those in peril on the seas.' For what seemed an eternity, but apparently only half an hour from start to finish, and other voices joined, and I felt a hand on my shoulder as the storm eased, and I opened my eyes and our dear horses were calm again, and after a while as the ship went smoothly they stood up slowly. I breathed a sigh of relief, and looked as I saw four crew members who had the guns, but they had put them down, and one just said, 'Thank the Lord we didn't have to shoot these great horses, I think the hymn helped, we'll be off Ma'am' as I thanked them, and noticed that at least two of these hardened sailors were blowing their noses.

The journey passed without further incident, except for one of the kids which had managed to escape and ran around the 'stabling' area, jumping and running around, almost getting under the horses hooves, but they just looked at him, and as Ellen and Henry were there and they managed to catch the little fellow, and put him back into the pen, and of course cleared up after him.

20th September 1936

Landfall at last! We were so relieved to arrive after such a long way. We had packed our bags and left the cabins, and after the rest of the passengers disembarked, we went to the stabling area and led the horses out down the ramp, and they were so good walking with a lead rein, but the goats were not so good and needed three of us to bring them out and one kid needed carrying, the one who ran around the deck. We tethered the horses, and Louisa with Mother H kept Scuffy on a tight lead, as keeping him away from people and other animals was very important now, in England for the rest of the year at least. We showed our passports, and paperwork for the horses, and there was a veterinary surgeon to check the goats and the horses, with Henry following him, and asking his opinion on the pregnant mare and the nanny goat, the veterinary surgeon thought that the nanny goat was close to birthing, and the mare seemed well, despite the storm halfway through the voyage, but he felt that she was close, and could foal any time during the next few days. After the formalities had been completed, and Gerard had spoken to the captain who had joined us in the shed, he (the captain) said to all of us, 'I'm glad that you all arrived safely, especially these magnificent horses,' he went over to them and stroked the muzzles of each one, and they did not react badly, 'The storm was a bad one, and we have had worse but was as if it almost seemed to calm down real quick, almost like divine intervention' he said with an American accent, but I was not very good at which one. He then asked Gerard where we were going, and he replied East Sussex, near Hailsham, and the captain nodded, Gerard asked him if he could give him some money to cover the clearing up of the deck where the horses were, and the captain was a little unsure for a moment, but Gerard took his wallet out and pulled out some US dollar notes and pressed them into the captain's hand, and I took my purse out and took out some English notes, two pound notes and a ten shilling note and gave them to the captain so that the crew could have a drink here, and Gerard gave the captain them as well and the captain lifted his hat to me, and turned and walked back to the ship.

There was still the matter of getting tickets for the train to Sussex, but Gerard took his document case out and showed me the paperwork for five adults, four children, seven horses, four goats and one dog, with some straw to go in to the rear carriage, which was a 'cattle truck' and some water. I was astounded, and he laughed and said, 'Well you did organise the sea journey, so I thought I would get your father to get the train journey set up, and he mailed these to me about two weeks ago.' I smiled and we arranged for our luggage to be taken to the train terminal and we led the horses, and the goats with Scuffy to the waiting train which was about ten minutes walk. The horses seemed to be content to walk as they had not moved very much for the past almost two weeks, and they skittered a little bit but not much, the mare who was in foal which moved a little slower, and Henry asked to walk her, and once we arrived at the station, we settled the horses and goats first, which we managed with little difficulty. Jarred asked to stay with Henry, who was quite concerned about Mary Ann's horse called Merrilees, who once in the truck appeared quite restless, I had my opinion about that, but stayed silent on the subject. They closed the ramp and the door, and I joined the others as we embarked on the train. Our luggage had been loaded in the goods van, and we found our seats not in first class but second class but I was not used to first class anyway. Gerard said that he had telephoned Mother and Father to let them know that we had arrived safely and were taking the train to the village, and anticipated arriving mid afternoon. I had to adjust to English time as we all did, and we changed our timepieces to 1.45 p.m. British Summer Time. As the train pulled away, I thought back for a moment on the sea voyage and it would seem that I was preoccupied with the horses, but everyone still managed to have time to enjoy the time, taking meals with others, but Scuffy had to remain in the cabin with someone and he went for walks below decks. Mother H had a cabin to herself, but she only went there for a rest or to sleep. Gerard and I made sure that we spent time together, and we talked about some memories of our life at the house in Moose Falls, which seemed so far away. I am happy to say that this time I did not suffer any seasickness, but perhaps that was due to my being in the early days of pregnancy on the way out.

I looked outside to see the scenery go by. I had not been in this part of Hampshire, then Sussex, as we passed through different stations, stopping at some and passing through others. After what seemed ages, but only about two hours, the train slowed down to a stop with a call, 'Three Gates Station' and we took our hand luggage off and disembarked the train. We seemed to be the only ones left on the train as it turned out, and as we helped Mother H down, with Gerard and Harry and Ellen with Louisa and Scuffy close behind. As the steam cleared, we saw two people standing together near the exit, and as we walked towards to them, I recognised the woman, and Mary was at my elbow, as I said, 'That's my mother!' and she said, 'That's my father.' 'And my father too!' I said with a happy cry.

As we walked towards to each other I noticed that my mother's frame had thickened, and her clothes were not very expensive or new, and she was holding a pair of spectacles which she had removed just as we saw each other, but what else I noticed as she was with our father, was that she is very content and no longer strained. We closed the gap and putting propriety aside, I ran into my Mama and hugged her and hugged her, and she hugged me back, and Mary ran to Henry and hugged him also. With tears in my eyes, I could not speak properly as she held me at arm's length and looked at me, 'Oh my Darling Anna, you have grown into a beautiful woman, I have missed you, can you forgive me?' and she looked so happy to see me. Regaining my composure I replied 'Considering the circumstances, I can understand, and to find that my best friend is my sister, well words cannot express how I felt.'

Mary Ann was talking quietly to Henry our father and there was a slightly awkward moment as we stepped back, and Mary Ann looked a little shyly at my mother and she said to Mama, 'You are my step-mother how shall I address you?' Mama looked at her and held her arms out to her, 'What would like to call me?' Mary Ann replied, 'Well I called my mother Mum, can I call you Mother?' Mama just said, 'If you wish dear Mary Ann, I have always looked on you as an adopted daughter, the moment you entered the household.'

With that they hugged each other and I felt so happy. I looked to Henry, my father, and he extended his arms to me, and I went to him and hugged him too, yes, the love was there. 'What will you call me Anna?' he asked, as we stepped back a little and I replied, 'Well father has bad associations for me, I would like to call you Dad, if I may.' He nodded, and then asked, 'Where are your husbands?' I pointed towards the back of the train as they were helping to unload the luggage, 'They will be here soon to meet you. Ellen is here, with Louisa, and my mother in law, Marie Claire Horan.'

Mama walked towards Mother H, and Mother H walked towards her, to my surprise Mama held her hands out to Mother H who reciprocated, 'My dear Marie Claire, how good it is to meet you at last, you are just like your photographs, but actually prettier.' Mother H replied, 'I am happy to meet you at last as well Eleonor, but we have aged a little.' I asked how they could be so familiar, and Mama replied, 'We have been corresponding over the years. Marie Claire has been keeping me aware of what has been happening as you have been busy bringing up your children.'

Mother H nodded and Mama introduced her to our father. Ellen with Louisa and Scuffy who had his ears cocked, and I introduced them to Mama and Henry, who commented on how Ellen looked like her father, she has become a very pretty accomplished young lady, as tall as I am, with her hair up, although she was wearing trousers with boots, she allowed herself to be embraced by her grandmother and grandfather, and she was happy to call them so. Louisa stood close to me, with her and our beloved dog Scuffy, and I took her hand and introduced her to Mama and Henry, (I will get used to calling him Dad) and said that she is our adopted daughter, and sister to Ellen and Jarred, she looked up at them and said, 'Are you my grandmother and grandfather too?' Mama replied, 'If you would like to call us so, yes dear Louisa.' Louisa nodded, and clung to Mama who put her hands on her shoulders as Louisa clung to her and as Louisa only came up to Mama's chest, and Mama stroked Louisa's long dark hair, which hung in a single plait. Louisa introduced them to Scuffy and I was a little worried because of the conditions that we were able to bring him, but he sniffed their hands, and allowed himself to be stroked, ah another introduction. I looked towards the back of the train, as the ramp was lowered at the back carriage of the train, and I called to Mama, 'Mama, there is something else, I have brought back something for you, please come with me,' and as we reached the carriage, Jarred called out, 'Mama, Mama, come see!'

I rushed to the entrance of the ramp, and looked inside, 'No! When was it born, I saw in the half-light a small form was standing there towards the back of the carriage. As they brought out the goats, plus a kid newly born, being carried, Mama said, 'Goats, you brought goats!' And I laughed, 'Louisa needs goats milk, and then as the horses were led out one by one, then Mama gasped, 'You brought your horses back!'

278

Then I asked young Henry as Merrilees was led out and her new born foal, which was black just like Jasper, when Merrilees had foaled, and he replied as we passed through Lewes.

As we left the station, I spoke to the guard, mentioning that there were two extra passengers on the train, meaning the kid and foal, and asked him how much was owed, and he just said, 'Babies go free,' and he chortled, and commented on my accent, I explained that I had lived in Canada for the past 18 years, and he said, 'Are you the lady from the big house who went away in disgrace?' I said perhaps yes, but had come back to claim my inheritance or at least restore it. He just said, 'That would be good, it needs someone to put some life back into it.' I thanked him, and gave him some pound notes for his mates on the train, as the back carriage would need clearing out, and he doffed his cap and thanked me.

I went to join the others as the luggage was loaded onto a truck and some furniture, as we led the horses to the blacksmith who had a field out at the back of his premises where we could lodge the horses temporarily, and then on to the schoolmaster's house for tea, before we went to the small hotel. I was happy that we were not far from the horses, who seemed content with their temporary home, and the blacksmith's home, and the blacksmith said in passing, 'I s'pose he will demand our respect.' I responded firmly but quietly, 'No he will earn your respect he is a good man!' He looked at me and smiled, 'From what I recall, he was a nice young medic; you are right, he will.' I walked on to Mama's home, and joined Gerard and the others and felt happy, we were home.

Present day

Sara put down the journal, and almost cried with relief and emotion, she had been so taken up with the diaries, that she had tried to read them every opportunity, and considered typing them up on her computer, rereading them as she typed, but she wondered if this was the end of the story, so she looked in her grandmother's papers and belongings, and to her delight and relief, she found a big package containing several more journals in the same handwriting, she looked forward to reading them.